A BOOK OF Spirits AND Thieves

A BOOK OF Spirits AND Thieves

MORGAN RHODES

razor bill

An Imprint of Penguin Random House

razOr
bill

An Imprint of Penguin Random House
Penguin.com

ISBN: 978-1-59514-760-8

Printed in the United States of America

1 3 5 7 9 10 8 6 4 2

To everyone who believes that books are magic.

Chapter 1

CRYSTAL

"Be careful where you point that thing, young lady. It'll get you in trouble one day."

The old man Crys had been stalking for twenty minutes glared at her through the lens of her camera. The deep wrinkles she'd found so fascinating now gathered between his eyes as he creased his forehead.

She snapped a picture.

"Thanks for the advice," she said, flashing him a grin before she quickly made her escape.

It would be a great shot, one of her best yet. Eyes that had seen at least eighty years of life. A face, weathered and aged, with a thousand stories to tell. Definitely portfolio-worthy.

Crys passed a bank with a digital clock in the window and winced when she saw the time. *Becca's going to kill me,* she thought.

The last class had let out at three o'clock, but because she hadn't gone to school today, she'd completely lost track of time. She could smell spring in the air, finally, after such a long, cold winter. The cool breeze felt fresh and clean and full of possibilities, even beneath the scent of cement and dust and exhaust fumes.

It was five minutes to six when she finally made it to her destination. Five minutes to closing.

The Speckled Muse Bookshop was located on the west edge of the Annex, a Toronto neighborhood adjacent to the U of T campus and the Royal Ontario Museum. Busy streets, a young crowd—thanks to the proximity to the university—lots of restaurants and little independent shops.

Crys paused and snapped a shot of the weathered sign out front—she'd taken the same pic from nearly every angle possible over the last couple of years. Along with the name of the shop written in quirky, painted letters, there was an illustration of a little girl with big glasses, pigtails, and a sprinkling of freckles, sitting on top of a stack of books.

It was a caricature of Crys from when she was five years old, before she even knew how to read. Before she got contacts for her annoying nearsightedness and used her thick glasses only when she absolutely had to.

Back when the Hatchers were a whole family, not just three-quarters of one.

Something warm brushed against her leg, and she lowered her camera with a frown. "Who let you out, Charlie?"

Charlie, an adorable black-and-white kitten, replied with a tiny *mew* that seemed to have a question mark attached to it.

"Come on." Crys leaned over and picked him up, pressing him against her chest. "You're way too close to the street out here, little guy."

A month ago, when it was early March and still freezing cold, she'd found the kitten next to a garbage can a block away from the store and next to her favorite sushi place. He'd been no bigger than the palm of her hand, and looked forlorn and miserable.

She'd brought the shivering handful home and insisted they keep him.

Her mother had taken one look at him and said no. But Crys's younger sister, Becca, immediately stepped in and argued on behalf of the tiny feline's fate. Between her two daughters' joint arguments, Julia Hatcher finally relented. It was the first time in ages that Crys and Becca had agreed on anything. Becca then named him Charlie after *Charlie and the Chocolate Factory*, one of her favorite books.

Now Crys pushed open the glass front door, triggering the familiar, melodious chime of the doorbell that signaled a customer had entered. Immediately, she felt the heat of Becca's glare from across the shop.

Yeah, I know. I'm late, she thought. *What else is new?*

The mail lay on a small table near the door in an untouched heap. Several brown cardboard boxes of books were stacked next to it.

The Speckled Muse was housed in a historical three-story building—one of the oldest in Toronto, dating to the mid-nineteenth century. Crys's great-grandfather, a man of wealth and influence in the city, had purchased the building seventy years earlier and given it to his book-loving wife so she could open a bookstore. The current sign was relatively new, but the name of the shop was more than sixty years old.

If only great-granddaddy hadn't squandered his fortune on poor investments, leaving nothing for his family line apart from the bookshop itself.

The Speckled Muse—a Toronto landmark. One of the oldest bookstores in one of the oldest buildings and, as many ancient edifices were, rumored to be haunted. Crys had yet to see evidence of a ghost—apart from hearing the occasional groans and creaks that are normal in any old building.

All of this, both truth and rumor, helped to coax customers through the front door and into the maze-like shelves and nooks and crannies of the shop, which, contrary to its small and quaint storefront, had a massive interior that magically seemed to go on and on.

The first floor of the building was dedicated to the store, and the upper two made up the Hatcher family home, accessed by a winding iron staircase at the very back of the main floor. Three bedrooms and a bathroom on the top floor, a kitchen, a living room, and another bathroom on the second. Plenty big enough for the three of them. And now Charlie, of course.

"Thank you so much for coming in." Becca handed change to a customer from behind the register. She wore her honey-blond hair off her face, in a loose braid that fell across her right shoulder. There was a pencil tucked behind her ear that Crys would bet she'd totally forgotten about. "I hope you enjoy the book."

"Thank *you* for helping me find it!" The woman—a redhead with ruddy cheeks and a toothy grin, whom Crys immediately recognized as a regular customer—clutched the plastic bag bearing the store's logo to her chest. "My mother read this to me when I was just a little girl. It's an absolute treasure. And such a good price!"

With a bright smile, and a friendly nod in Crys's direction, the woman left the shop with her reasonably priced treasure firmly in hand.

"Becca Hatcher—making dreams come true, one book at a time," Crys said with amusement.

She received no response, just an intensified glare as her

younger sister moved from behind the long wooden counter toward the door, sidestepping the books that had piled up and needed to be logged and shelved. She flipped the sign to CLOSED.

It smelled musty in here—like old paper and leather. It was a smell Crys used to love, since it smelled like home, but now she thought they needed to give the shop a good airing out.

"No greeting for your favorite sister in the whole wide world?" Crys pressed.

"You were supposed to be here two hours ago."

Crys shrugged. "I was otherwise occupied. I knew you could handle things on your own."

Becca groaned. "Unbelievable. You don't even care, do you?"

"About what?"

"That you . . . *you* . . ." Becca's cheeks reddened with every sputtered word. If there was one thing that could be said about the Hatcher sisters, it was that they didn't try too hard to keep their emotions hidden.

"I . . . *I* . . . ?" Crys prompted. "What? Forced you to spend two extra hours around your favorite objects while Mom's out doing her daily chores?"

"You made me miss book club."

Crys inwardly cringed. Becca loved her stupid book club like a six-year-old loved gummy bears. "You know, you really should try to find a hobby that has nothing to do with books. Expand and grow. Live a little." She gestured toward the front window, which looked out at the always-busy Bathurst Street. "There's a whole world out there to discover."

"You're right. I do need another hobby," she replied. "Maybe I should take up *photography*."

She said it as if it were an insult.

"Whatever."

"You're so much like Dad—you know that?" Becca added.

Great, Crys thought. *Twist that knife in just a little more.*

Suddenly, Crys wanted to put down the camera—a Pentax from the eighties that took film that had to be developed in a dark room. It wasn't fancy, and it definitely wasn't digital. The flash had broken long ago and been discarded, which, because Crys liked using natural light for her shots anyway, didn't make any difference to her.

Instead, she held the device up with one hand while still cradling a purring Charlie with the other and snapped a picture. Becca raised her hand to block her face, but it was too late.

"You know I hate having my picture taken!"

"You should get over that." Crys had found that most people hated having their picture taken, which was why she much preferred taking stealth shots of strangers all around the city. She had no idea why Becca was so camera-shy. The girl could be a model. The lion's share of the good looks in the family had gone to the younger daughter, a fact Crys tried very hard not to let bother her.

"You're such a jerk. You know that?" Becca replied. "You only think about yourself."

"Bite me." Despite her bravado, a trickle of guilt soured Crys's stomach, like always. It was definitely time for a subject change. "Did you know Charlie got outside?"

"What?" Becca glanced at the kitten, and her face blanched. "I didn't even realize . . . If he'd been hit by a car—" She reached across the counter so she could gently pet the top of his head. "Oh, Charlie, I'm sorry."

"He probably just slipped out with a customer. It's fine. He's fine." The kitten began to squirm, so Crys gently set him down on the floor. He flicked his tail and sauntered away, down a long aisle of crammed bookshelves toward his favorite napping spot in the mystery section.

Becca swept her serious gaze across the front of the store until it fell again on Crys. Her dark blue eyes narrowed, and she cocked her head as if seeing her sister for the first time today. "You changed your hair again."

Crys twisted a finger around a long pale lock. Normally her hair was a medium ash blond, just like their mother's. A year ago, she'd started to dye it whenever she felt a whim, and it had since been black, dark brown, red, and, for a short time—and much to their mother's dismay—bright purple.

Last night she'd gone platinum blond. Her scalp still burned from the peroxide, and she resisted the urge to scratch it, hoping her hair wouldn't start falling out from the abuse she'd heaped upon it.

Although . . . bald might be cool to try out for a while.

"Yup," she said. "You like?"

"Sure," Becca replied after a moment. "It makes your eyes look even lighter."

"Thanks, I think." Crys didn't know if that was a compliment or simply an observation. She had the same eyes as their father—icy blue and so pale they nearly lacked any color entirely. Some people said her eyes were spooky.

She was okay with this.

"Mom'll be back in an hour," Becca said, glancing down at her watch.

"Let's get some sushi in the meantime. I'm starving." Walking around all day would do that, and Crys had forgotten to have lunch.

"I'm sick of sushi. Let's figure out dinner after we finish with the store."

How could anyone ever get sick of sushi? Crys could happily eat it for breakfast, lunch, and dinner if given the option. "Fine. Just tell me what to do, boss."

"Sort the mail." Becca gestured toward the pile near the front door. "And I'll . . . I guess I'll shelve these." She grabbed a cardboard box and hoisted it up onto the counter. "A customer came in and had a bunch of used children's books she wanted to unload. Mom wasn't here to vet them as quality, so I took them all. I don't know why anyone would want to get rid of all these books, but I guess it's good for business, right?"

"Sure," Crys replied distractedly, eyeing the mail. She'd spotted a suspicious-looking letter at the top of the pile and started walking toward it. "Shelve away."

The letter was addressed to her mother, and it was from Sunderland High—Crys's school.

She ripped it open without a second thought and scanned the contents, which informed Mrs. Hatcher that her daughter, Crystal, had a questionable attendance record. She'd missed three weeks' worth of classes since the year began. The principal wanted to meet to discuss her frequently truant daughter's choices and how it could put her graduation in June at risk.

Crys ripped the letter into tiny pieces and threw it in the garbage can. She didn't need to graduate with top marks to be a photographer. And ever since her two best friends, Amanda and Sara, had both moved away in the last six months, classes held no interest for her anymore.

She only needed to survive until June to leave school behind her forever.

And in seven months she'd turn eighteen. That number meant the freedom to do whatever she wanted, whenever she wanted.

Eighteen meant she could finally leave Toronto and travel around the world, taking pictures, fleshing out her portfolio, so she could get a job at a magazine such as *National Geographic*.

That was both the dream and the plan. And only a matter of months and the occasional annoying letter from school stood in her way.

Along with letters and bills there was a larger parcel, wrapped in brown paper and tied with string. It was covered in what looked like European stamps. She recognized the sender's handwriting immediately.

It was from her aunt Jackie.

Again ignoring the fact that the parcel was addressed to her mother, not her, Crys tore off the paper, curious to see what her aunt had sent. Crys felt it'd been forever since she'd seen or talked to Jackie, who lived in Europe most of the time, exploring and having adventures and romances and getting into trouble like the free spirit she was. Jackie hadn't graduated high school, either, and her aunt was the coolest and smartest person Crys had ever known. She'd received her education from living life, not from reading textbooks.

"And you've sent us . . ." Crys pulled the object out of the packaging, her enthusiasm quickly fading. ". . . a book. Hooray."

The book did look very old—which meant it might be valuable on the secondhand market. That was one point in its favor. Its cover was smooth brown leather. Handmade, by the feel of it. It was the size of an old atlas and as thick as a dictionary. As heavy as one, too. It had cost Jackie a small fortune in postage to send this overseas.

Affixed to the cover was a metal relief of a bronze bird, its wings spread in flight. Crys traced it with her index finger.

There was no title, and nothing was written on the weathered spine.

A piece of paper fell out as Crys opened the cover. She snatched it up off the worn hardwood floor.

This is it, Jules. I finally found it. Grandma would be proud. Keep it safe, and I'll be in touch as soon as I can. —J

Crys opened the book. It appeared to be a one-of-a-kind text, similar to the ones ancient monks slaved over all their lives, with decorative calligraphy, careful penmanship, and intricate paintings. The pages felt as fragile as onionskin, but the words inside were crisp and clear, the illustrations of flowers and plants, green landscapes, robed figures, and unfamiliar furry animals as sharp as if they'd been rendered this week.

The language, however . . . Crys frowned down at it. It wasn't recognizable to her. Definitely not Latin. Or Italian. Or Chinese.

The alphabet was odd, made up of curls and swashes instead of discernible letters. There were no breaks between words; the text looked like lines of gibberish and nonsense rather than an actual language. But it was all rendered with a fine hand as if it might make perfect sense to someone, somewhere.

Some of the text was printed in gold ink, some in black. The gold ink shimmered even in the most shadowy areas of the overstuffed shop as Crys walked it back to the children's section, easily navigating the maze-like shelves without looking up.

Becca was there, on her knees, sliding the new books into place after noting them in the open ledger beside her. Crys glanced around at the shelves, which were painted pink and blue and green in this area, rather than the standard brown and black in the rest of the store. Kid-sized chairs and a small sofa, both upholstered in bright polka-dotted fabric, were there for reading comfort. A decade ago, on the wall next to the large, round window that made this alcove the brightest part of the shop, her father had painted a mural of a fantasy land with a golden castle and two princesses who looked a great deal like Becca and Crys. The painted words *Imagination is Magic* curved around the fluffy white clouds in the bright blue sky.

Daniel Hatcher used to organize and host readings every Saturday in this kids' nook, free for all children and parents. He always made sure there were drinks and snacks available. Local children's authors would visit and talk to the kids and sign books. And this had also been the place Crys and Becca had lounged for hours in their childhood, spending time together reading and discussing book after book after book.

Times had changed. The nook, once a place of magic and fairy tales, now looked weathered and old. The only ghosts to be found back here were memories of a different time.

"What's that?" Becca asked, drawing Crys out of her reverie.

"Good question. Jackie sent it. I don't know what it is, but I hope it's worth big bucks."

Becca stood up and brushed some dust off her jeans. "Let me see it." Crys handed it over, and Becca's eyes widened as she took it. "Wow. It's beautiful. Absolutely beautiful. I wonder how old it is."

"*Very* old," Crys replied. "That's my professional opinion."

Becca sat down on the small sofa and began to carefully flip through it. "I wonder what language this is."

"No idea whatsoever."

"This is like something you'd find in a museum."

"Do museums pay lots of money for ancient books no one can read?"

This earned Crys a sharp look. "It's not all about money, you know."

"Let's go ahead and agree to disagree on that."

Becca traced her hand lightly over a fully gold page, the writing so tiny and cramped that there was barely any of the thin paper showing. The ink shone bright in the light from the window, even as dusk had started to descend over the city.

"Don't get your greasy fingers all over it," Crys said. "It'll decrease the value."

"Quiet." Becca's voice was hollow now, distracted, as she peered at the pages, her brows drawing together.

"What's wrong?"

"I don't know."

"You look constipated."

Becca shook her head, not bothering to respond to Crys's smart-ass comment with even a glare. "This book . . . I feel like I can . . . I don't know. *Sense* something from it."

"Sense something?" Crys laughed and looked up at the ceiling. *"Spirits, come to us now! Speak to us through the pages of this weird old book."*

"Shut up. It's not like that. It's not . . ."

"Not what?" Crys prompted when Becca fell silent.

Becca's breathing quickened, her chest rising and falling rapidly.

That was alarming. "Becca, what's wrong?"

"This book . . ." Becca whispered hoarsely, as if the words were getting stuck in her throat. She began to tremble. "It's doing something . . . to me. I can feel it . . . pulling."

"Pulling? Pulling what?" In seconds, a chill spread through Crys, bringing with it a dark and heavy feeling of dread. "You're starting to freak me out. It's just a dumb book. Give it back to me."

She held out her hand and waited for her sister to hand it back to her. "Come on! What are you waiting for?"

Becca lurched up to her feet off the small sofa. "I can't seem to let go of it. I'm trying, but I can't."

The golden page began to glow.

Crys swore under her breath. *What the hell was going on?*

She reached forward to grab it out from her sister's grip. The moment she touched the book this time, a violent shock tore through her, as if she'd jammed her hand into a light socket. It knocked her backward, and she fell flat on her back on the far side of the alcove. The wind had been knocked from her lungs, and she struggled to find her breath. As fast as she could, she scrambled to her unsteady feet.

"Get that thing away from you, Becca!" she gasped.

Becca's eyes had filled with the bright golden light from the book. "I don't know what's happening. What . . . what is it doing to me? Help me!" Her voice broke with fear. "Please, Crys, *help me*!"

Crys lunged toward her sister just as light started to stream out of the book, momentarily blinding her and making her stagger back again. She blinked, rubbing her eyes, only to see that sharp beams of this impossibly bright light had wrapped around Becca, slithering around her chest and arms and face like a thousand golden snakes.

Becca screamed, and the bone-chilling sound drew a frightened shriek from Crys's throat. The book finally dropped from Becca's hands as she crumpled to the floor in a heap next to it.

Crys scrambled to Becca's side and grabbed her sister's shoulders, shaking her. "Becca! Becca, look at me! Look at me!"

The golden glow from the book coated her skin and gathered in her eyes for a moment longer before it finally extinguished.

Becca stared straight ahead, her expression slack.

"Please!" Crys yelled, shaking her harder. "Please say something!"

But her sister didn't respond. She stared, she blinked. She breathed. But Becca Hatcher was gone—mind and soul.

Gone. In an instant.

Leaving Crys behind, alone . . . with the book responsible.

Chapter 2

FARRELL

The Raven Club wasn't his favorite bar, but it was the noisiest one he knew. Silence meant thinking. And thinking meant remembering.

Tonight he wanted to forget.

Half a bottle of vodka also made forgetting a lot easier. And the club offered its fair share of dark-haired beauties to help take his mind off the date on the calendar.

"You are *very* helpful, you know that?" he said to the girl on his lap, weaving his fingers into her long hair, which was stiff with hair spray. She wore a low cut, sparkly top and a skirt short enough to get her arrested in many places around the world. Luckily, Toronto wasn't one of them.

She brushed her lips against his throat. "I aim to please."

"Aim a little lower, would you?"

"Anything you want."

He did another shot and glanced at the time on his phone. Midnight. He'd successfully made it through the third of April.

Suddenly, the sickly sweet scent of the girl's floral perfume had begun to chase his buzz away. Girls, thinking it made them smell like money, piled that garbage on way too thick for his taste.

"Enough," Farrell said as he pushed her off his lap.

"Oh, come on. We've barely gotten started." She stroked his chest and unbuttoned the top of his white Prada shirt. "Here we are, all alone, just the two of us. It's destiny, baby."

He tried not to laugh. "I don't believe in destiny."

The private lounge he'd reserved offered a sliver of privacy, but Farrell would hardly call them *alone*. Only twenty feet away, through a shimmering curtain, was the rest of the club. The sound of throbbing music had begun to make his head ache.

He'd kill for a cigarette, but he was trying to quit.

The brunette had caught his eye when he'd gone to fetch a bottle of Grey Goose from the bar. He had no idea how old she was under all that makeup. Maybe twenty. Maybe thirty. He didn't really care.

"The night's still young," he told her. "We have time, Suzie."

"It's Stephanie."

He gave her one of his best smiles, which never failed to work wonders with difficult females. Right on schedule, her serious expression faded and her eyes sparkled with interest. He didn't have many talents, but effortless charm and a way with women were two of them.

Also, the public knowledge of Farrell Grayson's upcoming inheritance helped get him all the female attention he'd ever want.

One hundred million dollars of his grandmother's vast estate, left to him in her will—with a stipulation: He didn't get his hands on it until he turned twenty-one.

Only 576 days till he finally had the freedom to do as he pleased without being caught under his parents' thumbs, totally dependent on his monthly allowance.

"Suzie . . . Stephanie . . . Sexy . . . come back over here, whoever you are," he said, patting his knee. She did as requested, smiling now.

Her tongue tasted like rum, he thought absently. And Diet Coke.

His phone vibrated and he glanced down at it. It was a message from his kid brother, Adam.

im in big trouble can you come get me

It included an address to one of the seedier neighborhoods downtown.

Another text message swiftly followed: *never mind im fine*

Yeah, right. Farrell slipped the phone into the inner pocket of his jacket. He grabbed the bottle of vodka and took a swig from it, feeling the pleasant burn all the way down his throat.

Fun was over. Duty called.

"Got to go," he said.

Stephanie's eyes widened with surprise. "What? Where?"

"I need to deal with a family thing."

"I'll come with you."

"No thanks," Farrell said without hesitation.

"Oh, come on." She traced her long fingernails up his arm. "We're having such a good time. You really want it to end so soon?"

"I really couldn't care less." He kept his smile fixed as her expression fell. "What? You thought this was an open casting call for the role of Farrell Grayson's girlfriend? Sorry to disappoint you."

Her surprise faded and her eyes flashed with anger. "Asshole. Everything they say about you is true."

She got up from his side and stormed out of the lounge, shoving the curtains out of her way, but her arms and hair still got caught in them in her furious need to make a dramatic exit.

Fine with him. He'd never liked the taste of rum anyway.

Since having his license suspended four months ago, Farrell had had to get used to having a chauffeur. It was either that or take public transit—and both of his parents were appalled by the thought of a Grayson riding the subway.

Not that any of this was their fault; it was entirely his. Wrapping his Porsche around a tree had totaled the car, landed him with a DUI the family lawyers were still sorting out, and sent him into the hospital with a serious concussion.

You're damn lucky you didn't hurt anybody else, the voice of his conscience snarled. It sounded exactly like his older brother, Connor. All their lives, he'd been the one offering up such pearls of wisdom, whether Farrell wanted them or not.

When the limo reached its destination, Farrell, unsteady on his feet from the amount of liquor he'd consumed, approached a low-rent apartment building.

Out front, several of the streetlamps were broken, casting the treeless area in darkness, apart from the light of the nearly full moon. Shadows moved to his left across the concrete parking lot, but he paid them no attention. He wasn't looking for trouble—not tonight.

"Wait here," he told his driver.

Farrell went upstairs and knocked on the door to the apartment number Adam had texted. After a moment, it opened a crack.

"Sorry, we didn't order any," the kid said with a smirk.

Farrell smiled at him, then kicked the door open, breaking the security chain. "Where's my brother?"

The kid scrambled backward. "Hey, I was just kidding around. I was going to let you in. Farrell, right? I'm Peter." He nodded toward the corner. "That's Nick."

The other boy, Nick, watched the two of them warily, taking a shaky step backward as Farrell fisted his hands and moved menacingly toward the first kid.

"Where is Adam?" he growled. "Don't make me ask again or you'll regret it."

"Back room," Peter said, then cleared his throat. "It's cool you're here. You're welcome to join the party. We don't mind sharing."

Farrell moved through the small apartment toward the closed door at the rear. It opened before he reached it, and Adam's nervous face greeted him.

"Oh, hi," Adam said.

Yes, his brother definitely looked nervous. Nervous *and* guilty. "What the hell's going on?"

"Nothing." Adam rubbed a hand through his light brown hair. "I mean, everything's fine. You should go back to whatever you were doing, and I can . . . fix this."

"Fix what?" When Adam didn't answer, Farrell shook his head. "I'm taking you home. It's after midnight. Isn't that your curfew?"

Adam scowled. "I'm too old for curfews."

"Our beloved parents might disagree with that. I know they did when I was sixteen. Let's go." He blew out a breath. Maybe he was taking the wrong approach. "I got the latest KillerMan movie all loaded up. I know you want to see it as much as I do."

One thing the brothers shared was their love of Korean action movies. Never dubbed, always with subtitles. They watched at least one a week together in the Graysons' home theater.

"But the party's not over yet," Peter whined.

So these were Adam's new friends. Both of them gave Farrell a deeply uneasy feeling.

"Party, huh?" he said. "Three kids out late on a Friday night in some sketchy apartment. Doesn't seem like much of a party to me." He was met with silence, and he returned his attention to Adam. "What's in the room?"

Adam grimaced. He held the door open only wide enough for him to look at Farrell, not wide enough for Farrell to see beyond.

"I told you not to come."

"Yeah. Right after you said you were in trouble. *What's in the room?*" he repeated.

"Nothing."

Farrell already felt his hangover circling like a mean-spirited vulture. "Show me right now."

"Yeah, let's show him." Nick, with a big, sleazy grin on his face, approached slowly. "The fun just got started. Adam's first, but you can go second, if you'd like."

Farrell pushed the door open to reveal a small bedroom. The bed was unmade, the curtains askew. It smelled sour, like unwashed clothing.

An unconscious woman lay on the bed.

"Explain," he bit out through clenched teeth. *"Now."*

"She was looking to party—she just needed a bit of a push." Peter shrugged. "Led the three of us back here before she passed out. It's her place."

She was at least ten years older than the boys. Her red lipstick was smeared, and she smelled like cigarette smoke and alcohol.

"Who drugged her?" Farrell asked as evenly as he could, flicking a glance at Adam. "You?"

Adam shook his head, his expression bleak.

"Did you touch her?" She was still wearing all her clothes, even her panty hose and stiletto heels. But he had to ask.

"No," Adam replied in barely a whisper.

"He's been in here for half an hour," Peter said with a laugh. "We were getting bored waiting for him to get started."

Farrell ignored him, keeping his attention on Adam. "Were you going to?"

A shadow of fear and uncertainty slid behind Adam's eyes.

Nick shook his head, grinning. "We tried to help your brother pop his cherry, and this is what—"

Farrell couldn't hold his anger in anymore. He exploded. He grabbed Nick by his throat and slammed him against the wall, rattling the cheap framed art. "Listen to me very carefully. If you ever—*ever*—get my brother involved in something like this again, I'm going to kill you—both of you." He sent a death glare toward Peter before returning his attention to the kid in front of him. "You hear me?"

Nick's eyes bugged. "Whoa, wait—"

"If you come anywhere near Adam again, I will personally slit you open and watch your guts spill onto the floor, and I'll enjoy every minute of it. And if I hear that you ever do this to another woman, you will deeply, deeply regret it. Understood?"

Nick nodded frantically. Peter's acne stood out like bright red dots on his pale face. They both answered in unison: "Understood."

Farrell finally released Nick. "Get the hell out of here, both of you."

The two boys scrambled to leave the apartment without another word of protest.

Adam had pressed himself back against the wall, as if wishing he, too, could run away. "Farrell . . . I swear I wouldn't have—"

"Shut up. Just shut your mouth." He looked down at his hands to find that they were shaking. He clasped them together as he moved toward the woman on the bed. She groaned and shifted on the sheets. A tacky necklace with a big, fake ruby hung around her neck. Her hair was a brash yellowy blond, with an inch of black roots.

Her fake lashes fluttered, and her eyes opened a crack. A drunken smile stretched her red lips. "Hey, baby. You ready to have some fun?"

"I've had my fun for tonight." He grabbed a blanket and pulled it over her. "Sleep it off. You'll feel better tomorrow."

He caught another whiff of cigarette smoke. Farrell made a mental note to stop somewhere for a pack of smokes. He needed nicotine in the worst way. He'd gone three days without a cigarette. That was more than enough.

"Farrell . . . ," Adam began again, his voice choked.

"Just tell me why you'd want to get involved in something like this." Farrell didn't look at him as he moved through the apartment toward the open door. Adam trailed after him like a ghost.

"It's been a year tonight, you know that?"

Farrell froze. "You're using *that* as your excuse?"

"It was a mistake."

"You're damn right it was." He should know what mistakes were. He'd made so many of them himself he'd lost count.

"Ever since Connor died, you've been so distant. Mom and Dad . . . they've practically ignored me. I don't feel like I belong anywhere. And Nick and Peter wanted to be my friends. I know it was wrong—and I know I wouldn't have done anything to her or let them do anything. But tonight . . . for a moment I felt like I belonged somewhere. Like I had a group to call my own."

One year since Connor died.

It would be so nice to forget. But it didn't matter how much he drank. That image of Connor was always there, burned into his brain.

"I get it, kid. I do. The need to belong, to have people to depend on through thick and thin. But losers like Peter and Nick aren't going to give you that. I know what you need."

"What?"

"Dad was going to tell you over breakfast, but I'm more than happy to spoil the surprise. The next society meeting is tomorrow night, and you're on the list. You're going to be initiated."

Adam gaped at him, his eyes wide. "Are you serious?"

"Yup. You're in."

"I mean, I know practically nothing about it."

Farrell shrugged. "What happens at the Hawkspear Society stays at the Hawkspear Society. But you'll learn soon enough."

Adam just stood there, shaking his head in disbelief, before a gigantic smile spread across his face. "This is amazing."

"Congrats." Farrell couldn't help but smile at his little brother's exuberant reaction. It wasn't every day that someone got initiated into a secret society made up of Toronto's most elite and powerful.

Adam had no idea what lay behind those locked doors, but Farrell knew it would most definitely make him feel like he belonged somewhere. Somewhere incredibly special. Somewhere powerful.

Somewhere *magical*.

Sixteen was the minimum age for members, but it was still very young. Farrell wasn't totally certain his brother was ready for what he'd witness tomorrow night.

But rules were rules. And family was family.

Adam Grayson was about to grow up fast. Farrell could only hope like hell that he wouldn't end up like Connor.

Chapter 3

MADDOX

NORTHERN MYTICA—
YEAR 15 OF THE GODDESS VALORIA'S REIGN

If he valued his life—and he most certainly did—then he needed to hurry. He'd already kept Livius waiting far too long.

The journey from his mother's small village to the city of Ravenswood had been nearly impossible to complete in only two days while still taking the time to rest and eat. His mother had begged him to stay with her another day, saying she'd cook him a stew from the rabbit she'd caught in her snares that morning. Though his stomach had protested giving up such a fine meal, he'd kissed her quickly on both of her cheeks and embraced her tightly.

"I promise I'll return the very next chance I get," he'd told her.

If he hadn't left, he wouldn't earn enough to pay the taxes owed on her small cottage. She'd be cast out by the lord of the land, and, like many poor women in the North, she'd be forced to become a beggar.

He'd never allow that to happen.

So he made his way quickly to the city, a treacherous journey across roughly hewn paths and dirt roads, through forests thick with criminals, stinging insects, and beasts with sharp teeth. He had no weapon—he wasn't allowed to have one of his own—so all he had to aid him were his wits.

At the edge of the forest less than a mile from the city, Maddox's pace slowed to a halt as he came across an old man lying next to a tipped-over wooden cart, his face and shirt bloodied.

"Boy . . . ," the old man moaned, reaching out toward Maddox as he approached with apprehension. "Please—please . . . help me."

"Of course I'll help you." He would never ignore someone in dire need like this, even though the sight of blood made his stomach lurch. "What happened here?"

The man's white hair was sparse, his mostly bald scalp red from the blazing sun. "Thieves stopped my cart. They attacked me and left me for dead. Come closer. You must help me to my feet, help me get to the city."

Maddox scanned the tree line, now nervous that thieves might be lying in wait. "What direction did they go?"

"Take my hand, boy."

Maddox hesitated only another moment before he clasped the old man's hand and helped him to his feet. "You've lost a great deal of blood."

"Not nearly as much as you'll lose if you don't do exactly as I say." The old man produced a dagger and held the sharp edge of steel to Maddox's throat. "A trusting youth, aren't you?"

Trusting. Or stupid. In Maddox's experience, they seemed to be interchangeable when it came to many of his choices.

"Give me all your coin." The old man's lips peeled back from broken teeth. His breath smelled like rotting vegetables. "Or I'll slit your throat."

Stupid. So very, very stupid.

"Sorry to disappoint, but I don't have any coin on me." Maddox grimaced as the man pressed the blade harder and warm blood trickled down his neck. "If you let me go, I promise I can get you plenty."

"Promises don't work for me."

"You've obviously confused me with someone else, someone with coin to spare. Do I look like someone who carries bags of gold and silver with me?"

The old man peered at him. "You're well dressed enough."

Today he wore tailored leather trousers, a suede vest, and a fine shirt made from linen imported from across the Silver Sea. At first glance, Maddox Corso might be mistaken for the son of a lord.

Which made sense. These clothes had been *stolen* from the son of a lord.

"How old are you, boy?" the thief asked.

He hesitated before answering truthfully. "Sixteen."

"Where is your family?"

"In the city up ahead," he lied. "They're the ones with the gold." He racked his mind in search of a way to escape this predicament. "So tell me, do you lie in wait at the side of the road like this often? Is this a hobby or a profession? Is it profitable?"

His questions only got a jab from the blade to silence him.

Maddox then tried to clear his mind, to concentrate on the man and nothing else. To will the thief into unconsciousness with the strange and nameless power inside him.

Unfortunately, his magic failed him today, which wasn't surprising. It almost always did any time he actually *tried* to use it.

Another voice cut in. "What are you doing with my son?"

The old man wheeled around to face the intruder, taking Maddox with him. "*Your* son, eh? So it would appear your father has come looking for you."

"So it would appear," Maddox mumbled.

But Livius was his *guardian*, not his father.

Livius, who was dressed every bit as well as Maddox today beneath his long, hooded cloak, swept his gaze across the otherwise vacant road until it finally landed on the man's overturned cart. One of his eyes, as always, was covered by a black patch. "Does this setup work well for you? Drawing hapless flies into your sticky web?" he asked.

"Works like a witch's charm. I find many of those willing to help an old, dying man also have pockets heavy with gold. I only wish to unburden them of that weight."

Livius's gaze locked on Maddox, his good eye dark in his tanned face. "The boy is young and naive. He's susceptible to deception."

"And I am very grateful for that weakness." The thief's grin widened. "You have the power to stop this peacefully. I'm happy to release him . . . provided you show me what I want to see."

Livius reached into his leather satchel and pulled out a handful of golden coins that glittered under the sun. "Something like this?"

From his current position, Maddox could only guess that the thief's eyes also glittered.

"Yes, something exactly like that." The thief roughly poked Maddox in the center of his back. "Take the coins from your father, boy. Take them and put all of them in my bag. Only then will we part ways."

Maddox did as instructed, the blade pressed to his throat the entire time. He avoided eye contact with Livius, who watched him patiently, his arms crossed over his thick chest. Five handfuls of gold coins made their way into the thief's worn sheepskin bag.

"Excellent." The thief shoved Maddox away and picked up the

bag from the ground. "Be on your way now, the both of you. And don't look back, or you'll regret it."

"You think you can steal my gold and just walk away?" Livius clasped Maddox's shoulder, his fingertips biting into his flesh.

"Seems that way, doesn't it?" The old man turned away with a sneer.

"Not to me." Livius let go of Maddox, closed the distance between him and the thief in two steps, and sank his blade into the man's back.

The thief collapsed to the ground, real blood now mixing with the fake substance he'd used to lure Maddox to his side.

With a last hiss, he closed his eyes forever.

"He was old and weaker than you," Maddox mumbled. "He was going to let me go. You could have taken back the coins without killing him."

"What did you say?"

Maddox turned to Livius and was greeted with a strike to the side of his face.

A good blow, too. He saw actual stars behind his eyes as he stumbled backward on the loose soil, tasting coppery blood in his mouth.

"You take your own sweet time getting here when you know I'm waiting for you," Livius growled, "and get yourself in trouble along the way. What else is new, you pathetic little brat? If I hadn't finally lost my patience and come looking for you, what do you think would have happened? I'm sick to death of dealing with your insolence."

So don't deal with me at all, Maddox thought, ignoring the sting on his cheek and the tightness in his chest. *Leave. Go away. Never look back.*

But he knew that would never happen.

He'd tried to escape from Livius before, but his guardian was a masterful tracker. He'd barely survived the beating he'd received, and he remembered Livius's voice, low and calm, promising that he'd murder Maddox's mother very slowly if he ever tried to run away again.

Maddox knew Livius was a man of his word.

He swore he'd protect his mother until his last breath. After Livius was through with him, after he'd used Maddox's special skills to help pay his many debts, Maddox prayed that he'd be freed to start a life far away from the cruel, heartless monster.

Until then, he knew he had to play along.

"Let's make haste." Livius's words were cold. "Defy me again, brat, and I swear to the goddess I'll break both of your arms."

"Yes," Maddox said slowly. "I can feel it. Your villa is besieged by an evil spirit that has escaped from the dark land beyond death."

Lord Gillis gasped, holding his hand to his mouth. "I knew it. I knew it! I heard it over and over in the dead of night. It's frightened my family nearly to the point of madness. A . . . just an evil spirit? Are you sure that's all it is?"

"Positive," Maddox lied. "Why? Did you believe it to be something else?"

The lord twisted his hands. "This villa has only recently come into my possession. Years ago, the gardens in the back were allegedly used as a meeting place for immortals to work their magic."

"Allegedly?" Livius repeated.

"Yes. I, of course, did not witness such sacred meetings myself."

"No, of course not." Livius smiled patiently as if dealing with a foolish child who chased butterflies and called them demons. "What an honor and an accomplishment to have purchased such a valuable landmark."

"Yes. Yes, it is."

Maddox had no time to think of the immortals, who were said to exist side by side with the citizens of Mytica before he was born. Once the goddesses arrived and took their thrones, there had been no more talk of any other immortals sighted anywhere in the land.

Regardless, Maddox preferred to focus all his attention on spirits—whether or not they were real.

"I can rid your home of this dark presence," Maddox said.

Lord Gillis nodded enthusiastically. "Yes, wonderful. Please do."

He hadn't yet seen the gardens, but Maddox now walked along the hallway of one of the grandest villas he'd ever been invited inside. The floor was a mosaic of bronze and silver tiles that must have cost several lifetimes of a regular working man's earnings. Portraits of Gillis and his ancestors lined the walls.

Livius stood nearby, his arms crossed over his chest, watching. Waiting.

"Allow me a few more moments to strengthen my contact with the spirit," Maddox said. "We can't merely scare it away or it will disappear, only to return again to torment you after we've left."

"Yes, yes," Lord Gillis said, running a nervous hand over his bald, sweaty scalp. He wore robes—dark orange with elaborate gold embroidery—that swished around his fat legs. "Please, take all the time you need."

Maddox returned to the hall where the lord had said he first sensed the malevolent entity, and glanced up at the high golden ceiling. Seeing the difference between this elegant home and his mother's modest cottage caused bitter disappointment to rise in his throat. He would never be able to afford such a fine home for her.

"The spirit's presence is strongest in this room," he finally said.

"Do you know who it is? Perhaps this spirit has some sort of grievance with me?"

"Do you have many enemies?" Livius asked.

"No. I mean, I don't think so." Lord Gillis glanced nervously at Livius. "None I can think of offhand who'd choose to haunt my home."

"Maddox?" Livius prompted, his face in an expression of patience and encouragement. He faked sincerity with such ease that sometimes he fooled even Maddox.

"Well," Maddox began, "even if it *is* someone you know, once a spirit is devoured by the land of darkness, their essence becomes twisted and malformed. Even if they manage to escape, they're never the same as they were when they were mortal. They're dangerous."

A shiver went down his spine as he spoke these words aloud. It might have been standard, rote dialogue for such appointments as these, but it was also the absolute truth.

"Can they . . . *kill*?" Gillis asked, his voice tense.

Maddox actually wasn't sure if they could, but it was a logical question. "They can, indeed."

The lord let out a shuddery breath. "Then you must do everything in your power to dispose of this spirit immediately!"

Maddox nodded gravely. "I will try my best."

"He will do more than try," Livius said with pride. "He will succeed as he's done for many before. How else would you have heard of Maddox's stellar reputation as a spirit vanquisher if not from a satisfied customer?"

"When I first heard of the boy's unusual powers," Gillis said, his voice low, as if they might be overheard, "I couldn't believe my own ears. I've heard of no one else who can do what your son is capable of. I swear on my own life, I will keep his secret until I meet my grave. Just like you asked."

"Very good." Livius clasped the man's shoulder. "However, please do feel free to tell those who are trustworthy and may require our help. It's what we do. We help those who have nowhere else to turn."

Maddox tried very hard not to roll his eyes.

Lord Gillis nervously wrung his hands as he followed Maddox around the room so closely that he could feel the man's warm breath tickle the back of his neck.

He wanted to get this over with, but if he was too quick about it, the procedure wouldn't be believable. Too long, and it would strain the patience of everyone involved.

The timing had to be just right.

"This line of work must be so dangerous for you both, though . . . ," Gillis said after a moment.

"Dangerous?" Livius prompted.

"What the boy can do is so much more than what a witch is capable of. And even witches must protect their secrets."

Livius's jaw was tense. "The goddess *has* become rather strict of late, hasn't she?"

Gillis laughed nervously. "Yes, I'd say that demanding the head of every accused witch in the North qualifies as rather strict. But what can we do? Defy her and face her judgment ourselves?"

"Have . . . have you ever met her?" Maddox asked, his words now tentative. "The goddess?"

Gillis turned to him. "Indeed, I have. She is as beautiful as the sunrise. She is absolute perfection in every way, and I shall worship Her Radiance every day of my life."

"As will we all," Livius murmured, the standard reply for such praise of the goddess.

Maddox mouthed the same response while wondering if Gillis was lying. Very few had seen the goddess in person. She allegedly preferred to remain within the grounds of her huge palace a full day's journey west of Ravenswood on the very edge of the sea.

"Luckily for us," Livius continued, "witches are known to be female. I've never heard of the goddess's wrath accusing a male witch."

"And yet your son is one."

Maddox wanted to protest being referred to as a witch—as well as the constant assumption that Livius was his father—but he held his tongue.

He wasn't a witch. Witches had the powers of the elements—earth, fire, air, water. His powers . . . well, he didn't know what they were, other than utterly useless and unreliable most of the time.

"His gifts are very special and must be protected. That's my job . . . to protect him." Livius paused. "Are you ready to begin, Maddox?"

Maddox didn't feel very special right now, or protected, but he knew what to do. He'd done it many times before. "I am. You might want to stand back, Lord Gillis. I don't want you to get hurt."

Lord Gillis immediately took a giant leap away.

Maddox tried not to smile at the man's dramatics as he pulled a silver box the size of his palm from his satchel. "I will trap the spirit in this box. . . ."

"With your very special power over the dead," Gillis finished breathlessly.

"Yes." He tried to inject confidence into the single word.

"Amazing."

It was good that Gillis needed no further convincing—he was a believer from the start. That made everything much easier. After this, whatever creaking or knocking heard in the middle of the night that had disturbed the Gillis family enough to seek his help would be considered nothing more than what they actually were: knocks and creaks in a large house on the edge of a tall, windy cliff.

Maddox sensed no actual spirits here, only a family of rich cowards. But to admit this would be to forfeit payment.

He held the box in his hand and closed his eyes.

"Come to me, spirit of the dark. Leave these good people alone. Come to me. Come to me now."

He waited a few moments, then tapped into the ability he knew he *could* easily control, which was to summon a shadow from the corner of the room, drawing it toward him in a ribbon of darkness. The shadow swirled in front of him in a dramatic display before he drew it fully into the box.

He closed the lid to trap it inside.

"It is done," he said solemnly.

Gillis stared at him with utter amazement, which was a completely normal reaction. The trick had impressed many over the three years Maddox and Livius had been traveling together, separating many lords and nobles from their gold.

"Incredible," Gillis said with awe.

"Your worries are now at an end," Livius said. "The spirit has been successfully removed from your home, and we shall dispose of it so it will never trouble you again."

Gillis clasped his hands. "Much gratitude, kind sir. To you and your incredible son."

I'm not his son, Maddox thought darkly. *I'm nothing more than a slave to him.*

A slave he could use to make enough coin to pay back the moneylenders to whom Livius owed a small fortune. Livius had once been a gambler, one with very bad luck. The last time Livius hadn't been able to make a payment, one of the moneylenders had taken his left eye as punishment.

"No gratitude necessary," Livius replied. "Except, of course, the second half of the fee that we agreed upon."

"Yes, of course. Of course! Please, follow me."

Maddox turned toward the entrance to see that a girl now stood by the golden archway leading into the huge room. She gazed around, her eyes wide.

"Don't worry," he told her. "The spirit is gone."

She stared at him. "What?"

Likely, she was Gillis's daughter. Though, Maddox thought, she really was far too lovely to be the daughter of such an ugly man. Perhaps her mother was a rare beauty. The girl's clothing was unusual, to say the least. The top half of her ensemble was made from wool, but was dyed an incredibly unnatural, bright shade of rose. And he'd never seen a girl wearing trousers before. These trousers were not the baggy style that Mytican men wore; they were close-fitting and made from some sort of finely woven blue material. He forced himself to stop gawking at her long, lean legs.

"Who are you talking to?" Livius growled at him.

He nodded toward the entryway. "The girl."

"*What* girl?"

Maddox blinked. "Lord Gillis, your daughter. . . ."

Gillis shook his head. "No daughter. I have only sons, and

they're out for the day at the festival. Now, come with me, both of you. I will pay you and we will part ways as good friends."

The girl still stood by the entrance, looking around at the large room as if seeing it for the first time and finding it horribly confusing.

"Where am I?" she asked Maddox. "I—I found myself out in the garden a few minutes ago. How did I get here?"

Lord Gillis approached the girl, but as he got closer, he didn't slow down, nor did he acknowledge her presence. Maddox opened his mouth to say something, but before he could, the lord walked right into her.

No, he didn't walk *into* her. He walked straight *through* her.

As if she wasn't even there.

Livius shot Maddox a glare sharp enough to cut. "Get that stupefied look off your face, you fool. Let's finish this and leave."

The girl watched them as they passed. Maddox couldn't take his eyes off her.

"You can see me," she said. "They can't, but you can!"

Maddox forced his attention away from her, focusing instead on his footsteps. His heart began to pound harder.

"Please, look at me." The girl kept pace with him. She had long, honey-golden hair worn in a braid and blue eyes the color of the sea at dusk. She looked afraid and confused . . . but incredibly determined.

He would not be fooled by her beauty. It seemed as if Lord Gillis was correct after all. His villa *was* haunted.

Be gone, dark spirit, he thought fiercely. *Leave me in peace.*

"I don't know what's going on, but something bad happened to me." She tried to touch him, but her hand passed right through him like a wisp of smoke. He tensed up but felt nothing, which surprised him. The spirits he typically encountered left him chilled to the bone, shivering.

She stared down at her hand with horror. "Oh my God, what's going on?"

Maddox kept his lips pressed together, tempted to give her another glance, but stopping himself just in time.

"I *know* you can see me," she said, her voice quavering a little but remaining strong otherwise. "Don't try to pretend you can't!"

He blinked rapidly, dismayed that Livius and Gillis had stopped and were now blocking the entryway, preventing his escape from the spirit girl. They now stood face-to-face as Livius took a pouch of coins from the lord. The two clasped hands.

"Look at me, will you?" the girl cried. "Please!"

Her fearful tone pulled at him, and he finally met her gaze.

A whisper of relief moved through her eyes. "My name is Becca Hatcher. I don't know what's happened to me, where I am, or how I got here, but I know one thing. You're going to help me get back home."

Chapter 4

CRYSTAL

It was all a blur.

She called 9-1-1. The ambulance arrived quickly, its lights flashing and siren blaring. She forced herself to hit the right buttons to call her mother and left a hysterical, rambling message. Then there was the ride to the hospital and the doctor asking her what happened. . . .

It was a question Crys wasn't sure she knew how to properly answer.

"A b-book," she stammered. "She was looking at a book at the store. It—it did *this* to her."

"Are you saying that something she read upset her?" the doctor asked. "What book was it?"

"I don't know. She—she just . . . I don't know what it was! You have to help her!"

"We'll do everything we can," the doctor assured her. "She's stable at the moment. It's possible she'll snap out of this catatonic state all on her own."

Catatonic state. It sounded so clinical.

Her mother arrived within the hour and gave her a tight hug. "It'll be okay," she whispered into Crys's hair.

Then she disappeared into Becca's room. It was a while before the doctor left, and Crys brushed past him to go inside. Her mother sat in the chair next to the bed.

Becca's eyes were still open, and she stared straight ahead. Every now and then she blinked.

"Becca?" Crys ventured.

"I don't think she can hear you," her mother replied softly. "It's getting late. You should go home."

Crys ignored her. She went to Becca's side and gently took her hand, cringing at the sight of the IV inserted into a vein and covered with tape.

"You told the doctor there was a book," her mother began.

"There was. There . . . there *is*."

"I know. I went to the shop before I came here and put it somewhere safe." She sighed and rubbed her temples. "You shouldn't have opened that package, Crys. It wasn't addressed to you."

Her mother's calm demeanor infuriated her. "No kidding. Message received, loud and clear. But I thought the worst I'd get was a paper cut, not . . . not this. What is this, Mom? What's happened to Becca?"

Julia Hatcher's lips thinned. "Jackie never should have sent that thing to the store."

That *thing*? "There was something in that book. Something . . ." Crys shook her head, trying to remember clearly. "I didn't recognize the language. It was old, ancient-looking, strange. And it literally glowed when Becca was holding it. The note from Jackie inside said that you know what that book is, so just tell me. Tell me so we can help Becca."

Crys waited for her mother to laugh and remind her that she'd been ignoring her sister's existence lately, but here Crys was, refusing to leave her side as if they were inseparable.

She wouldn't need the reminder that she'd been a lousy sister lately—ever since their dad left—but it didn't mean she'd ever want anything bad to happen to Becca.

But her mother didn't say anything of the sort. Instead, she let out another shaky breath. "Please, Crys. Go home. Get some sleep. Let me handle this."

"But why won't you tell me anything even though you know what's going on?"

"I don't know what's going on. There's nothing I can tell you right now that could help."

Crys sighed. She knew she wasn't going to get anything else from her mother tonight. Julia Hatcher was every bit as stubborn as she was.

"Fine, whatever." Crys stood up, still touching Becca's hand, her attention now fully on her sister.

She knew she'd let Becca down countless times in the last couple of years when she'd needed a sister's support and attention. She wouldn't let her down this time. She had to learn more about that book.

On the way home, Crys bought some sushi—a spider roll, which was actually made with crab. Once, she'd jokingly told Becca it was made with real spiders. The horrified look on Becca's face had made her howl with laughter at the time.

Tonight, she only picked at the food for an hour before she finally threw it into the trash.

It was after midnight by the time her mother got home. Crys was in bed but wide awake, Charlie's small, furry body curled up next to her. Julia came by her room, pushing the door open to look inside. Crys pretended to be asleep, lost in a pile of sheets, blankets, and cat. The door closed a moment later, shutting out the sliver of light from the hallway, leaving only the glow of the clock radio for her to stare at.

Over and over in her mind, she tried to remember exactly what had happened. Opening the package, paging through the book. Touching the bronze bird on the cover, the smooth brown leather. Walking it to the back, handing it to Becca . . .

The page of strange gold writing that started to glow. The glow in Becca's eyes. Then it was as if the golden writing itself had reached out and grabbed her. . . .

But that was impossible. Things like that didn't happen in real life.

The phone rang, and Crys jumped as the unexpected sound cut through the darkness.

Maybe it's the hospital. She grabbed for the phone next to her bed and held it to her ear.

Before she could say anything, she heard her mother's harsh whisper. "You shouldn't be calling the landline."

"I don't have my cell. This is the only number I know by heart." It was her aunt Jackie.

Crys's heart skipped a beat, and she moved her hand across the mouthpiece so she wouldn't be heard.

"What's going on?" Jackie asked. "You sounded frantic in your message."

"Frantic, yes. I'm definitely frantic. Your package arrived today."

"And . . . you're welcome." Jackie sounded very pleased with herself. "Am I not amazing? Are you not impressed with how fantastic my detective skills are when I fully put my mind to something? You seriously don't want to know what I had to do to get my hands on that thing. Finally, after all these years, we're the ones with the power. We can draw that bastard out of his safe hiding place and make him pay for everything he's done."

Crys's mother didn't reply. Silence stretched across the phone line.

"Jules?" Jackie prompted. "Don't tell me you're having second thoughts about this. Please tell me you still have a clear head about everything."

"Never been clearer."

"Good. Always remember: Markus King stole everything from us—including your damn husband—and now I've stolen something from him."

Crys stifled a gasp as her grip on the phone tightened.

"Stop, Jackie. Listen to me," her mother said, voice hoarse. "Becca touched the book before I could get to it. She opened it up, and something in it . . . affected her. She's in the hospital, catatonic."

All Crys heard on the other end of the line was utter silence for several taut moments.

"What? *Becca?* But . . . I . . . I didn't know that could happen," Jackie whispered.

"Of course you didn't. Neither of us did. But it's happened, and now she's . . . I don't know what it's done to her. I don't know how to help her." She hesitated. "Markus would know."

"Jules, no—"

"If I could talk to Daniel . . . Despite everything that's happened between us, he wouldn't want anything to happen to either of the girls. I could meet with him, talk to him. . . ."

"No. Stop right there. I know you still have hope for him," Jackie said, "but he's been swallowed up by that monster's secret society long enough for us to know he's lost to us."

"I know" was Julia's barely audible reply.

"That book is the key to *everything*, Jules. Even after all these years, I know Markus would do anything to get his hands on it. Don't get weak on me, okay? I'll figure out how to help Becca. I swear I will."

"You better."

"I said I *will*."

Click. The conversation was over, though Crys couldn't tell which sister had hung up first. It took another minute before Crys could place the phone back in its cradle, her hands shaking.

She reached down to pet Charlie, needing to feel his soft fur and warm little body to help ground her.

"What's going on, Charlie?" she whispered, her throat tight. "What the hell is going on?"

Crys and Becca had never been given a good reason for why their father left. One day he was there, the next he wasn't, and their mother had gone along with it all with seemingly stony acceptance, never truly opening up to her daughters about it except to say that "some marriages just don't work out."

Had Daniel Hatcher abandoned his family for a secret society?

She grabbed her cell phone and her glasses off her bedside table and started searching for information.

She typed: *Markus King. Secret Society. Toronto.*

The search yielded plenty of hits about many men with the name, but absolutely nothing useful. Nothing seemed to refer to the kind of man whose name her mother and aunt had just hissed over the phone.

Crys pulled her black-rimmed glasses lower on her nose and rubbed her eyes. A glance at the clock told her it was nearly three in the morning, and she'd still uncovered nothing on the Web. Finally, she gave in to her exhaustion. She fell asleep for five hours, waking up with her glasses askew and Charlie still snoring on her stomach. She sat up, and he mewed in protest before tumbling off. Her stomach wrenched as she immediately remembered the events of last night.

"Markus King, who are you?" she said aloud as she got out of bed and pulled on her bathrobe.

She slowly made her way to the kitchen and poured herself a glass of orange juice before sitting down at the table.

It had been just over two years since Daniel Hatcher left. Her father. Her hero. Her friend. Her mentor. The man who'd shared with her his love for animals and photography. He'd even been the one to introduce her to sushi, which her mother despised.

He'd left her with only memories, one in particular that had continued to replay itself over and over again.

"Tell me, Crissy." He always called her Crissy, a nickname she wouldn't allow anyone to call her. "If I ever went somewhere—somewhere else—would you want to come with me?"

"Of course I would," Crys replied without hesitation.

"Even if your mom and sister couldn't come, too?"

She blinked, confused. "Why couldn't they?"

He grinned that mischievous grin of his, the one that always made her smile in return. "They can always join us later if they wanted to. But first it would be an adventure, just you and me."

"Then, sure, I'd go with you," she said, shrugging. "Sounds like fun."

She had wondered, more than once, whether she really would have gone with him if he'd really asked. But he hadn't asked.

Two whole years. She'd kept his cell number on her phone all this time. If he ever called, she'd planned to answer it just so she could tell him to go to hell.

Before she could think twice about it, she began scrolling through her contacts list, rushing by name after name of all the people she couldn't reach out to. There were Amanda and Sara, her best friends who'd moved far away at the beginning of the school year, one right after the other. Her sister. Her mother. Dozens of random acquaintances, including a boy she'd liked last year but hadn't summoned up the courage to ask out before she'd quickly lost interest in him . . .

DAD

According to Jackie, Markus King, whoever he was, wanted that book. He would know what it was and, possibly, what it had done to Becca. Would he also know how to help her just as her mother had suggested?

Heart racing, Crys jabbed the entry in her phone and composed a quick text.

Are you still in Toronto? I miss you, Dad. Will you please meet with me today?

Her chest grew tight as she realized it was the truth. She missed her father so much it hurt.

She hesitated only briefly before pressing Send.

Then she put the phone down on the table and pushed it away from her, as if it had sprouted horns and a tail. Charlie sauntered into the kitchen and started to eat from his dish of cat food, glancing up at her between bites as she now curled herself up on the wooden chair, hugging her knees to her chest.

Five minutes later, her phone chirped. She pulled it closer and warily eyed the screen.

Yes, I'm still here. Of course I'll meet with you, but it will have to be tomorrow. Just tell me when and where.

Crys shut off the phone and tried to ignore the sick, twisting feeling in her gut.

She felt as if she'd just made contact with the dead.

Chapter 5

FARRELL

If there was one thing Farrell struggled with the most, it was properly tying a bow tie.

"Finally," he muttered as his clumsy fingers managed the proper knot at last. He pulled on the black jacket of his Armani tuxedo and took a swig of vodka from his silver flask.

He slipped the flask into his inner jacket pocket and then fastened a gold pin to his lapel—a small crest of crossed spears behind a hawk.

The society's signet was so literal it used to make Farrell laugh out loud.

He leaned forward, eyeing his reflection in the mirror, and pushed his dark brown hair back from his face. He glared at the birthmark beneath his right eye with displeasure. One day he'd get around to having it removed. He honestly hadn't paid it much attention until a local magazine did a photo spread on the family and someone in the art department had taken the liberty of airbrushing it out.

A physical flaw in the House of Grayson. Can't have that.

He turned on the heels of his tight, Italian leather loafers and left his room.

"Have you been drinking?" His father's deep voice greeted him in the hallway.

He gave Edward Grayson a wry look. They wore identical tuxes—same designer, same size. "Honestly, Dad. Would I drink on an important night like this? It's baby brother's initiation."

His father's lips quirked up, almost into a smile, and he absently raked both of his hands through his graying hair. It was another trait they shared—an unconscious gesture they made when not entirely at ease. "I'm counting on you to keep a close eye on Adam tonight."

"I will."

"I mean it. He's so excited about his initiation, and . . . well, I hope everything goes smoothly. Your mother's concerned that his reaction to his first meeting will be . . . unpredictable."

His mother was always concerned about something. "How about my first reaction? Was it unpredictable?" Farrell asked.

His father studied him. "You are always unpredictable."

He decided to take that as a compliment. "I try my best."

"Adam cannot embarrass himself or this family." It was Isabelle Grayson's voice that now sliced between father and son. Farrell glanced at his mother as she approached, her four-inch Louboutin pumps clicking on the marble floor. Her jet-black hair was pulled into a tight coil at the nape of her neck. Her lips were bright crimson, her eye makeup applied flawlessly. She wore a dark blue gown that brushed the floor and diamonds on her wrist, fingers, neck, and ears.

Her current expression held no discernible emotion. That could be because of her chilly personality or her most recent visit to her favorite Botox syringe, Farrell thought.

"He won't," Farrell said. "Adam will be fine."

"I hope you're right." His mother swept her appraising gaze

over him before moving down the staircase. Farrell watched her go with a tight feeling in his chest.

"Son . . . ," his father said, his voice softening a fraction. "Are you all right?"

Farrell blinked, glancing at him sideways. "Of course I am. Why wouldn't I be?"

A shadow crossed his father's concerned face. "You've been very quiet this week, which is unlike you. The anniversary of . . . well, it's been difficult for all of us, of course, but I know, for you, having found him like that, it must be—"

"I'm fine," Farrell bit out, shuttering up his emotions as best he could. Numb was best. Numb was always best. He felt the reassuring weight of the silver flask in his pocket. "We should go. Wouldn't want to be late, would we?"

Adam's face fell as soon as they got out of the limo.

"It's just a restaurant," he said blandly.

"Yes." Their father's eyes sparkled at the sight of the five-star restaurant where their attire wouldn't seem out of place in the slightest. "One of my favorites, actually."

"So, what? Do they reserve a room at the back for us? Like a birthday party?"

Farrell smirked. "Just wait till you see the balloon animals."

"Enough talking." Their mother's words were clipped. "Be silent. Eyes forward. Consider yourself blessed to have been allowed this opportunity at your young age, and don't embarrass me."

Adam clamped his mouth shut and met Farrell's gaze. The two nearly started to laugh. They might be unpredictable, but their mother certainly wasn't.

They entered the restaurant, practically vacant at nearly midnight. The familiar hostess's eyes flicked to their golden pins before she nodded.

"This way," she said, gesturing toward an elevator that slid open at the end of a short hallway. No party room or balloon animals in sight.

Adam kept quiet now, watching and waiting, as they got on the elevator together without a word. The doors closed, and they began moving down.

It wasn't very long before the doors opened again.

The hallway had fluorescent lights set into the ceiling about every fifteen feet. If Farrell stretched out his arms, he would easily be able to touch both sides of the narrow corridor. They walked two-by-two, parents in front, brothers in the rear.

Farrell had expected something much different than this on his initiation night—perhaps thick stone walls covered in mold and mildew, lit by blazing torches, leading to a cavernous hall with mysterious strangers in hooded robes. The scent of ancient traditions and history itself in the musty air.

Instead, he got something much less medieval and much more modern. This hallway reminded him of a narrower version of the city's PATH system: a maze of underground tunnels connecting the subway to stores and buildings in the business district so that commuters could avoid the slush and ice whenever possible during Toronto's harsh winters.

But this wasn't the PATH. These hallways were privately owned and maintained. Only a privileged few ever got to see these walls. But it *was* a maze of tunnels that led to many different places—or so he'd heard. So far, he'd only used them to travel from the restaurant to the society's inner sanctum.

Left turn, right turn, right, left, left . . . and so on. Farrell had never bothered to fully learn the route himself, because his parents had always been there to guide him.

"How far until we get there?" Adam asked.

"Not very," Farrell replied. Up ahead, he could see some other members headed to the same destination. "We're almost there."

Which was good, since his new shoes were killing him.

Finally, they came to a spiral staircase, which they ascended slowly and carefully. The staircase led to an iron door covered in mysterious symbols. Edward Grayson knocked—three quick, then three slow.

A moment later, the door opened, and they entered the society's headquarters.

"First we're at a fancy restaurant," Adam said loud enough for only Farrell to hear. "And now *this*?"

The disappointment and uncertainty had returned to his brother's voice.

Farrell knew that entering a grand theater dressed in formal wear, as if attending the latest touring Broadway musical, was not what Adam ever would have anticipated. "Just wait till showtime," Farrell replied under his breath.

Nearly two hundred other society members were already here, all taking their seats in the rows closest to the stage. This theater could easily seat six hundred, but the leader preferred to keep his numbers to a minimum.

Out of the corner of his eye, Farrell spotted a familiar face. Lucas Barrington stood at the very front near the wide stage and beckoned toward Farrell to join him.

"What the hell does he want?" he muttered to himself.

Lucas had been Connor's best friend for years, but Farrell had never liked him. He'd always been too . . . shiny. Too slick and polite and full of compliments, like he was trying to sell something. Farrell wasn't buying the suck-up act, so he usually tried to avoid the guy whenever possible and lately had only seen him at the quarterly meetings, every three months. They hadn't spoken a word to each other in six months.

"I'll be back in a minute," Farrell said to Adam. Then, without waiting for a reply, he walked toward Lucas.

"How are you doing?" Lucas asked.

"I'm fine."

"I hope you mean that."

"Why wouldn't I?"

"It's been a whole year now. I miss him, too. We all do."

Farrell's gut lurched. He wished he could find a way to turn off his emotions, once and for all. "Has it really been that long? Time sure flies. Is that what you called me over here to say?"

"No. Let's go over there. It's more private." Lucas nodded to the other side of the stage, where there was a small alcove away from the other members.

Once there, Farrell crossed his arms. "So, what's up?"

"I'll make this short and sweet." Lucas scanned the theater before his dark eyes met Farrell's. "You've been chosen."

"Chosen? For what?"

"For Markus's inner circle."

Farrell nodded slowly, not understanding. "Which is . . . ?"

"Markus's *secret* inner circle. It's always existed. Carefully selected members are chosen to help him on a more personal level. It's a huge honor."

Farrell covered his shock with a smirk. "Huh. A secret society within a secret society. Is it covered in secret sauce, too?"

Lucas snorted. "Markus wants to meet with you in private to discuss this further."

"I take it you're a member of this inner circle."

"I am."

His heart had started to race at this possibility. Very few members ever met with Markus in private. The man was a human question mark. "And why am I the latest chosen one?"

"Apparently, he sees the same potential in you that he saw in Connor."

"Wait. Are you saying that Connor . . . was he in Markus's circle, too?"

"He was." Lucas's expression turned grim and he shook his head. "I still can't believe what happened. And I know we've never discussed it before, you and I, but I guess this is as good a time as any. Did you have any idea he was having problems?"

"All I know for sure is he started acting differently after Mallory broke up with him."

"He took it hard when she left."

"To say the least." That was a short answer. The truth was, Farrell had heard Connor threatening his girlfriend of four years over the phone—telling her that if she didn't change her mind and come back to him that he was going to find her, hurt her. Make her regret her choice.

His voice . . . it had been so cold and dark and obsessed that it had made Farrell's blood turn to ice.

That hadn't been like Connor. The last couple of months of his life, he'd started to withdraw from Farrell, from Adam. He'd started acting like he had a secret, one he'd protect at any cost. . . .

Was it that he'd become part of Markus's circle?

"When does Markus want to meet with me?" Farrell asked.

"Soon. I'll notify you."

Farrell let out a slow, even breath. "Hopefully I'll be available at short notice."

Lucas grinned at Farrell's flippant comment. "Even you know to jump when he says so. And I hope it goes without saying that you'll tell no one about this."

Farrell's gaze moved to the audience of society members—some of the richest and most influential people in the city—all getting comfortable in their plush red-velvet seats and chatting politely to one another, as they did at the beginning of every meeting. Each one wore the same gold pin to show they belonged here. That they, too, had been chosen.

How many of them are also part of Markus's inner circle? Farrell wondered.

"My lips are sealed," he promised aloud.

Mind swirling, he returned to his seat.

"What was that all about?" his mother asked.

Farrell waved a hand. "Oh, you know Lucas and his girl problems. I told him he's way too young to be considering Viagra. Hopefully he listened."

"I will ignore your questionable attempt at humor." Her red lips thinned. "Speaking of girls, a friend of mine has a daughter I'd like you to begin dating."

"Really." He raised an eyebrow. "My mother, the matchmaker."

"Felicity Seaton is beautiful and poised, goes to an excellent school, and comes from an exemplary family."

"She sounds so shiny that I'd need sunglasses to date her."

"I've set up a dinner for the two of you at seven o'clock, Tuesday evening at Scaramouche."

Before he could protest, the lights began to dim and the theater went silent. A spotlight shone down on the brocade curtains as they parted to reveal the figure of a man. Like all the men here, he wore a tailored tuxedo that perfectly fit his tall frame.

"Who is that?" Adam whispered to Farrell.

"Our illustrious leader, Markus King," he whispered back.

Adam's eyes widened. "Seriously? *That's* our leader?"

"Uh-huh."

Markus King, the leader and cofounder of the Hawkspear Society, an organization that had existed for sixty years. A man who stayed out of the public eye and who cherished his absolute privacy, trusting very few.

Those who saw him for the first time always had the same reaction: disbelief followed by complete awe. Farrell had formed his own expectations as a young initiate. He'd imagined a wise, old man who watched over his society and its members with sharp eyes and no sense of humor.

Or, perhaps, a senile, old man who muttered to himself, and whom no one wished to upset by asking him to step down from his place of power after six decades to make way for a newer, younger leader.

Farrell quickly learned that Markus King could not be summed up by the naive expectations of a sixteen-year-old mind.

Tonight, he regarded their enigmatic leader with bottomless curiosity about what their private meeting would entail.

"How old is he?" Adam asked, his voice hushed.

"No one knows for sure."

Markus had bought this theater soon after he'd arrived in Toronto. In the 1950s, he closed it down, choosing not to reopen it to the general public. To anyone walking along the street, the theater would appear as nothing more than a sad old building. This was one of the reasons why it was accessed by the tunnels. If anyone noticed that two hundred men and women in tuxedos and evening gowns were entering an abandoned theater once every three months at midnight, there might be some difficult questions asked.

"I welcome you, brothers and sisters," Markus began. The acoustics of the theater helped make his deep voice all the more majestic. "I welcome you, one and all, with open arms. Thank you for coming here tonight. Without you, I would not be able to share my knowledge and my miraculous gifts. Without you, there is no past and there is no future. Without you, I would be lost in a sea of enemies. Together we are strong. Together we can make a difference in this world today, tomorrow, and always."

It was the credo of the society, which everyone repeated in unison: *"Today, tomorrow, and always."*

In all the meetings he'd ever attended, Farrell had never paid as close attention to the standard greeting as he did now. This powerful man had chosen Farrell to join his inner circle—just as he'd chosen Connor. Before his suicide, Connor had kept this secret—even from his own brother, with whom he once shared everything. What did it mean?

"Spring beckons in this great city, a season that promises new beginnings, fresh starts," Markus continued. "We will begin tonight, as always, with a report of our plans for the next few months."

He called up several members to the stage to speak, including Gloria St. Pierre, a woman who practically dripped diamonds in her wake. She spoke about an upcoming charity ball all members would attend and beseeched them to invite friends to buy pairs of expensive tickets, whose proceeds would go toward grants for struggling artists.

Farrell usually tuned out the first half hour of these meetings, but tonight he tried—emphasis on *tried*—to remain present and attentive.

Once Gloria was finished, Bernard Silver, the owner of a popular string of local coffee shops, spoke of a meeting he'd had with the mayor of Toronto. Bernard had attempted to sway him on a policy that would pull funding from several homeless shelters, and he was proud to say that he had been successful.

"Charity and politics?" Adam said to Farrell under his breath. "Is that all this is about?"

"It's a large chunk, but not all. Just wait. The boring part's almost over."

It was a rule that new members were not supposed to be told about the inner workings of a meeting before their first visit. Farrell wasn't a fan of rules, but he knew which ones not to break.

He valued his membership more than any of his many possessions. And he knew Adam would, too.

Once Bernard finished speaking, Markus again took center stage.

"We have a new member joining our numbers tonight," he said. "Adam Grayson, please stand."

With a nervous glance, prompting a nod of encouragement from Farrell, Adam rose to his feet. The spotlight moved to light his face, and he blinked from the glare of it. The members seated behind Farrell began to murmur with approval about the handsome, young Grayson boy.

"Join me onstage, Adam," Markus said, beckoning to him.

All went silent, except for Farrell's loud heartbeat, which hammered in his ears as he watched his brother move toward the side of the stage, climb the six steps up, and walk over to stand next to the society's leader.

The real meeting was about to begin.

"Welcome, Adam," Markus said, then gave a dramatic pause, "to the Hawkspear Society."

"Thank you, sir." Adam's voice remained strong.

Farrell felt a burst of pride, which helped ward off the whisper of uneasiness circling his gut.

"Have you been told anything about what we do here?" Markus asked.

"No, sir. Nothing."

"But you are aware that this organization must remain hidden from the world at large."

"Yes, sir."

"These people"—Markus spread his hands out toward the audience—"are essential to my life's mission. They have seen the truth that my existence brings with their own eyes, and they know it is important, that it is the most crucial gift I can contribute to this world."

Adam didn't reply right away. It was, after all, a rather cryptic statement.

After a moment, he found his voice. "What is it that you do, sir?"

"My purpose . . . my mission, Adam . . . is to help protect this world from evil—true evil—that would do irreparable harm without my interference. Eradicating that evil helps to shine a light on that which is good. You've heard much talk of that already tonight: charity balls, politics with purpose, the building and nurturing of strong relationships. We take a stand, collectively and separately, to do what we can to make a positive difference in this city and also work toward protecting the world at large. And what we do here, at these meetings, is essential to bringing us together as one mind, one heart. One purpose."

He paused, as if leaving space for a question. Had Farrell been unaccustomed to how Markus spoke, he would have likely laughed out loud at such grandiose speeches that didn't answer any questions in a completely satisfying way.

Perhaps Markus had been a politician in a previous life.

Adam's brow was furrowed. "How exactly do you protect the world from evil, sir?"

Markus nodded as if to acknowledge an excellent question. "When I first came to this city sixty years ago, I met a man who befriended me when I was alone and had no one. By the time I met him, he had already begun undertaking the insurmountable task of protecting this city. Together we formed the Hawkspear Society. A hawk, because it watches from high above. It sees all—nothing escapes its attention. And a spear, the weapon that, to us, represents protection and defense. We are an organization committed to truth and justice."

Adam sent an uncertain glance at Farrell, who nodded, trying to will strength toward his brother.

You can handle this, kid. Don't be nervous.

"Watch," Markus said. "Observe. And then decide if you are ready to be a part of my mission from this day forward."

Two of Markus's helpers—perhaps they were also part of his inner circle, Farrell thought—led a bound, gagged, and blindfolded man to the center of the stage. He had black hair that was graying at the temples and wore a dirty T-shirt. His face had a week's worth of stubble on it. One of the helpers removed the gag and blindfold. The man's dark, glittering eyes scanned the silent audience with both confusion and outrage.

"Where the hell am I?" he demanded, squinting at the bright spotlight.

"Tonight," Markus said, walking a slow circle around him, "John Martino, forty-eight years old, appears before us. A man who has been in and out of prison since he was eighteen."

"So you know who I am." John eyed Markus with disdain, then glared at the two men who stood on either side of him like silent sentries. He turned back to Markus. "Who are you?"

Markus ignored him, keeping his gaze fixed on his audience. "John is an executive in a very profitable industry—the illegal drug trade. Twenty dealers work under him. He supplies them with product, which they push on the streets to addicts and other victims of substance abuse. One of his recent shipments of ecstasy was laced with arsenic—"

"I had nothing to do with that!" John protested.

"—which caused the deaths of six people, including the daughter of one of our loyal members. After an investigation by the grieving father, her possession of the drug was linked to you, Mr. Martino. My loyal colleague asked that you be tried for your crimes here, tonight, so you will not harm anyone else in the future. Do you deny what you've done? Do you accept your guilt and your punishment? Only then can you be purged of the evil that taints your mortal soul."

"Who are you?" John's expression had grown even more wary. "You're not the police. This isn't a court of law."

"The girl who died—the girl you *murdered*—had a bright future. She wanted to be a doctor, who would have made a difference in this world someday. She was only fifteen years old."

"She was the one who swallowed the pill. She made her choice."

"And you've made yours—over and over again." Markus paused and then turned to address his members. "How many murders is this monster responsible for? Dozens? Hundreds? Thousands?

And how many more will he be responsible for if we were to set him free without answering for his crimes?"

"Just give me the chance," John snarled. "You're next, you son of a bitch."

"Pass your judgment," Markus instructed the audience.

Silence fell over the theater.

A moment later, a man in the front row stood up. "Guilty," he said.

Slowly, others stood and repeated the word. Another moment later, many more rose together, including Farrell and his parents, their voices rose in unison.

"Guilty."

Markus glanced at Adam, who was watching all this with wide eyes. "And you, Adam? What is your verdict?"

Adam looked at John, really looked at him for a long searching moment. John stared back at him, as if trying to intimidate the kid. Then John threw his head back and laughed, the sharp sound cutting through the silence.

"You're just a little kid, aren't you? What, your babysitter wasn't available tonight?"

Adam's eyes narrowed. "Guilty," he said.

"Great!" John was still laughing. "Guilty, guilty, guilty. How about I get a lawyer and sue all your asses for kidnapping me?"

Markus regarded the audience. "How can I protect the world from the darkness this murderer brings with him wherever he goes? The harm he dispenses with every selfish choice he makes? How shall John Martino be punished here tonight? What will cleanse him of the evil inside him that darkens this world wherever he goes?"

"Death," the audience said in unison. Farrell felt the word leave his lips as it had at every meeting before.

This man before them was evil. Judgment had been passed by the Hawkspear Society.

And that judgment was final.

"What? What are you talking about?" John now struggled against the men who held him firmly in place. "Let me go!"

Markus approached him slowly, reaching beneath his jacket to pull out a golden dagger.

"I free you from this life of pain," Markus preached to John. "I free you from this life of darkness. You can rest now. You will never harm anyone else ever again."

"Wait, what is this? You can't—!"

Markus thrust the dagger into the man's chest. John gasped in pain and shock, then shrieked as Markus twisted the blade.

"Blood for blood, death for death," Markus said, yanking the dagger from the man's flesh.

"*Blood for blood, death for death,*" the society repeated.

John dropped to his knees, staring up at Markus. For a moment, it looked as if he were a wounded peasant kneeling before a conquering king, begging for mercy.

Then he fell to his side, blood welling next to him in a shallow crimson puddle.

Farrell felt it then, the same powerful sensation that overcame him four times a year after each execution.

Magic—Markus's magic—strengthened by the spill of blood.

It charged the room like a whisper of electricity, raising the hair on Farrell's arms and the back of his neck. It brought with it a sense of serenity, of righteousness. Of power.

"It is done," Markus said solemnly. He pulled a handkerchief from his pocket and wiped the blood from the blade.

Farrell's gaze shot to Adam to see his reaction to witnessing a public execution with no prior warning. His brother's face was unreadable, but he stood rigidly, fists clenched at his sides, his attention fixed on the dead body.

"Adam Grayson," Markus said solemnly. "Will you accept the invitation to join my society as an official member, and in that capacity, will you agree to contribute heart, body, and mind to my mission to protect this world from evil? Will you keep our secrets and do all you can to serve the Hawkspear Society? Will you accept that the sacrifices made here are symbols of our focus on the greater good of this city, this country, and this world?"

Adam hesitated for only a moment. Then he raised his chin and, without looking in Farrell's direction again for encouragement, spoke the words that would seal his destiny.

"Yes, I will." His voice was strong and filled with determination.

Farrell let out the breath he hadn't even realized he'd been holding.

It was the right answer, of course. The only answer.

"Remove your jacket and pull up the sleeve on your left forearm," Markus instructed.

A frown of confusion creased Adam's forehead, but he did as asked, letting his tuxedo jacket fall to the floor. He fumbled with the button at his left wrist and then pushed the crisp white sleeve up to his elbow.

Markus took Adam's wrist and, without warning, he touched the sharp tip of the golden dagger to Adam's flesh and pressed down.

Adam inhaled sharply but didn't flinch or make a single sound of protest.

"The mark I give you now," Markus said, "binds you to my society. It will also free you from any human ailments you may have previously been susceptible to. No disease, no sickness, for as long as you remain one of my trusted members. This is my gift to you." He continued to trace the dagger across Adam's forearm in a precise pattern—a circle, or was it a triangle? Farrell had closely watched as it had been cut into his own arm three years ago, but he couldn't seem to recall what symbol it was. The memory was a blur.

Bright red blood dripped to the stage floor. With every drop, the charge of magic pulsing through the gathered members strengthened. The air itself seemed to shimmer with it.

When it was done, Markus pressed his hand against the wound. White light began to glow around his hand, and when Markus let go of Adam, the wound had been completely healed. It left no scar.

"There," Markus said. "You are now one of us."

Adam looked down at his arm with amazement. "Thank you."

Once again, Farrell thought back to the night of his initiation. His fear, his anxiety. His doubt. There he stood before everyone, with Connor in the audience, watching and worrying, just as Farrell did for Adam tonight.

He'd seen the grimness on Adam's face upon witnessing the execution from only steps away. His little brother knew he'd just made a serious commitment to a society dedicated to saving the world from evil. That what they did here was important. Necessary.

Farrell had already seen behind the first curtain.

Now he'd been chosen to see what hid behind the next.

Chapter 6

MADDOX

"I know one thing. You're going to help me get back home."

Right after the spirit girl said this, she'd vanished into thin air, leaving Maddox turning around in circles, confused by everything he'd seen and heard, until Livius barked at him that it was time to leave Lord Gillis's villa.

Thankfully, it seemed as if the strangely dressed girl had only been a figment of his imagination.

It was entirely possible that such hallucinations had been caused by Maddox's not getting very much sleep lately. He'd recently begun having nightmares. Always the same one, too—the horrific experience of seeing his first spirit.

The shadowy creature moved toward him in the dead of night . . . chilling his heart the closer it came. Maddox pulled his blanket up to his nose as he stared out with horror at what approached him, lit only by the flickering candle on his bedside table.

It had black eyes so dark and bottomless he was certain they could devour his soul.

"Help me," the horrific thing screeched.

Maddox screamed and screamed until the spirit withdrew from him, as if in horrible pain, and faded into the shadows. His mother was at his side a moment later, pulling his small body into her arms and holding him tightly until he stopped sobbing.

"You're stronger than any creature of darkness, my sweet boy," she whispered. "These troubled spirits . . . they're drawn to your magic, like nightflies to a campfire. But they will never hurt you. I promise they won't."

He wasn't sure it was true, but her promise helped him be brave.

By the time he turned twelve, Maddox had learned that he had the ability to trap the dark things that visited him in the night in silver containers that he would then bury deep in the earth.

"Why can I do these things, Mama?" he asked her one evening when she was in the middle of making a potato and pheasant stew. The pheasant had been killed by the man she'd recently claimed to have fallen in love with. Livius was very handsome and seemingly full of enough kindness, charm, and wit to get him through the door of their cottage and into Damaris Corso's bed.

"I don't know." It was her constant reply whenever he asked, but somehow it always rang false to him. He sensed that she *did* know something, although she refused to say what it was. "But you must tell no one of your magic. Other people wouldn't understand like I do."

However, it was Damaris who confided in Livius about her son's abilities a year later. Afterward, Livius had shown them his true self, which was made up almost entirely of greed and deceit. He was an opportunist and a con man hiding in their village to escape the moneylender he owed.

But he decided his luck had finally changed as soon as he learned Maddox's secret.

Once Livius discovered that real hauntings were rare and that noblemen who believed their villas were plagued by spirits were quite common, he began to rely on Maddox's ability to summon shadows to trick customers who were made gullible by fear. And it was a very good trick: No one ever doubted Maddox's abilities as a vanquisher of dark spirits.

The day after they left Lord Gillis's villa, Livius took Maddox to the local festival. With the crowds so large that it was impossible to estimate their numbers, it appeared as if all citizens who lived within a twenty-mile radius were there to celebrate the goddess's fifteenth year of ruling Northern Mytica.

Maddox was just an infant when the two radiant and powerful beings first came to Mytica, but he'd heard all the stories. He'd lived his entire life under Valoria's rule.

Two goddesses made their home Mytica. One in the North, one in the South.

Valoria of the North was the goddess of earth and water. She commanded both elements, and her displays of magic were, as the stories went, as beautiful as they were terrifying.

The goddess of the South was Valoria's sworn enemy. Contrary to the legends of Valoria's beauty, she was said to be horrifically ugly and sadistically cruel to her subjects—rich and poor alike. Many claimed she was a glutton who ate the children of those citizens who crossed her. She commanded the elements of fire and air. She was never mentioned in the North by name, for it was against the laws of the land. But Maddox had heard whispers of her name many times before. Cleiona, a beautiful name for a repulsive goddess.

Some said the goddesses came from another world entirely—far apart from this one. That, despite the fact that Mytica was a small realm compared with the larger kingdoms across the sea, they had chosen it because it was a land of incomparable beauty—where their magic could rule.

Magic had once existed more plentifully here. Golden and flawless immortals—the same immortals Lord Gillis believed once used his gardens—were said to have once walked side by side among mortals.

All Maddox knew for sure was that there were no golden immortals in Mytica anymore—at least, none whom he'd seen with his own eyes. There were only two powerful goddesses to worship.

But there were some who wished to worship neither. A handful of rebels had risen up a decade ago but had been easily defeated by the goddesses and their armies.

In Central Mytica was a large swath of unsettled land that was considered neutral ground. Those who chose to live there did so in exile, without the protection or guidance of the powerful leaders to the north and south. Central Mytica was a wild and lawless land, one Maddox had no interest in ever visiting.

A fat woman festooned with flowers tucked into her hair and fastened to her dress merrily greeted Maddox and Livius as they entered the crowded festival. "Welcome to the Celebration of Her Radiance, the Goddess of Earth and Water!" She placed a daisy chain around each of their necks. "There is cider in the blue tent, and in the red tent, we have roasted chestnuts, seared goat, baked figs, fried fish tails—so much to eat! Have a wonder-filled day!"

"Thank you," Maddox said, amazed by the mass of colorful tents, the delicious scent of freshly seared meat and just-picked delicacies, and the hundreds of people out enjoying the day of sunshine. Dozens of banners waved, adorned with the image of the goddess and the symbols of her elements—wavy lines for water, a circle within a circle for earth.

"Good sirs." Another man approached with an ear-to-ear grin.

"Allow me to show you my very special product." He held up a clay pot filled with a brown substance, whose stench wrinkled Maddox's nose. "This is manure from my favorite cow, who I believe to be a bovine witch that can conjure up earth magic in a rather creative way. Purchase this from me today, and I will guarantee your crops will grow better than—"

"Remove yourself from my sight," Livius growled, shoving him out of the way. "Come on, Maddox. We don't have time for such nonsense."

"He says his cow is a witch."

"He's an idiot. Besides, we're not here to take a pleasurable stroll through the vendors' tents. We're here for business."

Maddox's steps slowed as they approached a small yellow tent, just past a trio of jugglers in colorful garb and a pen of pigs and chickens. He'd rather inspect magical manure all day than help Livius with this task.

"Do I have to come in with you?" he asked.

"Yes," Livius hissed. "Stop asking stupid questions."

There were other questions Maddox wanted to ask. Such as: *Why do I have to meet the man to whom* you *owe money? Do you think I'll protect you with my magic?*

If he could find a way to properly control and harness his magic, he certainly wouldn't use it to protect Livius.

He cast another wistful look at the jugglers, all laughing as they performed for an enthusiastic audience. It looked like fun for both the audience and the performers.

Livius took a deep breath before he pulled back the flap and entered the tent. Maddox reluctantly followed him into the dark interior.

Two large, intimidating bodyguards stood by the entrance like a duo of ugly tree trunks, their thick arms crossed over their broad chests. Another man sat at a wooden table, attended by a buxom, young blond woman who served him food and drink.

"Livius!" The man smacked his lips after devouring a juicy rib of some unknown animal—likely from the pen of depressed-looking swine they'd passed—and wiped his greasy fingers on the loose silk ties of his shirt. "It's been a long time."

"Cena." There was no apprehension or fear in Livius's voice, only confidence—even if it was false. "Yes, far too long."

Cena leaned back in his chair. His bushy eyebrows joined in the middle of his forehead, looking like a fat caterpillar that had attached itself to his face. "For a while, I thought you were dead. Or that I'd have to send my men into the land of darkness to drag your arse back here."

Livius laughed as if this were the funniest thing he'd ever heard. His fingers twitched as he stroked his eye patch. "No need to attempt such a journey."

"And who is this?" Cena gestured toward Maddox.

"This"—Livius squeezed Maddox's shoulder hard enough to make him wince—"is my son, Maddox."

Maddox needed to bite his tongue not to argue with such an introduction.

Cena pursed his lips. "Your son looks nothing like you."

"He got his looks from his mother. His brains from me." Livius reached into his satchel and pulled out a heavy bag of coins, which he then placed next to Cena's plate of food. "This is part of what I owe you."

Cena glanced at the bag. "When will I get the rest?"

"Soon."

"How soon?"

Livius's jaw tensed. "Very soon."

"I'd almost forgotten how much you like to give vague answers when you know I'll only be pleased by specific ones." Cena fixed him with a predatory smile. There was a strand of meat stuck between two of his yellowish teeth. He glanced again at Maddox. "You're the one I've heard about, aren't you?"

Maddox didn't like so much attention on him. "Me?"

"The witch boy who can speak to the dead."

That was the trouble with secrets. Once they started to spread, they ceased being secrets at all.

"It's all a con," Livius said quickly. "The boy has no talent other than a keen ability to earn his old man the coin I need to pay you back."

"A con, is it? From what I've heard, it's a rather successful one." Cena kept his attention on Maddox, which made him feel exceedingly uncomfortable. It didn't seem to be in his best interest for this man to know the truth.

A sharp intake of breath drew Maddox's attention to the right of the tent. His stomach lurched to see that the spirit girl had reappeared.

"You again!" she managed. Her gaze frantically moved through the tent. "For a moment, I thought I'd gone home, but I'm still here. And, again, trying to find my way in this strange place has led me straight to you."

"Livius, your son suddenly looks rather unwell," Cena observed.

Livius's expression was tense. "He's a sickly boy. Some days I wonder how much longer he has to live."

The lie was so quick to leave Livius's mouth that Maddox wondered if it might be the truth. Something behind the words sounded like a threat.

"Go, boy." Cena flicked a finger at him. "Go outside and get some sunlight on your face and some air in your lungs. Let me talk to your father for a while in private."

Maddox didn't have to be told twice. He felt Livius's glare on him as he departed the tent without another word. He walked fifty paces through the festival grounds before he stopped and slowly turned around.

The spirit girl—Becca Hatcher was what she'd called herself—stood directly behind him. She looked the same as she had the day before, in her strange woolen tunic and trousers, so unlike the other girls her age attending the festival.

How old had she been when she died? About his age or a little younger?

All he knew for sure was that she was the most beautiful girl he'd ever seen in his entire life.

He blinked with surprise at the thought. *No. Spirits aren't beautiful. They're dark and evil.*

"Are you going to talk to me, or what?" Her dark blue eyes flashed with impatience. "You're starting to make me feel like I've gone completely mad."

That made two of them, actually.

"Where am I?" she asked, glancing around at the busy festival. "This is all so weird."

He understood most of her words, but some of them seemed as unusual and foreign to him as her clothing. "You need to leave me alone, Becca Hatcher."

She turned a smile on him this time, a bright smile that made a warmth rise within him. She certainly didn't look anything like the shadowy creatures he'd encountered before. "Just Becca is fine. And thank you."

Livius doesn't let me talk to girls, he reasoned with himself. *That must be why I'm so distracted by this one.*

No, not a girl. A spirit. Dark and evil, remember?

Now he was annoyed.

"Thank you for what?" he asked, crossing his arms tightly.

"For acknowledging my existence."

He eyed the people milling past him with uneasiness. "I'm acknowledging nothing."

"If you say so. Who are you? What's your name?"

"I'm not telling you anything," he said sharply. He had to take control of this situation. He wasn't defenseless against such creatures. She'd best be wary of how far she pressed his patience. "You need to go. Now."

"Go *where?*"

"Back to where you came from."

"That's exactly what I want to do, but I have no idea how. It's . . ." She drew in a shaky breath. "It's so hard to explain. All I know is I was in the shop with Crys, and that book . . . I swear, this is all because of that book!"

"What book?" He didn't want to ask, but he couldn't help himself.

"The *book.*" She gestured wildly as if this would help explain. "It was written in some sort of bizarre language I've never seen before. And then I felt something grab hold of me, and the next moment, I'm here. Or . . . I was outside that big house. When I went inside, I saw you. And you saw me." She frowned. "Hello? Are you even listening to me?"

She spoke so quickly all he could do was cock his head and try his very best to follow along. She wore a necklace—a silver rose suspended on a thin silver chain—which she played with, twisting it between her index finger and thumb. Her fingernails were colored with paint, a bright rose shade like her knitted tunic.

When he realized he was staring, his gaze shot back to her face. "I'm listening."

She studied him for a moment. "You haven't told me your name yet."

"It's Maddox." He groaned at his mistake. He hadn't meant to tell her his real name.

"Maddox," she repeated.

The odd whisper of pleasure he got at hearing her speak his name aloud only made him more annoyed than he already was.

"Tell me where I am, Maddox," she said.

"This may be difficult for you to understand, but you're a spirit. Somehow you've managed to escape the land beyond death and return to the mortal realm . . . where you've somehow maintained your mortal form. This is very rare." In fact, it was the very first time he'd encountered such a spirit.

A man passing Maddox gave him a strange look that made him cringe. It would be better that no one listen in—otherwise, it would appear as if he were conversing with thin air.

She frowned at him. "You're trying to tell me I'm a ghost. That I'm dead."

"Apologies if this is a shock to you, but . . . yes."

"I'm *not* dead," she said, raising her chin. "I'd know if I were dead."

"Would you?" He decided to be bold and waved his hand through her form. She stared down at herself with dismay as her body momentarily turned to smoke wherever he touched. "Does that seem normal to you?"

Now she looked ill. "No. Not even slightly."

"Then I've proved my point."

Slowly, she took a deep breath and regained an expression of steely resolve. "Okay, before I completely freak out, I need to make something crystal clear to you. I don't know what's going on, but I know I'm not dead. I'm not a ghost. I've been . . . zapped. By . . . magic or . . . something. I obviously don't know exactly what happened. But the fact that you can see me, the fact that I found you again among all these people, leads me to believe that you're the one who can help me."

Help her? He couldn't even help himself. "I assure you, I can't help you."

"You *can*." Becca reached for him, but her hand passed right through his arm. She clenched her hand into a fist, her expression turning pained. "If you'd just try!"

"Listen to me, would you? I don't need trouble. I have enough trouble as it is."

If that was so, then why did something inside him want to help her? She must be so scared, but she was hiding it well. The girl was brave.

No, *not* a girl. A spirit.

Maddox sighed. She was also a girl.

A girl who was asking him to help her.

Finally he sighed. "Try how? I don't know what you think I can do for you."

"Before I first met you, I felt . . . weightless. I felt a terrifying nothingness. But when I'm anywhere near you, I feel something. It's the same sort of shivery sensation I got when I touched the book. Something—I don't know. Magical?" She tried to meet his gaze, but he looked away. "That book is the reason I'm here—I know it is." She looked down at herself, then gave him a squeamish look. "Yes, I'm seriously going to freak out."

He grimaced. "I don't know what that means, exactly, but don't do it."

"Please," she said, her voice now quavering. "Please, help me."

Curse it, he swore inwardly. He did want to help her if he could.

Suddenly, he thought of that first spirit he'd ever encountered, the horrible, dark creature that had reached for him in the night.

What would have happened if he'd agreed to help it instead of hiding from it? If he'd opened his heart to something so clearly in pain, rather than cower in fear from it?

Perhaps it had been every bit as frightened as he was.

A terror-filled scream from somewhere nearby drew his attention away from the spirit girl.

"Wait here," he told Becca.

A crowd had quickly gathered. Maddox now began to run toward the commotion to see what had caused it.

"What's going on?" he asked a woman at the edge of the crowd with two children at her feet, clutching her skirts.

"A witch," the woman told him. He peered over the shoulders of those in front of him to see that a young girl had been grabbed by a man wearing the uniform of Valoria's private guard: brown leather tunic and trousers, red cape, and golden helmet. "She's been accused of using her magic in an attempt to summon a storm to ruin the festival."

Maddox looked up at the cloudless blue sky. "There's no storm."

The woman shrugged. "As I said, it was an attempt."

It was rumored that Valoria arrested and imprisoned witches with minor abilities in elemental magic, reasoning that the use of such spells made her own powers seem less incredible and fearsome to her subjects. Another rumor was that she didn't want these witches to gather in large groups, pooling their magic in any attempt to usurp her throne.

"So now what?" Maddox asked the woman. Despite his command that she stay behind, Becca had come to stand next to him.

"There will be a public execution," the woman said.

"What?" Becca exclaimed. "They're going to kill that girl just because someone accused her of being a witch? What is this, old Salem? You're kidding me, right?"

"It's the way of this place," he told her under his breath. How could she not know this?

"The way?" she sputtered. "What backward, messed-up, whackadoodle place is this? That girl doesn't deserve to die. She didn't do anything wrong!"

He agreed with her, despite not fully grasping her truly bizarre language. He'd always found such knee-jerk decisions to be cruel and unnecessary. But what could he do about such matters? The goddess decided the laws—it was up to her citizens to abide by them.

He shook his head. "An accusation is more than enough to condemn her, no matter how"—he paused—"*whackadoodle* it might seem."

When he turned from her, she darted back into his view. He groaned. She was as persistent as a buzzing honeybee.

"Then you need to help her," she insisted.

"I need to do no such thing."

"You mean, you'd just stand here and watch them do whatever they're going to do to her? Like it's nothing?"

Her words were like a stinging slap to his cheek. "I don't think it's nothing."

"Who are you speaking to, young man?" the woman asked, frowning.

"No one," he growled, his anger over his own powerlessness triggered by the mouthy spirit girl. "No one at all."

"Nice," Becca said, although her tone told him she meant anything *but* nice. "Ignore me. You can try, but I promise I'm not going anywhere. I will haunt you for the rest of my life if you don't help her!"

The threat made him grimace.

In the center of the crowd, the girl screamed again as the guard yanked her hair.

"This foul witch," the guard announced, loud enough for all to hear, "has shown rebellion and evil intentions against our great leader, Her Radiance, the Goddess of Earth and Water. Such a crime cannot be tolerated. It will not be tolerated. Her sentence is death."

Maddox looked on, his fists tightly clenched at his sides.

"No, please!" the girl cried out. "I'm not a witch! I'd never do anything to challenge Her Radiance!"

She could easily be lying. And even if she wasn't, Maddox couldn't just freely roam about North Mytica, helping every wrongly accused witch he came across. Livius would never agree to that.

"Do something!" Becca yelled at him, right in his ear. "You need to help her!"

His cheek twitched.

He didn't doubt Becca's threat. She would haunt him forever.

The guard pulled his sword from its sheath, his expression impassive. He raised it above his head, ready to bring it down to end the witch's life.

The guard then let out a harsh gasp and staggered back from the girl. He dropped the sword and clutched his throat, his face turning bright red in an instant. He tried to reach for his weapon as spittle flew out of his mouth and dripped down his chin as if he were choking on a piece of roasted goat meat.

The gathered crowd stared at the guard in shock.

"This is true magic," the woman next to Maddox whispered in awe.

Yes, it certainly was.

"You did that," Becca said, watching him with wonder. "You stopped him, didn't you?"

Maddox's magic rarely worked on command, so this unprecedented moment had astonished even him. Better not to waste it now that he had a momentary hold of it. The guard would undoubtedly continue with the execution the moment he recovered.

Maddox focused again. The guard froze in place, his eyes rolling back into his head, and fell over backward in a heap.

The accused witch stood there like a frightened deer.

"Run, would you?" Maddox yelled at her.

She didn't need to be told twice. She turned and ran, and was quickly swallowed up by the crowd.

Becca stared at him with awe. "You're amazing."

"This is all your fault," Maddox mumbled, never more infuriated with anyone in his life as he was with the spirit girl.

"*My* fault?"

He had no idea if the guard was dead or simply unconscious. All he knew was that he had to get out of there before anyone suspected he had something to do with this.

"Maddox, wait—" Becca began.

He turned and slammed into the chest of a large man in a guard's uniform and looked up at his ugly mug of a face.

The guard narrowed his eyes. "Care to explain what just happened, boy?"

"What? That, with the witch?" Maddox gave the guard his most innocent look. "I had nothing to do with—"

The guard hit him in the head with the hilt of his sword.

Darkness fell for what felt like hours . . . or perhaps it was only moments . . .

Slowly, very slowly, he opened his eyes.

Becca. Where is Becca? It was his first thought, but he couldn't move enough to even search for her.

From his position flat on the ground, his cheek pressed to the dirt, he saw Livius ten paces away, gesturing at him and yelling something to a group of guards. The fat moneylender, Cena, stood much closer.

"Yes, he's the one you've heard about," Cena said, looking down at Maddox. "The witch boy who can talk to spirits. Information like this must be worth a nice reward, yes?"

"You'll get a reward if your information is true." A guard crouched next to Maddox, peering at his face with curiosity. "We won't execute him just yet. The goddess will want to speak with him first."

Chapter 7

CRYSTAL

Every other Sunday, from the time she was nine to the time she was fifteen, Crys and her father would go to the Art Gallery of Ontario. Becca never really cared about art the way Crys did, always preferring to stick her nose in a book and keep it there all day long. Even though most shops were open on Sundays, it was the day the Hatchers had decided to keep the bookstore closed so they could have family time.

Family time. It sounded so quaint, thinking about it now.

So Becca would read in the living room with her mom or hang out at a friend's house those days—things that Crys would do on Saturdays. But Sundays were reserved for father-daughter art-appreciation sessions.

She'd seen plenty of incredible exhibitions over the years. Andy Warhol, da Vinci, the impressionists, the Group of Seven, and tons of modern art—which Crys loved, but at which Daniel Hatcher always cocked his head, uncertain how to interpret two bands of color worth over a million dollars.

Currently the AGO was hosting a history of photography exhibition. It was called *Light and Shadow: Photography from 1839 to Present Day*.

Crys hitched her heavy bag higher on her shoulder as she explored the once familiar hallways and alcoves of the AGO. She kept her mind off her nerves by focusing on the paintings and sculptures in the permanent collection before wandering into the special exhibition rooms.

Displays of old cameras—far, far older than her trusty Pentax—and one-of-a-kind shots of landscapes, architecture, and solemn faces posing for early photographs were good distractions. Crys noted happily that there weren't too many perfectly coiffed model-types around a century ago.

"They aren't smiling, because they had to sit for a very long time, frozen in place like that," a deep, familiar voice behind her said. "Hard to keep a smile looking genuine for that long."

Her shoulders tightened, but she didn't turn around.

"You look wonderful, Crissy," he said. "So grown up."

Finally, she glanced over her shoulder. And there he was, looking very much the same as he had the last time she'd seen him. Two whole years ago.

It felt more like ten.

Eyes that were duplicates of her own stared back at her, that spooky light blue color they both shared framed by dark lashes. A smile curved up one side of his mouth. "Nothing to say?"

"I have plenty to say," she managed. "Just trying to find my voice."

"Texting is easier, isn't it?"

"Texting is always easier."

He wasn't wearing his usual glasses (she'd inherited her bad eyesight from him). Maybe light eyes were naturally weaker than darker ones, she'd often wondered. Her contacts had pissed her off that morning, and she'd thrown them across her bedroom after several unsuccessful attempts at putting them in, then had stepped on them during her search. So glasses it was today. But she didn't blame the contacts. She blamed being close to the edge of Anxiety Cliff all week.

"So let's talk about photography," he suggested, crossing his arms and studying the display in front of them. "You know what this is called?" He pointed to a self-portrait of a man staring into the camera. The image had been printed on a shiny surface, very unlike the matte photo paper Crys used in the makeshift darkroom she set up in the house when she needed to develop film.

"It's a daguerreotype," she said, pushing her glasses up higher on her nose. She had already known the answer, but there was a descriptive plaque right next to it that explained everything, which she read from. "'Named for Louis-Jacques-Mandé Daguerre, the daguerreotype is an early photographic process that uses an iodine-sensitized silver plate and mercury vapor.'"

"Sounds like a lot of effort."

"Too much. I wonder what this guy would have thought of digital."

"Maybe he would have looked happier about the whole situation."

"Maybe." She swallowed hard, barely seeing the impressive image before her, barely caring about being so close to a historical artifact of her favorite subject.

"You're still wearing your funny T-shirts," her father observed.

She looked down at herself. Her vast T-shirt collection was simply clothing to her, not a conscious attempt at daily humor through fashion. The one she'd randomly chosen today was a cartoon of an anthropomorphic piece of sushi with the caption: THAT'S HOW I ROLL!

"I'm a fashion plate, what can I say?" She bit her bottom lip. "Can we go somewhere a little more private to talk?"

"Sure." He nodded. "The café?"

More memories. Lunch and dessert at caféAGO. Coffee for him, Coke for her. She always chose key lime pie if it was available because she believed it was the best pie in the universe—like a vacation on a plate. While they ate, they would discuss what they'd seen so far. What paintings and photos they loved the best, which sculptures were the most inspiring and meaningful. The days they spent at the gallery always flew by.

On the way to the café, they fell into an uncomfortable silence.

Crys had been so determined to focus on whatever she had to do to learn more about Markus King that she hadn't taken into consideration the emotional impact that seeing her father for the first time in two years would inflict. In the mere minutes she'd spent with him so far, she felt as if she'd regressed in age by at least ten years. She was now seven years old, following her daddy out of the photography exhibition, down the stairs, and around the corner until she could smell the delicious food—sandwiches, salads, pastries.

Scent helped her summon up the past as perfectly as any time machine—or photograph—could.

All she selected for lunch was a chocolate chip muffin and a bottle of water. Daniel got a chicken sandwich and a coffee and paid for everything at the register.

Neither of them even glanced down at the food once they'd chosen a table as far away from the other diners as they could find.

She'd expected to feel only anger at seeing him again. But what she truly felt was . . .

She didn't actually know what she felt. There was no perfect word for it, she realized. A blend of nostalgia, curiosity, and, oddly, a sharp edge of relief. All mixed together into a messy batter along with only a few tablespoons of anger.

She consciously tried to bottle up all her emotions and shove them into her fuchsia leather bag for safekeeping.

"I know you have questions for me, Crissy," he said, his fingers curling around the edge of the table.

If it were anyone else, she'd protest the use of that cutesy nickname, but it sounded right coming from him. Just like the good old days.

"I know you must be furious with me," he said when she didn't start talking right away. "All I can say is I'm sorry, but I know that's not nearly good enough."

"I just . . ." Crys squeezed her bottle of water, the cold condensation sliding between her fingers. "I can't believe you've been in Toronto the whole time. You've been so close, and I didn't know."

"How did you find out?"

She considered her words. "I overheard Mom and Jackie on the phone. Your name came up."

She wasn't going to tell him everything. The book, what had happened to Becca—that was too precious, too fragile. This was an information-gathering mission only—information-*giving* was not on today's menu. And as much as her heart was in turmoil over this meeting, her brain was focused on what mattered.

She hoped very much the ratio would remain that way. Hearts and brains didn't always get along so well.

"Eavesdropping," he said. "So things at home are the same as always, huh? You're still a troublemaker."

It wasn't said as an insult but rather more with grudging admiration. "It's one of my talents."

"What were they saying about me?"

"Something about Mom still believing in you, but Jackie telling her you're old news."

She watched closely to see if this would get a reaction, but there was nothing in his expression to give her any clue what he might be thinking. Not even a blink or a twitch.

"Jackie never liked me," he allowed. "What else?"

"They said you're part of some exclusive society," she ventured tentatively.

He's been swallowed up by that monster's secret society long enough for us to know he's lost to us had been Jackie's exact words. They'd been branded into Crys's memory verbatim.

"Did they." He said this flatly and not as a question.

His bland reaction infuriated her. "Is it true? You left us because of some secret group you joined? What is it, like a cult that brainwashes its members to leave their families?"

Yeah, she *definitely* didn't have her emotions properly bottled up today.

She forced herself to take a shaky sip of her water.

She liked to think she had a talent for reading faces, after studying so many at a distance through her camera lens. Most people wore their emotions openly on their faces—anger, sadness, happiness, disappointment. Emotion was beautiful, no matter what it was. The more powerful the emotion, the better the picture turned out.

It felt a lot different not being the one behind the camera.

An uncomfortable silence fell between them, and she began picking at her muffin.

"It's not what you might think," he said finally. "I am involved in an important organization . . . one that I believe in with all my heart and soul. It's a good thing, Crissy. The only bad thing about it was that I had to make an extremely difficult choice I never wanted to have to make."

"So this society made you choose them or us."

"No. Your mother is the one who made me choose. And I know you'll never fully understand why I had to make the choice I did, but maybe you will someday. I don't expect your forgiveness. I would be too embarrassed to even ask for it."

"Wait." Crys's brain began to swim. "You're telling me that *Mom* made you choose."

His lips thinned. "I could never make her understand how important that organization is to me. It's about life or death, Crissy. I know that sounds far-fetched, but it's true. The good I'm doing, the good I'm a part of—"

"What? Are you saving the world or something?" she said, trying to find a joke somewhere in all this and move away from how blindsided she felt to learn that her mother had been the one who'd issued the ultimatum that had caused her father to leave them.

"It would sound crazy to an outsider, but . . . yes. In a very large way I believe I am."

She stared at him. "You're serious, aren't you?"

"You're old enough for me to try to explain it to you, but you won't truly understand unless you're a part of it." He absently stirred his coffee. "How are you doing in school, anyway? You're graduating in June, aren't you?"

"And you're trying to change the subject."

"Temporarily. Indulge me by answering my questions, and I might answer yours in return."

She exhaled slowly, reminding herself that she had to stay calm and not push him too hard. Otherwise this meeting might end much sooner than she wanted it to. "How am I doing in school? I've been going to as few classes as possible ever since Amanda and Sara moved away, and I've found myself with few friends and no interest in dealing with teachers," she admitted. "Actually, I'm thinking about officially dropping out to pursue photography full time. I don't need a diploma for that, do I?"

The look of shock on his face almost made her grin. "Please tell me you're lying."

"I don't really like lies. I prefer to tell the truth whenever possible. It's much easier to keep track of."

He frowned at her. "Crissy, you need to focus on school. It's important."

"I disagree. What are you going to do? Call Mom to have a friendly discussion about my future?"

He sighed and pushed his sandwich away. "Maybe I should."

"Aunt Jackie didn't graduate."

"Jackie is rude and reckless, and has never taken any real responsibility for her poor decisions."

Crys shrugged. "I think she's awesome."

"Most likely because you obviously don't know everything about her."

His acidic tone made her want to argue on behalf of her aunt, but Crys fought the urge. She didn't have time to get distracted. "You should be proud, though," she said. "I'm still using your camera. I'm really good, too. I've even placed in the finals in a couple of contests." She pulled the Pentax out of her bag to show him.

He reached over and took it from her, turning it over in his hands. "Did you ever get a flash for it?"

"No reason to. Light and shadow—that's all I need. Besides, flashes are expensive." Time to turn this conversation back around. She summoned up her courage and reached across the table to grab his hand. He looked down guardedly. "Listen to me, Dad. You told me once that you wanted to take me with you. Was this what you were talking about? Leaving Mom to be a part of this secret society of yours?"

"I didn't know what I was saying back then. I was confused."

"I hated you for a long time for what you did. I still do." The truth of the words left a sour taste in her mouth. "You left and you didn't even try to contact me . . . not even once! I could have kept it a secret. I wouldn't have told Mom if you didn't want me to."

"I've tried my best to respect her wishes."

"Well, Mom and me . . ." She bit her bottom lip. "We don't get along that well. I know she thinks Becca's the perfect one, and she's probably right about that."

It hurt Crys to say that because she believed this. It seemed as if her mother raved over every A-plus essay Becca brought home, over every accomplishment. Becca had been the one to figure out the new computer system to organize the shop and its accounting. The two talked about the books they'd read for hours on end while Crys tried to watch TV.

Practically the only time her mother ever spoke to Crys directly these days was to comment on something she'd done wrong.

"That's not true," her father said, shaking his head. "She loves both of you girls equally. Some of her rules might seem harsh, but they're because she loves you."

"Whatever. She expects too much from me. I know I'll never

make her proud. I would have said yes, Dad. I would have gone with you. I would have joined this society that's making such a big difference in the world."

His jaw tensed up as he studied her, a frown creasing his brow. "You have to be sixteen to be invited in. You were only fifteen at the time."

"Well, I'm seventeen now and . . ." She took a deep breath. "And I want in. I want to be a part of your life again, Dad."

His brows drew together tighter. "Crystal—"

"I want to know more." She cut him off so she could finish making her case. "Is there someone I can meet with? Someone I can persuade to let me join? I want this, Dad. I want to be a part of your life again. And if what you're saying is true—that you're, like, literally helping to save the world by being a part of this secret society, then I want to help, too."

As she said it, she realized she wasn't lying. She wanted to be part of her father's life, and she wanted to know everything about this group that had stolen him away from his family.

Maybe he was right and her mother was wrong.

It wouldn't be the first time.

Three years ago, when cash began disappearing from the till—five to twenty dollars a few times a week, Julia had accused Crys directly because she'd once been detained at the Eaton Centre on suspicion of shoplifting (which had actually been her friend Sara, not her). Her father had defended her. He and Julia had had a huge argument, their raised voices easily heard through the thin walls of the apartment.

It turned out that a part-time clerk had taken the money. She was fired, and since then, the running of the Speckled Muse had been kept in the family.

Her mother had never apologized, and Crys had never forgotten. Or forgiven.

Daniel Hatcher pulled his hand away from Crys's, put the camera back on the surface of the table, and leaned back in his chair. "You mean this."

"With all my heart." Then she closed her mouth. She'd had her say, and now it was up to him.

Had she moved too fast? Would he think she was up to something?

"There is someone I can talk to," he finally said. "His name is Markus."

She went very still when she heard the name.

Markus King stole everything from us—including your damn husband—and now I've stolen something from him.

It was him. The man her mother thought might be able to help Becca. The man Jackie had somehow stolen the book from.

The man who had the answers Crys desperately needed.

"And I promise I will talk to him," her father continued. "The society welcomes family members and . . . you're my family, Crys. You're my blood. I'll do what I can to arrange a meeting, but I'm not promising anything beyond that. I can't make demands; I can only make requests. The ultimate decision is out of my hands."

She nodded, her heart pounding. "I understand."

"I'll be in touch as soon as I can." He glanced at his wristwatch. "But I have to go now."

"Okay."

She stood up as he did, and, after a brief hesitation, he leaned over and kissed her cheek. "I've missed you, Crissy," he said.

She watched him walk away until he was out of sight. "Me too."

Chapter 8

FARRELL

The sound of persistent knocking woke him.

Morning light streamed through the sliver of window his blinds didn't cover. He groaned and tried to sit up, shielding his eyes.

What time was it?

A glance at the clock on his bedside table informed him it was eight.

Eight?

Considering he hadn't gotten in until almost five A.M., he was ready to kill whoever had stolen his sleep.

The door opened, and his father strode inside, went to the window, and pulled the blinds completely up.

"What are you doing?" Farrell demanded.

"Enough of this laziness," Edward Grayson snapped. "It's gone on for far too long. Get up."

"I'll get up when I'm finished sleeping. Not there yet."

"You need to start thinking about your future, Farrell."

He fell back down against his pillow and stared up at the ceiling. "Today?"

"It's been a difficult year. It's been hard for all of us. But it's time to be a man, time to start taking responsibility."

He couldn't deal with this right now. "How about I take responsibility in a few hours?"

His father moved toward the bed and, in one quick motion, yanked the covers off his son. "Get up. Or else."

The words *Or else what?* rose in his throat, but he swallowed them back down before he could speak. What? Were they going to disown him? Cast him out onto the streets without a cent until he turned twenty-one and got his inheritance?

Not a chance.

"What do you want me to do?" he asked.

"School or work. Pick one, but you need to make a decision."

"And I have to decide at this very moment?"

"No. But at this very moment you can make yourself useful by talking to your brother. He's in his room, claiming he's sick. He doesn't want to go to school. It's unacceptable."

"If he *is* sick . . ."

"He isn't." His father's lips thinned. Beneath the storm in his eyes, Farrell could see the worry there. "He isn't taking the events of Saturday night as well as I'd hoped he would."

Farrell took this in and then swore under his breath. "So what does that mean?"

"It means he needs his brother."

Adam had kept to himself on Sunday, and Farrell had been out for most of the day and night anyway, partying with a friend who'd come home from college for the weekend. Most of Farrell's friends had left town, scattered to schools all over the continent, leaving him mostly on his own to meet new friends each night he went out, whom he usually forgot by morning.

Farrell didn't bother getting dressed. Wearing only his loose black pajama bottoms tied with a drawstring at his waist, he left his room barefoot and headed for Adam's. Ignoring his throbbing head, he knocked on his brother's door.

"Who is it?" Adam asked sullenly.

"Me. Can I come in?"

"No."

Farrell pushed open the door. "Thanks so much. Good morning, sunshine."

"I said *no*."

He shrugged. "I'm a rebel."

Adam sat in a chair by the window on the other side of the expansive room, which was decorated in the style of the rest of the Grayson estate—expensive and to their mother's tastes, via her favorite interior designer. Only a couple of rock band posters taped to the gold-and-bronze designer wallpaper claimed the space as Adam's.

"So what's the problem?" Farrell asked, taking a seat on the edge of Adam's messy king-sized bed.

"I don't know." Adam raked his hand through his light brown hair. Farrell's was several shades darker and always a mess—luckily, it was a look that was currently in fashion.

In last year's photo spread in the *FocusToronto* magazine, Adam had been referred to as the "angel" of the Grayson family because of his innocent, boyish looks and polite demeanor. Connor had been the "gifted artist." Farrell hadn't been referred to as anything except "the middle child" of one of the richest men in Toronto. And this was the publication that had removed his birthmark without question or consultation.

Asses.

"Come on," Farrell prodded when Adam fell silent. "Talk to me. Something's up."

"I can't stop thinking about when Markus stabbed that guy. I don't want Dad to know I'm still messed up because of it, but . . . I don't know. I don't know what to think."

"'That guy' was a murderer," Farrell reasoned. "A drug lord. Who knows how many people he would have killed if he hadn't been eliminated?"

"Okay. Maybe that's true, but it's just . . ." Adam hissed out a breath. "Why not call the cops? Give him a real trial? Life in prison?"

"That's not how the society works," Farrell explained calmly. "Everything has a reason, kid. Trust me on that. How's that arm of yours feeling today?"

"Sore." Adam ran his fingers over his forearm, frowning hard. "What was that symbol he carved into me? What does it mean? What does it do?"

Farrell spread his hands. "It's protection—it keeps us from getting sick. No cancer, no diabetes, no nasty debilitating diseases. It's his gift to us, exactly what he told you."

"Who is he? I mean, *what* is he, that he can do something like that?"

They weren't supposed to discuss any of this outside society meetings, but Farrell felt that he had to reassure Adam that everything was okay. "You don't have to worry about any of this, Adam. Markus is what he is."

"Which is? What? A wizard?"

"I don't think he went to Hogwarts, no."

"I can't believe you're joking around about this."

Farrell sighed, then sat down on the edge of Adam's bed.

"Look. I don't know for sure what's myth and what's real, but the story goes that the original cofounder of the society once had a dream about a god of death. He took the dream as a prophecy and started hunting down murderers and other bad people and going all vigilante justice on their asses. Then he met Markus, the very same god he had dreamed about. They partnered up, started the society as a more organized venture, and recruited members—rich ones, since they both knew that money talks when it comes to trying to make a difference in the world."

Adam stared at him as if he were a complete stranger. "You're saying that Markus King is a god."

"I don't know. You've seen him. You've seen what he can do. . . . Don't you think it just might be possible?"

"I don't know what I think right now. How are you okay with all this, like it's no big deal? You're the one who's always asking questions about everything. Why is this different?"

Farrell shifted his bare feet uncomfortably. Was he okay with it? Yeah . . . he was. He'd made his peace with what happened at the meetings because he believed in Markus's mission—to protect the world from evil.

But he'd had three years to come to accept it as something right and good. Adam had barely had a weekend.

"You'll get used to it," he said. "I promise you will."

"I don't want to get used to seeing people killed right in front of me, no matter who does the killing, or why."

Farrell tried to stay calm, but the thought that his kid brother was having a meltdown over this troubled him deeply. This could cause serious problems, not only for Adam personally, but also for the Graysons as a family.

"I get that you're feeling uneasy," Farrell said, forcing himself to sound calm. "I sort of felt similarly after my first meeting. But you need to hear what I'm saying to you. Are you listening?"

Adam turned his pale face to Farrell. "Yes."

"You agreed. When Markus gave you the choice to stay or go, you chose to stay. You got to the point of no return, and you went beyond it, kid."

Weakness was unacceptable. The weak didn't survive very long—not in the society, not in the world at large.

He hated that Adam's attitude this morning had started questions coursing through his own head, questions that had faded in the time since he'd been initiated.

Who was Markus King? Who was he *really*? Where had he come from? And how was he able to do the things he did?

Maybe he'd learn the truth if Markus accepted him into his inner circle.

The thought sent a shiver of anticipation down his spine.

"Always keep one thing clear in your head, Adam. The magic that Markus can do—it's for good."

"Good magic. Public executions. Prophecies. Gods of death." The pain and doubt on Adam's face had swiftly been replaced by fierceness. "Do you even hear yourself? Taking the law into your hands, whether you're waving around a magic knife or not, isn't *good*. It doesn't make him any less evil than that guy he had on the stage."

Farrell rubbed his temples. It was too early for this talk, and it had succeeded in making his hangover that much worse. This conversation was pointless, but he had to keep trying. He didn't want his little brother to get himself in trouble by asking too many questions.

He narrowed his eyes and threw some fierceness back at Adam.

"It's over. You need to accept that you made a binding agreement to the man who gave you this." He squeezed Adam's forearm and his brother gasped in pain. Even though there wasn't a scar or mark, Farrell remembered how extremely tender his wound had been for weeks afterward. "You're going to screw it up, for yourself and for all of us, if you don't get a grip on yourself. Hear me?"

Adam's face had gone pale, his dark eyes standing out like burning coals. "I'm done talking about this."

"You might be pissed at me right now, but I'm here for you whenever you need me. I'm your brother. I'll always be your brother. Remember that, okay? Now quit this sick act and get to school before Dad comes in and dishes it out way worse than me."

Farrell left the room feeling furious and helpless and like he'd only made Adam feel worse than he already did.

He made his way down the hallway, then froze as he reached a closed door at the end. He eyed it before trying the handle. It was unlocked.

He pushed the door open and glanced inside Connor's old bedroom. He felt at the wall for the light switch and flicked it on.

His mouth went dry.

This was where Farrell had found him, lying on that bed. Now it was made, its sheets and duvet perfect and pristine.

A year ago, they'd been covered in blood.

Other than that, the room was exactly the same. Even Connor's art, including an unfinished oil painting propped on an easel by the window that looked out at the back garden of their Forest Hill estate, hadn't been changed. It was a shrine to the firstborn Grayson. The perfect son. Talent, looks, intelligence—a triple threat. That was his big brother.

He went to the easel and looked at Connor's last painting.

If there was one flaw the eldest Grayson kid had, it was vanity. His paintings were almost always self-portraits.

Connor had been painting this one as if it were a Renaissance commission by a king or a wealthy lord. Chiseled jawline, curved lips, straight nose, and hair the same shade of brownish-black as Farrell's—only Connor wore his hair long, to his shoulders. Black eyebrows slashed over hazel eyes that, even though they were created with dabs of paint, seemed to pierce Farrell right through his soul.

"Miss you, brother," he whispered. "Miss you bad."

"I always thought it was his best piece." A voice startled Farrell, and he turned to see that his mother had entered the room, her gaze fixed on the canvas. "It seems to come alive the more you stare at it, doesn't it?"

He was surprised that she'd greeted him like this instead of with harsh words about his daring to enter her shrine to her lost firstborn. "He was talented," he said.

"I know he would have become a very famous artist." Her brows drew together a fraction, but then she shook her head a little and a cool smile stretched across her lips. Her attention remained on the canvas, as if she could reach in and stroke the hair back from her eldest son's forehead. "One year. I can't believe it's been that long. I sensed his deep sadness after he and Mallory ended their relationship. If I'd known his heartbreak was so great, I would have made an appointment for him with my therapist. I could have stopped him from doing something so final."

A trip to the therapist was his mother's standard solution for any emotional conundrum.

"Why didn't he finish it?" Farrell asked. There was no background behind the painted figure, only white canvas. Pencil marks showed what he'd meant to paint. A window. A sky. A wall.

She frowned. "What do you mean?"

He stared into his brother's painted eyes. "The Connor Grayson I knew always finished what he started. The Connor I knew never would have taken his own life, either. He loved life."

She looked at him sharply. "Until he didn't love it anymore. We change just like the seasons change. He wasn't any different."

"Don't you ever think there could be another explanation for what happened?"

"No," she said with finality. "He was a sensitive artist who had his heart broken. He chose to take his own life when he fell into despair. Over the last year, I've accepted that that's what happened. For you to question it . . ." Her lips pressed tightly together. "It's too painful."

Guilt cut through him. "I'm sorry." He didn't get along with his mother very well, but he didn't want to hurt her. He crossed his arms over his bare chest and forced himself to change the subject away from something that was still so raw. "Dad spoke to me this morning."

"About Adam?"

He nodded. "I tried talking to him. He's upset."

"I hope he'll quickly make peace with what he saw at the meeting."

"He will," Farrell said with a confidence he didn't completely feel.

"Good."

This was, officially, the single longest conversation he'd had with his mother in well over a year. *May as well go for a lifetime record,* he thought. "Dad also told me that you two want me to start thinking about the future," he said. "And I agree. I have to decide about school. Either I enroll somewhere and take some courses, or I start working for him."

If Farrell didn't go for a college degree, it would be an early entry into Grayson Industries. Stiff suit, tight tie, miserable business lunches, pretty secretary. Buying and selling other businesses. Being cutthroat. Making billions.

It wasn't Farrell's scene. The secretary part sounded all right, but the rest didn't interest him in the slightest.

He wished he knew what to do.

Isabelle Grayson's small smile remained fixed on her lips. "Actually, it's your father who's insisting on this decision. It doesn't really matter to me."

"Really?" Suddenly, he was hopeful that he and his mother didn't have as much distance between them as he'd thought. Maybe she understood him, understood what he'd gone through. Understood the nightmares he'd had to endure nearly every night since finding Connor's body.

"Yes, really. With Connor, I had such high hopes—that he would be a famous artist, that he'd soon get married and give me grandchildren. That he'd carry on the Grayson name. For Adam, his teachers say he has an incredible mind, that he's meant for medicine, law, business. Whatever he chooses, they believe he'll be successful. But you . . ." Her discerning gaze swept him from head to toe. "I have no reason to think you'll ever amount to anything of note. Therefore, I expect very little from you."

Farrell's throat was raw from listening to her little speech. "Thanks so much for clearing that up for me, Mother."

He stood there, dumbfounded, as she left the room. He wasn't sure why her words had blindsided him. He already knew what she thought of her middle-born son: nothing at all.

This only proved it.

He swept a gaze through Connor's room one last time before he went back to his own.

"What the hell do I care?" he muttered to himself, angry now. "Her opinion means nothing to me."

Back in his bedroom, he checked his phone to see he had a text message from Lucas.

Markus will meet with you tonight at 8.

Markus's inner circle.

It might be a secret inside of another secret, but it was something special and überexclusive. It was proof that Farrell wasn't nothing, wasn't nobody. That he'd been chosen by a powerful, enigmatic man to be included in something incredible.

Something Connor had been a part of before his death.

Something that would show his mother that he wasn't as worthless as she believed.

Chapter 9

MADDOX

The sound of a slap and the sting of pain drew him out of the darkness. He sucked in a big mouthful of air and sat up sharply.

Someone held him by the front of his shirt. Another slap brought more clarity.

Livius. It was Livius who was hitting him.

"Wake up," the man snarled. "Wake up and see what mess you've gotten us into now."

Maddox stared around at the small, shadowy room they were in, memories of what happened at the festival coming back with the force of another blow. "Where are we?"

"Where do you think we are? In the palace dungeon."

He said this as if it should be common knowledge, but Maddox had never been in a dungeon before. It was dark, smelly, and dank, with stone walls and a black metal door. He'd also never been inside the palace; he'd only seen it in the distance, a massive and foreboding black granite structure that rose out of the earth like a giant crystal shard, visible for miles and miles.

"Why are you here, too?" Maddox asked, stunned.

"Because Cena told them I'm your father. Because I protested your arrest. And here we are. Because of your stupidity." Maddox opened his mouth, but Livius raised a hand as if to strike him again. "Keep quiet. You've done enough already. Let me do the talking when the time comes."

"When the time comes for what?"

"For introducing the witch boy to the goddess."

Maddox shuddered with fear at this possibility. "But what if—"

"Shut up, you idiot. I don't want to hear another word leave your mouth, or I'll personally cut out your tongue."

Maddox pressed his lips together.

"Can you get us out of here with your magic?" Livius asked when silence lapsed between them for a long moment.

"Don't answer him," Becca said, and Maddox's gaze shot to the corner to see her standing in the shadows. She twisted her rose charm necklace nervously. "He just said he'd cut out your tongue if you speak again. I really don't want to see how he'd do that—they took his weapons away back at the festival."

He was surprised that seeing her again had quickly cast a measure of lightness into this gloomy dungeon cell.

"You're still here," he said, fighting a smile.

"What?" Livius snapped. "Of course I am, you fool."

Becca shrugged. "I did say I'd haunt you forever, didn't I?"

Maddox ignored his guardian and focused on the girl. "You said you would if I didn't help the witch."

She drew closer, her worried gaze locking on his. "I thought for a while I was only having a bad dream and that I'd wake up eventually, but this is real. You're real. He's real. . . ." She glanced at Livius, her expression souring. "He's a total dick, by the way. How can you let him abuse you like that, without getting fed up and kicking his ass? You're not five years old. You're, like, my age. At least."

Kicking his ass? He responded to this suggestion with an involuntary laugh. Livius didn't own a mule.

"You're talking to yourself." Livius peered at him with his good eye. "Are you mad, boy?"

"That would be an excellent explanation," Maddox said, nodding.

"Or perhaps . . ." Livius scanned the cell. "You see a spirit in here, don't you?"

"Yeah, he does, you jerk," Becca said, her hands now on her hips. "I swear, if I could, I would knee you so hard in your—"

"I don't see anybody in here but you," Maddox said quickly to Livius before Becca could finish.

He pointed at the door. "Break it down and get us out of here."

"You know I can't control my magic that easily. Even if I could, I don't think I could use it to break down a heavy dungeon door."

"If you controlled it at the festival, then you can control it now."

"In case you were wondering," Becca said, "the guard woke up. Let's just say he was *really* pissed off." She shot Maddox a smile, but it faded as quickly as it had appeared. "But I didn't realize it would get you into so much trouble. When the guard hit you . . ." She studied his temple with a pained expression. He touched it, feeling the dried blood. "I—I thought they were going to kill you, and all I could do was stand there and watch."

"They didn't kill me."

At least not yet, he thought.

She played absently with her honey-colored braid as if she couldn't keep her hands still. "My aunt taught me and my sister some self-defense moves once. I tried to punch him, but it didn't work. My hand went right through his ugly face. I was so scared you were going to die."

No one had ever been afraid for his life before. It made him oddly happy that this strange and beautiful girl seemed to care about him. That was, until he gave it a little more thought.

"Why were you scared I might die?" he began. "Because if I did, I wouldn't be able to help you get back to your home?"

Her concerned expression vanished and was replaced by annoyance. "That wasn't what I meant."

"I thought that was all you wanted from me."

She crossed her arms tightly over her rose-colored tunic. "Actually, it is. But you never agreed to help me. Remember?"

"If I were dead, I couldn't agree to anything. I'd be dead."

This earned him a sharp glare. "If you're trying to be funny right now, I'm not laughing."

He glared back at her. "I'm not feeling all that amusing at the moment, actually."

Livius regarded him sourly. "You've either gone mad as a nightbird or you are communicating with a spirit in an oddly friendly manner. Which is it, boy?"

"Madness or maddening spirits. Neither can help us at the moment." Maddox tore his gaze from Becca's and went to the door, in which a small, fist-sized window allowed a modest glimpse at the dark hallway. He could hear the moans of fellow prisoners coming from other cells.

"Is there a spirit in here or is there not?" Livius's tone turned icy. "You're avoiding my question."

His annoyance at being trapped in a dungeon with two of the most frustrating people he'd ever known grew. "Me? Avoid your incredibly important question that helps us not at all, Livius? I'd never do such a thing."

"You insolent little bastard." Livius grabbed Maddox and slammed his head against the hard, metal door. Fresh pain screamed through him. "If I hadn't come into your life, you'd be nothing. You'd have nothing. You would have starved to death long before now."

"Wrong. My mother provided for me fine before you arrived."

"Ha! Before she lost her looks, she made most of her coin by taking men to her bed. I imagine your real father was just another face in the night."

Blood dripped into Maddox's narrowed eyes from Livius's most recent blow. "My mother is not a whore."

Livius grinned, an unpleasant flash of white teeth. "If you believe that, you're more of a fool than I thought you were. How do you think we met? She offered herself to me for two pieces of silver. A very good deal, I thought. She was worth at least three."

Maddox turned a look of pure fury on the man, and then, as if a large, invisible hand shoved him, Livius staggered backward and hit the stone wall. He gasped and clutched at his throat.

"See?" Livius said, coughing and wheezing as he recovered from the blast of Maddox's magic. "You *do* have control . . . and much greater strength than I'd have guessed. Perhaps this magic of yours can't be used on the door, but it will work on the guards. When they return, do what you just did to me, but worse. Kill them."

A moment of heated emotion had triggered that burst of magic, just as it had at the festival, but it didn't mean he could do it again on command. And stealing shadows, his simplest trick, wouldn't help them at all today.

"Even if I could," he snarled, "I wouldn't. I'm not a murderer."

Becca had watched all this in silence. "What kind of magic is this that you can do?"

His jaw was tight. "I honestly don't know."

Mere moments later, a group of guards entered the cell and marched Maddox and Livius out of the dungeon and into the palace. Becca kept pace with them, never straying out of Maddox's line of sight.

He didn't want to show her how afraid he was, so he concentrated instead on the painful grip the guards had on his arms and the fast pace they maintained, at times literally dragging him across the black stone floors.

He tried to use his magic again, but fear was the only emotion he felt, and it wasn't doing anything besides making him even weaker than he already felt.

Up until they reached the throne room, everything in the palace had appeared to be chiseled from black granite: floors, ceilings, walls, staircases. There was no art, no decorations or statues or tapestries. Nothing to make the goddess's residence or the dark jewel that was the Northern Mytican landscape inviting. A shiver sped down Maddox's back. Sunlight shone down from the small windows onto the floor of the tall and wide hallway like ghostly spears.

They reached a set of large black doors. The two guards standing before them each opened one to allow the prisoners and their escorts silent entry into the throne room.

"Okay, this is different . . . ," Becca said in a strained tone.

That was an understatement, to be sure.

The throne room was easily a hundred paces by a hundred paces square and twice as high, the ceiling a mosaic of colored glass. The floors were made of hard-packed earth.

"The goddess of earth and water . . . ," Livius mused under his breath, eyeing the room with barely guarded awe. "Incredible."

It was as if they'd entered an exotic forest—something the likes of what Maddox had heard tales of from far away. Intense heat pressed down on them in waves. Trees grew from the earthen floor, reaching up thirty, no, fifty feet toward the ceiling, thick and lush, with leaves the size of Maddox's body. Large, colorful insects with translucent wings chirped and buzzed as they flitted through the air. Flowers—red and yellow and purple—bloomed, beautiful and beckoning nearby.

Becca moved closer to one of the flowers, as if to smell its honey-like scent up close, but before she could try, its thick petals snapped shut on a passing butterfly like the maw of a beast in disguise.

A butterfly-eating flower, Maddox thought, his stomach turning. He would rather not know what else these plants would like to feast upon.

The pathway, overflowing with beings of both life and death, led to a dozen steps precisely chiseled into black rock. At the top was a large obsidian throne.

On the throne sat the goddess.

Valoria.

Maddox stopped breathing at the sight of her. The rumors of her beauty were all true. The woman was flawless, with raven-black hair and skin like pale gold. Her eyes were green chips of emerald, the same color of the leaves and foliage that surrounded her. Her gown, with its lengthy train that trailed down several steps, was crimson.

Maddox's eyes were drawn to a sudden movement under the silk of the train. Then he saw something slither out from beneath it.

He gasped.

"Yes," Valoria said, and Maddox could feel her smooth voice sink down to his very bones. "That is the reaction Aegus usually gets from my prisoners. But don't be afraid. He only bites at my command."

His heart pounded. He'd never seen an actual cobra before. Only in books—illustrations of incredible creatures found in other lands, other kingdoms—had he encountered these beasts. This serpent was much bigger than he would have ever imagined, easily six feet long.

He'd heard that the goddess had an affinity for serpents. That she used earth magic to command the creatures that spent their lives with their bellies pressed to the dirt. Lizards, beetles, rodents . . . but snakes were her favorite.

The cobra eyed him, its tongue tasting the air, before it turned its cold gaze away and slithered beneath Valoria's gown again.

"Welcome to my palace, young man," Valoria purred. Her hands, bejeweled with rings and golden bracelets, grasped the arms of her black throne. "I've heard some interesting tales about you."

He kept his eyes to the mossy floor.

"The only question is: Are these tales true or not?" She stood up and slowly descended the stairs to where Maddox was forced to his knees before her. She touched under his chin, her skin as cold as marble despite the heat of the room. Perspiration trickled down his forehead as he raised his gaze to meet hers.

"Do you fear me?" she asked.

Yes, very much so, he thought.

He wondered what response she wanted. "No, my goddess."

"Good." She smiled. "I don't want you to be afraid. I want us to be friends."

Becca stood to the side, clenching her hands together.

"I'm here," she whispered. "I'm not going anywhere."

Despite Valoria's vast wealth of fearsome magic, she didn't seem to notice the otherworldly entity in the room with them.

Having Becca nearby helped him to be brave.

"We are honored to be in your presence, Your Radiance," Livius said. He, too, had been forced to his knees beside Maddox.

"You are the father of this boy," she said.

"No, I am his guardian," Livius admitted. "But he is like a son to me."

"I see." Valoria's red skirts flowed behind her like a trail of blood. Her guards had stepped back, giving her room to move freely.

The large cobra began to slither down the steps, drawing closer to Maddox, its tongue darting out like a small but deadly whip. It finally reached him and it sat up, its hood fanning out, and it stared at him.

Had Becca not been close, he knew he would have shrieked like a little girl.

"Don't move," Becca urged.

Great suggestion, he thought. *Thank you so much.*

"Fear," Valoria said, a smile in her voice. "It's so very motivating, isn't it? One sees a snake, and one is afraid. But snakes are no more frightening than any other beast. A rabbit's bite might lack lethal poison, but it can be every bit as deep and dangerous as Aegus's. But one sees something pleasant to the eye, and the fear vanishes, the guard drops. Appearances can be deceiving."

Just like a beautiful goddess. She might lull her subjects into obedience with her attractive appearance, but everyone knew she was as deadly as poison contained within a beautiful bottle.

Maddox glanced at her hands to see the symbols for earth—a

circle within a circle—and water—parallel wavy lines. One on each palm, as if branded there.

She held her hands out to him. "Interesting, yes?"

"Yes, Your Radiance," he agreed quickly.

"I am the immortal embodiment of earth and water magic. But you . . . I've been told you have more mysterious abilities. Abilities that go beyond elemental magic. You possess a different form of magic never seen before in this realm."

"Tell her," Livius said. "Share with our goddess all that you can do, son."

"No, tell her nothing," Becca argued, crouching down next to him. "Play dumb. Her guards were going to execute that girl at the festival just for being accused of using magic. What do you think she'll do with you once you show her what you can do?"

A dilemma. Should he do what an abusive, manipulative arse tells him? Or should he do what Becca Hatcher, the beautiful girl whom his heart wanted to trust after only a handful of moments, suggested?

"I'm afraid there's been a misunderstanding," Maddox said, forcing confidence into his voice. "My greatest apologies, Your Radiance, but I am not what you may believe me to be."

"Maddox," Livius growled. "What are you saying? My goddess, he is afraid. His words fail him, so allow me to provide whatever knowledge you wish to glean about my young charge."

She pursed her lips and flicked her gaze toward Livius. "Is it true that he can summon the spirits of the dead from the land of darkness?"

Livius nodded. "He can."

A lie. Maddox had never summoned a spirit before—at least, not on purpose. He could only draw closer a spirit that was already in the mortal world.

"And he can imprison them in silver," Livius continued. "He can also incapacitate and choke a man twice his size with only the power of his mind. It's incredible."

"Indeed, it certainly sounds so," Valoria said with growing interest.

Maddox wanted to retch. His deepest secrets were being revealed so bluntly, and he hated it.

"The only witches I've known have been females," Valoria said. "But you are most certainly not a girl, are you? Why are you different from the others, I wonder?"

Coming from Valoria's cool tone, these were not questions; rather, they were more like musings. Maddox didn't say a word in response.

"A spirit visited him earlier in the dungeon," Livius said. "He spoke with it at great length."

Maddox's heart sank, and he exchanged a brief, worried glance with Becca.

"Is this true?" Valoria asked.

"What do you want from me, Your Radiance?" Maddox asked, avoiding having to speak of Becca. He might not be able to help her get home, but he at least wanted to protect her from this powerful goddess who might mean her harm.

Her brows shot up. "Such candor. Such boldness. It pleases me to see that you're in possession of a backbone. I had begun to wonder."

Jaw tight, he studied the ground by her feet, feeling very much like a butterfly being watched by one of the goddess's hungry, carnivorous flowers.

"I want very little," Valoria said. "Only two things have managed to evade me throughout my reign. I seek a girl, sixteen years old, who is possessed by great magic, but I have failed at every turn. Perhaps she's been hidden away in the South, or perhaps even in another land far from here. But it's the lack of knowing that vexes me to no end."

Find a lost girl? Why did she think *he* could assist in such a matter?

"What do you want with her?" Maddox dared to ask.

"Her magic," Valoria said plainly. "I need it to find someone else—someone who was lost to this world years ago. Someone who stole something very important from me that I want back."

"I don't know how I can be of help, Your Radiance."

"After such a long search with no success, I have come to believe that this young girl could be dead. If she is, I want her spirit summoned here to answer my questions and to aid in my search for the thief. You could do that, if what your guardian says about you is true."

A young witch and a thief stupid enough to steal from a goddess. Both somehow attainable only by Maddox's magic.

A guard approached through the thick tangle of foliage, the hard heels of his boots sinking into the mossy ground with every step. "Apologies, Your Radiance, but I wanted to report that we've finally captured the madman and locked him away."

Valoria's expression hardened as if the softness had never been there in the first place. "Why do you interrupt now?"

"I know you wanted to know. He won't be a bother around the palace any longer."

"And what about you?" she asked the guard sharply. "Will *you* be a bother?"

"No, Your Radiance." He bowed so deeply his forehead touched a patch of daisies as he backed away.

Valoria was quiet for a long time before she turned to ascend the stairs and sat again upon the throne. The snake, Aegus, slithered up her skirts to settle in her lap. She stroked the top of his head absently as she gazed down at Maddox, assessing him from top to toe.

"Speak," she finally said. "Tell me that you are honored by this opportunity to help me."

But Livius spoke first. "He is at your command, as I am, my goddess. Whatever we can do. Whatever you need, we are your most loyal servants."

Her eyes narrowed. "I was speaking to the boy, not to you."

Livius lowered his head. "My humblest apologies . . . but it would be much better if you take *my* word regarding the boy's abilities. He is but a young fool who needs my constant assistance. I am grateful every day that I've been able to guide him, since on his own, he is stupid, irresponsible, and, quite frankly, apart from his magic, completely worthless. I have helped to give his life meaning, something that he should be eternally grateful for. We are here to serve you, Your Radiance. I assure you this is true."

A most uncomfortable silence fell as Valoria stared down at Livius. Then she picked up Aegus and whispered something to the snake, before kissing it on the top of its scaly head.

It slithered off her lap and down the stairs again, heading right toward Livius.

"He is a truly beautiful serpent," Livius said, his voice tight.

"Yes, he is," she agreed. Her eyes brightened, as if lit from within by emerald flames.

Aegus rose up, fanning out his hood, weaving his head back and forth as if responding in time to a distant melody. In mere moments, the snake grew before Maddox's eyes to three times its original size.

Livius gasped as the now giant snake slid up past his lap, curled around his shoulders, and sank its fangs into his neck. He screamed and batted at the cold-blooded animal before his eyes rolled back into his head and he fell to his side, twitching violently.

The cobra detached itself, shrank back down to its regular size, and returned to his mistress's lap.

Valoria stroked the top of Aegus's head as one might do to a kitten. "That man was very annoying. And entirely unnecessary to me."

Maddox knew his knees would have given out had he been standing. As it was, his vision swam as he watched the guards drag Livius's dead-but-still-twitching body away.

Becca had her hands clamped over her mouth, as if to muffle a scream. He wanted to get up and do something, say something, to comfort her. But he didn't dare budge an inch.

"This woman is evil." Becca's voice quavered. "She's a murderer."

She surely came from a place far different from Mytica. Though Maddox was shocked by what he'd just seen, sudden, violent death was normal here. Expected, really. Every day and every moment.

Survival depended entirely on keeping one's wits about them.

"Do you wish I'd spared your guardian's life?" Valoria asked, studying him with a serene expression.

"No," Maddox replied hollowly.

"You hated him. I could see it in your eyes every time he spoke."

He drew in a shaky breath. "He wasn't kind to me."

"And now he's gone, and you're free from the unpleasantness for which he was responsible."

He wondered if she expected gratitude.

"Now," she said, "you will answer me. Can you help me summon the spirit of the young witch? Was what has been said about your magic the truth?"

He quickly tried to figure out the best way to answer her question.

"Spirits are . . . drawn to me," Maddox began. "Contrary to what Livius asserted, I've never consciously called them to me from the land of darkness itself. But those spirits that are close by can find me. And, yes, I can trap them when they do. That's all I really know about my magic."

He chose not to confirm that he could choke a man from a distance if he was properly motivated.

The goddess considered this in silence. "Do you think that you could summon the witch's spirit if you tried?"

"Say yes," Becca urged. "She doesn't want any other answer. We can figure it out later. I mean, we don't even know if this girl is dead."

He nodded slowly. "Yes, Your Radiance. I can certainly try."

"Good. I will give you until tomorrow to rest and gain your strength, and then you will do as I ask of you."

"And . . . apologies, my goddess, but what will happen if I fail?" he ventured.

"If you fail, I'll have no further use for you." She smiled as she continued to pet Aegus's scaly head. "And you will follow your guardian to his grave."

Chapter 10

CRYSTAL

Whenever Crys needed time to think, she developed film. Something about being in the darkroom—mixing the developing solution, the stop bath, and the fixer, and then the tricky-but-all-important moment of getting the film out of the canister and onto the reel in total darkness, popping it into the tank, timing everything just right—helped to clear her head.

Today she developed twelve rolls of film and made prints of her favorite exposures.

The ornery old man she'd stalked on Friday afternoon was a great shot, just as she'd known it would be. She decided to call him Ralph. Angry Ralph. Did Ralph have any idea how interesting his face was?

The last shot she'd taken in this batch was of Becca, just before the book had changed everything. It was slightly blurry since her sister was moving, trying to block her face before Crys could click the shutter. Becca's dark blue eyes—which were translated on the black-and-white film to an intense charcoal—flashed with annoyance, and half her face was in shadow. Her thick blond braid was in motion like a bolt of lightning. She looked ready to take on the world.

Stop looking at life through that lens, Becca seemed to be saying. *And talk to me. Be my friend again, not a stranger. Stop pushing me away. I need you.*

Guilt slithered through Crys.

Why wasn't she at the hospital? Why was she wasting time in the darkroom when she should be with her sister?

She quickly cleaned up—since the darkroom also doubled as the main family bathroom, she knew she couldn't keep her chemicals in the bathtub and live to tell the tale. Then she headed for the hospital.

It seemed Crys wasn't the only one who'd had this idea. She arrived at the room to see that her mother had already claimed the padded chair by Becca's side. She sat there reading a book—one of her favorites, a fourth-edition copy of *To Kill a Mockingbird*. If she'd had a first edition, she would have definitely kept it under glass to protect its value.

Crys had read *To Kill a Mockingbird* at least five times, back when she was a voracious reader like Becca was now. She'd stopped reading novels in her free time shortly after her father left, associating him with the bookshop since he had always been there working from open till close.

How stupid to abandon something I loved because someone I loved abandoned me.

"Did you feed Charlie?" were her mother's words of greeting.

Crys hadn't spoken to her since Saturday. She hadn't said a word about going to the AGO, feeling the need to process everything her father had told her in private.

"Yes," she replied. "He's got a feast that will last him days. He's going to get nice and fat."

"A quarter cup of food per day is all he's supposed to have at his age."

"I'm kidding, of course." Crys sighed and studied Becca's pale face. Her sister's eyes were closed today, so Crys tried to fool herself that she was only sleeping. "Any change?"

"No."

Crys tried to will Becca to wake up. To pop open those indigo eyes, stretch her arms above her head, and say, *"Why does everyone look so worried?"*

But she didn't. That book—whatever it was—had done this to her. It had made everything that made Becca *Becca* vanish from the world, leaving behind only a shell.

"What is it, Mom?" Crys asked.

She put her book down and looked at her daughter wearily. "What is what, Crys?"

"That book."

Julia Hatcher's expression tensed up as she stood. She went to the window, where she pushed the curtains aside to gaze out at the cloudy sky and the cityscape of tall gray buildings and people down on the sidewalk, hustling around like ants. "Don't mention that here. Someone might be listening."

Her mother had a talent for summoning Crys's frustration like a psychic with a wandering spirit. "Yeah, you're right. Someone might hear me mention . . . a book. I'm sure that would strike anyone as a bizarre conversation topic for a bookshop owner and her daughter-slash-employee."

"You should go home."

"I just got here."

"Crys, please. I'm tired—"

"I just want to understand what's going on. You know more than you're telling me, I know you do. What's wrong with Becca?"

"I don't know."

"I don't believe you."

Her mother sighed with frustration. "I think you enjoy baiting me. You're as argumentative as your father."

Crys couldn't keep her secret in another moment. If she did, she was going to explode, and that wouldn't be pretty. She shoved her glasses higher on her nose. "I spoke to him yesterday."

The room seemed to grow ten degrees colder in seconds as Julia turned from the window to face Crys. "You *what*?"

Crys hated the lump that had knotted itself up in her throat. She wanted to be strong while she confronted her mother about this. "Why didn't you tell me he was still in Toronto?"

"Unbelievable." She rubbed her forehead as if a migraine had just landed. "You were listening to me and Jackie the other night?"

"Nefarious methods, Mom. Sometimes they're necessary."

"Fine. Yes, your father is in Toronto, but he may as well be a million miles away. He doesn't want to see you or Becca—"

"But I did see him. He met me at the art gallery yesterday."

Her mother gaped at her, her face going nearly as pale as Becca's. "I don't know what to say to that. I have no words."

"I have words. Plenty of them." Anger burned now, bright as a small sun trapped inside her chest. "You gave him the ultimatum. *You're* the one who made him choose between us and his society."

"Yes. I did," she said, raising her chin. "And he chose wrong."

"But *why* did he have to choose? Couldn't he—?"

"No, he couldn't have both." She cut Crys off, her tone harsh. "You have no idea what you're butting your nose into, young lady. No idea at all."

"Really? Don't I?" Crys pointed at Becca. "I was there when this happened. You weren't. I have a pretty good idea that there's something insane going on that you know about, and you're not telling me a goddamned thing!"

"Language," her mother growled. But if she wanted Crys to be a prim and proper lady who never swore, she was living in the wrong century. "So, what lies did your father fill your head with, Crystal? Did he try to turn you against me?"

"No. But maybe now that I've heard his side of things, I'm wondering if I wouldn't be better off living with him."

She blanched. "Over my dead body. If you knew the truth about him . . . about us . . ."

"News flash, Mother. The truth is exactly what I'm trying to learn." Crys laughed, a dry, brittle sound that held no humor. "What would you care if I left? You barely ever look at me. You haven't even noticed I changed my hair again."

"Of course I noticed." Her mother shook her head. "You can be so dense sometimes. So goddamned dense."

"Language," Crys replied mockingly, but her mother's words had hit her like a punch to the gut. "You know what? It's fine. I don't need you to tell me anything. I can figure all this out without your help, thanks. Maybe from . . . oh, I don't know. The great leader of Dad's mysterious group? Markus King himself?"

This time it was Julia who flinched. Her eyes widened. "No, Crystal. No way. I forbid you from ever seeing that man."

"Oh, okay, if you *forbid* it." Crys shrugged, forcing a smile. "Clearly, I trust what you say since you've been *so* forthcoming with me. Cross my heart, I will never, ever try to do whatever I can to get the answers you're not willing to give me."

Julia Hatcher's face had gone from pale white to bright pink in moments. Her hands were actually shaking. "You're impossible to reason with."

Crys pointed at herself. "*I'm* the impossible one?"

"Leave this alone, Crystal. I'm warning you."

"Or what?"

"I . . . I need to get some air." Julia moved toward the door and, without another look at Crys, left the room.

Crys stared, mute with rage, wanting to run after her and keep arguing, to get her to break. To get her to talk and share what she knew.

To force her mother to trust her with the truth.

But no. It was the same as it always was with her.

She slumped down into the chair her mother had abandoned and stared at Becca's face, which was nearly as white as the crisp hospital sheets surrounding her. Her heart monitor let out a soft, continuous beep. When Crys reached over to take her hand, her sister was cool to the touch.

Crys's eyes burned, but she refused to cry. She refused to feel hopeless and helpless and totally alone.

"Please come back, Becca," she whispered. "I'm sorry I've been so lousy to you lately. I didn't mean it, really. It wasn't you; it was me. I know that sounds like something people say when they're lazy and making excuses, but it's the truth." She inhaled shakily. "I always thought I'd hate Dad forever and that if I ever saw him again, I'd spit in his face. But it wasn't like that. He didn't want to leave us. Mom made him. He says he's doing something good for the world with this society of his. So what does that mean? Is this Markus guy some saint who helps people in need? Could he help you, too?"

Becca's chest hitched a little, and a soft gasp left her lighter-than-usual lips. Crys's heart skipped a beat, hoping this would be the dramatically wonderful moment she'd been dreaming of, when Becca would open her eyes.

She tightened her grip on Becca's hand. "If you can hear me . . . open your eyes. Wake up, right now. *Please.*"

Another intake of breath gave Crys an irrational burst of hope, but Becca's eyelashes didn't so much as flutter. Her eyes didn't open. Her fingers didn't curl and tighten around Crys's.

A phone rang, its shrill sound piercing through Crys's rib cage like an arrow. She jumped and spun around, searching for the source of the noise, and saw her mother's cell phone, wedged into the side of the chair.

Crys looked down at the call display, then grabbed it before it went to voice mail.

"Jackie," she managed, her throat raw.

There was a long pause. "Crys? Is that you?"

"Yeah, it's me."

"It's so good to hear your voice, sweetie. Where's your mom?"

"She's outside, getting some air. We're at the hospital."

"Becca . . ." Jackie's voice caught and then grew very soft. "How's she doing?"

"The same."

Jackie swore under her breath. "I had no idea the book could affect her—or *anyone*—like this. Why did I send it directly to the store? I didn't even consider it. . . . I didn't think it through. . . ."

"What is it, Jackie?"

Instead of avoiding the topic or changing the subject like her mother had, Jackie sighed. "What do you already know?"

"Not much, thanks to Mom. She doesn't want me to know anything."

"Of course she doesn't. She's protecting you."

"From what? All I know is that there's a secret society that Dad's a part of; a weird, old book that put my sister into a coma;

and a boss guy named Markus who you think is a monster who's at the center of it all."

"Crys . . ."

"Do *not* try to tell me that I need to forget about this, Jackie. I won't let go of it. I'm in pit bull mode. I'm latching on and not letting go until I get to the truth. About everything my mother has been keeping from me—about Dad, about the book, about everything."

"Not all pit bulls are like that, you know. It's all in the upbringing. Kind of a good metaphor, really, now that I think about it."

"You're changing the subject. You're just like Mom."

Jackie gasped. "How dare you!"

She said it so theatrically, in such a quintessentially cheerful Jackie-voice, that it brought everything back to normal between them. Jackie and Julia were as different from each other as Crys was from Becca.

"Look, sweetie, I don't entirely agree with my big sister. You're not a kid anymore. You're a young woman, and, quite honestly, I think you could be a great help to us."

"A help with what?"

"With my plan to destroy Markus King." There was a pregnant pause, and Crys wasn't sure if Jackie was being serious or still putting on a theatrical show. "That sounded epically melodramatic, didn't it?"

Crys tried to compose herself because, yes, it sounded like the proclamation of a storybook warrior heading out on a quest to slay a dragon. "Well, according to Dad, Markus is one of the good guys. He's set up this society of his to help save the world."

"Oh my God. Kill me now. You've spoken to your father about this?"

"Yup. But don't worry. I didn't say anything about Becca or the book."

"And what did that asshat say to you?"

"Jackie—" An unexpected burst of laughter escaped from Crys's throat.

"Okay, okay. I'm sorry for saying that out loud," Jackie said. "But he *is* an asshat, and that's me being extremely gentle with my language. He told you Markus is a stand-up guy, did he?"

"He did. Only not in those words."

"I'm not surprised he's still fully on Team Markus, but he's wrong. Look *evil* up in a dictionary and there will be a picture of Markus." She went silent for a moment. "I know your mother can be an asshat, too, sometimes, and we don't always see eye to eye—to say the least. But trust me—she's only being an asshat because she loves you. She wants to protect you from . . . this."

Trust me.

"If you want me to trust you, I need you to tell me everything you know about that book. What is it? Where did it come from? And why do you think Markus wants it so bad?" Crys reached for Becca's hand again while cradling the cell phone on her shoulder.

"There's too much to tell and no time to tell it."

"This is not helping."

"You're a smart-ass, you know that?"

"I inherited that trait from my favorite aunt."

Jackie laughed, a genuine sound from her belly. "Look, I'm trying to get back to Canada, but I'm having a bit of a problem leaving Paris."

"What sort of problem?"

"Uh, let's just say I'm currently wanted by certain . . . authority figures."

Crys's brows shot up. "Because you stole the book?"

There was a pause. "Because I steal a lot of things. Some shinier than others. Stay in school, sweetie. Get a good education and you won't end up like your crazy aunt."

"Too late for that advice."

Jackie groaned. "A subject to discuss in further depth when I finally get my butt across the ocean. And I will. But in the meantime—and know that I'm going out on a limb here because your mother would murder me if I told her I was bringing you on board—you need to go see someone named Dr. Uriah Vega at his office tomorrow. He's a professor of linguistic anthropology at the University of Toronto, and we go way back. Mention my name and tell him I said to give you the full monty on the book. He'll know exactly what to tell you to help clear a few things up. Go after lunch since he teaches all morning."

A name and a location. It was the best lead she'd had so far. "Thanks," Crys said. "I'll do that."

"Hey . . . remember when I gave you and your sister those self-defense lessons?" Jackie asked.

"Like it was last summer." Which it had been. "Why? Will I need them?"

"You never know. Just remember my number one lesson, because it's the most important and useful one of all." She swore again loudly. "Sorry, I need to scram. I'll call again as soon as I can, okay?"

But Crys couldn't remember which lesson was the number one. Right now all she could recall was that a knee to the groin and a finger to the eyeball were very effective methods for suppressing an attacker.

What was the first lesson?

"Wait, Jackie—"

The line went dead, and Crys stared down at the phone in disbelief.

A few moments later, Julia returned and stood at the doorway. "Did I just hear you talking on the phone? Who was it?"

"Jackie," she said, her voice hushed. "But she's gone now."

Her mother snatched the phone out of her hand and stared at the home screen with dismay. "What did she say?"

"To not trust anyone but you and her."

"Good advice for once," Julia said, though the way she was looking at Crys told her that she was more than a little suspicious about what Jackie might have divulged. "Let's go home. We can't do anything more for Becca today."

Her mother took hold of her arm, and Crys didn't protest or try to squirm away.

They didn't get along most of the time, but Crys had always thought she at least knew her mother. Jackie said her sister was hiding the truth because she loved Crys. But Crys had to wonder: Was that love? Was that trust?

Frankly, she wasn't sure who this woman directing her out of Becca's room and into her silver Mazda hatchback in the parking lot really was. Julia Hatcher had more secrets than Crys ever would have guessed.

Two could play at that game.

Chapter 11

FARRELL

Farrell tried to read while he waited for the call from Lucas. He'd bought the entire Walking Dead graphic novel series but still found that flipping through images of zombies and a plethora of blood and guts and angst did nothing to distract him.

"Farrell . . . you busy?"

He glanced at the doorway of his room to see Adam silhouetted in the frame.

He set the books aside on his bed and put his arms behind his head in a lounging position. "Come on in."

Adam took a seat on the side of the bed, eyeing the graphic novels. "Walking Dead?"

"You can borrow them."

"Are you finished with them?"

"With these two." He nudged the first volumes toward his brother, who took them, staring at the covers with interest.

"Awesome," Adam said. After a pause, he looked up from the books to his brother. "Look, I know I overreacted and bitched you out this morning. I'm sorry."

Farrell frowned. "Wait. Are you really apologizing right now?"

"I've been thinking a lot about what happened Saturday night, and . . . it was just a shock. That's all."

"I know."

"I wasn't expecting that, especially not with me on the stage, so up close and personal. But—that guy, he was dangerous. If we had let him go, he'd have gone out and caused the deaths of tons of other people. If he went to jail, it probably wouldn't have been for nearly long enough. There was no other answer." Still, his face looked bleak and haunted about this harsh realization.

"I get it, kid. I do." Farrell leaned forward and gripped his brother's shoulder. "And you don't have to apologize to me for anything. Ever. Okay? I should have been more understanding."

Adam blinked. "Wow, is this, like, a sentimental brotherly moment? Should we hug tenderly?"

Farrell laughed. "I don't give hugs out liberally, especially not to family."

Adam grinned in the lopsided way that made Farrell know that his happiness was genuine.

Farrell's phone buzzed, interrupting this rare peaceful moment. It was Lucas.

"Gotta take this, kid," he said, bringing the phone to his ear. "Yeah?"

"It's time," Lucas said.

He covered the receiver with his hand. "Adam, why don't you take the whole set? I won't be reading them anytime soon."

"Really? Okay." Adam gathered the books and headed for the door. He hesitated there, as if he still had something more to say. But after a moment, he left the room, closing the door behind him.

"It's time, is it?" Farrell said. "Cryptic, much? Is there a secret handshake I should memorize before I leave the house?"

Lucas snorted softly. "Always with the jokes. I'd probably curb that tendency a bit tonight if I were you. Markus's sense of humor is . . . singular."

Whatever that meant. "I'll be on my bestest behavior—cross my heart," Farrell said.

"You don't have to be nervous."

"Do I sound nervous to you?"

"I would be, if I were you." Lucas told him where to meet in half an hour.

Farrell left the mansion and directed his driver to the address, which was a large cathedral on the west side of the city that looked more like a castle, with tall spires and towers and stained glass windows that sparkled despite the overcast day.

"Shall I wait here for you?" Sam, his driver, asked.

Farrell had tried very hard not to start to like him, or even get to know him. Sam, who was somewhere in his midtwenties, had been hired as a temporary solution to the problem that was Farrell Grayson's lack of a driver's license. But Farrell would be back in a brand-new Porsche the first moment that the lawyers sorted out his DUI, and then Sam would be nothing more than a distant memory.

"Don't make friends with the hired help," his mother had shrilly told him a decade ago when she'd caught him playing with one of the maid's kids.

But Sam had been a huge help in the last few months, and it was hard not to think of him as a friend, rather than just someone his parents paid to drive him around.

Farrell smiled as he recalled a conversation from a recent night out.

"Ever think about, oh, I don't know, not drinking?" Sam had asked as he waited for Farrell to stop puking at the side of the road.

"I've thought about it," Farrell had replied, wiping his mouth. "And . . . nah."

"Just asking." Sam grinned and shook his head. "It's your liver."

Sam was reliable and friendly and went above and beyond to help him out. Farrell appreciated that more than he'd ever admit out loud.

"No, Sam. Don't bother waiting, since I have no idea how long I'll be," Farrell said now. "Go get yourself some dinner. I'll call when I'm all done."

Not one minute after Sam had driven off, Lucas approached Farrell on the sidewalk. He offered his hand, and Farrell grasped it and shook it.

"You ready for this?" Lucas asked.

"Hell yeah." Farrell eyed the intricate building and gestured up at it. "Do I need to confess my sins first? I admit—it's been a while, and I have quite a few."

Lucas grinned. "Follow me."

He led Farrell around to the back of the cathedral, where they found what looked like an unmarked subway entrance blocked off by construction tape and wooden panels. He shoved away a panel, which revealed a trapdoor beneath.

"After you," Lucas said after lifting the door.

Farrell raised an eyebrow, intrigued. "Looks dark down there."

"Yes. Very dark." Lucas waited patiently, as if issuing an unspoken challenge. *Are you a coward, Grayson? Or are you worthy?*

"Let's do this," Farrell mumbled, then stepped through the trapdoor, grappling in the darkness to find the stairs. He braced himself with his hand against the cool concrete wall as he slowly began his descent. The door slapped back down into place as Lucas fell into step behind him.

"It'll just take a few moments for my eyesight to adjust," Lucas said. "Then I can get us where we need to be pretty quickly."

"Yeah, sure. My eyes will take a minute, too."

"Not like mine. Not yet, anyway."

"Oh, I love it when you talk in riddles. It gives me tingles." Farrell kept moving down the stairs, taking them slowly so he wouldn't fall and twist his ankle. Finally he reached what he was pretty certain was the ground floor. He saw the glow of fluorescent light from about fifty feet ahead and he followed Lucas in that direction.

"So how many are in this circle?" Farrell asked, trying to make conversation to distract himself from thoughts about the unknown destination before him.

Lucas shook his head. "I can't talk details with you. Not till you're officially in."

"What happens then? Do I get a prize? A chest tattoo of, I don't know, a hawk and a spear?" The prospect of getting a tattoo didn't bother him. He already had two. One—a quote from his favorite Korean action movie (in Korean, of course)—*Bright is life. Dark is death.*—on his left side over his ribs. And on the inner bicep of his right arm, he'd gotten a crown to remind him that he was the king of his own life, that no one controlled him.

"No tattoo," Lucas said. "You'll see."

"You're so helpful. Anyway," Farrell started, ignoring Lucas's ban on questions, "who got into the circle first? You or Connor?"

"Me. I was invited two months before Connor was. I suggested him, actually, but Markus had already been considering him."

"Did he handle it well? Being chosen like that?"

"I thought he did."

"He had started to become a real prick before . . ." Farrell had to force himself to say it. "Before he died. It was like his personality did a one-eighty."

"Really? I didn't notice anything."

"Yeah, he went from being a nice guy to being a total dick. Could it have been the circle? Did it do something to him?"

"Like what?" Lucas eyed him sideways. "Like make him want to kill himself? Is that what you're insinuating?"

"You're right. It doesn't make sense. I'm still just trying to figure it all out."

"Trust me, Farrell. Nobody wants your brother alive more than I do. I was his best friend. I didn't see it coming, even when Mallory dumped him. And if I did, I damn well would have done whatever I could have to stop it.".

The words were there, the words Farrell needed to hear from Lucas. But his tone was off. Lucas spoke without any emotion, like he didn't care one way or the other. Like he was paying lip service to shut Farrell up.

A horrible thought rose to the surface of Farrell's mind. *Did you have something to do with my brother's death, Lucas?*

"I think you and I could be friends, now that we're about to have a lot more in common," Lucas said. "Which is interesting, since I always thought you were a prick."

"Ditto." Farrell had no idea how to interpret this conversation, but he knew he didn't want to push Lucas too far. It would be best to befriend him, to get to the real story of his brother's final days. He needed to coax the truth—if there was any new truth to tell—out of the guy as smoothly as possible. "But I need more friends in my life. I've almost run out of people to braid my hair and talk about cute boys with."

They both laughed, Farrell trying to sound as natural as possible, as they navigated the maze of tunnels. The hallways now had better lighting, but they were still much dimmer than the tunnels under the restaurant leading to Markus's theater.

"Do all these tunnels connect?" he asked.

"I don't know. Maybe."

Farrell glared at him for giving yet another nonanswer. "How about I ask you all these questions again after I'm in?"

In the faint light, he saw Lucas's lips quirk up. "Good idea."

They walked in silence for a while, Lucas leading the way as the tunnels got narrower, then wider, then narrower again with each turn they made. Finally, Farrell ventured to speak again. "Any advice when it comes to my meeting with His Majesty?"

"Sure. Be honest. Answer his questions with nothing but the exact truth. He'll know if you're lying."

"I don't know. I lie really well."

"He'll know. But you should also be honest about what you want. If you don't want in—"

"I do," Farrell interrupted before Lucas could finish his sentence. Failure was not an option. He'd come this far, and he refused to leave without being accepted into the circle. Every step he took was one his brother had also taken. One way or another, Farrell was determined to get to the truth.

Lucas shrugged. "Then I don't see a problem."

Farrell absently played with the gold society crest he'd pinned to the lapel of his blue shirt, beneath his leather jacket. It was incredible to know that the circle had existed for decades, yet he had never heard of it before Saturday night. "How long has he been considering me?"

"A year," Lucas replied.

So as long as Connor has been gone. The thought made him grimace but also brought up another question. "So am I taking my brother's place?"

"I thought so to begin with, but apparently not. Markus believes he sees something special in you."

Farrell considered that. *Special, huh?* That would be news to his mother. "What's in it for you? What do you get out of being part of the circle?"

"I get to serve Markus," Lucas said, as if it were obvious.

"Is that it? Why not just serve at the Red Lobster, then? Way less blood and death to clean up there. More tips, too."

Lucas's gritted teeth glinted in the torchlight. "Keep walking, Grayson."

They walked for what felt like a mile, passing flickering lights set into the ceiling every twenty feet. It was damp down there and as cold as winter—like walking through a meat locker. The floor was slippery, coated thinly by patches of ice.

Finally, they reached an iron spiral staircase, nearly identical to the one that led to the theater, except that this one was painted red instead of black.

"Up we go," Lucas said.

With trepidation, Farrell eyed the stairs leading up into more darkness. "If I'd known this would be a major hike, I would have worn my Nikes."

Up and up the staircase went, until the air grew warmer again. Finally, they reached a silver door that bore the Hawkspear crest.

Lucas knocked. Two quick knocks, four slow knocks: a different sequence from the one used at the theater. Farrell filed that bit of information in his head for future reference.

The door creaked open, and a man Farrell recognized from the society meetings peered out at them. He wasn't sure of his name; he'd never really paid much attention to the particularities of society life before.

"We're here," Lucas said.

The man opened the door wider to allow them entry, and suddenly Farrell found himself out of the dark stairwell and inside a warm building that was, judging by the walk through the tunnels, at least a mile from the cathedral. It must be accessible by secret passageway that also connected to the theater and the restaurant, Farrell thought.

"This way," Lucas said, leading Farrell through the dim interior.

The place was huge, at least as large as the Grayson mansion. The floors were stone and the walls plaster, with original oil paintings that looked as if they'd hung there for a century. Just past an archway at the end of a hallway, Farrell's gaze landed on what appeared to be a massive library where there were floor-to-ceiling bookshelves filled with leather-bound books.

Facing the door, in the center of the room beneath the skylight, was a large, heavy-looking wooden desk. Markus sat behind it, wearing a black business suit, white shirt, red tie. His elbows rested on the desk, and his fingers joined in a steeple before him.

"Come in, Mr. Grayson," he said, his voice clear and precise. "Thank you, Mr. Barrington. You may wait outside."

"Yes, sir." Lucas bowed his head and then left, closing the door behind him.

Farrell wasn't afraid.

Intimidated, however? Yes, he was definitely that.

He hadn't been this close to Markus since his first society meeting three years earlier, at which he'd stood on the stage before the audience just as Adam had the other night, with the spotlight in his eyes.

Markus never socialized with the society members after meetings. He didn't attend the charity functions or political rallies organized by his followers to help shape a better Toronto. He only ever addressed his gathered membership from his lofty position on the theater stage, where he brought forth prisoners and conducted their trials. Once certain guilt had been determined—and it always was—Markus performed the executions himself with his golden dagger, while the rest of the group beared solemn witness. Then he would slip out of sight, like a shadow, while his followers stayed behind and lingered for some time, engaging in whispered conversations that couldn't be held in broad daylight.

There were so many whispered rumors about the man, the recluse, the genius . . . the *god* . . . that Farrell couldn't count them, let alone remember them all and keep rumors straight from what he knew to be the truth.

"Thank you for coming," Markus said. "I'm honored to have you visit my home."

"It's *my* honor, sir." A thousand questions rose up in his throat, but he didn't say any of them aloud. Not yet. He might be reckless and irresponsible at times—well, most of the time—but he knew when to keep quiet.

He wasn't 100 percent certain about what Markus *was* that allowed him to have such power, but he didn't underestimate the man for a single moment.

"I'm sure Lucas has already let you know that I believe you would make an excellent addition to my small, exclusive group."

Farrell nodded, willing his heart to stop pounding so hard. "Yes. And anything I can do to prove myself to you, sir, I'll do it."

"Please, call me Markus. Your being here grants you many privileges that aren't extended to others in my society. It makes you my friend. Would you like that? To be my friend?"

"I would . . . Markus." He wisely chose not to blurt out anything about hair braiding or boy gossip. *No jokes,* he thought.

"Do you think you're special, Mr. Grayson?"

That was a loaded question if ever he'd heard one, especially now, when he was still sore from his conversation with his mother. Farrell took a moment before answering this powerful man.

"Yes, I do," he finally said, opting for simplicity.

No elaboration, just confidence. And he hoped his tone conveyed more than he currently felt.

"Good." There was a smile on Markus's lips. "I agree. Your brother was also special. It's unfortunate that he ultimately proved himself unworthy."

A muscle in Farrell's cheek twitched, but he bit his tongue so as not to reply, afraid of what he might say. It probably wouldn't be smart to get in an argument with a potential god of death.

"I know," Markus went on, "that my speaking this way about your dead brother must seem very disrespectful to you. However, despite any familial loyalty you feel, you must admit that Connor took the coward's way out of his single, precious life."

The words stung. "He had his problems."

Did any of those problems stem from being in your circle? Farrell thought.

"Of course. As we all do. But it's how we deal with life's challenges—both internal and external ones—that define us. Do we face them fearlessly, with courage and a sense of justice? Or do we run from them, seeking any easy answer to help hide from the harsh truths of life? Everyone is different, and it's difficult to tell who's who until one is tested. Which type are you, do you think?"

The type who likes vodka too much for his own good, he thought. *But you'd probably consider that a strike against me.* "I don't hide from anything," Farrell said aloud.

"And what do you want from this life you've been given, Mr. Grayson?" Markus asked. "Many claim that they simply want happiness. Some say they want peace and serenity. Some want money. Power. Sex. Excitement. What is it that *you* want?"

Farrell would be the first to admit that he hadn't given his future a whole lot of thought. He scanned the shelves laden with the largest private collection of books he'd ever seen in his life as he considered his reply. "I want to be respected. I want to be powerful. And, yes, I want to be special. I want to leave a mark on this world so no one forgets who I was."

He hadn't even realized it was the truth until he spoke it out loud. He felt as if he'd just purged something dark and cold inside him by giving it a voice.

Markus regarded him silently. "Do you feel conflicted in any way about how I choose to deal with my prisoners?"

Farrell remembered his argument with Adam about how being judge, jury, and executioner of criminals wasn't any less evil than the crimes those prisoners were accused of.

Of course Farrell had had his doubts in the beginning, but he'd come to accept that there was no other way. Markus's mission, if somewhat extreme, was important to the world.

Four executions a year wasn't that many. And they were symbolic. They meant something. They gave the society the motivation to go out and do good for the world around them whenever possible.

"I don't necessarily enjoy witnessing those people die," Farrell said, "but I know it's important and necessary, and I'm honored that I've been given the chance to be a part of it."

Lucas said Markus could sense a liar, so Farrell had not even tried to speak untruthfully. He had no idea what Markus could be thinking right now, or how Markus was judging him.

Was he saying the right things?

When Lucas first told him about the circle, he hadn't been absolutely certain he wanted any part of it. He'd mostly just considered it as a means to trace Connor during his last days, taking his last steps. But being here, face-to-face with a man who emanated waves of power from anywhere he was, Farrell realized this venture was more than just an investigation into his brother's suicide. He actually wanted this for himself. He *needed* this.

His mother thought he was nothing, especially compared with the perfect genius Connor was or the full-of-potential angel Adam was. But Farrell was *not* nothing, and this proved it in black and white.

This was his destiny.

"I have no reason to think you'll ever amount to anything of note. Therefore, I expect very little from you."

One day, he'd force Isabelle Grayson to eat every last one of her words, as if they were ingredients in a rancid soufflé.

"Do you have questions for me?" Markus asked.

Perhaps he should have just said no, but Farrell couldn't resist the opportunity to gather more information.

"How many are in your circle?" he asked.

"It would be six, including you. They become my eyes and ears in the world beyond these walls. I need those I trust without question to assist me."

"Are there always six?"

"Now, yes," Markus said. "At one time, years ago, there were eight, but two chose to leave the society and return to their regular lives. I require quite a lot of dedication from society members, and even more from those in my circle of trust, but neither needs to be a lifelong commitment, unless one chooses it to be so. One can always leave if they wish."

Farrell considered this. It was a strange relief, knowing that the commitment to the society wasn't forever if one chose a different path. "So you trusted my brother."

Another nod. "I did."

His heart ached at remembering Connor, at walking in his older brother's footsteps. "How long was he part of your circle?"

"Only a few months, I'm afraid."

Farrell cast away the memory of his brother's bedsheets, covered in blood from the cuts on his wrists. "And what does your trusted circle do for you that the other society members do not?"

Markus folded his hands on the desktop. "Their most important task is to search the city for specific criminals to be tried at our meetings. These searches can sometimes take quite a while, as the evil ones among us prefer to hide in the shadows, away from the glare of judgment." Markus paused, as if giving Farrell time to consider the gravity of what he'd just said. "And of course my circle also completes various other tasks and errands for me when required."

He didn't go into further detail, but Farrell got the impression that he shouldn't ask any more questions, and that he'd learned enough for today. If he were to join the circle, he'd need to capture criminals and bring them to the theater, knowing fully that he'd be leading them to their deaths. He would be responsible for claiming lives so that the society could grow stronger in their efforts to watch over the city—the world—to keep it safe from evil.

At the thought, he felt a rush of power similar to what he felt every time Markus spilled blood on the stage.

"Are you really a god of death like they say you are?" Farrell asked under his breath before he realized what he'd said. He half hoped that Markus didn't hear him.

"I am," Markus replied plainly and without hesitation.

Farrell's eyes snapped to his. He hadn't expected an answer from the mysterious man, let alone a perfectly clear and simple one, but there it was: confirmation that Markus was so much more than a secret society leader with a few magic tricks up his sleeves.

"Knowing this to be true, will you accept your position as a trusted member of my circle?" Markus asked. "And will you pledge to do whatever I ask of you, whenever I ask it?"

"I will." The words left his mouth before he realized it, an echo of his original commitment to the society.

"Good. Your agreement means that you will also accept a generous gift from me, one that will aid you in your service."

Then Markus fell silent for a full minute, watching Farrell with dark eyes.

Finally, he rose to his feet. He pulled his infamous golden dagger from a hinged mahogany box on his desk, its lid ornately carved with the Hawkspear emblem set against a backdrop of mountains, and inlaid with gold. "Give me your arm."

Was he about to give Farrell a second mark? Is that what Lucas had meant during that whole tattoo discussion?

The first mark had gifted Farrell with perfect health—he hadn't been sick a single day in the last three years (though, unfortunately, Markus didn't seem to have any power over hangovers).

What gift would this second mark bring?

He wanted to ask but knew this was not the time. Instead, he unbuttoned and rolled back the sleeve of his shirt, then offered his left arm to Markus.

Don't flinch, he reminded himself.

Markus grasped his wrist, then cut deeply into Farrell's forearm, guiding the tip of the dagger along his flesh. Farrell gritted his teeth, forcing himself not to react to the pain as he watched the blood flow from the wound, drip to the floor, and flow over the symbol that Markus etched into his skin.

When it was done, Markus placed the dagger on his desk and pressed his bare hand against Farrell's arm. A healing white light began to emanate from the wound, and Farrell felt a burning sensation—horribly painful, nearly as much as the cutting itself had been.

Moments later, Markus drew back from him. The wound had healed, and Farrell's skin was unmarked.

"Do you feel it?" Markus asked.

"Feel—?" Farrell started to ask but then closed his mouth.

He felt it.

He could hear the tick of the clock in the adjoining room. He could hear Lucas, who stood waiting for him on the other side of the door, tapping on his phone as he wrote a text or answered an e-mail.

He could smell bread baking in the kitchen, somewhere in the house. He could see with perfect clarity each and every title written in gilded gold and silver and bronze on the spines of the books throughout the room.

"My senses . . . ," he breathed.

"Are much improved," Markus finished. "This will help you in countless ways."

So this was how Lucas had been able to see in the near-pitch darkness of the tunnels, unafraid of tripping over his own feet. Now Farrell could do that as well.

"Thank you, Markus," he said, lowering his head in deference.

"How do you feel, Mr. Grayson?"

"Incredible." It was true. He'd never felt so good, so healthy, in his entire life.

Another nod from Markus. "Good. I have officially accepted you into my circle with this second mark. If you prove your worth fully to me, I will give you a third."

A third mark? What gift would that give him?

"Now. I have an assignment for you, Mr. Grayson."

My first assignment already? Farrell had barely begun to recover from the amazing effects of his new mark. He needed a drink. A big one. Straight up.

Still, clarity of mind shone through him. Above all else, he wanted to prove himself to this powerful god—the sooner the better.

"What is it?" he asked.

"There's a girl who I believe is attempting to seek information about me and the Hawkspear Society. I feel her particular investigation could be problematic, for many reasons we don't need to get into now. I want you to get to know her, make her trust you, find out what she's hiding, what she knows of the society, and what she may want from me in particular. And I want you to report back everything you find."

Farrell blinked. "You want me to spy on a girl."

"Yes. Will you do this for me?"

He'd been hoping for some epic task that would allow him to prove his worth. Spying on some girl playing at being Nancy Drew sounded simple enough, but it wasn't remotely groundbreaking.

Still, there was only one answer he could give, and he knew what it was.

"Of course I will, Markus."

Chapter 12

MADDOX

The guards threw Maddox back into his dungeon cell, laughing as they slammed the door shut behind them. Maddox lay on the dirt floor, staring up at the low stone ceiling, stunned by the harsh treatment and by everything he'd witnessed.

"Maddox . . ." Becca crouched down next to him and peered at his face with concern. "Can you hear me?"

"No. I can't hear anything anymore."

"Clearly you can hear me if you're answering me."

"She ordered that snake to kill Livius. A big snake with fangs . . . that grew even bigger. Did you see it grow?"

"I saw." She nodded. "So she's really a goddess, huh?"

He finally met her gaze. "You're accepting all this much more calmly than I would have expected."

"Do I seem calm? Because I'm not. I'm screaming on the inside, but I'm trying to keep it together because losing my mind will not help either of us right now." She exhaled shakily. "I'm sorry Livius is dead."

"I'm not."

"He was horrible to you, but nobody deserves to die like that."

He raised an eyebrow. "You're far too kind. You really aren't from Mytica, are you?"

"No," she replied. "I'm *really* not."

He forced himself to sit up, pressing his back against the hard wall. He regarded the spirit girl in silence for a long time—so long that she began to twist the end of her golden braid around her index finger.

"What?" she asked.

"I'm thinking."

"You're staring. Staring makes me nervous. I don't like being the center of attention. I even dropped out of Drama Club last month because of stage fright, which is strange because I'm normally very self-confident."

He blinked. "You say a lot of words that don't make any sense to me."

"Sorry, your tourism bureau didn't supply me with a dictionary upon arrival."

"What's a dictionary?"

"It's a book that . . . oh, it's not important right now." She stood up and went to the door to peer out of the tiny window that looked out at the hallway. Moans and coughs and the occasional shriek could be heard from other cells. "We have to get out of here."

"We?" he repeated. "I don't know why you're even still here. You could walk through that wall and leave this place far behind you."

"That wouldn't solve anything, would it? I need you out of here, too. You're the only one who can help me."

A fresh burst of frustration blossomed in his chest. "Why are you so sure I can help you?"

"Because you're the only one who can see me and talk to me! And you can work spirit magic."

He held his head in his hands and looked up at her. "Are you sure you want to call it that?"

"I do. Yes, let's call it spirit magic. There has to be a reason why I first appeared in the very place you were. It's all connected. *We're* connected, Maddox. Don't ask me how I know it. I just do. You can help me get back home."

"You're setting yourself up for disappointment."

Becca didn't reply but instead moved closer to him—so close that only a few inches separated them—and studied his face. Now *he* was the nervous one. He tried not to look away. Tried to hold her blue-eyed gaze. In the dim light of the cell, her eyes reminded him of the clear night sky. And her pink lips were so very . . .

"You don't believe in yourself," she said, shattering his concentration. "But you should. I saw what you did at the festival. I saw what you did to Livius here in this cell."

"My curse, you mean." It was how he'd come to think of his magic over the years.

"It's not a curse. It's a gift. Are there others in this place who can do what you can?"

He shook his head. He'd never heard of anyone in Mytica who possessed the same kind of magic he did. "There are witches, said to have the blood of the immortals in their veins. They can work with elemental magic in small amounts. Blood can strengthen their power when they've gotten weak. I've never met a real witch, so all my knowledge springs from the rumors I've heard."

"Witches with the blood of the immortals? Seriously?" she said, then raised a hand when Maddox opened his mouth to explain further about the golden beings said to have walked side by side with mortals before he was born. "No, let's put a pin in that for now and focus on you. Okay? I want to know everything there is to know about you."

Her current proximity to him made him feel half excited and half uncomfortable. If she were flesh and blood, he could easily reach out and touch her. The texture of her strange woolen tunic mesmerized him. It looked so soft.

He gulped. "There isn't much to tell. Livius always said I was duller than a dirtworm."

"Well, Livius was wrong. You're anything but dull to me. You're . . . fascinating." She actually smiled, a beautiful smile that sent a pleasant shiver running through him.

"I've never been fascinating to anyone," he admitted.

"Wow, we really need to work on your self-confidence, don't we? We have a good section of self-help books at the shop back home. I wish I had a couple to quote from right now."

Maddox frowned. "You're wasting your time, Becca Hatcher. When the goddess learns that my magic is not controllable and that I'm unable to summon the spirit of someone she's only *guessing* is dead, she'll have me put to death. I have a day to live, if that."

Her smile fell away. "If I could slap you right now, I would. Really hard."

This reaction coaxed a nervous laugh from him. "Apologies if it sounds grim, but it's the truth. I'm going to die, and there's no one here to help me. Without Livius, I'm all alone."

"You're not alone. You have *me*, and I'm not going anywhere," she said firmly. Angrily. "When the going gets tough, I believe in one thing, Maddox. My gut. It tells me which book to read next, even if it has lousy reviews; which movie to see, even if no one else wants to see it; which friends to hang out with, whether they're popular or loners or smart or dumb as bricks. And my gut tells me that you're not going to die. You're important to this world. And you're important to *me*. Got it? You and me, we're friends now. And friends help each other out in bad, snake-monster, scary-goddess times."

Friends. He mouthed the word. Of course he knew what it meant. However, he'd never really had a true friend before. Not one he could depend on, or trust with his secrets. With his life.

"Now, stop being a coward," Becca went on, "and let's get a plan together to get you the hell out of here."

He lurched up to his feet, his eyes blazing—going from feeling awkward to furious in a single moment. "*Coward?* I'm not a coward. How can you say I'm—"

"Finally, a little passion! Good to see it." She was grinning now. "And I don't actually think you're a coward. I just said that to get a reaction. Anyone who could face that Valoria woman and her magic snake and not crumple into a sobbing heap is brave. *You're* brave, Maddox."

The moment of outrage passed as quickly as it arrived. He wasn't brave, not really, but he chose not to correct her. But if she really did believe in him, maybe he could try to believe in himself. And if by some miracle he could help her as she thought he could, then he would do so without question.

"Tell me more about this book you mentioned before. The one you believe sent you here."

Becca began speaking about the leather-bound manuscript with the unfamiliar, unreadable gold and black lettering and painted illustrations but was interrupted by the sound of a metal key in the lock. The cell door swung open.

Two guards shoved a dirty man wearing ragged clothes inside. His face was bloody, as if he'd recently been beaten, and he smelled like he'd just been rolling around in a pile of cow manure.

"Here's some company for you, witch boy," the smirking guard told Maddox. "If you live through the night with the likes of him in here, the goddess will see you first thing tomorrow."

"Wait, no—" Maddox began, but they closed the door, and the small cell was plunged back into shadows.

The man stood in the center of the cell, staring at Maddox, his eyes shiny orbs in the center of his dirty, bloody face.

Maddox exchanged a wary, worried look with Becca.

"Today," the man said. "Tomorrow. Yesterday. All of them. All in a row. And here you are, and there we go. Dancing along. Happily and merrily, tra-la-la."

Maddox heard the guards cackling outside the cell, then saw a bloodshot eye appear at the window, peering in at them.

"Enjoy your new friend, witch boy," said a guard. "Perhaps Crazy Barney will tear you apart and eat you piece by piece before dawn, sucking the marrow from your bones. Sleep well!"

"Yes, the marrow," Crazy Barney said, raking his fingers, black with grime, through his long, tangled hair. "My favorite part. Slurp, slurp! Eat it all up!"

Maddox dodged past him to get to the door, and he pounded on it until he was sure his fist would bruise. "Let me out of here!"

The guards just laughed. On his tiptoes, he peered out the window to watch them as they strolled away down the hall, looking in on other prisoners.

"Don't panic," Becca said, her attention fixed on their new cellmate. "There's a way out of this."

"Really? Suggestions, please?"

"Well, there is that shove-and-choke magic trick you did before. I know you say you can't control it, but maybe if your life is in jeopardy. . . ."

He chewed his bottom lip. "Any other ideas when that doesn't work?"

"Ah, he talks to the spirits," Crazy Barney said, staring up at the ceiling, which was only an inch or two above their heads. He held his arms out to either side, palms up. "Spirits, come to us. Present us with your offerings. We will accept them with gratitude."

Then he spun around in a slow circle, laughing maniacally.

Maddox stared at him.

Crazy Barney stopped turning and cast a curious look at Maddox. "Are they gone . . . those who listen in? Those who cast their ears in our direction and take pleasure in our discomfort? Silly them, silly us." He cocked his head. "I'm very hungry. Will dinner be served soon?"

Maddox pressed his back against the wall. "I'm sure they'll be back any moment with a tray."

"Yes, yes. Yes. Of course they will. Wouldn't want to let their prize prisoner talk too long with someone like me without something to quell my appetite."

"Talking is good," Becca said, her expression squeamish. "Keep him talking. He looks seriously crazy."

Yes, it would seem that Crazy Barney came by his nickname honestly. "We can talk as long as you like . . . Barney. May I call you Barney? I'm Maddox."

"I know who you are." Barney moved toward the door, and Maddox jumped out of his way. The man glanced through the tiny window.

"It's an honor to meet you," Maddox said. Becca was right, keeping him talking was probably the best thing to do. If Barney was busy talking, he wouldn't be busy craving bone marrow. "Tell me about yourself. From where do you hail? Here in the North? Overseas, perhaps?"

"No time for unimportant questions." Barney turned around and swept his gaze over Maddox from head to toe.

"Your magic?" Becca stood next to him, fists clenched, as if she was ready to assist him in a fight. "Now would be great."

"I'm trying. It's not working," Maddox growled. His head already hurt from concentrating so hard.

"Try again," she insisted.

And so he did. He tried to summon his inner strength to shove Crazy Barney backward, cutting off his air supply, hopefully enough to knock him out until the guards returned.

"Can't feel a thing," Barney said, cocking his head. "But you're still very young. Your magic has yet to manifest fully. Is the spirit attempting to guide you?"

"Yes," Maddox said slowly. "A beautiful spirit girl is guiding me. And she's telling me that you're very special, Barney. Very special indeed."

"Did you say *beautiful*?" Becca asked.

Curse it. Maddox tried to concentrate only on the madman. "You and me, we're going to get along just fine. We're going to be good friends. And, um . . . friends don't eat friends."

Barney regarded him patiently. "Let's get a few things straight right away, *friend*. I'm not crazy. My name is Barnabas, so you can quit with *Barney*. And you're going to help me with two very important tasks."

What just happened? "Excuse me?"

"First you're going to break us out of this dungeon. And second we're going to use your magic to destroy Valoria and save the world."

Chapter 13

CRYSTAL

The University of Toronto was so close to the Speckled Muse that in mere minutes after she left the bookshop, she found herself among the buildings and residences of the expansive St. George campus that was integrated into the heart of the city like just another neighborhood surrounding the green-and-blue football field.

Jackie hadn't given her much to go on, just a name and a department, so she did her best. But it wasn't long until she had to admit she was overwhelmed. A campus like this made the halls of her high school look like a dollhouse in comparison. She'd never had a great sense of direction to begin with, so even with the YOU ARE HERE signs, she had a difficult time finding her way along the labyrinthine streets and pathways.

"Do you know where I can find Dr. Vega?" Crys asked a student, who ignored her completely, keeping her attention on the screen of her phone.

She asked someone else.

"Who?" the girl asked distractedly.

"Dr. Vega. He's in the Anthropology Department?"

The student flicked her hand but didn't slow her steps. "I think it's over there somewhere."

"Over . . . where?" Crys began, but the girl had already walked away.

She stopped in her tracks and tried to compose herself by snapping a few pictures of the ornate, multilayered Romanesque arch over the south entrance of the main University College building on King's College Circle. So beautiful, like something she'd expect to find in Europe, only a short walk from her own home.

But admiring pretty stone archways wouldn't help her current situation.

"Breathe," she told herself. "You're not lost or in over your head, you're just dealing with a momentary setback. One more picture, then let's go find one of those maps again."

Another student walked through the shot just as she took it.

"Hey!" she protested grumpily.

"Sorry." The male student raised an eyebrow. "Are you lost? Anything I can do?"

Crys lowered her camera. The guy was twenty, maybe twenty-one. Blond hair, dreamy dark blue eyes, completely gorgeous, like a model or an actor. She searched his face but couldn't find a single flaw.

"Is it that obvious I'm lost?" She tried to sound as calm as possible. "Vega. I mean, *Dr.* Vega. I'm looking for his office in the Anthropology Department. Can you help?"

"Of course I can," he said.

"My hero." She groaned inwardly. If she didn't watch it, she'd be giggling in a minute.

Crystal Hatcher didn't giggle.

He turned and pointed. "Head through here and turn left on Saint George Street and then right on Russell. The Anthropology Building will be on your left. You'll find Dr. Vega's office there." His smile widened, showing off perfect white teeth. "Closer than you probably thought you were, right? Never lose hope."

She breathed a silent sigh of relief. "Thank you so much."

"Any time I can be a hero for a beautiful girl like you, it's my honor. Have a good day." With another smile, he turned and began walking in the other direction.

A beautiful girl like me? Nobody had ever called her beautiful to her face before; that was a compliment usually reserved for her sister.

She took another snapshot of the guy, noting that he looked good from both the front and the back.

Maybe she'd have to rethink her original plan to not go to university.

Crys shook her head, trying to clear it. She wasn't usually so quickly smitten by guys just because they were good-looking.

Whatever, she told herself, and then headed confidently in the right direction.

In the Anthropology Building, she finally found a list of offices. Dr. Uriah Vega was on the second floor.

She took a deep breath before getting in the elevator, then navigated the gray hallway, before she found the door that held his name placard. After only a slight hesitation, she knocked.

When the only reply she heard was a grunt, she knocked again.

"Well, come in, then," a grudging voice said. "And be quick about it."

She turned the handle and eased the door open.

A man sat behind a desk piled high with stacks of paper surrounding an old computer covered in colorful sticky notes. He had reddish-blond hair, thinning across his scalp, round wire-rim glasses, and an unfriendly scowl on his face.

"If this is about the paper due today, I'm not taking anyone's excuses. If you're late, you'll be penalized."

Her heart thundered. "Dr. Vega?"

"Who else would I be? And to remind you, students need to make appointments to see me outside of my listed hours. Check the door."

"I'm not a student."

His scowl deepened. "Then who are you and what are you doing here?"

"Jackie Kendall told me to come and see you."

His eyes bugged out. A moment later, he jumped up from his desk and reached the door in three big steps, pulling her farther inside. "Jackie sent you?"

It was like Dr. Jekyll and Mr. Hyde, a complete personality change in a split second. "Yes, I'm . . . I'm Crys Hatcher. Her niece. She said this would be a good time to talk."

"Why didn't you say that to begin with?" He pushed the door shut and locked it, then pressed his back against it. "Were you followed?"

The question made her feel queasy. "Uh . . . I don't think so."

He went to the small window behind his desk and peered outside, scanning the area before yanking down the blinds. "You must know these things. You must always be vigilant."

Jackie hadn't said anything about watching for stalkers—although, she had mentioned self-defense. Was Dr. Vega totally paranoid or was he simply being cautious, like Jackie?

She nudged her glasses back up her nose. "I'll remember that in the future. Promise."

He sat down with a heavy thud behind his desk and signaled for her to take a seat on the rather uncomfortable-looking wooden stool across from him. The professor reminded Crys of a youngish Albert Einstein: frazzle-haired, wild-eyed, eccentric.

Hopefully nearly as brilliant.

"Where is Jackie?" he asked.

"In Paris, I think. She's trying to get here as soon as she can."

"Really? She's coming here?" He leaned back in his chair, his expression now wistful. "I haven't seen her in over a year, not since our last meeting in London. A beautiful woman, your aunt. She's . . . quite remarkable. I look forward to every e-mail she sends me."

Crys could practically see the little cartoon hearts popping up over his head. He wouldn't be the first, or even the fiftieth, man who'd fallen hard for her free spirit of an aunt.

Vega's frown returned slowly, popping the cartoon hearts like soap bubbles. "Jackie always informs me of any news or changes. She didn't mention anything about you." He swept a skeptical gaze over Crys. "How old are you?"

"Seventeen."

"Let me see your ID. I have no proof that you are who you say you are."

Definitely paranoid. She fished around in her bag and pulled out her Sunderland High School student card. "Good enough?"

He pursed his lips as he studied it. "Hmm. I suppose." He leaned back again and eyed her guardedly. "What do you want?"

How was she supposed to get information from a man whose mood swung so wildly from minute to minute? "Jackie said that you'd give me"—did she really have to say it out loud?—"the . . . *full monty* on the book."

The bug eyes returned. He whipped off his glasses and wiped the lenses on his rolled-up shirtsleeve. "She said that? Those words exactly?"

"Um, yes."

"Does this mean that you have it?" Vega asked, his voice hushed to a hoarse whisper.

"Have what?"

"The Bronze Codex."

He was speaking another language, and she tried to keep up. "What's the Bronze . . . ?" And then it clicked. "That's what the book's called, isn't it?"

He drew in a ragged breath. "So you *do* have it?"

She wasn't going to admit anything. Not now. "I didn't say that. Jackie just said you'd tell me what it is and what it can do. Can you do that?" Jackie hadn't been that specific, but he didn't have to know that.

"The Bronze Codex is my life's work. Of course I can." He stared into her eyes so deeply she thought he might be trying to see her brain. "Very well, if Jackie says the full monty, the full monty's what you shall get."

He stood up and went to his bookshelves, then pulled a full set of volumes off a midlevel shelf, tossing them carelessly to the floor. They had hidden a safe behind them. He worked the combination lock until it clicked, then opened the door and pulled out a thick black binder, nothing more extraordinary than something she might carry around at school.

He brought it to his desk and placed it down gently.

"Jackie sent me digital photos of each page when she first acquired it." He flipped through the photos, and Crys watched with amazement as images of the pages that had been burned into her memory flitted across her eyes as three-hole-punched black-and-white printouts. "It's incredible, isn't it?"

"You said it's your life's work."

He nodded. "It was my father's obsession first. The Codex was brought to him by its original owner many years ago for an initial assessment of the language and origins. My father named it the Bronze Codex, after the bronze hawk on its cover, a symbol that is repeated on twenty-four of its pages." He flipped through the binder, brushing his index finger over every hawk illustration he came across.

"So your father saw the book in real life. Who was the owner?"

Vega's brows drew together, studying Crys as if to second-guess how much of the "full monty" he should actually divulge. "A Toronto woman who had been a classmate of my father's. She trusted him more than anyone else. He is the one who persuaded her, after a time, to get rid of it."

"Why?"

"Because, while he was unable to translate it himself, he still knew it was dangerous. So, yes, the book has been lost to us for well over twenty years."

"Didn't your father know where it ended up? Or the woman who brought it to him, at least? Couldn't you have asked?"

"Both of them died fifteen years ago."

Crys's chest tightened. "They died . . ." She hated to ask, but she had to. "From natural causes?"

"No. The woman . . ." He swallowed hard. "She fell from the twenty-fifth floor of a high-rise building. My father . . . he drowned. Which is suspicious considering he was a silver medalist for the Canadian Olympic swim team in his youth."

A chill swept over Crys, raising the fine hairs on her arms.

"You're saying that you think they were murdered because of this book."

"Yes, I do. I believe they were murdered by Markus King."

Her breath caught in her chest.

Dr. Vega raised a bushy eyebrow. "You know the name, don't you?"

All she could do was nod.

"And you know that your aunt wants to use this book to draw King out of his hiding spot—wherever that is. To make him pay for his many crimes."

"I don't know all the details, but yes." She chewed her bottom lip, staring down at a black-and-white sketch of a hawk parting a column of indecipherable words with its wide wings. "How did she find it, after all this time?"

"Nothing more than a lucky break. We found a listing of it in the online archives of an exclusive auction house. I received a tip that a—quote—'unreadable book' had been secretly sold into the private collection of a British family who had no idea what they had actually acquired. The family had simply placed it in a curio as if it were nothing more than a valuable first edition to display in their library. It had been hidden there in plain sight for at least a decade, lost to the world, until Jackie found a way to procure it from them."

"You mean she stole it."

He shrugged. "Procured. Stole. Your aunt certainly has her ways to get what she wants."

Crys could easily picture her pretty blond aunt talking her way into a stately British home, scanning the shelves while she flirted with whoever stood in her way, wearing a short skirt and stiletto heels that showed off her long legs. Then the moment their backs were turned, Jackie would have disappeared from the home like a puff of smoke, the book tucked under her arm.

"But what *is* it, Dr. Vega?" Crys asked, knowing she had yet to uncover the most vital information about the book. "What is the Bronze Codex?"

She expected him to brush off the question, just as her mother had, to change the subject to something safe and distracting. But instead, he studied her for exactly five seconds before pulling a scientific journal out of his lower desk drawer, flipping through the pages, and turning it around so she could read the heading.

Obsidia: A Magical Language from Another World
By Dr. Uriah Vega, PhD

The article was dated fifteen years ago.

"I wrote this shortly after I completed my doctorate," he explained. "So foolish, looking for credentials and praise, ignoring the potential danger that going public with such information would cause."

Crys read the heading three times, not understanding. "Fifteen years ago. So around the same time your father and that woman were killed."

His expression darkened. "That's right. That's why I feel personally responsible for their deaths, and why I'll never forgive myself."

This article had potentially caused two people with direct knowledge of the book to be murdered.

It's possible all this was just a coincidence, Crys thought. Or, if it wasn't, that Markus King isn't responsible.

But then who was this man to whom her father was so loyal?

"Obsidia is the language in the book?"

"Obsidia is what my father called it. I have retained that name as I try to translate it. I will admit that most of the scholars who've read this paper have ridiculed my hypothesis."

"Your hypothesis that Obsidia is a magical language from another world."

"Yes."

She had to admit, it did sound completely insane.

"Here's what I believe, Miss Hatcher," he said gravely. "Are you ready for my theory—a theory that your aunt also believes?"

"More than ready."

"Sixty years ago, this book appeared in Toronto, out of nowhere. Because of some other . . . strange circumstances in her life, the woman who found it believed it was something she needed to hide from others seeking it. So hide it she did, holding her secret to her chest for years before she trusted my father enough to share it with him.

"My father told me that the moment he saw the Codex, the moment he touched it, he knew that it was incredibly rare and special. He had worked with rare books—so-called *grimoires* and spell books from many cultures and ages—but he'd never come across something that affected him at first sight as this one did. This language, he believed, could potentially unlock the mysteries of the universe—and could imbue great power on anyone who can read and comprehend such a language. This . . . the Bronze Codex . . . is a book of spells from another world, Miss Hatcher."

Crys felt the color drain from her face with every word he spoke. Her hands were cold, clammy.

A book of spells. Real magic . . . from another world. Did she believe that?

"What does Markus King have to do with this book?" she asked, breathless.

Dr. Vega placed one palm flat against the binder, his other on top of the paper he'd written. "All I can say is, I know that he wants it and he's more than willing to kill for it."

When she didn't reply right away, the words sticking in her throat at this flat proclamation, he flipped further through the binder to an illustration of what looked like an ornate stone wheel. "Such detail. It's incredible, don't you think?"

Crys moistened her dry lips with the tip of her tongue before she found her voice. "You said this book is not from our world."

Vega nodded gravely. "That is both my father's and my hypothesis, yes."

Crys realized she was clutching the strap of her bag, still slung over her shoulder, so tightly that her fingers had gone numb. She loosened her grip. "Are you talking about outer space and, like, intergalactic travel?"

He shook his head. "No little green men here, Miss Hatcher. Many believe our world to be the only one, but this is arrogant thinking. Then there are those whose minds are open to more flexible possibilities. It would be best and easiest for you to picture these other worlds as . . . parallel dimensions. And I believe the Codex . . ." He caressed the binder as one might do to a lover's cheek. "It must explicate the means to create a magical gateway between these worlds, which is how it got here in the first place."

"A *magical* gateway?" She couldn't keep the disbelief out of her tone. "You know that sounds crazy, right?"

He nodded now, as if in partial agreement. "So most have told me, but that's done nothing to change my mind." He flipped to the middle of the binder. "I've studied my father's notes and sketches for years, and I've been poring over these photocopies ever since Jackie sent them to me, giving me my first glimpse at the book itself. This language—just as my father always claimed, it's like nothing I've ever seen before. Nothing even comes close. I'm familiar with hundreds of languages, both modern and ancient. I learned ancient Babylonian in a month. I can translate hieroglyphics while simultaneously chewing gum and standing on my head. But this? This is the greatest undertaking of my life."

"Because you can't decipher it."

"Don't be so quick to assume, Miss Hatcher. Your aunt believes in my abilities; otherwise she never would have shared so many secrets with me. I believe with enough time, I can crack the code. Here." He touched a page with one large line of script on it, surrounded by hawks and a drawing of a meadow with what looked like a glass city in the distance. "This word. I believe it could be *evergreen*. Perhaps *never-ceasing . . . perpetual . . .*" His gaze moved to hers. *"Immortal."*

"Immortal," she repeated, her mouth dry. "Maybe . . . maybe this is all just some sort of a hoax. There have always been con men throughout history who've tried to fake one-of-a-kind artifacts, right?"

He actually grinned at that, the maniacal smile of someone who doesn't sleep much and who compensated for it daily with gallons of caffeine. A quick glance at the professor's desk confirmed Crys's hunch: There were multiple coffee mugs and Styrofoam cups strewn across the surface. "A fair assessment, but I know I'm right about this. Down to my very soul, I know." He flipped forward again and pointed at an illustration of what looked to Crys like a squirrel, but with very long ears. "For example, this particular species does not and has never existed in our world."

"That's just a drawing. Mickey Mouse isn't actually a real mouse, either, you know."

An edge of annoyance entered his gaze. "You want to deny what I'm saying, but I see in your eyes that you believe it could be true."

"If it is," she allowed, "do you feel safe here having those photocopies in your office? I mean, after what happened to your father?"

"I haven't been visited by members of Markus King's society for well over a decade. I haven't published a thing about the Codex since my original paper, and I'm sure they're well aware that any subsequent attempts to shed light on the matter have been mocked by my peers at every turn, all but discrediting any work I've ever done in the field. They believe my work in this area has ceased. That I am just a humble university professor with eccentric theories."

"But they're wrong," she said.

He nodded. "It's best that they think I'm nothing more than a fool."

"I don't think you're a fool." She had to confide in him. If Jackie trusted him, she would, too. "Dr. Vega, you have to help me. My sister, Becca, she's in trouble."

"What do you mean? What kind of trouble?"

"The Codex . . . she saw it. She touched it."

"Oh my," he said, leaning back in his chair. "So Jackie did manage to get the Codex back to Toronto. She is a woman no one should underestimate."

So much for being vague. Dr. Vega was a whole lot savvier than he had originally appeared. He didn't underestimate Jackie . . . and Crys wouldn't underestimate *him*.

"Becca's in a coma from touching the book. She started off catatonic, but now it's turned into a full-blown coma." A shiver sped down her spine. "The book did it to her. I need to know how to wake her up again."

His brows drew together. "I'm sorry you have to deal with all this at your young age."

Crys waved his concern away. "I held the book for as long as she did, and nothing happened to me. Why would it affect her and not me?"

His lips thinned. "I honestly don't know. I'm sure many people have had physical contact with the book in the past, but this is the first I've heard of it having a tangible and negative effect on its handler."

"So what do we do?"

Dr. Vega riffled through his top drawer, pulled out a lined notebook, and scrawled something into it with a blue pen. His handwriting was nearly as unintelligible as the Codex's. "I will make haste in my attempt to translate these pages. In the meantime, I'll try my best to come up with some hypothesis of what's happened to your sister."

Anxiety welled in Crys's chest. "You'll try your best? I thought you were the expert here. You have to give me more than a maybe."

"I am the expert. But it doesn't mean that I know everything about it, especially having only had these photocopies in my possession for less than two weeks. I can't possibly unravel an enigma like that in such a short amount of time." His expression softened. "I'm sorry, Miss Hatcher. I wish I could tell you something that would ease your mind."

Crys stood up, her legs now weak. "Me too."

Of course she wouldn't find an answer so easily. Dr. Vega might have a bunch of theories about the book, but if he didn't know it was capable of doing something like this, he might not be as useful as she'd hoped.

But yet again Markus King's name had come up in a conversation about the book. The way Jackie and Vega talked about him made him sound terrifying and evil, but it didn't make sense. Why would her father not only trust him, but also think he was capable of saving the world, if he were such a monster?

It didn't match up.

"I promise to call as soon as I have more information," Dr. Vega promised.

All she could do was nod. Just then, there was a knock at his door. Dr. Vega tentatively moved toward it, unlocking it and peering outside. It was a student, asking for time to talk about an assigned paper. Without another word, Crys slipped past them and left the office, her head in a fog.

She'd received so much information, but none of it helped.

Magic languages. Spell books from other worlds. Immortals.

If this were any other week, she might laugh off everything Dr. Vega said as ridiculous ramblings—just another fantasy from one of Becca's favorite books.

She shoved open the main door and emerged from the Anthropology Building into the cool air. It was overcast again, no blue sky showing at all. The city seemed gray and bleak. And to think, only a week ago little green buds were emerging on flowers and trees. Now it felt as if winter was threatening to return.

A hand on her arm stopped her in her tracks. She turned, finding herself face-to-face with a boy wearing a black leather jacket and a red scarf.

"You know . . . ," he said. Fashionably messy, mahogany-brown hair, hazel eyes, a killer smile. "You look really familiar to me. Do I know you?"

"I don't think so." Although, she had to admit, he also looked vaguely familiar to her, too.

He'd caught her at a moment when she was incredibly close to the edge of her patience, but she didn't want to take out her frustration on a stranger.

"I'm thinking about taking a few classes here," the boy said. "I could use some tips from someone in the know. Are you free right now? This might sound crazy or impulsive, but can I buy you a coffee? I'd love the chance to talk to you."

His smile was charmingly lopsided. He had a mark under his right eye, which some might think marred his looks but which Crys found interesting. His nose seemed a little crooked, as if it had been broken once or twice. But that, combined with the birthmark, kept his face from being too perfect, too symmetrical.

Comparing him with the golden boy from earlier, she found this one much more interesting, and definitely worthy of her camera. She'd love the chance to take his picture.

But not now. Not ever, actually—she had far more urgent needs to focus on.

"I don't go to school here," she said. "Sorry."

"But—"

"Someone else will help you, I'm sure. Good luck."

Before she turned to walk away, she couldn't help but notice that his friendly and flirtatious expression had darkened a shade.

It was then that she knew where she recognized him from.

Farrell Grayson—the middle son of one of the richest men in Toronto. She remembered paging through *FocusToronto* magazine last year and seeing the feature on the Grayson family and their three gorgeous sons. But something was different . . .

The mark under his eye. He didn't have it in the pictures.

I can't believe I remember something like that, she thought.

Farrell Grayson, the overprivileged rich kid whose handful of arrests and bad boy ways landed him regularly in the Toronto headlines. Yes, she definitely knew who he was by reputation alone.

Crys glanced over her shoulder at the boy in black and red standing in the same spot she'd left him. Perhaps she should have taken it as a compliment that he wanted to buy her a coffee, even if just to pick her brain.

But she had way more important things to do than pay attention to boys. Especially ones who had trouble written all over them.

Chapter 14

FARRELL

It didn't cost much to bribe high school students for information. Sixty dollars, and Farrell had everything he needed.

Tuesday morning, he went to Sunderland High and learned that Crystal Hatcher had managed (barely) to maintain passing grades, despite missing nearly three weeks' worth of classes since January. Her favorite and best subject was art and her worst and least favorite was calculus.

She lived with her sister and mother in the apartment above the Speckled Muse Bookshop, a small local business that had been in Crystal's family for several generations. The bookshop was a downtown tourist attraction not only because the building that housed it was one of the oldest in the Annex, but also because it was rumored to be haunted. Sales had slowed in the last few years with the growing popularity of e-books and the lower prices and larger selections of big bookstore chains and online retailers.

On a more personal level, there was some speculation among her classmates over whether or not Crystal had seen her father since her parents separated two years ago.

Out of the six senior students Farrell had questioned, only two considered Crystal a friendly acquaintance, but not a close friend. Crystal's two closest friends had recently moved to Vancouver and Miami. Three informants admitted they didn't know her very well at all. And one—a girl with a sneer and a sour attitude—thought she was a "total bitch."

That one caught his interest.

Crystal Hatcher, the bitchy loner who liked art and not much else. According to her friendly acquaintances, she didn't have a boyfriend, but one girl noted that she'd mentioned somebody named Charlie with great affection in recent weeks.

And none of them had seen her at school since last Thursday.

He'd found a yearbook photo of her that showed an unsmiling girl with jet-black hair and unusually pale eyes. He tore it out and pocketed it, then headed over to Bathurst, a little north of Bloor Street, to lurk outside the bookshop until he saw her leave.

She looked a lot different from her yearbook photo. Her long hair was tied in a messy ponytail that cascaded down her back, and it was bleached so blond it was nearly white. She wore black-rimmed glasses that were far too large for her face. Faded jean jacket, ankle-length black skirt, black steel-tip boots. A flash of color came from her bright fuchsia bag. As she passed him without even glancing in his direction, he caught the scent of strawberries.

Strawberries were his favorite fruit.

Feeling confident, he followed her to the U of T campus, then waited for her to come out of the building she'd disappeared into before going in for the kill. When it was time, he approached her with his very best smile in place and poured on the charm. . . .

And was quickly discarded like yesterday's news.

This never happened to him.

As such, he wasn't sure what to do about it other than stare after her in disbelief as she walked away.

Darkness stirred within him in reaction to his failure, and the scent of strawberries stayed with him for hours afterward as he tried to figure out what he'd done wrong.

"Are you listening to me?"

Felicity Seaton gazed across the table at Scaramouche—a high-end French-inspired restaurant with a stunning view of the city—over her glass of club soda and cranberry juice.

"Of course I am," he replied, indicating to the waiter that he wanted another vodka on the rocks. It would be his third since this blind date began.

He wasn't sure why he hadn't canceled. It wasn't as if his mother could be any more disappointed in him than she already was.

For some reason, this had seemed like a good idea. A date with a suitable girl who could give him the air of respectability that he sorely needed, in the eyes of both his parents and everyone else in the city.

Felicity raised a thin, penciled-in eyebrow at him. "Then what did I say?"

"That you're going to France next week."

She smiled. "That's right. You've been there, of course?"

"As a child. I don't remember much except being dragged around to art galleries and having to eat a lot of cheese."

"You must go again. Marseille at this time of year is an absolute jewel."

"I'll take your word for it." He gave her an even smile in return, one that he only felt on the skin-deep level, and tried to ignore the rancid scent of her perfume. The scent likely cost hundreds of dollars an ounce, but Farrell thought she should save her money and buy something cheaper and less offensive.

Something more . . . fruity.

Was Felicity every bit as beautiful as his mother had claimed? Sure. Even though she did have sharp features that reminded him of a fox. Felicity had modeled at sixteen, but decided it didn't truly interest her. Instead, she wanted to devote her life to charity work. She had perfect shoulder-length blond hair with subtle highlights that likely came from the salon rather than from the sun, and makeup so precisely applied it gave the impression that she was naturally flawless.

She wore a black satin dress that was a tad too elegant for an eighteen-year-old on a Tuesday evening, but to each their own.

As they made pleasant conversation, Farrell felt that he was suitably holding up his end of this deal with his mother, even though his mind was a million miles away. Finally they finished with dinner, and then turned down dessert.

"If I eat another bite I'm going to burst," she claimed.

She'd barely picked at her plate of sea scallops.

Farrell tucked his credit card into the bill holder, not bothering to glance at the amount on the check.

"It's been so wonderful getting to know you," she said.

He resisted the urge to yawn. "I couldn't agree more. I hope to see you again soon."

"Yes, absolutely."

He fixed another cool smile on his lips during the drive to her parents' Rosedale estate. "Till next time," he said.

"Next time," she agreed.

"Unless," he began, "you don't want this night to end so soon?"

She turned and met his gaze with interest. "You couldn't stay here tonight. My parents would lose their minds to find a boy in my room—whoever he is. We'd have to go to a hotel."

He widened his eyes. "Why, Miss Seaton, whatever did you think I was suggesting?"

Her cheeks flushed. "I . . . I mean, I—"

He leaned closer and gave her a chaste kiss on the cheek. "Best to take things slowly, I think. If that's all right with you."

"Of course. More than all right."

He walked her to her front door, said another gentlemanly good-night, and then made his escape.

Girls were all the same. It was so much fun to toy with them.

The unexpectedly wicked thought made him grin.

"She seems nice," Sam said as he stood by the open back door of the limo.

"Yeah, she's a peach." Farrell swung himself into the backseat. "Let's go get some drinks."

"I can't drink, sir. I'm driving."

"Then you can drink chocolate milk and watch me drink vodka."

"Very well," Sam agreed. "Chocolate milk it is."

On the way to the Raven Club, Farrell decided to check up on his little brother, maybe see if he wanted to catch a late movie.

The phone rang twice before Adam answered.

"Yeah?" he yelled. The music was so loud on the other end that Farrell could barely hear him.

"Where are you?" Farrell asked.

"What?" Adam shouted, and Farrell let out a frustrated sigh.

"Where. Are. You."

"Firebird! I'm at Firebird with some new friends! They're great!" Adam's words were slurred.

Firebird was a new dance club on Lake Shore Boulevard near the exhibition grounds, one that Farrell knew for a fact didn't cater to the underage crowd.

His grip tightened on the phone. "You're drunk."

"You're, like, psychic! Hey, everyone, my brother is psychic. He knows I'm wasted!"

"I'm coming to get you."

"Oh, please. Are you seriously giving me a hard time about this? So I've had a few drinks and maybe, I don't know, maybe I did a line or two. I'm having fun."

A line or two?

Farrell reached forward to knock on the partition, which then rolled down immediately. "Sam, head to Firebird instead."

"Yes, sir."

"Adam, stop whatever it is that you're doing," Farrell said into the phone. "Go outside and wait for me."

"No way," Adam replied. "I'm not going anywhere. Why are you being such a jerk about this? You party all the time. I'm just following in your footsteps. You should be proud of me."

At the beginning of the call, Farrell thought he'd be furious at his little brother, but a cool sensation flowed over him instead. A calmness that slowed his heartbeat and ramped his senses up. He smelled gasoline, the rubber of the limo's tires. He could pick out individual voices beyond the blare of music. "I expect better from you, and so do Mom and Dad."

Adam just laughed and hung up without another word.

Farrell and Sam arrived at the dance club fifteen minutes later.

"You need help?" Sam asked.

"No, stay out here. This won't take long."

Farrell entered the club, wincing as the loud dance music

assaulted his enhanced sense of hearing after the comparable silence of outside.

Firebird's decor lived up to its name. Everywhere he looked, he saw flames—painted on the walls, flickering in the gigantic digital displays hanging over the bar, stitched into the fabric of the chairs and sofas. Under the strobe lights, the dance floor was a glittering mosaic depicting a phoenix, its feathers made of fire as it rose from the ashes.

The place was packed, the scents of body odor and cheap cologne assaulting Farrell's sensitive nose. He scanned the club, trying to hear his brother's voice and pinpoint his face in the crowd.

And there he was, in the center of the dance floor, grinding against some trashy-looking girl who was at least twice his age.

He made a beeline for Adam and grabbed his arm. "Time to go, kid."

His brother turned a sullen, unfocused glare on him and yanked his arm away. "I'm not a kid."

"You're right. You're actually acting more like a baby right now."

"I'm having fun."

"I don't care."

"You can't make me leave."

"Sure about that?" He grabbed Adam's arm again and pulled him off the dance floor. Adam swore and swung his fist but didn't make contact.

"You're hurting me," he yelped.

Farrell let go of him, noticing that his fingers had left red marks on his brother's arm. "Sorry."

Adam rubbed the marks. "I don't know why you're being such a dick. You do this all the time. You did this when you were my age."

"Maybe I want better for you."

"Maybe I don't care what you want."

Farrell studied him. The kid's face was flushed and sweaty, his pupils dilated. He wasn't just drunk; he was high.

"Who gave you the coke?" he asked, his voice low and even.

"What does it matter? I could get it anywhere, anytime, if I wanted it. As long as Markus doesn't kill off every drug dealer in the city."

Farrell glanced around to make sure no one was listening. "I know you're still having a hard time with what you saw at the meeting, but that's no reason to lose control of yourself and act so recklessly."

"That has nothing to do with this."

"Doesn't it?" People always turned to vices to escape, to forget. Farrell knew that better than anyone.

Adam was visibly messed up after seeing that execution. Farrell had understood to a point, but now he had no idea why it had affected his brother so deeply, far deeper than it had ever affected him. No other society member he knew of had reacted like this to the trial and Markus's dagger marking.

Adam sneezed.

"That's what happens when you stuff white powder up your nose," Farrell said.

"I think I'm getting a cold. Or the flu. Something's going around."

Farrell eyed him, confused. "That's impossible."

Adam had been given the gift of Markus's first mark, which meant he should be in perfect health from now on. He shouldn't be able to get the common cold ever again.

"What's happening over here?" A guy Farrell had never seen before joined them, his grin toothy and unpleasant.

"Who are you?" Farrell asked.

"Adam's good buddy. Michael." The grin widened. "You're Farrell, Adam's brother. Glad to meet you. I've heard a lot about you."

"How old are you?" Farrell asked, ignoring the introduction.

"Twenty-one."

"And you're hanging around with a sixteen-year-old?"

Michael shrugged and slung an arm around Adam's shoulders. "Adam's my boy. He's a part of my pack now."

"Is he."

"Come on, man. Let's go back to my table. I got some candy there I'm happy to share with my friends."

"Candy."

"*Nose candy*. You know what I mean."

"Yeah, I do."

Farrell grabbed Michael and drove his knee into his gut. Michael let out a grunt of pain, his gaze clouding over with confusion.

All thoughts escaped Farrell's mind, leaving only cold certainty. This kid had given Adam drugs, encouraged him to use them frequently. To party. To have fun.

And Farrell wanted to kill him.

"Wait, what are you—?" Michael began, but Farrell was there, yanking him to his feet.

"Stay the hell away from my brother. Hear me?" Farrell punched him in the throat.

Michael gasped and sputtered, clutching his neck. As Farrell came at him again, Michael tried to fight back, but he was at a disadvantage.

Senses, strength, clarity.

A cold and precise purpose: *Protect Adam.*

Farrell threw Michael onto the dance floor, which cleared

immediately. The shrieks and yells echoed in Farrell's ears. His fist connected with Michael's nose, and he felt it break. Michael screamed.

A few more punches, and the kid collapsed to the ground. Farrell jumped on top of him, hitting him in the face over and over until all he saw was blood.

Someone grabbed hold of his arms to stop him. "You're going to kill him!"

It was the club's bouncer. He was strong and managed to drag Farrell up to his feet.

Michael just lay there, convulsing, whimpering.

"Don't get up," Farrell warned him.

"Trust me, buddy," the bouncer said. "He's not getting up anytime soon."

Farrell turned a cool, calm look on the bouncer, sizing him up. He was larger than him, taller than him, and looked like trouble.

"Here." Farrell pulled out his wallet and tucked five one-hundred-dollar bills into the bouncer's shirt pocket. "Take care of this for me, okay, pal?"

The bouncer grabbed the money, frowning down at the bills.

Farrell didn't wait for a confirmation. Money talked; it always did.

He grabbed Adam and pulled him out of the club, ignoring the stares from those who'd watched the one-sided fight. He didn't let go of his brother until they were outside.

"Get in the car, kid."

Adam just stared at him. "What the hell was that?"

"What was what?"

"You . . . what you did in there. You didn't have to nearly beat him to death."

"He gave you drugs."

"So what? He didn't force them on me. He offered, I took them. I wanted to see what it was like."

"That's how it starts."

Adam eyes were wide. "What is wrong with you?"

"Nothing. I feel great. Actually, I've never felt better." He flexed his fist, expecting to see bruised and bloodied knuckles, but his hand was unblemished.

"That wasn't you," Adam said, shaking his head. "That was a . . . a *monster*."

"Enough melodrama. Let's go." He moved toward Adam, who flinched away from him as if he couldn't bear to be touched.

"Who *are* you?" he whispered.

"I'm your brother," Farrell said, relishing the cool sensation within him that made him see the world clearly. "And I only want to protect you."

Chapter 15

MADDOX

When the guards arrived at dawn to take him to his second audience with the goddess, he was ready.

"He's coming with me," Maddox insisted, nodding toward Barnabas.

The blond guard glanced at "Crazy Barney" and laughed. "Bonded overnight, did you?"

"You'd be surprised."

"He can't come with you."

"The goddess wants me to use my magic to help her. And my magic—it's very unpredictable. But with Barney around, it's much easier to control. How can I explain it?" Maddox tapped his chin, as if thinking deeply. "Have you ever had a good luck charm?"

The dark-haired guard nodded. "I had a hen's toe that my grandfather once gave me. Brought me great luck until I lost it."

"Yes, exactly. *He's* my hen's toe," Maddox said, nodding. "If he's not in the same room, I might not be able to access my magic. And I don't think the goddess will be pleased if I tell her that my humble request was denied."

This earned him groans and dirty looks from the guards, but after much debate, they decided to bring Barnabas, in chains, along with them to the throne room.

That went smoothly, Maddox thought. Perhaps Livius taught him how to lie better than he'd ever realized.

Barnabas had refused to share any real details about his plan. "Get me in that throne room and be ready for our imminent escape," he'd said. "And I also have a task for your spirit friend while we're otherwise occupied."

Later, after he'd fallen asleep and started to snore, Becca regarded Maddox with disbelief.

"I don't trust him," she said. "He's crazy."

"It's an act."

"Who would break into a *dungeon,* even if it's to get to you?"

"A madman."

"Exactly. He knows too much about what you can do. He only wants to use you."

"If he can get me out of here alive, I might be all right with that."

"I like a nice walk," Barnabas said now, his chains clanking with every step, drawing Maddox's mind back to the present. "Good for the bones. Good for the marrow. Makes it glow at night like fire-sprites, which, confidentially speaking, are a delicious treat with a nice goblet of wine to help douse their flames."

"Fire-sprites? Quiet, you crazy bastard," the blond guard growled. "Or I'll gut you where you stand."

"No," Maddox said quickly. "No gutting. He needs to be fully intact to be my hen's toe. Be quiet, Barney."

"Yes, my young friend. I shall be quiet. It has been far too long since I last feasted my eyes upon Her Radiance's golden flesh. I tingle at the thought."

"Shut up," the blond guard growled, shoving him forward along the hallway.

Maddox wasn't sure what to make of Barnabas, not yet, but since no one else was there to assist him in this particular time of need, he had no choice but to hold tightly on to optimism.

He wished Becca were walking by his side—that would help bolster his courage greatly. But Barnabas had given her the task of locating a specific room in the palace ("We could do it ourselves, but better to have an invisible friend help us," he'd said), so she'd gone in the opposite direction.

They were brought to the front of the tree-and-plant-filled hall to kneel at the bottom of the steps before Valoria, who sat on her throne.

"What is this?" the goddess said with displeasure. "What is this filthy creature you insult me with?"

"Greetings, radiant being." Barnabas nodded into a deep bow, his forehead brushing against the moss. "It is an honor to breathe the same rather humid air as you on this lovely, vine-entangled morning."

"The madman," the blond guard explained. "The witch boy claims that he needs him here to do his magic, as a good luck charm."

"Does he, now." She considered them one at a time. "I suppose it doesn't matter. His stench will be removed from my presence before too long. Now, boy. Can you do what I ask of you?"

Aegus slithered out from beneath Valoria's gown. Today her long skirts were black and trimmed in crimson.

"Such a beautiful creature!" Barnabas exclaimed. "One would never guess how cold-blooded it is."

Maddox grimaced, knowing Barnabas wasn't speaking only about the snake.

Aegus hissed, his forked tongue darting out from his mouth.

"Speak, boy," Valoria commanded, ignoring Barnabas.

He'd spent most of the previous night worrying about how he would answer her. How did one respond to a goddess requesting an impossible task?

With as many lies as required, of course.

"Yes, Your Radiance, I can help you. Whatever you need. We will find this girl's spirit and conjure it back from the realm of death, if that is where she is."

"And can you extract her magic? So we can use it to reclaim what was stolen from me?"

Another addition to her list of impossible tasks. "It might help if I knew what the stolen object is that you're seeking," Maddox said.

"A dagger," she said. "A very special golden dagger that has been long out of my reach. I also, of course, want the thief to pay dearly for his many crimes."

A golden dagger. That was what all this was about?

"This young witch," Maddox continued, willing confidence into his words. He thought of Livius again. He hated him for the three years they'd traveled together across the land, bilking nobles out of their coin, but he had been an excellent con man. "What does she look like? What is her name?"

"Her appearance? Her name?" Valoria's eyes narrowed. "If I knew those things, I would have been able to find her myself. All I know for sure is that at the time she died—if she is indeed dead—she was a beautiful and very powerful young witch. She is the daughter of my dead sister, after all."

Maddox's eyes widened. "The daughter of . . ." He gulped.

He hadn't known it was possible for immortal goddesses to have dead sisters.

Barnabas went rigid beside him, watching quietly, his gaze never leaving Valoria. "Do what you do to help Her Radiance, my young friend," he said. "Do it now so she can get what she most deserves."

"All right." Maddox closed his eyes and raised his palms. "There are spirits around us all the time," he lied. "I will now implore them, ask them for more information about this witch."

Valoria nodded. "Very good. Go ahead."

"Spirits, come to me. Answer my questions." Maddox opened his eyes and glanced around at the tall trees that reached up toward the high ceiling and the monstrous flowers that snapped at any insects that crossed their paths. "Yes, yes, they are here. The spirits are curious about what you seek." He drew in a sharp breath. "Oh . . . oh my."

Valoria leaned forward. "What is it? What do you see?"

"There is a spirit here who is cautioning the others not to help you."

"Who is this spirit?" Valoria hissed.

"King Thaddeus." It was the name of the former king of Mytica, a kind and benevolent man who had welcomed the goddesses with open arms, willing to share his kingdom with them.

But as the story went, it wasn't long before Valoria had turned him into a pile of dirt with her earth magic.

"Vanquish him! Send him back to the land of darkness," Valoria instructed. She didn't seem too concerned by this imaginary complication. "Do you require a box of silver to trap him?"

"No, Your Radiance. It must be a gold box." Maddox found the lie very easy to tell.

Valoria glared down at him. "I don't have a gold box here. Based on what your guardian said, I believed silver would be sufficient."

Maddox tried to look both thoughtful and regretful. "Alas,

he didn't know nearly as much as he thought he did about my abilities. Apologies, my goddess."

"Very well." She sent a withering look at the guard. "Fetch me a golden box immediately."

"Yes, Your Radiance."

But before the guard could leave, Maddox fixed a frown upon his face and shook his head as if listening to the dead king. "No, I can't tell her that," he said.

"What? What does he say?" she demanded.

"I . . . don't want to tell you."

"Tell me, or I will have your lucky charm killed."

"Tell her," Barnabas urged. "Now would be good."

"Well, King Thaddeus says that he forgives you," Maddox said, cocking his head as if the spirit spoke directly into his ear. "He says he knows you're very sad, very lonely. He's heard that you mean to add to your ban of all storybooks and tale-telling by forbidding such simple pleasures as singing and dancing. That you also want to outlaw the consumption of ale and wine. You don't want your people to have access to life's simple pleasures. He says that you do this because you are deeply unhappy."

This was only a guess on Maddox's part. Valoria was cruel and sharp on the outside, but there was something faded and gloomy in her green eyes that made him think his guess might be correct. The only time those eyes lit up with pleasure was when she gazed at her cobra, her dangerous, beloved pet.

"He forgives me, does he?" she said softly.

"Yes, Your Radiance."

"How very, very . . . unlikely." Her eyes narrowed. "Do you play me for a fool, witch boy?"

Uh-oh.

There was a commotion at the back of the throne room. Six guards ran in, quickly navigating the winding pathway through the thick interior forest.

"Apologies, Your Radiance," the lead guard said, "but a substantial problem has developed in the dungeons this morning. Twenty prisoners have broken free."

"*What?*" she snarled. "How did this happen?"

"I don't know." He bowed deeply. "I wasn't there, but . . . I don't believe this issue can be contained without, well, without . . . your intervention."

"Weak, pathetic, useless mortals!" she hissed. She slipped Aegus into a large porcelain jar beside her throne, and then descended the stairs. "You," she said to the two guards who'd brought Maddox and Barnabas before her, "stay here with them until I return."

"Yes, Your Radiance," the guards said in unison, their heads lowered.

"Who is responsible for this?" she demanded of the others.

The guard who'd given the news of the dungeon break glanced nervously at his partner.

"You're both utterly useless." She pointed at him, the long, loose sleeve of her black dress swishing. There was a crackle in the air and both guards let out pained gasps. Maddox watched in shock as their skin turned to bark, their fingers to leaves, their feet to roots. In moments, they were nothing more than two six-foot seedlings to join the rest of the goddess's indoor forest.

As she passed them on her way out of the hall, Valoria shoved one of the new trees, breaking a branch off in her wake.

All was silent for several heartbeats after she left.

"I must admit, the woman does have a remarkable green thumb," Barnabas said under his breath.

"Are you ready, Barnabas?" the dark-haired guard with the lucky hen's toe asked.

"Ready as I'll ever be." He leaned backward and placed his hands on the mossy floor.

The guard swung his sword, slicing through Barnabas's chains.

"What is the meaning of this?" the blond guard asked. "What is—?"

The other guard swung his sword again, permanently halting his compatriot's voice.

"An escape, that's what it is," Barnabas informed the dead guard.

Ah, Maddox thought. This must have been the part of the plan that Barnabas had neglected to share with him.

He glanced back and forth between the two men. "You know each other."

"Yes, indeed." Barnabas grinned, his teeth stark white in the middle of his dirty, bearded face. "This is my brother, Cyrus. Cyrus, this is Maddox."

"A pleasure to meet you." Cyrus wiped the blood from his blade.

Maddox saw Becca appear through the ivy-covered wall to his left. She looked back at it in amazement. "You're right. I can walk through walls. That's useful." She skidded to a halt at the sight of the dead guard, her eyes growing wide. "Um, the plan . . . ?"

"Went, uh, quite well?" Maddox replied. "Did you find the room?"

"Of course I did." She tore her gaze from the fallen guard to meet his eyes, then gave him a weak smile that lightened his heart in a mere moment. "Did you expect me to fail?"

He returned the expression. "Not for a single moment."

"Your spirit friend must certainly be a girl," Barnabas observed. "That moony look on your face right now confirms it."

Maddox's smile fell, and he cast an impatient look at Barnabas. "We need to leave before the goddess returns."

"Yes, excellent idea." He clasped Cyrus's gloved hand. "Much gratitude, brother."

Cyrus gave Barnabas his sword and the dagger from the sheath at his side. "Take these weapons. I'll send message when I can."

With Becca leading the way, Maddox and Barnabas moved swiftly out of the throne room and along a narrow passageway.

"It's not far," Becca said. "Barnabas's intel was right; it's the only plain door in this entire hallway."

All the doors they passed were carved with intricate, ornate patterns, but Barnabas had told her to look for an unadorned one. Plain oak.

"Stand back, my young friend," Barnabas said. He kicked the door. The lock splintered and the door swung open.

Maddox gave him a surprised sideways glance.

"He's strong," Becca said, eyeing the man skeptically, her arms crossed over her chest. "Keep in mind, this only proves he's a thief who will kill to get what he wants."

"Wonderful," Barnabas said gleefully as he entered the room. "It's exactly as I was told it would be."

Maddox followed, gasping at the room full of treasures in which he now stood. Gold and silver coins, necklaces, bracelets, rings, handfuls of colorful jewels . . .

Barnabas went directly toward a gilded copper box, two feet tall and wide and studded with gemstones. There was a latch on its side and he tried it, but then pulled his hand away as if it had been burned.

"The lock's enchanted," he said. "It's infused with fire magic."

"*Enchanted*," Becca repeated in a breathless whisper. Then louder, "What's inside?"

Maddox repeated her question out loud as he drew closer to Barnabas, awed by all the treasures in this secret room.

"Something very special that will help us," Barnabas replied.

"You're not going to tell me, are you?" Maddox said with annoyance.

"No. But you'll find out soon enough. Grab it, would you? But avoid touching the lock."

Maddox knew their time before discovery was limited, so he grabbed hold of the box, pleased to find that he was able to lift it without great effort.

"Good," Barnabas nodded.

They turned toward the door.

"The snake!" Becca shouted.

His stomach sank at the sight of Aegus, who now blocked their path. The cobra hissed and grew before their eyes until it was as tall as Maddox and twice as wide when it sat up and flared out its massive hood.

Barnabas swore under his breath. "Forgot all about him. My mistake."

The snake set its attention on Maddox, as if attracted by the torchlight glinting against the jeweled box in his arms, and began to slither closer. Maddox tried to will his magic to the forefront, to render the snake unconscious so they could escape.

Nothing happened.

"Barnabas . . . ," he growled. "Do something!"

The snake lashed out toward him, fangs at the ready, but when it lunged all it met with was the tip of a sword. Barnabas swung the weapon, slicing off Aegus's head in one clean cut. It dropped to the ground, heavy as a ripe, oversize melon.

Maddox's legs nearly gave out.

Becca let out a sigh of relief.

The collapsed snake's tail twitched in agony.

"Remember, it's a magic snake," Becca said shakily. "It might be able to grow another head. Let's leave before we find out, all right?"

"I couldn't agree more," Maddox replied. "Barnabas, let's get out of here. Now."

Without another word, the three of them, two thieves and a spirit, slipped out of the room and made their way down the hallway, searching for the nearest exit.

"Excellent," Barnabas said. "We're closer to ending Valoria's reign with every step we take."

"Is this not the first time you've tried to assassinate her?" Maddox asked.

"Assassinate an immortal goddess? It's not as simple as putting a dagger through her cold black heart. She's powerful, smart, and deeply paranoid. Her only weaknesses are her obsession with that niece of hers, the thief who stole her dagger, and, well, that snake I just sliced into two scaly pieces."

"And you believe that what's in this box will help destroy her."

"Yes, I do. And now we need to bring it to the person who knows how to get through that lock."

Barnabas kept saying "we," as if he and Maddox had suddenly become a team. "I never agreed to help you," Maddox said.

"That's right." Becca nodded. She stayed close to his side, so close that he'd be able to feel her warmth if she were more than a spirit.

"No promises made. You can lose him the second we get out of here."

Barnabas was quiet for a moment. "I can help you find the answers you seek, Maddox Corso. I know a great deal about both you and your magic."

He'd never told Barnabas his surname. "How?"

"I knew your father."

Maddox's steps halted. "My father."

"Yes. I can tell you about him and how he met his final fate."

"He's . . . dead?"

Barnabas stopped as he turned the next corner. "I believe that's the servants' entrance up ahead. We'll talk about this later. For now, let's keep moving."

Just a few short words had made his mind reel.

His father.

Maddox's father.

"Don't let this distract you," Becca said. "He could be lying, leading you on, saying whatever he needs to say to get you to keep following him. All he's giving you are words, not proof."

She was right. He had no reason to trust Barnabas or any promises that came out of his mouth.

Barnabas shoved open a creaky door. "Interesting. Perhaps this isn't the servants' entrance—more like their *exit*—but it will do just as well."

The door led outside and into a graveyard with small, modest stone markers.

"Tread with care and in silence, my young friend." Barnabas began to walk, slowly and with precision, over the grassy area. A hundred paces ahead, Maddox saw stone gates and, beyond those, blue skies, green hills, and forestland. Freedom.

Maddox tried not to think about the dead that were just underfoot. He needed to concentrate on something else. "Barnabas, please tell me more about—"

"I said silence."

Maddox frowned. "Why do you keep saying—"

Something grabbed his ankle.

"Maddox!" Becca shrieked. "The ground!"

Skeletal hands had begun to emerge from the earth, pushing up desperately through the dirt.

Maddox gasped. "Valoria is the goddess of earth and water. . . . This must be earth magic. She's enchanted this graveyard to keep anyone from escaping."

"Wrong," Barnabas growled. "This is your doing."

"*My* doing?"

"Don't you know? Summoning spirits, trapping spirits and shadows . . . raising the dead. You are a necromancer, my young friend."

"A *what*?" he exclaimed.

"Death magic is your gift." Barnabas grinned broadly as if he'd just presented Maddox with a delicious pudding for dessert. "Now, let's run very fast before we're torn into pieces, shall we?"

He didn't have to be told twice. Maddox ran, chasing after the surprisingly swift Barnabas, dodging the clawed hands of the rising dead. He focused only on the stone fence before them. Once they got there, Barnabas scaled it without a problem, even while juggling the sharp sword and dagger.

Maddox had the copper box tucked under his arm and did his best not to touch the enchanted lock. "I can't climb a wall with this. I'm not sure I can even climb a wall *without* this."

"Throw it!" Becca suggested. "And do it quickly! They're coming!"

Heart pounding, Maddox shouted, "I'm throwing it to you!"

"Go ahead!" Barnabas called out.

Maddox hauled himself back and launched the heavy box over the stone wall. He heard a pained grunt from Barnabas's side, which told him it had been successfully caught.

"Now go. Go!" Becca urged. "Hurry!"

He felt at the wall, trying to get a handhold. He managed to get several feet up before his grip slipped and he fell back down to the ground.

"Not good." Becca wrung her hands. "Either climb faster or send those things back to their graves."

"I don't even know how I raised them!"

"Then that leaves you with one choice. Climb! Now!"

"Talk, Becca. Say something—say anything—to help distract me." His hands shook as he tried to grasp the jagged stones, and he began to bleed from the effort. How had Barnabas done this with such ease?

"Okay." She blew out a breath. "Hey, you know what? Your world is a complete mess. It's violent and cruel and bizarre and scary, and I hate it. There's, like, literally only one thing I like about it."

He wasn't surprised that she despised this place where she was trapped. He wasn't so fond of it himself. One day, when he had the money and the means, he would travel somewhere far away and never look back. "What's that?"

"You," she said simply, and as he locked gazes with her, her smile managed to enchant him utterly. But then her smile turned quickly to a scowl. "Now, hurry up, would you? Go!"

Hand over hand, he climbed the wall, this time not slipping

before he got to the top. Two dozen corpses covered with rotting flesh stumbled and crawled toward him, reaching up to try to grab at his ankles. If he'd taken even a moment longer, they would have been successful.

When he jumped down to the other side, Becca was already there waiting for him.

"Luckily, it seems as though the dead can't climb," Barnabas observed. The box sat next to him on the ground, undamaged. "We're safe, but we need to keep moving. It won't be long before Valoria learns we've escaped. It'll take her a little while to deal with the newly undead, so that buys us a small amount of time."

Maddox wasn't budging from his spot. He crossed his arms. "Did my father tell you that I'm a . . . a nacromincer."

"Necromancer," Becca corrected.

"*Necromancer,*" Maddox repeated firmly.

Barnabas nodded. "He did."

"Why can I do this . . . death magic, as you called it? Why can't I do magic like others—like witches?"

"That, I can't tell you. What I do know is that you're powerful, and I need your magic to aid me."

"I don't even know how to harness it properly. How can I help anyone else?"

"You agree that Valoria is evil?"

"Of course I do."

"And she needs to be stopped?"

"Yes, but that's impossible. You can't stop an immortal goddess—not here and not in the South. It's well known that many rebels who remain loyal to King Thaddeus's legacy have tried and have died in their attempts. And even if you were successful in vanquishing Valoria, there's still Cleiona to contend with."

Barnabas flicked his hand in dismissal. "I'll deal with the other one later. One goddess at a time, my young friend."

"I'm not your friend. I don't even know you. You need to tell me what your plan is right now or I refuse to go a step farther."

Barnabas glared at him for a long, uncomfortable moment.

"Fine. We're taking that box to the most powerful witch I know, the one who told me it existed in the first place. Its contents harbor the means to send someone from one world to another."

Maddox shot a look at Becca. Her eyes were wide with shock at Barnabas's claim.

"Other worlds." Maddox couldn't believe his own words. "Such talk is . . ."

"Madness?" Barnabas grinned. "Perhaps. But there's only one way to know for sure."

"This is it. This is what I need." Becca drew closer to Maddox. "If he's being honest, this could be the answer we need to send me back home."

He met her gaze and nodded. "It certainly could."

"I've had my say," Barnabas said after a moment of silence passed between them. "And I'll understand if you wish to part ways. But I'd much prefer you to join me in my quest."

Other worlds. Death magic. A chance to help a beautiful girl—his first real friend—who truly needed him. Who believed in him when he didn't believe in himself.

Finally, Maddox nodded. "Then let's get going."

Chapter 16

CRYSTAL

After a brief visit to the hospital on Tuesday evening, Crys went to school on Wednesday, but barely paid attention to her classes. After school, she took over at the bookshop so Julia could visit Becca. After Crys closed up shop at six, she headed to the hospital again.

Becca appeared to be peacefully sleeping. Crys sat down heavily in the now familiar bedside chair.

She'd avoided saying more than a few words to her mother all day, knowing she'd be furious if she learned Crys had gone to see Dr. Vega behind her back.

Julia Hatcher didn't like it when her eldest daughter broke the rules.

All day Crys's thoughts had stewed and simmered as she tried desperately to come up with a plan—something a seventeen-year-old girl who didn't know anybody important could do to help her sister.

It all came back to Markus and the Bronze Codex.

It had been days since she'd met her father at the AGO. Three days with only silence as she waited for him to reach her with news about meeting the mysterious man in the flesh.

"I'm trying to figure this out," Crys told Becca in the last few minutes before leaving for the night. "I refuse to sit back and wait for other people to make decisions for you or for me."

As she headed home, she was distracted by the bright screen of her phone. She was composing another message to her father, which she'd deleted a dozen times, changing a word here and there, then writing it over again and again.

I'm still waiting. And hoping. Call me.

She felt just about ready to press Send. She hoped her message conveyed the right balance of patience and daughterly whimsy. How could he ignore that? And if he came back with a *No, my boss won't meet with you,* then at least Crys would have an answer. Besides, her father couldn't be the only way to get to the society leader.

"Hey, blondie. Nice phone."

Crys slowed down at the nearby comment and glanced to her left to see a tall boy with dark hair studying her with a smirk.

"Gee, thanks," she replied drily.

"I need a new phone."

"Yeah? Then you should probably go to the mall and get one."

"Let me rephrase that. I need *your* new phone."

At first, she didn't understand what he meant. Her head was in the clouds, so focused on the task of composing her message. "What?"

"And your bag, too." The boy shrugged. "Now would be good."

She swept her gaze around to see that, while the sidewalk wasn't extremely populated, she and her new friend weren't totally alone, either. This jerk didn't seem to care that they had an audience. "Go to hell," she said.

His smirk only got bigger as he came at her, fast, snatching the phone out of her hand and yanking her bag off her shoulder.

She got a hold of her bag and tried to pull it back. "Let go!"

"I'll break your fingers if I have to, bitch. *You* let go."

With another yank, he pulled her leather bag away completely, turned, and began running away.

Crys stared in shock at a couple of alarmed-looking people passing by. "Did you just see that?"

"Be careful," a woman called to her. "He looks dangerous."

"Thanks for the warning."

She started running after the thief. Her phone—not to mention her bag—had her entire life in it. E-mails, texts, bookmarks. Addresses. Photos.

The guy had long legs and he was a fast runner, but she refused to give up that easily. He now had her wallet. Her money, her bank card, her ID.

And her Pentax was in that bag, along with six rolls of undeveloped film.

"Stop, thief!" she yelled, hoping someone might help her before she lost sight of him.

And someone did. Another boy stepped in front of the thief, who staggered to a halt. The new boy grabbed for the fuchsia bag.

She recognized him immediately, even from a distance. It was the boy from the university—the one who'd asked her questions. The rich kid . . . Farrell Grayson.

The thief slammed his fist into Farrell's face, sending his head snapping to the side.

The thief went to hit him again, but Farrell ducked and punched him in the gut.

Crys caught up to them and jumped the thief, ready to use Aunt

Jackie's "groin and eyeball" self-defense lesson. Her momentum took him down, hard. Her phone dropped to the sidewalk, and the contents of her bag tumbled out. When the thief scrambled to grab it again, she kicked him in the face.

He yelped in pain, covering his nose, and sent a chilling look at her before he took off.

"Yeah, you run!" she yelled after him, outraged. "Run fast, asshole!"

Farrell helped her stuff her wallet, phone, and other items back into her bag. Then he picked up her Pentax, which had smashed against the sidewalk.

It was in pieces.

Time stopped as she registered that her beloved camera had been destroyed.

"No." Her throat rapidly thickened to the point that she couldn't swallow. A hot tear slipped down her cheek.

"Hey, don't cry," Farrell said. "It's only a camera. And, no offense, but it looks like it belongs in a museum. How old is this thing?"

"It's old," she managed, her breathing coming out in shaky gasps. "But it . . . has . . . sentimental value."

She'd tried to be strong all week, to not cry, and now she was having a full-blown emotional breakdown in front of Farrell Grayson.

"Then I'm very sorry," he said.

She shook her head, pulling her glasses away so she could wipe her eyes. "Damn it. I don't cry."

"Could have fooled me."

"I don't *normally* cry." She let out a shuddery sigh. "Look—thanks for stopping him. I appreciate it."

"I only slowed him down. With my jaw." He rubbed his chin.

"Besides, I think you could have taken him down just fine without me. You're tougher than you look."

"Thanks, I think." She took the broken pieces of the camera from him and put them into her bag, not ready to throw them away quite yet.

He cocked his head. "I know you, right?"

She sniffed. "Funny. This time the line actually works."

"What?"

"The university. We briefly crossed paths yesterday."

Recognition dawned in his hazel eyes. "Right. You're the girl who didn't have time to talk." He reached into the pocket of his black leather jacket and pulled out a pack of cigarettes, tapping one out without even glancing down, as if he'd done it a thousand times before. He placed it to his lips, and brought a silver lighter up in his right hand. Then his gaze snapped to hers. "I know we're outside, but I feel I should ask anyway. Do you mind if I smoke in front of you?"

"Normally I would, but since you're the only pedestrian who tried to help me out when I got mugged, I'll allow you to go ahead and damage your lungs in my presence."

"Don't worry. My lungs'll be just fine." He grinned that charmingly crooked smile of his and sparked the lighter, touching the orange flame to the tip of the cigarette.

Out of the three million people in this city, she'd happened to run into this same guy twice in as many days. That was a crazy coincidence.

"Do you live around here?" she asked.

"No."

"Didn't think so. Not many fancy mansions in this neighborhood."

His grin widened. "Lucky guess? Or do you magically happen to know who I am?"

Interesting word choice, she thought. If only he knew about the education she'd just received from Dr. Vega. "I'll admit that I saw your photo spread in *FocusToronto* last year. And, I mean, your face is already well known in the city."

"My mug shot did get some press a while back." He eyed her curiously as he took a deep inhale of the cancer stick and blew out the smoke, though happily he did so in the direction opposite her face. "Aren't you going to ask why I happened to be here, tonight, ready to jump in and get my face pounded by some random thug?"

"Okay." She eyed his jaw, which was slightly swollen now and red, and grimaced with sympathy. "Why?"

"Because I really need a drink. And one of my favorite bars in the whole wide world is right around the corner from here." He paused. "I think you need a drink, too, after busting out that little ninja move. That was impressive, by the way. Remind me never to get on your bad side."

She shrugged. "My aunt taught me a few moves."

"Lethal weapon, table for two." He nodded farther up the sidewalk. "What do you say?"

Her heart was still pounding from the fight with the thief, so it took her a moment to process what he was suggesting. "I'm only seventeen. I can't drink."

"I'm nineteen. The law says I'm legally allowed to order and consume alcohol. And even if it didn't, money speaks volumes. They'll serve you, promise."

She didn't have time for drinks with boys, even cute, rich ones who'd just saved her from a big-time jam. "I don't know . . ."

"If it helps your decision, you should know I'm not hitting on you. This is a 'we survived a violent crime together so let's have a celebratory drink' drink. That's all."

She eyed him skeptically. It's not like she'd leap to assume that someone like Farrell Grayson would be interested in her *that* way, but he was being suspiciously friendly. "I didn't think you were."

"Actually, I could really use a friend right now, if you're willing. 'Safe and platonic' is my middle name." He cocked his head. "Am I successful in tempting you to stray to the dark side?"

There was that crooked grin again.

Crys bit her bottom lip and studied him for a moment longer as he smoked his cigarette and shivered in the cool evening air in his thin, but probably very expensive, leather jacket. It was night now; the clouds had cleared away to reveal the black sky studded with stars and the bright sliver of the new moon.

"Fine," she relented. "One totally illicit drink, and then I have to get home."

He nodded. "Modestly daring. I approve. What's your name, anyway?"

"Crystal. Crystal Hatcher. Everyone calls me Crys."

He offered her his arm. "Allow me to lead you into temptation, Crys Hatcher."

The bar was small and exclusive. Everyone there was well dressed and well coiffed. Crys twisted a finger through a long pale lock of her hair and tried not to regret the faded jeans and novelty T-shirt she had on under her coat.

She'd never cared much about fashion. Why should she start tonight?

They got a booth in the corner and the waitress came over. Farrell ordered a double vodka on the rocks for himself.

Crys eyed him. "That's a serious drink."

"I'm a very serious guy." The amused expression on his face led her to believe he was anything but. "What would you like?"

"I have absolutely no idea."

"Salty? Sweet? A shot? Wine?" Farrell studied her pensively as she kept him waiting for an answer. "I'm thinking we'll go with a whiskey sour."

"All right," the waitress said, throwing an appraising glance at Crys but not asking for any ID. "I'll be right back."

Crys shrugged out of her jacket.

"Cute," Farrell said, his gaze now on her chest before his eyes snapped to hers. He smirked. "I mean your T-shirt, of course."

"Thanks." She looked down at herself to remember which one she was wearing.

It was a dinosaur that'd awkwardly tipped over onto its nose, with the caption T. REX HATES PUSH-UPS.

Classy.

A minute later, the waitress returned with their drinks.

"A toast," Farrell said, raising his glass. "To Crys, a kick-ass girl who's nobody's victim."

"I'll enthusiastically drink to that." She clinked glasses with him and took a sip of her cocktail, not sure what to expect. It was sour, but still sweet, kind of like lemonade with a kick of liquor that heated her throat as she swallowed. "I like it. I think."

"I'm an expert at matching the right drink to the right person. It's one of my gifts."

She wondered what his other gifts were if he considered *that* one of them. "You said you're nineteen, which means you're only recently legal. Yet you're already an expert?"

"I took a crash course in debauchery." He swirled his drink, his pleasant expression fading just a little. "That was a poor choice of words. I have a driver now, only a phone call away, because I can't drive myself at the moment. Made the mistake of doing a little too much of this"—he indicated the drink—"and then getting behind the wheel. Luckily, I'm the only one who ever got hurt."

That was quite a confession for him to make to a near stranger, but she appreciated the honesty. "Everyone makes mistakes. As long as you learn from them, I guess."

"My mistakes have to be pretty big for me to learn from them, but I do eventually. So, where do you go to school, if it's not at the university?"

She took another sip of her drink. "Sunderland High."

"I'm assuming senior year?"

She nodded.

"Planning for college? Is that why you were at the university yesterday?"

"No, I—I mean, I like to keep my options open. I'd rather travel for a while. See the world. Figure out my future before it's figured out for me."

"Good plan. Let me guess, you're an aspiring photographer."

"I am. An aspiring photographer, now without a camera."

Farrell appeared to consider this. "You can always use the camera on your phone."

"It's not even remotely the same. That camera was retro, but it took professional-level shots." She looked down at the ice cubes in her drink, trying to put the loss out of her head. "What do you want to do with the rest of *your* life?"

"No idea. But I've been considering a few options lately." He leaned forward. "I have to know . . . what perfume are you wearing?"

"Perfume?" She shook her head. "I'm not wearing any perfume."

"No way. I smell strawberries—like, a field of them, warm under the summer sun."

"I use a strawberry-scented soap."

"That must be it. Just soap. Huh. What do you know?" His lips quirked up as he downed the rest of his drink in one swallow. "Why don't you tell me about your family? Do you get along with them?"

She tried not to laugh. "I feel like I'm being interrogated."

"Sorry, I like to talk. Ask questions. Get to know people."

"All right." Another sip of her whiskey sour and she found that it was almost gone. "Well, I have a younger sister named Becca, and we live with our mother above the Speckled Muse Bookshop."

"That sounds like fun."

"Sometimes. Are you a reader?"

"Do graphic novels count?"

"Sure."

"Then yes. I'm practically a bookworm."

She watched him, feeling more comfortable in his presence the longer they sat there. "How about you? Do you have any siblings? No, wait. I already know you from that photo spread. You have a younger brother and an older brother."

A shadow of pain crossed his expression. He signaled for the waitress to bring over another vodka.

Crys eyed him carefully, now worried that she'd said something wrong.

"Good memory," he finally said. "Yeah, two brothers. I'm the middle child with all the psychological baggage that comes along with that position."

Whatever sadness had passed across his face had now disappeared. Maybe it had been nothing at all. "Are you planning to go to college here?"

"Thinking about it. Not sure campus life is my scene, though."

"So what is your scene?"

"Good question. I'm currently at a crossroads. What choice should I make today that will affect my entire future? Talk about pressure. I'm not a fan of pressure."

"Me neither."

He leaned forward after a few moments of silence passed between them. "Tell me your biggest secret, Crys. And then maybe I'll tell you mine." His expression turned mischievous.

She couldn't help but laugh. "You're trouble, aren't you?"

"The worst kind."

She considered him in silence, this boy she never would have met had coincidence not brought them together twice, before she spoke again. "Do you believe in magic?"

"Actually, I do."

Her gaze snapped to his again with surprise. His hazel eyes were so lovely—one moment stormy and intense, the next sparkling with humor.

Forget about his eyes, she told herself firmly. This wasn't a date. This was a conversation with a potential new friend who could be very useful.

She had no idea what kinds of contacts the Graysons had, but if they were as rich and powerful as Crys believed they were, they were sure to know a lot of equally influential people.

They might even know a man like Markus King.

"I mean, I'm not talking about card tricks," she clarified.

"Me neither." He shrugged. "I don't know what I believe, really. I just know I'm open to the possibility that there's more to this world than meets the eye."

"Exactly." She bit her lip, feeling a giddy urge to confess all her secrets to him.

After one cocktail, she didn't think she was drunk, but she wasn't quite sober, either, especially since she hadn't eaten anything since breakfast.

"So . . . let's talk magic." Farrell glanced at a couple in a nearby booth, their lips locked in a passionate kiss. "There are so many strange things in this world. Why can't it be possible that magic is real? Agree?"

Maybe their paths had crossed on purpose . . . like it was some sort of universal plan. Fate.

Maybe they were soul mates.

Go home, her brain told her. *You are drunk.*

"I totally agree," she said instead.

He raised an eyebrow and leaned forward conspiratorially. "Do you know something, Crys Hatcher? Or are you just making conversation?"

If he only knew. What would his reaction be if she told him about Dr. Vega's theories about the magic language? About the Codex? But just before she opened her mouth, she closed it again and glanced down at the time on her phone. It was already after nine o'clock. Her mother had texted her twice, wondering where she was.

"You know, I should probably get going. I said one drink, and I managed to devour it in record time." She stood up. "Thanks, Farrell. For the help . . . and for the company. I needed a distraction tonight."

"I aim to distract. You're not planning to walk, are you? I can get my driver to take you home."

"I'm fine. Really. What happened with that mugger . . . that, like, doesn't usually happen in this neighborhood. And home is only a couple of blocks from here."

"Can I see you again?" At her startled look, he tempered his words with a fresh grin. "As just a friend, of course. Capital-P Platonic."

Crys tended to be wary of things that seemed too good to be true. And Farrell, despite his DUIs and his interest in cigarettes and vodka, was just that. "Maybe."

"I can accept a maybe." He reached across the table and grabbed Crys's phone. "Here's my number. Text me if you ever want to hang out, talk about magic, confess your deepest, darkest secrets. I'm available twenty-four-seven."

"Really. Twenty-four-seven?"

"What can I say? I get bored easily and I'm not a big TV fan." He handed her phone back, and his fingers brushed against hers as she took it. "But it's funny. You don't bore me, not one little bit. That's rare."

"Ditto," she said.

Yes, she said *ditto*. Like something out of a dumb old movie.

With a mumbled goodbye, she left the bar and let the cool air pull her out of her slightly tipsy state. Alcohol—not a great idea. She'd almost told him everything.

It would be smartest not to contact him again. She knew one thing for certain: He might not have anything to do with magic books or secret societies, but Farrell Grayson was definitely dangerous.

Chapter 17

FARRELL

Once again, Farrell's hypothesis had been proved: Deep down, all girls were the same. Flash them a smile, buy them a drink, make them feel important.

Putty in his hands.

Despite her disinterest that first day on the university campus, Crys Hatcher was no different from the rest. Too bad he couldn't get her to stay a little longer. A couple more whiskey sours and he was sure he could have gotten all the information he needed to satisfy Markus.

His target was cute enough, he supposed, but a tad too artsy for his usual taste in girls. Still, he had to admit there was something about her that intrigued him. Maybe it was the way she bit her bottom lip when she was nervous. It made him wonder if that mouth of hers also tasted like strawberries.

The only new information he'd managed to learn about Crys was that she believed in magic. That was a big clue as to why she might matter to Markus. Maybe she'd taken an incriminating photo with that old camera of hers. Maybe she'd inadvertently discovered some dangerous information about the society.

He knew he wasn't nearly finished with her just yet.

Farrell texted Lucas on his way home from the bar.

Thanks for the help tonight, but you didn't have to hit me so hard, you dick.

Lucas returned the text almost immediately.

Your new girlfriend broke my nose.

He grinned as he typed his response. *The best laid plans . . . often lead to pain. But it worked perfectly. She was all over me.*

What are you doing now? Lucas texted next.

Nothing.

I'm going out. Got a tip on someone that M will want to invite to the next meeting. Usually would wait on this, but don't want to let him slip away.

A tip on a criminal they could capture for the next society meeting, the first one since Farrell had been accepted into Markus's circle. He wondered where the evildoers were kept as they waited for the next gathering.

The thought of participating in a capture excited him.

I'm in.

"Saw the video of you at Firebird," Lucas said when they met up at Yonge and Dundas square, across from the Eaton Centre. The downtown Toronto mall and tourist attraction had closed over an hour ago, but the sidewalk outside was full of pedestrians and the street was jammed with cars. Neon store signs pulsed and glowed from up above, lighting up the night. This was the heart of the city, always busy. Always alive and throbbing with energy.

"Yeah?" Farrell had his hands jammed into the pockets of his leather jacket.

"Love how you managed to tilt it. Rich kid protects brother from evil drug dealer . . . quote, unquote."

"That wasn't my *tilt*, just a lucky break."

Michael, the guy Farrell had beaten up, was a known drug dealer currently on parole. Someone had uploaded the video of the incident to the Internet and had taken Farrell's side, calling him an "avenging angel."

No charges were pressed—at least not against him.

Adam, however, hadn't said a single word to him since. Farrell had decided to give his kid brother the chance to cool off, a chance to realize he'd only done what he did to help.

His brother had stayed at home all day, tucked into bed nursing a head cold. Their parents didn't discuss Adam's current health with Farrell. He'd overheard them, however, discussing it with each other.

"The mark will take care of future *illnesses, won't it, Edward? This is just . . . what? A virus he contracted before the meeting?"*

His father had nodded firmly. "I'm sure that's all it is. That would also explain why he's had such difficulty coming to terms with the trial."

"Yes, of course, darling. Time. That's all he needs."

"There he is," Lucas said now, nodding toward a cluster of pedestrians to their right. "Tall, bald head. Nose ring."

Farrell spotted him easily. The man looked like a biker, rough and dangerous. The cobweb tattoo on his throat was a well-known gang symbol.

"What did he do?"

"Serial rapist. Got off on the last charge on a technicality. Someone in Hawkspear brought Markus his name, told him that this douche is responsible for attacking her cousin and nearly killing her. We heard he was in New York, but he took a flight here two days ago. Lucky break for us."

"Yeah." The thought of capturing the guy filled Farrell with fevered anticipation. "You think we can take him down?"

"Maybe not gently, but we'll take him. For now, we'll follow and see where he goes. This can't happen in public." Lucas had already shown Farrell the special ring he wore on his middle finger. Pull off the top and a syringe appeared with a small dose of etorphine at the ready. One jab to the neck and seconds later they'd have an unconscious prisoner.

Farrell had been promised his ring in the next couple of days. He didn't usually wear jewelry, but he'd make an exception this time.

They trailed after the guy for a minute in silence.

"Question," Farrell asked.

"Yeah?"

"Did all of your senses improve after you got the second mark?"

"Hell yeah. Amazing, isn't it? Like waking up from a coma and seeing the world for the first time. Like Dorothy entering Oz and everything's in color."

"No one warned me what a killer bright light would be, though." Farrell winced as he remembered the unexpected pain he'd felt yesterday morning when he pulled up the blinds in his room. "I have to wear sunglasses all day."

"Don't you normally?"

"Sure, but I don't *have* to. You know? I'd prefer not to go blind just by walking around in broad daylight if I can help it."

Lucas nodded. "Same with me. We're hypersensitive now. We've *evolved*." He grinned. "But those quick moments of discomfort are a small price to pay for the chance to see in the dead of night, right?"

There was no argument there. "Absolutely."

"So you feel good?"

"I feel *renewed*." There had to be a better word for it, but it was the best he could come up with. "And I'm stronger. I know I am. It was no effort at all to smash in that scumbag's face." As he said it, he realized he didn't feel even a sliver of remorse about that unplanned violent act. Just the opposite, actually. "I liked it. I liked seeing his blood flow and hearing his nose break. I liked knowing I was the one who'd hurt him. Is that wrong?"

"Not at all. Bastard got what he deserved, I'd say."

Their target paused and moved his black-eyed gaze through the crowd. He made a right at the next intersection to follow a woman who'd broken away from her group of friends.

"Looks like he's chosen his date for the evening," Lucas said under his breath.

They kept at a healthy distance so they wouldn't be noticed.

"Connor used to do this with you?" Farrell asked.

Lucas nodded. "Only once, but we made a good team."

"Did he have any problems with it?"

"Not that I noticed."

Other than the coincidental timing, Farrell hadn't been able to find any real proof that Connor's suicide had been related in any way to his induction into the circle.

So it had to be the girlfriend. Mallory had come to the funeral, her eyes red and puffy. The rest of the family had shunned her, but not Farrell.

"This is all my fault," she'd whispered. "I shouldn't have made things so final with him. I just needed some space to think about everything. But he'd been so cruel to me lately. . . . I don't know. I thought he *wanted to break up."*

"Don't blame yourself," Farrell managed to reply. "He made the choice. He could have asked for help."

"I'm so sorry."

"Me too."

Farrell pushed the memory out of his mind and drew a pack of cigarettes out of his jacket pocket. He lit one, his mind drifting now toward his younger brother. "Here's another question for you. Ever heard of the initiation mark not working properly?"

"No. Why?"

Farrell fought to keep his expression neutral. "Just wondering," he lied. "You never know if someone might be immune to Markus's magic."

Lucas shrugged. "I guess it's possible."

"What would happen to them?"

"Good question. Maybe he'd try again? It would suck to miss out on the gift of staying healthy for the rest of your life."

"Does the mark do anything else other than the health thing?"

"What do you mean?"

Would it keep someone from freaking out over witnessing executions four times a year? he thought, but didn't say out loud. "I don't know. Just making conversation. We'd better focus or we're going to lose him." The bald man and his potential victim turned the next corner. It took a minute for Farrell and Lucas to catch up, but when they turned onto the next street, all they could see was the woman, fiddling in her purse for her keys. She let herself into a townhome and closed the door behind her, safe and sound.

"Where did he go?" Farrell asked.

"Good question. He's got to be around here somewhere."

They began to search, passing the woman's house and peering down alleyways.

"There he is," Lucas said, nodding up ahead. A shadow

disappeared behind a building lit by a bright streetlamp. He picked up his pace.

Farrell jogged to keep up with him.

"What? Can the guy walk through walls?" Farrell asked, frustrated, when they found no one there.

"The hell? Where did he—?" Then Lucas grunted with pain as he staggered forward, dropping hard to the ground. He'd been struck, hard, right below his kidneys.

"Are you following me?" the man asked, his voice a low growl. He'd crept up behind them, unseen and unheard. "That's rude."

"We don't want any trouble." Farrell raised his hands, trying to appear as if he wasn't a threat. He wanted to give Lucas enough time to pick himself up and get the syringe ready.

"Could've fooled me." He clamped his hand around Farrell's throat and slammed him against the wall. The man's cold black eyes narrowed as his grip increased.

The world began to bleed away at the edges of Farrell's sight.

Then Lucas came at him, the sharp needle on the ring aimed for the rapist's neck. The man knocked his hand away and slammed his fist into Lucas's face, letting go of Farrell.

Farrell slumped to the ground, wheezing. His ears rang, his lungs burned.

But he didn't hesitate. Farrell got back up and attacked.

Together, he and Lucas fought, punching and kicking the rapist as a team until they finally got the advantage.

The man did his share of damage in return. Farrell tasted the copper tang of his own blood. Lucas got an angry cut over his left eyebrow when he was slammed into the wall.

Finally, the man dropped to his knees, his face as bloody as the Firebird drug dealer's had been.

Farrell saw the flash of metal: Instead of the syringe-ring, Lucas now brandished a knife.

"He's too dangerous to take in, even unconscious," he said. "He'll never last three months till the next meeting, but we can't leave him out on the streets preying on the innocent."

"You're just a kid," the rapist muttered, his black gaze fixed on the weapon. "You have no idea what you're doing, playing with shiny things like that."

"Don't I?" Lucas moved behind the man and gripped his forehead. "I find you guilty and I sentence you to death."

He sliced the blade across the man's throat. Blood spurted from the gaping wound.

The man clutched his neck, his eyes wide and staring, before he fell face-first onto the pavement.

Farrell just stood there, stunned, as he watched the puddle of crimson grow. "You killed him."

"Damn right I did. One less evil piece of garbage to deal with in the future." Lucas flicked a look at Farrell as he wiped the blade off on a handkerchief he'd pulled from his pocket. "You got a problem with that?"

The man was dead and the blood still flowed. No shiver of magic, no gratifying feeling that the society was working as one united force against evil. This was just Lucas, Farrell, a knife, and someone deserving death.

So much blood. The sight filled Farrell with a cool satisfaction.

A smile curled up the side of his mouth. "Nope. No problem at all."

"Good."

He'd accepted the society executions as a necessary evil, but he'd never before been *excited* by the sight of death. To hold another person's life in one's hands, to control his fate . . . now *that* was ultimate power.

Farrell craved more.

"Saving the world," he said, finding that his mind was every bit as clear as his conscience. "One day at a time."

Chapter 18

MADDOX

They walked northeast from the goddess's palace for hours until they reached a thick forest. Their path through the forest narrowed, and the canopy of leaves and branches became as thick above their heads as it had been in Valoria's throne room. The air smelled fresh here, scented by evergreens and flowering trees. As they silently walked, focusing on their footsteps, the forest came alive with the songs of birds and the buzz of insects.

"I'll admit it," Becca said. "It's beautiful here."

"It certainly can be," Maddox replied.

"Do you have seasons here?" she asked. "At home, we just got through winter. It was an extra cold one with tons of snow."

"I've heard of kingdoms that experience changing climates. Mytica isn't like that. This is how it is all the time. We have rain and thunderstorms, of course, and it can get cooler at night. But it's always warm during the day." He gazed around at the trees. "I can't imagine this kingdom covered in snow and ice."

"Lucky you," she mused.

"I don't know. I think it would be nice to experience something different. So maybe you're the lucky one."

"Maybe," she allowed.

"We're going to stop for a rest here," Barnabas announced as the forest thinned out to reveal the edge of a small lake about fifty paces away, its surface like glass reflecting the blue sky. He put his weapons down on the grassy ground. "Our destination is still a day's journey from here, so I do want to keep going while there's still light. We'll stop again at dusk and make camp."

Becca still looked fresh and lovely despite having kept pace with them all day. Perhaps as a spirit she didn't experience fatigue like Maddox did. He knew he must be a sight—a sweaty, disgusting mess.

Barnabas began to remove his filthy trousers.

"Um, why is he taking his clothes off?" Becca asked.

"Barnabas, what are you doing?" Maddox asked as the man's pants hit the ground. Becca turned her back to the scene, her expression turning squeamish.

Barnabas glanced at Maddox. "I'm going to take a bath. The first one I've had in, well, by the smell of me, far too long."

Off came the shirt.

"A bath," Maddox repeated.

"Yes. A long one." He nodded. "And I'll wash my clothes as best I can, too. I suggest you do the same. A couple of days in the dungeon doesn't do anyone any good."

Without another word, he wadded up his clothing into a ball and walked toward the lake, completely nude.

"Be careful of lake monsters!" Maddox called after him. Barnabas replied with a laugh.

Becca cringed. "There are lake monsters?"

He wondered if there were lake monsters in her world. He shot her a grin. "They're just a legend."

"Lots of legends around here, aren't there?" She swept her gaze over him and bit her bottom lip. "Are you going to have a bath now, too?"

"I can't argue that it's not an excellent idea."

Still, he didn't make a single move to start taking off his clothes.

"Why don't I wait over there?" She gestured to a grassy clearing and raised an eyebrow. "I promise I won't watch."

"Can I trust you to keep that promise?"

Her smile was mischievous at the edges. "Cross my heart."

He frowned. "Does that mean yes?"

"Yes, I promise. I won't peek at the two handsome skinny-dippers. Have fun."

He watched her walk away, certain he'd heard her wrong. *Handsome?*

His grin returned, and he quickly stripped and tucked his clothes beneath his arm. The water felt cold but invigorating as he waded into the lake. When he was submerged to his waist, he started to wash the dirt from his skin. It felt wonderful.

Barnabas floated by on his back, spitting out lake water as if he were a fountain. "I'll go hunting when we make camp later and bring us back some dinner. Unless you'd like the honor."

Maddox had never had a father to teach him how to hunt. He'd helped his mother with her snares and her vegetable garden, gotten their bread from the local market, but that hardly counted as practice. "I'm not much of a hunter."

"That makes one of us. When I was your age, I was the best hunter in the entire kingdom."

And the most modest about it, too, Maddox thought. "I'm sure you were."

"We'll also take some time this evening to test your magic."

"Test it how, exactly?" Maddox scrubbed his shirt, attempting to remove the more stubborn stains.

"Don't worry too much about your clothes, my young friend. We'll steal more the first chance we get." Barnabas dove underwater and came up again a moment later, sliding his fingers through his black hair. "As far as the test . . . I haven't yet seen any real proof of your abilities."

"You said I was the one who raised the dead in the palace graveyard. Wasn't that proof enough?"

"That was just a guess. An educated one, but still, only a guess. Did Livius ever help you practice your magic?"

He remembered how Livius would grow disgusted and threaten him whenever Maddox disappointed him. "No. But he got angry when it wouldn't work on command in front of clients. Luckily, we encountered very few real spirits during our partnership."

"Partnership, huh?" Barnabas vigorously scrubbed his hair and beard. Now that he was clean, Maddox saw that he was younger than he'd initially guessed. Perhaps only twice Maddox's age. Barnabas's smile had fallen away, and he now wore more of a scowl. "You were saddled with him for far too long. I'm surprised your mother was such a poor judge of character when it came to him."

"What do you know about my mother?" Maddox asked, now guarded. "Do you know her because you knew my father?"

"You could say that."

"And is that how you know about Livius? I don't think I ever mentioned him by name." Maddox watched Barnabas very carefully for his reply.

"Everyone knows about Livius. There was a reward for his capture, you know, for crimes of his past. A good one, too. Damn goddess stole my chance to line my pockets with gold when she caught him and killed him." He eyed Maddox. "You don't believe a word coming out of my mouth, do you?"

"Not really," Maddox admitted.

"Smart boy. Never trust anyone until they've proved themselves to you. But give me time. I'll earn that trust of yours."

"Swear it on the goddess?"

"I'll swear it on King Thaddeus's name." He grew more serious in moments. "That's my ultimate plan, you should know. King Thaddeus's offspring has been kept hidden away for safekeeping since infancy, and I mean to put that rightful child on the throne when I finally do away with Valoria once and for all."

This seemed like an exceptionally honorable goal to Maddox. He never would have guessed that this crazy thief had such loyalty inside him. "You mean to steal the throne from a goddess and give it to a dead king's son. That's a dangerous plan."

"It's his *daughter*, actually." He raised his brow as he swam in a slow circle around Maddox. "You immediately assume the rightful owner of the throne is a boy, huh? What would your pretty little spirit have to say about that?"

The knowledge of Becca's existence still felt precious, like a priceless jewel he needed to guard.

Could he trust this man?

He was silent a moment longer, thinking hard. "She says she's from another world. She says she's connected to me somehow. . . ."

"Which, if you're a necromancer, makes sense." Barnabas lowered his brow. "Another world? Did she really say that?"

"She did." The skepticism he'd pushed away earlier now came

back with full strength. "I've never heard of a necromancer before."

"You're sixteen. I'm sure there are many mysteries in this world you're not aware of yet. Or that I'm not aware of, for that matter."

"You've met another like me?"

"Not exactly like you. No, my friend, you are most definitely one of a kind. But I know your magic is death magic. I've seen much proof of it already, but I know you can do more."

"How do you know?" He tried to piece it together in his mind. "Was it my father? Did he tell you? How would he know anything about me if he's never known me? Was he a necromancer, too?"

All the humor and openness remaining in Barnabas's face had disappeared. "There are some things I can't share with you right now, my friend. You're going to have to trust me for a while longer, no matter how difficult that request may seem."

Maddox pressed his lips together and glared at him.

Barnabas shrugged. "Don't give me that look. Remember, if it weren't for me, you'd likely be kneeling at the goddess's skirts, trying to figure out how not to become food for her snake or a new plant for her garden."

"I could have escaped without your help."

"Of course you could have." He nodded, but Maddox felt as if he were being mocked. "Now, back to the subject of your spirit friend. What does she want from you?"

Maddox wasn't sure that he wanted to share any more information with this strange man. "She thinks I can help her return to her world. And if what you're saying about whatever is locked within the box we stole is true, there's a possibility she might be right."

Barnabas nodded as if what Maddox had just said wasn't

madness itself. "If a beautiful girl asks for your help because she believes in you, you must help her. Simple as that."

Then he began to swim away.

"Wait," Maddox said. "You need to tell me more about my father. How did he die? And did he know about my magic?"

"Later," Barnabas replied. "We'll have plenty of time to talk about him later."

Then he dove under the water and disappeared from sight.

Maddox finished before Barnabas did and emerged from the lake, wringing out his clothes before sliding back into them. There was no time to let them dry first. He felt clean and determined as he went in search of Becca, frustrated and angry about his conversation with Barnabas.

He found her seated beneath a tall oak tree in the grassy clearing, her head in her hands.

When he realized she was crying, his heart wrenched.

"Becca, what's wrong?"

She pulled her hands away from her face to regard him with wide, glossy eyes. "You're back so soon. I . . . I didn't want you to see me like this."

"I didn't want to leave you on your own too long."

She laughed as a shimmering tear slipped down her cheek. "You think you need to protect me? I don't need protection here, not like you do."

He stiffened at the suggestion that he couldn't defend himself. "I'll have you know, I can take care of myself just fine."

"I didn't mean . . ." She sighed. "I know you can, okay? But you're flesh and blood, and I'm . . . I'm a spirit here. A sword could kill you, but it wouldn't hurt me."

Of course, she was right. She'd meant no offense. Why was he so sensitive to every word she spoke? "Apologies for being so harsh."

She shook her head. "That wasn't harsh."

"Why are you crying?"

"This meadow reminds me of one my sister and I went to once for a picnic. She thought it was a dumb idea, but I was really excited about it. I packed the lunch and we spent the day together. And it was fun. But ever since Dad left, I feel like all she does is ignore me. She's so into her stupid camera and her precious Charlie lately that I'm not even sure she knows I exist half the time. Still, I miss her so much right now that I can barely breathe. I miss when we were closer, when we were friends, not just sisters. When we went on picnics, even though she thought they were dumb. If I get back, I'm going to change things between us. I'm going to get to know her again, whether she wants to or not. I'll give her no choice." She raised a brow. "I can be very persistent."

"I believe it." He'd never had a sibling, at least not one that he was aware of. The relationship sounded both horribly complicated and wonderful at the same time. "What's her name?"

"Crystal," she said. "Crys."

"Crystal-crys." He nodded. "It's an unusual but quite lovely name."

"No, I mean, her full name is Crystal, but everyone just calls her Crys." She sighed. "Sorry, I don't usually act like this. I'm being weak. I need to be strong right now, not be a baby."

He crouched down next to her, wishing he could wipe her tears away. "Tears aren't just for babies. They're proof that you feel something and aren't afraid to show it. It's those who won't ever allow themselves to cry that are the weak ones."

She looked at him for a long moment, biting her bottom lip. "You're different, aren't you?"

"Different?"

"From other boys. From any boy I've ever met before."

His jaw tightened. "Perhaps you'd prefer to be around boys who don't say silly things like I just did."

A flash of annoyance lit up her blue eyes. "That's not even slightly what I meant. You're just . . . I can't even explain it. You say what you mean and you mean what you say. You're kind and generous and thoughtful. You're brave and strong and sweet, and I . . ." She bit her lip again and studied her hands, which were folded in her lap, before she locked gazes with him. "You make me feel, even though I haven't known you very long at all, that I could trust you with anything. Anything at all."

"You can." His words were hushed, his throat felt thick with unspoken feelings.

All the things she'd just said about him, was that really how she saw him? She made him sound like something special. Something better than he ever thought he could be.

She pushed herself up to standing and studied the grassy ground before she looked up, her blue eyes meeting his again. "While we wait for Barnabas, tell me something about you, about this crazy world you live in."

"What do you want to know?" he asked.

She shook her head. "I don't know. What about school? Do you take any classes?"

"Classes . . . I've heard of those, I think." He grinned. The girl had no knowledge about this world whatsoever. "They're for the children of lords and other nobles who can afford tutors. For a mere peasant like myself . . . well, my mother taught me how to read."

Her eyes lit up. "You have books here?"

"Of course."

"Like what kinds?"

"The ones my mother read to me were full of legends and stories of immortal beings and fantastic creatures from faraway lands."

"Do you remember any of the stories?"

"Some."

"Tell me about them."

The subject had seemingly managed to chase her sadness away. He wanted to keep that bright excitement in her eyes as long as possible.

"There's a tale I liked about a mortal boy who found a magic shell. He made a wish on it to turn his legs into the tail of a fish. He believed this would help him swim to the bottom of the sea in search of his one true love, the sea princess. After much trouble and many tests and trials, the fish-boy succeeded and—"

"They lived happily ever after."

He nodded.

"That's my favorite kind of story," Becca said. "Love stories with happy endings. I haven't told anyone, but my dream is to be a writer. To write romance novels that make people happy and entertained. My English teacher tells me I have a very creative imagination."

"So you wish to become a scribe of legends and tales." What an incredible thought this was to him. To be the one to write such wonderful stories.

"Something like that." She leaned back against the tree trunk. "Do you remember any other stories?"

The question brought back so many memories of happy times, when his mother would tuck him into bed and read to him late into the night, far longer than she'd planned to, because she'd become so taken with a story that she had to continue so he could see how it ended.

Not all stories ended happily, though. The sad stories always made her cry.

"There's another tale about a powerful, immortal sorceress who lost her magic and became mortal. She went on a quest to find the source of this magic, and she ended up saving a mortal prince, who'd been cursed into the form of a winged horse. They fall in love, the sorceress's magic is restored, and they go on to rule the kingdom together for a thousand years as king and queen."

"I love that. Although, how did the prince live for a thousand years if he was mortal?"

"I don't know. Maybe her magic made him immortal like her?"

"And when they fell in love, was he in horse form or prince form? How did she break his curse if she didn't have her magic?"

"Uh . . . I'm not sure I remember that."

"Sounds like a plot hole to me." She blinked. "You don't know what I'm talking about, do you?"

"Not even a little," he admitted.

"Still, it sounds like a great story. And the other one, too. Tales of fantasy and magic are the best."

He nodded in agreement. "Unfortunately, Valoria has created laws forbidding such stories. She feels they will deteriorate the intelligence of mortals. She issued an official decree that all books like that are to be burned. And they have been. So many have been destroyed."

"What?" Becca sputtered with outrage. "That evil bitch!"

When he'd first learned of the ban, he, too, had been furious. He'd made a promise to himself that he would hide every book he found from that day forward, to save it from destruction. It was a small act of rebellion, but it had given him purpose.

That was before Livius took him away from his home.

Barnabas appeared out of nowhere and breezed past them, headed toward the pathway. Thankfully, he was fully dressed in his much cleaner but still sodden clothing. "Let's get going, my friends. The sun will soon start to set, and I want to get to the next village before we lose the light."

"Friends? Can he see me?" Becca asked, surprised.

Maddox grimaced. "No, but he wholly accepts your presence as truth. He doesn't even entertain the possibility that you're not real and I'm crazy."

She rose to her feet. "That's very open-minded of him. No discrimination against lost spirits."

"He's full of surprises." Maddox eyed Barnabas with an edge of wariness. He wanted answers.

"I'm going to continue keeping an eye on him," Becca said. "If he does anything shady, I'll report back. I swear I won't let anything bad happen to you if I can help it."

He nodded as he collected the copper box and began to follow after Barnabas. "The feeling is entirely mutual, Becca Hatcher."

There was a village a short journey from the lake, where they found a stone cottage with a line of drying laundry.

"Here's one for you," Barnabas plucked a cotton tunic off the line and threw it to Maddox. "And here's one for me. Nice and clean. True luxury."

Suddenly, an alarmed female voice called out. Barnabas had spoken loud enough to attract the attention of the woman who lived there. She chased them off with a dangerous-looking broom handle after Barnabas had grabbed two pairs of trousers and an armful of apples from her tree.

At dusk, they made camp at the edge of the village and changed into their new clothes. Barnabas disappeared into the forest, returning shortly after with two rabbits he'd already skinned and cleaned.

"Impressive," Maddox had to admit.

"And very tasty when cooked properly." He set up a spit over the campfire to roast the meat.

Maddox sat down on the log next to him. Becca sat cross-legged across from them, studying the fire.

"Will you answer more of my questions now?" he asked, trying to sound as patient as possible.

Barnabas considered him for a long while. "Perhaps. What do you want to know?"

"Everything you can tell me about my father."

"He was a rebel who was loyal to King Thaddeus. He's the one responsible for hiding the king's daughter somewhere safe."

"Is the king's daughter the girl Valoria is searching for?" Becca spoke up. "The one with the magic she says she needs to find the thief who stole her dagger?"

Maddox repeated the question.

"I don't believe so," Barnabas replied. "The rightful heir to the throne has shown no signs yet of being a witch, but I suppose it could be possible. More reason to keep her hidden."

"What happened to my father?"

Barnabas poked at the burning embers with a stick before he answered. "Valoria tore his heart from his chest."

Maddox went cold at this blunt answer.

"Oh, Maddox . . . that's so horrible," Becca began. "I—I'm so sorry."

He couldn't say anything in response or even acknowledge her words. For a horrible moment, he was trapped in his mind, at the mercy of an image of the goddess cutting open a rebel's chest and pulling out his still-beating heart, watching the life leave his eyes. . . .

I'm sorry, Father, he thought, his own heart aching at the knowledge of this horrible truth. *I'm sorry for what happened to you. I'm sorry I couldn't know you.*

After several silent moments, he tried to find his voice. "Is he the reason I'm a necromancer? Did I get this from him?"

Barnabas shook his head. "Your father had no magic I was aware of."

"Neither does my mother." She would have told him otherwise—he was certain of it. "Perhaps I am cursed, just like I always thought I was."

"Perhaps," Barnabas agreed, his attention fixed on the roasting rabbits.

All these years not knowing the truth, and now here it was—so much all at once. He needed to do everything in his power to avoid harping on the untouchable past, and instead focus on the changeable present and future. "Who is this witch we're going to see? Do you trust her?"

"She's a friend. And, yes, I do trust her. She despises Valoria nearly as much as I do."

"Your grievances against Valoria go beyond your desire to reinstate King Thaddeus's daughter on the throne. You want vengeance for what she did to my father, don't you?"

"More than anything." The firelight flickered on Barnabas's

face, casting his grave expression in strange shadows. "And so should you."

He did. He'd merely feared Valoria before, but now he loathed her, too.

"I knew it," Becca said.

"Knew what?" Maddox asked softly.

"That air he put on—the fool, the jokester—it's all an act. This pain . . . *this* is the real Barnabas." She absently played with her silver rose pendant. "I'm not sure if this makes him more trustworthy or less, but at least it's genuine."

Perhaps she was right. There could be more to Barnabas than trickery and ruses.

The darkness slowly faded from Barnabas's expression. "We shouldn't wait any longer to practice your magic. Why don't you go ahead and try to summon a spirit right now? Prove to yourself and to me you can do this magic on command, and then send it back to where it came from."

Maddox immediately grew tense. "You make it sound like it's easy for me. I've never been able to consciously summon a spirit. The only ones I can commune with are already present."

"*I* believe you can do it—with ease, no less. You just don't believe it."

"You sound like Becca. . . ." Maddox then closed his mouth, regretting his words the moment he spoke them.

"Ah, so that's her name, is it?" Fresh amusement flickered in Barnabas's eyes. "Beck-ah? Are you there? Are you sitting next to young Maddox here? You must be a pretty lass, if he's so taken with you."

"Looks like his mask is back in place," Becca said, fighting a smile.

"It's not funny," Maddox said, annoyed that Barnabas kept saying such embarrassing things.

"What do you think, Becca?" Barnabas asked. "Do you think Maddox should show us and himself that he has more control over his magic than he thinks he does?"

"I absolutely do," she said, even though only Maddox could hear her reply. "I know you can do this. You can do amazing things and the only one who doesn't believe it is you."

Now it was two against one. That wasn't fair. "It's not that simple."

"Stop overthinking it and just do it."

They continued to encourage him to embrace the very thing that he was now certain was a curse. Finally, he became tired of resisting. "Fine. I'll try. But I need something silver to trap it, just in case."

"Have you ever tried trapping spirits in other precious metals? Or, perhaps, a mirror. Or . . . an apple." Barnabas threw one of his stolen pieces of fruit at Maddox, who caught it in his right hand.

Maddox took a big bite of the sweet, juicy piece of fruit, chewed, and swallowed. "I know it works with silver, so let's stay with that for now."

Barnabas glanced down at his hand. "Here." He pulled off his thick ring and tossed it at Maddox. "That's silver. At least, that's what the man I stole it from told me."

Maddox inspected the ring with doubt. "Normally I do it with a silver *container*."

"What difference does it make? Like you said, you can't even summon spirits on command. You won't even need to use it."

The challenge had been issued. He didn't want to fail with Becca watching his every move so closely.

"Fine." He closed his eyes, squeezed his hands into fists, and concentrated as hard as he could.

I'm not afraid of you, he thought. *Show yourself, spirit.*

Maddox pried open an eye to see Barnabas studying him, crunching down on another apple.

"Nothing interesting has happened yet," Barnabas informed him.

Becca had moved to sit on the fallen log behind him. "Keep trying," she suggested.

He squeezed his eyes shut again and tried to push away his doubt and fear.

He concentrated on the smell of the campfire. The sound of crackling wood. The cool breeze brushing against his arms and face. The sweet taste of the apple on his tongue.

Then: darkness before him, surrounding him. Darkness everywhere.

"Come to me now, spirit," he said aloud. "Show yourself. I command you to obey."

His voice was calm and confident, and he summoned the shadows as if they would respond to him. As if they would obey him.

Something shifted deep inside him. The brisk evening air grew colder.

Becca screamed. "Maddox!"

His eyes snapped open.

A shadow had risen from the ground, a formless, shapeless shroud of midnight. It edged closer to Becca, and she rose from her seat to stagger away from it.

"*So hungry,*" a ragged, broken, and pained voice said.

"No," Maddox gasped.

Barnabas shot up to his feet and dropped his half-eaten apple. "Did it work?"

Maddox didn't reply. Instead, he moved swiftly toward Becca, focused on nothing but saving her. He grabbed for the spirit, but his hands went right through it, the smoky substance of its form icy cold.

"What's happening?" Becca cried. Unlike him, she was able to make contact with the shadowy creature, Maddox assumed with growing panic, because they were both in spirit form. "How do I stop it?"

"She will make a fine meal," the spirit said. *"Much gratitude for summoning me here, necromancer."*

He froze with fear. This spirit had the power to devour Becca, to destroy her. To kill her.

And he had been the one to bring it here.

Becca shrieked as the spirit swirled around her like a thick black snake, pulling her up into the air. She fought against it but appeared to be weakening. Her punches and kicks slowed, her skin became pale and ashen in mere moments.

"Maddox . . . ," she managed. "Please . . . I believe in you."

His fear vanished and was replaced with steely determination. He would not let the spirit hurt this girl. He would not let *anyone* hurt this girl.

He held up Barnabas's ring and focused again, just as he had before the spirit was summoned. There was another shadow there, deep inside him. It was made of death magic. It called to the darkness.

"I command you, spirit! Leave her and come to me. Obey me now!"

The spirit stopped swirling, freezing in place. Then, letting out a horrible, ragged cry, it streamed toward Maddox, toward the silver ring he held. It collided violently with the metal, then disappeared.

Becca fell to the ground and Maddox rushed to her side. He tried to gather her into his arms, but of course his hands slipped right through her form.

"Apologies," he said, his eyes stinging as the fear and panic he'd been holding back now crashed over him again. He shoved the ring in his pocket, telling himself he'd bury it later, after he'd made sure she was all right. "A million apologies for putting you in harm's way."

She was a spirit who laughed. Who breathed. Who fell. Who got hurt. A spirit who believed in him when he didn't believe in himself. Who'd given him something to fight for when he didn't even know he was a fighter.

A spirit who'd come to mean so much to him so quickly that his heart ached at the thought of ever losing her.

"I'm okay. Thank God . . ." She reached up to touch his face, her trembling fingers hovering just over his skin.

He frowned down at her. "Trust me, I am no god."

"I know." She managed the slightest edge of a smile. "I forgot where I was for a second. But I'm not thanking any goddess."

"You confuse me."

"I don't mean to, really. And if I might say it again, you're amazing. You are *amazing*. Are you hearing me?"

"Amazing enough to nearly get you killed." He watched with unguarded relief as the color came back to her face. "I thought I'd lost you."

"I'm not going anywhere just yet. I'm haunting you, remember?"

Barnabas watched, his arms crossed over his chest, his expression grim, as Maddox and Becca slowly returned to the campfire.

"No more spirit-summoning tonight," Maddox told him fiercely.

He nodded. "But you did it. Of course I couldn't *see* anything, but it looks like it went well."

"Not well at all."

"I disagree. You summoned the spirit and then you trapped it, just as I expected you could. Do you now believe in the greater possibilities of your magic?"

Maddox and Becca exchanged a long glance before Maddox looked at Barnabas, nodding once. "I do."

Barnabas gave him a big grin. "Glad to hear it."

Chapter 19

CRYSTAL

"Excuse me, miss, but can you help me find a book?"

Crys turned from the bookshelf she was organizing to face a customer, a tall man with thick glasses. Her mother had closed the shop for four days, but it couldn't stay shuttered any longer than that. The doors opened for business again on Thursday, and both Julia and Crys were on duty—her mother at the front register, Crys shelving books and straightening up in the back.

"Sure, what are you looking for?"

"It's for my daughter. Something about a princess."

"Do you have anything more to go on?"

"I think there's a dragon in it? Also, the princess wears some sort of grocery bag instead of a gown."

Crys nodded. "That definitely narrows it down. It's *The Paper Bag Princess* by Robert Munsch, one of my all-time favorites. I think we have a few copies in stock." She showed him to the children's nook, where she located a copy. He inspected the cover happily.

"Thank you! Tracking down precious books must be your calling. My daughter will love this."

He went to pay for the book as Crys tried to figure out if that was a compliment or a curse.

She knew that working in a bookshop all her life wasn't her calling. Maybe Becca's, but not hers.

Still, as she shelved, a part of her—the part that had once loved this shop and its books with the same fierceness of the family members who'd founded it—rose to the surface. Surrounded by the intricate cover art, the grand-sounding author names, the intriguing titles that promised adventure and escape between the crisp covers . . .

"Crys," her mother called, breaking her reverie. "Come up here."

The *Paper Bag Princess* customer had left by the time Crys emerged from the maze of shelves. "Yeah?"

"A package just came for you." She nodded at a box on the counter.

Crys approached it cautiously. "From who?"

"I don't know. There's no return address." She paused. "Well, are you going to open it?"

"I haven't had much luck opening mysterious packages this week."

"At least this time it's addressed to you," she replied pointedly, one eyebrow arched.

Wincing at her mother's sharp tone, Crys began to open the parcel slowly and carefully, not knowing what to expect inside.

She pulled away the tissue wrapping to reveal something she had to blink twice to believe.

"You have got to be kidding me," she said aloud.

"Who on earth sent you that?" her mother exclaimed.

It was a Canon EOS Rebel DSLR camera, a top-of-the-line digital model. Unlike the old Pentax, this one came standard with a powerful auto pop-up flash. So out of her price range that she could never, ever even consider purchasing it on her own, at least until she had established herself as a professional photographer.

There was an envelope inside with Crys's name on it. She opened it up so quickly that the edge of the paper sliced her index finger. The unexpected paper cut stung terribly, and she sucked on her finger as she read the card.

I'm very sorry your sentimentally valuable camera got smashed. I know you'll take many incredible pictures with this one. Might this oh-so-shiny gift from your newest friend help change your maybe into a yes?—Farrell

Farrell Grayson had bought her a new camera. An amazing new camera she'd never dreamed she could have. While she had had a deep fondness for the Pentax and the memorable black-and-white shots she'd taken with it and developed herself, this one . . .

Well, *this* was too good to be true.

"Who's Farrell? I didn't know you had a boyfriend," her mother said, glancing at the note before Crys could tuck it back into the envelope.

"I don't." She bit her bottom lip.

"A suitor?"

Now her cheeks warmed. "Mother, nobody's used the term *suitor* in a hundred years."

Julia seemed amused that she'd successfully flustered her daughter. "He must be someone very special, and he must think *you're* someone very special, to send you something like this."

He *was* someone special—she wasn't denying that.

"I can't keep it," she said, staring at the camera box wistfully.

"Why not?"

"Just . . . I need to talk to him, I need to call him. I need to tell him that expensive gifts aren't necessary to be my friend." But now she knew that he definitely did want to see her again, that he wanted her in his life. The thought was just as scary as it was exciting.

Why did she have to meet this amazing guy in the same week that everything else in her life felt so out of control?

She checked her phone. He'd put his number into her Contacts under *F. GRAY*.

Her thumb hovered over the Call button, her heart pounding hard in her ears.

Then the phone began to ring.

DAD

Crys's eyes bugged. She quickly left the store to stand outside on the sidewalk so her mother wouldn't hear, and composed herself before she answered it.

"Dad, hi."

"Sorry it took me so long to get back to you. I wanted to wait for the right time and . . . well, it's done. Markus will meet you today. If the meeting goes well, he promises to consider you for initiation . . . if that's what you still want."

"Of course that's what I still want," she replied without hesitation, the lie spilling easily from her lips. "Thank you for doing this, Dad."

But maybe it wasn't a lie. Maybe she did want to be part of a society that held the key to a better world. Or maybe she'd learn that Jackie and Dr. Vega were right—that Markus King was a monster.

One way or another, though, she was closer to the truth than ever before.

"I'll pick you up in an hour," he said.

—∾—

He didn't pick her up at the bookshop, of course. He picked her up in front of the Tim Hortons around the corner at Bloor and Spadina, the spot where, once upon a time, the Hatchers used to go for hot chocolate, coffee, and donuts, as a family.

"What T-shirt is it today?" he asked when she got into his car. He wore mirrored wraparound sunglasses over his pale blue eyes.

"I just changed to a plain black one," Crys said. "I figured, if I'm meeting the leader of a secret society, he probably isn't the kind of man who appreciates whimsical fashion choices."

The corner of his mouth turned up into a small smile. "Don't be nervous."

"Do I look nervous?"

"Yes, you do. Extremely."

She managed a shaky grin. It still completely blew her mind that she was sitting in a car with her estranged father, on her way to meet with the leader of a secret society. "I guess I get nervous about things that matter to me."

"We have that in common." He shifted into gear and pulled away from the curb as Crys started to put on her seat belt.

"Where are we going?" she asked.

His lips thinned. "I can't tell you exactly. To be honest, Crissy, I can't tell you much about the society unless you become an initiated member."

He'd always been a careful driver, hands at ten and two, and it appeared that nothing had changed. Crys had her driver's license but rarely asked to borrow her mother's car. The subway or her own two feet worked fine to get her where she usually wanted to go.

"Does your mother know we've been in contact?" he asked.

"No," she said, watching him carefully to see if he detected her lie. His expression remained even, but she wished she could see his eyes to know for sure.

"How has she been?" he asked.

"Same as ever. Grumpy, always working at the shop, sometimes modestly pleasant to be around."

"And her cooking?"

"She still makes fantastic scrambled eggs."

He laughed. "So she hasn't bothered to learn how to cook."

"You were the great chef in the family. I think I've lost ten pounds since you left us." The sentence ended on a much heavier note than she'd intended.

"And Becca? How is she?" he asked after an uncomfortably silent moment.

"She's fine." She couldn't tell him about Becca. Not yet. She still had so many unanswered questions and was still uncertain about him. "She misses you, too. You should, I don't know, e-mail her. Or something. Just let her know you're okay and you're thinking about her."

"I'll consider it."

She pressed back in the seat. "Do you think you ever would have gotten in touch with me? I mean, if I hadn't been the first to text you?"

He was silent for a moment. "Your mother was adamant that I stay away."

"I usually take her adamant requests with a grain of salt, but that's just me."

Again, they went quiet as Crys tried to think of a question to ask that might actually get her some answers.

But he spoke first. "Crissy, there's something about this meeting that you're probably not going to like."

She braced herself, half expecting him to finally unburden himself and tell her everything. "What?"

"This." He pulled something out of the glove compartment. It was a long black piece of cloth.

"Is that a blindfold?" she asked uneasily.

He nodded. "You can't see where I'm taking you, and you can't know the route."

"Why not?"

He let out a long sigh. "Please, Crissy, just do as I ask. Don't argue or the meeting is canceled."

She regarded the blindfold with apprehension and considered her options. But nothing other than doing as he asked came to mind.

"Fine," she said. She took off her glasses, slipped them into her bag, and then put on the blindfold, tying it into a knot at the back of her head.

The world went dark all around her.

"This is all very cloak-and-dagger," she said, trying to sound natural, as if putting on a blindfold to meet someone like Markus King was totally routine for her.

He snorted softly. "If I'd known years ago that all it would take to get you to behave was to tell you that you might be able to join a secret society . . ."

"I really don't like the word *behave*. A lot of rules were meant to be broken." Crys bit her bottom lip. "Aren't you concerned that someone will notice that you're driving around with a blindfolded girl in your front seat?"

"Not particularly." His voice was now edged with amusement. "These windows are tinted."

After about fifteen minutes, the car pulled to a stop. She heard her father get out of the driver's side and come around to the passenger side to help her out.

"This way," he said. He guided her over a hard surface and up ten steps. A door creaked opened and they went through it.

The door clicked shut.

"Through here." Taking her elbow, he directed her twenty paces forward, opened and closed another door, and then came to a stop. "You can remove the blindfold now."

Crys didn't hesitate. She pulled the material off her eyes and blinked as she took in her surroundings, blurry until she put on her glasses. They'd entered a large room, with cherry wood paneling and antique furniture. Gorgeous oil landscapes graced the walls and were, she assumed, all original and more than a century old, like something she'd find hanging in the AGO. The rugs were embroidered with intricate detail. A crystal chandelier hung from the high, ornately molded ceiling.

The room struck her as one she might see in a landmark museum like Casa Loma, roped off and untouchable as tourists walked through it.

"This is his home, isn't it?" she asked.

"It is. He'll meet you in the library, where he does most of his work. This way."

Crys followed him through the door on the far side of the room, which led to a hallway. They went down a flight of stairs and then along another corridor. Finally, they entered a huge, lofted room with books displayed floor-to-ceiling and sliding ladders to reach the volumes on the uppermost shelves. The room smelled like leather, smoke, and roses.

There was someone leaning against the shelf to her left,

reading a book, near a multipaned window that looked out toward an expansive backyard with a large marble pool and sculptured bushes and trees.

She recognized him immediately.

"You," Crys said with surprise. "I know you."

It was the golden boy, the gorgeous blond guy she'd seen on the university campus, the one who'd given her directions to Dr. Vega's office. He turned his dreamy blue eyes on her and the corners of his mouth curved up into a smile.

"Hello again," he said as he slid the book back into place on the shelf.

"Do you live here, too?"

"Yes, I do."

Her father frowned with confusion, his gaze moving to Golden Boy. "You've already met?"

"Not exactly," he said. "Please, Daniel, introduce us."

"Crys . . . I'd like you to meet Markus King. Markus, this is my daughter, Crystal Hatcher."

Golden Boy walked toward her, reaching out his hand. "A pleasure, Crystal."

She didn't move to shake his hand, all she could do was stare. "Is this some kind of joke?"

He raised his eyebrows. "Joke?"

"You can't be Markus King. Not *the* Markus King, anyway. You must be his, I don't know, grandson? Great-grandson?" She turned to her father. "What's going on here?"

He shook his head. "This is Markus King, Crissy."

Crys turned to once again regard the guy, who looked like any college kid might. A college kid who also happened to moonlight as a male model, that is. "You're, like, twenty years old."

"I do appear to be that age," Markus agreed.

What was that supposed to mean?

This did not compute, and a sick, twisting sensation in her gut made her question her current hold on reality. She'd expected the leader of the Hawkspear Society, who had a rich history that included an intense conflict between her mother and aunt, not to mention with Dr. Vega, to be a senior citizen by now.

"You expected someone ancient," he said, as if reading her mind. "You were right to expect that."

In seconds, her mouth had become as dry as a desert. "How is this possible?"

Golden Boy nodded at her father. "You have permission to tell her. I think she'd have an easier time understanding if it came from you."

Her father nodded. There was absolutely nothing in his expression that made Crys think he was fooling around, playing some sort of epically unfunny practical joke on her. "I know that what I'm about to say will sound unbelievable to you, possibly even crazy, but . . . Markus is . . . immortal." He took a breath and studied her stunned reaction before continuing. "He is ancient and wise and powerful. He will never age, because he is a god."

And he said all this as if it made total sense.

Crys stared at him, unblinking. Her mind had gone utterly blank except for his words bouncing around inside her head as if they were in a pinball machine.

"He's an immortal . . . god," she repeated flatly, her throat nearly too tight to speak.

"Yes." He gazed at Markus with a reverent look in his eyes that told Crys he believed all this without question.

"This is . . ." Crys fought to find her voice. "I—I don't even know what to say. This was *not* what I was expecting."

Markus laughed, and the sound shivered down her spine. "And what were your expectations for today, Ms. Hatcher?"

She forced herself to tear her gaze from her father to look at Golden Boy instead. He watched her with his head cocked, as if curious for her reaction. "Only that I'd be meeting a super old guy who'd probably smell like cough medicine."

Her father's jaw tensed. "Crystal, you mustn't be so disrespectful."

The corner of Markus's mouth curved into a small smile. "It's all right, Daniel. I find her plain way of speaking to be rather refreshing. Now, if you'd please leave your daughter and me for a few moments in privacy, I'd greatly appreciate it."

Her father hesitated, but only for a short moment. "As you wish."

Without another word, he turned and left the room, closing the door behind him.

And Crys found herself all alone with an immortal god.

"Ms. Hatcher," Markus said, "please sit down with me. There's much I need to ask you if I'm to consider you for membership."

He indicated a small lounge area in the center of the room, next to a large ebony desk and directly under the skylight in the high ceiling. What was left of the natural light outside helped brighten the shadows that threatened to reach into every corner as the sun began to set.

Crys silently took a seat on a brocade chair and gripped the arms. She hadn't taken her eyes off Markus since her father left the room, still stunned by the thought that this was the leader of the Hawkspear Society. His clothing was nothing remarkable; he wore black pants and a white button-down.

He sat down across from her. "You're having a difficult time accepting your father's words, aren't you?"

She knew she had a lousy poker face. She'd have to snap out of her stunned fog and start really playing this game if she were to have any chance of winning.

"You mean the thing about how you're an immortal god? Um . . . yeah, you could say I'm a little stunned. I've never met anyone like . . ." She cleared her throat, finding it tightening by the second. ". . . Like you."

"I'm sure you have many questions, just as I have questions for you. I'd like to go first, if you don't mind."

She nodded, trying to keep her stare steady.

"How did you learn about the Hawkspear Society?"

Crys was a terrible liar, so it was her policy to go with the truth whenever possible. Plus, despite Markus's innocent, youthful appearance, there was something in his intense, wizened gaze that hinted that he was a pro at detecting cons.

"I overheard my mother and aunt on the phone talking about Dad and why he left us. I'd never known the truth before. Or anything about their separation, really."

"Your mother and your aunt. Julia and . . . Jackie Kendall."

"Yes." Of course he'd know their names. He probably knew everything about his members' families.

"And once you overheard this conversation, you immediately decided you wanted to join a society you knew nothing about?"

"Well, no. What I originally wanted was to have a relationship with my father again. But the more I learned about your society, the more interested I became in it."

"What exactly did Daniel tell you about Hawkspear?" His tone was even and pleasant, but Crys was not about to mistake this conversation for a friendly chat over tea and cookies. She knew that Markus was only gently grilling her to determine if she was worthy.

She needed to prove herself worthy. She needed to know more about the Bronze Codex, and to do that, she needed to gain Markus's trust.

"He didn't tell me much," she admitted. "He even made me wear a blindfold on the way here. But I do know he's committed to you. He chose this society over his family. My father never would have made a decision like that lightly. He believes in you. He believes in your mission. And if my father believes in you, then I know I can, too."

He sat there, silently assessing her. His narrow-eyed gaze moved over her slowly. "You look quite a bit like Daniel, especially your eyes. But I see a great deal of Julia in you, too. Both your appearance and your demeanor. She and her sister always used humor to help lighten difficult discussions."

This comment surprised her. "You've met my mother and Jackie?"

"Yes. I am quite acquainted with them both. They were once two of my most valued members."

Time skidded to a halt, and Crys had to clutch the sides of her armchair to steady herself in the moment.

She must have heard him wrong.

"I take it that this is news to you." A smile pulled at Markus's lips again as he regarded her unshielded shock. "I'm not surprised."

"You're saying that my mother and . . . and Jackie . . . were part of your society," Crys managed to repeat, her voice strained.

"They certainly were. Have they told you anything about your family history, Ms. Hatcher? Anything at all?"

Any confidence she'd walked into this room with was now

slipping through her grasp. She tried very hard to hold on to the small measure of composure she had left.

"I guess they haven't," she admitted quietly. "I know the bookshop has been in the family for a long time."

"Yes. Your great-grandfather, Jonathan Kendall, purchased the building as a gift for his wife, Rebecca. She adored books, so she turned it into a bookshop. And now it's all that remains of the Kendall fortune."

"Yes, that's pretty much the only story I know about him."

"So I take it that you're not aware that Jonathan Kendall also cofounded the Hawkspear Society with me."

She tried to keep the fresh wash of shock off her face but knew she'd failed. "No, can't say that's ever come up at the family dinner table."

"When I first came to Toronto, Jonathan invited me to stay with his family, for as long as I liked. Eventually he confided in me that he'd had a powerful vision. Of me. Before I'd arrived and before we'd ever met. He told me he'd known for some time that we were destined to start an organization together, that we'd be dedicated to protecting the citizens of this city from those who'd want to harm them. And so the Hawkspear Society came into being. Generations later, your mother—when she was still a Kendall—and your aunt were inducted. Julia was the one who nominated Daniel for membership after they met and fell in love. The rest, as they say, is history."

Crys had to take a moment to absorb this. It sounded like a piece of fantasy fiction, not the history of her own family. "But my mother and Jackie aren't members anymore."

"No. Unfortunately, we had a . . . falling-out. They chose to believe a series of unforgiveable lies about me. Once that trust between us had been lost, it couldn't be regained, so I released them from their ties to the society. Years later, Daniel returned of his own free will. He knew he was needed, and he wanted to continue to help with our mission."

Why wouldn't her mother have told her something as important as this? Did she think Crys wouldn't ever find out the truth?

If this *was* the truth.

Whatever lies Jackie and Julia had believed about Markus had turned their grandfather's closest ally into a monster in their eyes.

Appearance-wise, at least, Markus King was anything but a monster.

"Did my mother and Jackie believe you're a god, too?"

"They did," he replied without hesitation. "But I can tell that you don't. It's understandable, since you've seen no proof. I do have abilities that regular people don't possess. Would you like to see?"

She watched him in wary silence before finally nodding.

He held out his hand, and with a flick of the wrist, a bouquet of flames burst forth on his palm, rising up a foot, casting sparkling light into his dark blue eyes. He raised an eyebrow. "I'll admit, it's a bit too showy for my tastes. Any Las Vegas magician could do the same with the proper preparation."

Crys struggled to catch her breath. "So what else can you do?" she said, trying not to sound like that was the strangest, most captivating thing she'd ever seen.

He studied her carefully. "You've cut your finger."

She looked down at the bandage on her index finger. "It's just a paper cut. Nothing major."

He drew closer, crouching down in front of her. His demeanor was so calm that it helped to relax Crys a little, too. She didn't cringe away from him as he gently pulled the bandage off her finger and inspected the sore red wound beneath.

"I can help with this," he said, closing his grip around her finger.

She felt heat dance across her skin, penetrating deeper and deeper into her flesh. A strange, soft glow seemed to emanate from his hand. After a few more seconds, the sensation became unpleasant, but it couldn't be described as pain.

"There," he said, releasing her. "That's not something a magician can do."

She stared down in shock to see that her paper cut was gone, and that the previously wounded skin was unblemished.

No wonder his members believed he was a god.

"I'm going to need a moment to pick up my jaw off the floor," she allowed herself to admit.

"Of course." He returned to his seat opposite her, regarding her now with renewed amusement.

He'd healed her. No tricks involved, no smoke and mirrors. *Healed her* like some kind of miracle.

Crys had never been one to believe in the supernatural, but when she saw it with her own two eyes . . .

Was there another explanation? To admit that he might be a god . . . it was too much to wrap her head around in ten minutes or less. Ten *years* might not be enough time.

And there were so many questions that now bubbled up in her throat, when before she'd been stunned silent. This was a man who kept the location of his home a secret. She'd think the same sort of person—god, or *whatever*—wouldn't be one to simply stroll out in public.

"Why were you at the university that day?" she asked.

"Simply because I take classes there." When she raised her eyebrows at him, his smile widened. "Even immortals have healthy curiosities—not to mention many long days to fill. It was my pleasure to help you find your way to Dr. Vega's office."

"You already know him."

"Yes. And he knows me. Though I don't think he's aware that I'm a student in one of his classes. He doesn't pay much attention to his pupils."

Dr. Vega had accused Markus of murdering his father. But that wasn't exactly something she could blurt out right now. Still, the thought unsettled her deeply.

Would her father leave her alone in the company of a murderer?

"When you met with him, did he tell you what you wanted to know about the Bronze Codex?" Markus asked.

Crys froze.

He asked it as if it were a question, but his tone was more like a statement. He knew. Of course he knew. He seemed to know absolutely everything.

Could he hear her heart pounding now, as desperately as a trapped animal's?

He didn't wait for her to reply. "Dr. Vega is a paranoid and vain little man who is desperately in love with your aunt. I feel sorry for him sometimes, how seriously he takes everything."

"He . . . he seems to mean well."

"Yes, I'm sure he does." Markus's gaze remained steady on her. "I know Jackie Kendall has recently acquired the Codex. I also know that you and your mother are quite close with your aunt, despite the fact that her main residence is in England now. Do you know where the Codex is?"

Denying that Jackie got the book or saying she didn't know what he was talking about would be a waste of her breath, but at least she could answer with the absolute truth. "I have no idea where it is right now."

He pressed the tips of his fingers together. "The Codex was stolen from me a long time ago, but it is mine and I need it back, now more than ever before. It is filled with the magic I need to help protect this world from evil."

"You want to protect this world . . . with magic." Her father had left this part of Markus's mission out of their previous conversation.

"Yes." He paused, allowing his previous words to sink in. "If you really want to join my society, then you will do what I ask. Locate that Codex and return it to me."

She shook her head. "I'm sorry, but, like I said, I don't know where it is."

"Perhaps. But I believe that you—and possibly only you—can find it for me. I see in your eyes that you have the capacity and intelligence to understand how grave this matter is. You are very special, Ms. Hatcher. And I would be honored to welcome you into Hawkspear. If you agree to help me, if you stand by my side along with your father, you could make such a difference to the future of this world."

She bit her bottom lip and searched for a suitable response. Markus made her tongue-tied like no one else ever had.

He'd confirmed that the book was made of magic, just as Dr. Vega had theorized.

It was the Codex's otherworldly magic that had sent Becca into her strange coma. She'd known this deep down the whole time, but to have it confirmed by an immortal god himself . . .

"I know it's a lot to ask," Markus said gently. "I do. But promise me you'll try."

What could she say? *Let me think about it for a few days and I'll e-mail you?*

No.

"I'll try," she said quietly. "I promise I'll try."

She stood up, more than ready to leave this place, to escape into the fresh air where she could breathe and think.

"Thank you." Again, that smile managed to captivate her, leaving her head foggy and unclear, just as it had on the university grounds. He drew closer to her, taking both her hands in his. "I'll be in touch again very soon, Ms. Hatcher."

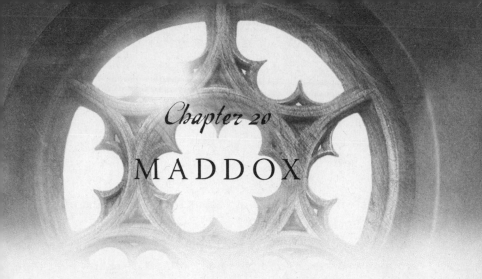

Chapter 20

MADDOX

Maddox, Barnabas, and Becca continued their journey to the witch's house. Maddox had been keeping a close eye on Becca ever since the events of the previous night, but she appeared to have fully recovered from the hungry spirit who'd nearly devoured her before his eyes.

"You keep looking at me," Becca said as they trudged across a wide, overgrown field covered in daisies. "I'm fine."

"Are you sure?" Maddox said.

"Positive."

"You were so brave."

"Yeah, right."

"You were," he insisted. "If something was to happen to you . . ."

"Maddox," Barnabas interrupted. "Leave the girl alone. You've inquired about her well-being at least a dozen times since breakfast."

Maddox glared at him. "You can't possibly understand our conversations from only hearing my side of them."

"I understand them well enough to wish for cotton to stuff in my ears."

"I'll find you something to stuff in your ears."

"What did you say?" Barnabas glanced over his shoulder with a conspiratorial grin.

"Nothing," he grumbled. "Are we nearly there?" They'd crossed through the field and now found themselves at the edges of a small village.

"We are indeed. Camilla lives somewhere around here."

"You don't know where?"

"No, not exactly." He paused and stroked his beard, turning around in a circle to survey the area. Cottages dotted the landscape before them, which led up a grassy hill. Two hundred paces ahead was the village center, where they could see a tavern and a busy market.

Becca and Maddox shared a look and continued to follow Barnabas as he randomly weaved through the village, peering in windows and knocking on doors.

Finally, a helpful passerby pointed him in the right direction.

Just in time, too. Maddox's feet were getting unbearably sore, and he was more than ready to rest. "So which cottage is hers?"

"We will know when we get there."

"What do you mean, we'll know when we get—" Maddox felt something tighten around his leg. A fierce yank pulled him up off his feet, and suddenly he was swinging from his ankles, viewing the world from upside down.

Barnabas, now also upside down, glanced up at the rope that had ensnared him. "We'll know because she's sure to have set traps for intruders. We're here!"

Becca regarded them both with lighthearted concern. "Wish I could help."

"Me too," Maddox replied as he swung on the rope.

A ring of fire then snaked around both Maddox and Barnabas, trapping them inside its ten-foot radius.

"Camilla, my darling!" Barnabas shouted. "It's just me, your devoted compatriot Barnabas, and a friend! Greetings to you! Please don't kill us!"

The flames rose higher, the oppressive heat pressing closer and closer.

"She means to cook us alive!" Maddox exclaimed.

But suddenly, the flames were extinguished, leaving a scorched, smoldering black ring around them.

Barnabas nodded. "Yes, that's much better."

"You've finally arrived!" a lovely, melodious voice called out from behind Maddox.

"Camilla, my beauty," Barnabas replied. "You are a sight for sore eyes. But, please, if you could release us from your ingenious trap, I'd be so appreciative. I'm afraid I've already lost all feeling in my right foot."

All Maddox could see as he continued to swing gently from the rope was a flash of blond hair, a few shades darker than Becca's, and then Barnabas, tumbling down from his snare. He got up quickly and brushed off his newly stolen clothes.

Camilla then went to Barnabas for an embrace. From this angle, facing her back, all Maddox could see was that she wore a purple cloak that hugged her curves.

"It's so wonderful to see you," she said, and then turned around to look at Maddox. "And who is your new friend?"

Maddox couldn't hold back a wince as the ugliest woman he'd ever seen swept her gaze over him.

Her hair was patchy and balding in the front, and she had no eyebrows to speak of. One bloodshot eye was set much lower than the other, and her chin sported a full beard of warts.

"This, Camilla, is Maddox Corso."

She inhaled sharply. "The witch boy."

"That's right," Barnabas said proudly.

"I'd really prefer a different nickname," Maddox said.

Camilla patted Maddox's cheek with her gnarled hand. "Shall we get you down from there, dearie?"

"I would be eternally grateful for that."

She held up a knife with an alarmingly large blade, but before he could utter a word of protest, she had hacked through the rope in a single swipe.

Maddox dropped to the ground like a sack of potatoes, then looked up to see Becca gazing down at him, her hands on her hips.

"Very graceful," she said with a grin.

"I do try."

"Excellent," Barnabas said, nodding. "Now, let's go inside and talk revolution."

Inside the witch's cottage, Barnabas placed the copper box on a wooden table.

Camilla shook her head in disbelief. "I can hardly believe you retrieved it."

"I can hardly believe it, either, to tell you the truth. It was difficult enough getting *into* that dungeon and locating young Maddox here, let alone getting *out* of it with all our limbs intact."

"I always knew you were a wily one, ever since you were a wee thing, Barnabas." She rubbed her hands together with glee. "That you stole it right from under her evil nose gives me such joy, so much I find I cannot express it. Finally, we have the chance to make Valoria pay for all the pain that she's caused."

"I hope you're right," he replied. "Now, remember, the lock is enchanted."

"I remember, of course. I was the one who told you!" She wiggled her fingers and leaned closer to the box. "Now let me just test exactly how enchanted this little box is. . . ."

She pressed her fingers against the lock and held them there. There was a sizzling sound, a sharp crack, and then Camilla fell over backward.

Maddox looked down at the witch, who was now unconscious on the floor of her cottage, as she began to snore. "My guess would be . . . *very* enchanted," he said.

"Yes." Barnabas crossed his arms. "Well, it seems we have a little time on our hands. I'm going to see if she has any wine."

After a short while, Camilla began to rouse, groaning as she opened her crooked eyes. "Oh my," she managed. "That was quite unpleasant. But I do have my answer. As soon as I regain my strength, I will be ready to break the spell that keeps this box and its treasure out of our reach."

"What do you think?" Becca asked. She sat cross-legged on the floor by the fire. "Are they going to tell you what's inside or keep you guessing forever?"

She was right—he was tired of being kept in the dark.

"What's in the box?" Maddox asked aloud to the room. "I believe I have a right to know, since I helped to steal it. Barnabas says it can pull someone from one world to another. Is that true?"

"You think I'd lie to you?" Barnabas pressed a hand to his chest as if stunned by this insult. Then he laughed. "Kidding, of course. I lie to everyone. But that was not a lie."

"He's told you nothing else?" Camilla asked, clearly surprised at how tight-lipped Barnabas had been.

"He's told me lots of things. I don't exactly know which of them to believe."

She glanced at Barnabas, who gave her a nod. "Feel free to educate the boy," he said. "Within reason."

Within reason? What was that supposed to mean?

Camilla gave the copper box a wary look and then placed her hand on the top of it. "The contents of this box once belonged to a sorceress named Eva. She was an immortal from a world apart from ours, the first immortal whose job it was to watch over this mortal realm. She possessed several specific tools to aid her in this task, and what rests in here is one of them. When Eva was murdered by fellow immortals, ones whom she once trusted but who betrayed her, these tools were scattered, and then stolen by thieves who wished to use their powers for their own gain. This box has remained locked away in Valoria's secret armarium ever since she seized the throne from King Thaddeus. She wishes to use it to gain access to another of Eva's tools, a golden dagger that she believes has fallen into yet another world. Sadly for Valoria, she doesn't possess the right kind of magic to achieve this goal, so for all these years, she has been searching for other solutions."

"The young witch Valoria believes is dead," Maddox said aloud, as the pieces of this puzzle, scattered up until now, began clicking together for him. He glanced at Barnabas. "She possesses the magic Valoria requires to get the dagger back."

Barnabas gave a shallow nod. "That is what the goddess believes."

"Come with me, young man. I have something to show you." Camilla directed Maddox out of her cottage to a garden surrounded by a tall stone fence. Barnabas and Becca followed closely behind.

In the garden was a tangle of weeds and wildflowers, a rickety wooden shed, and, dead center, a stone wheel as tall as Maddox.

"What is it?" he asked.

"A stone wheel," Camilla replied.

"I can see that. But what does it do? Why is it here?"

"Eva used wheels just like this, which she placed in strategic locations around Mytica. They are vessels that hold gateway magic. This magic can remain in the wheels for centuries because of the high density of the stone." She gave the wheel a hard knock as if to prove this. "We mean to use this wheel in the same way and create a gateway to send Valoria out of this world forever."

"Truth be told," Barnabas said, eyeing the wheel, "I thought it would be much bigger."

Maddox shook his head. "Wait. Even if you're able to create this gateway, how do you plan to get Valoria here, to your home? And then, on the off chance that you *could* get her here, how would you manage to then push her, a *goddess*, through a gateway to a . . . another world? It would be next to impossible."

"One thing at a time, my young friend," Barnabas said. "First we need to access the proper magic, and then . . . we'll figure out the rest."

A solid plan, Maddox thought, if an early and very painful death was the end goal.

Still, he considered everything he'd been told so far. If Barnabas and Camilla were right, if they could get the wheel magic to work without any help from the girl Valoria sought . . .

He turned to find Becca standing behind him, wringing her hands. Their eyes met and hers now shone with hope.

"Could this magic retrieve a spirit who has been displaced from her world?" Maddox asked Camilla, without turning his attention fully from Becca.

"What a strange question," Camilla replied, scratching her lower eye. "But I don't see why not."

"This is it," Becca whispered. "This is how you can help me get home again."

"It could be," he agreed.

"Now," Camilla said, "come back inside and let's have some soup. I made it fresh just before you arrived."

They went back inside for some soup that tasted like potatoes and dirt. Camilla cleared the dishes when they were done.

"I feel much better," she announced. "Let's try again."

Maddox watched tensely as Camilla focused again on the copper box. She posed with her hands on either side of it, as if trying to sense and harness its energy.

"I'd suggest she doesn't touch the lock this time," Becca said.

Maddox fought a smile.

"Ah, yes," Camilla gasped. "I feel it now. I must concentrate. Oh, here it goes. Here it is . . . yes, almost there. And"—she inhaled sharply—"and *done*."

The locked popped open.

Maddox's eyes widened. "You *are* a witch."

"And proud of it, young man." Camilla grinned. "Now, stand back. There could be another trap inside."

They backed away as Camilla slowly . . . very slowly . . . opened the lid. Maddox didn't know what to expect, but when nothing happened, and no one started to scream or run away, he let out a long sigh of relief.

"Oh, it's incredible," Camilla breathed. "I already feel its power, waiting to be unlocked next."

She reached into the copper box and pulled an object out.

Maddox cocked his head. "Huh. I expected something much shinier."

Camilla held in her hands a book. And not even a particularly spectacular-looking one, at that.

Becca staggered back at the sight of it, her hand flying to her mouth. Maddox looked at her, alarmed by her reaction.

"What's wrong?" he asked.

"That book . . ."

He glanced again at the brown leather-bound book, its cover emblazoned with a bronze hawk. "What about it?"

She looked stunned, as if completely petrified. Finally, she opened her mouth to speak.

"That's the book that sent me here."

Chapter 21

CRYSTAL

Her father drove her back to the Tim Hortons where he'd picked her up. As soon as he gave her permission to do so, Crys peeled the blindfold away from her eyes.

"You all right?" he asked. They'd been silent for nearly the entire ride.

"I will be." She rubbed her eyes, pulled her glasses out of her bag, and slid them back on. "You believe in Markus and his vision for the future, don't you?"

"Yes. Without any reservations, yes," he replied, those mirrored lenses still covering his eyes. "And now that you know all the things I could never tell you before, I know you're going to make the right choice."

Crys nodded and leaned forward to give him a quick hug. "Thanks, Dad."

He patted her back. "Now, go. Your mother will wonder where you've gotten to."

She got out of the car and watched him pull away. She stood there until he drove around a corner and his car disappeared from view.

Instead of going home or even heading to the hospital to check on Becca, Crys set out on a walk along Bloor Street. She needed time to think, to work everything out in her head.

Her entire world had shifted on its axis over the last week. So much of the information she'd learned was so far-fetched that it seemed impossible. She'd never been the type to read horoscopes, to get excited about visiting psychics, or to believe in the possibility that the rabbit hadn't been in the magician's hat all along.

This—this answer she'd received after meeting Markus herself—had been completely unexpected. What he'd shown her of his magic was real, and she couldn't deny it even if she wanted to.

She looked down at her healed index finger and rubbed it with her thumb.

An immortal god, she thought. *Did I really meet an immortal god today?*

She stopped at the intersection of Bay and Bloor, waiting for the light to turn green and the pedestrian sign to switch on. Then something caught her eye. A black limo, its back window rolling down so someone inside could flick out a cigarette butt.

The window was tinted and didn't roll down all the way, but it gave her enough of a view inside for her to see a face.

Farrell's face.

Her heart skipped a beat.

But then, in the split second before he rolled the window back up, she noticed that he wasn't alone. Someone was sitting next to him. Someone she recognized, but it took her a moment to place the face. And when she did, it made no sense to her.

It looked like the boy who'd tried to steal her bag.

Why would he be riding in a limo with Farrell? Her eyes must be playing tricks on her.

The light turned green, and the limo drove away.

She tossed and turned in bed all night as she wondered about Farrell, about her father and mother, about Markus.

The next morning, she went to the kitchen and sat down at the small table. The coffee had started to brew thanks to its automatic timer.

Soon, a bleary-eyed Julia Hatcher entered the room and headed straight for the coffee.

"Exactly what I need," she murmured, pouring herself a mug and adding cream and sugar. "Good morning. You're going to school today, I hope?" Crys just looked at her, her expression an exact translation of the concern she felt in her heart. "What's wrong?"

"I know, Mom."

Her mother sat down across from her and took a sip from the mug. "Know what?"

It was time to get it all out, come what may. She braced herself and took a breath.

"I know about the Hawkspear Society. I know that you and Jackie once belonged, too, along with Dad. And I know about the Bronze Codex."

Her face went pale. "And let me guess. Your father told you all this?"

"Some of it," she admitted. "But I learned the rest from Markus King."

Her mother shot up to her feet so fast her chair skittered backward. "That's impossible."

Now, that was a reaction that told her plenty. If Crys had received a bland *"That's nice, dear,"* she would have known that her mother was still doing her playing-dumb routine.

"Markus met with me. He invited me to his home."

Her mother shook her head. "I don't believe you."

"He's young and handsome. At least, he looks that way. He says he's an immortal god. Then he created fire from thin air and healed a cut on my hand like it was nothing, so, yeah, I think I believe him."

Her mother's eyes widened with every word she spoke. "Everything he says is a lie."

"So you and Jackie weren't part of Hawkspear? My great-grandfather wasn't the cofounder of Markus's society?"

Panic had crept onto her mother's face. "You have no idea what you're getting involved in, Crystal. You don't know what he really is, what he's capable of." She raked her hands through her hair. "No, this can't happen. I won't let you get hurt because of my choices. Everything I've done to protect you and Becca over the last fifteen years . . . and he still got to you."

She'd never seen her normally calm-and-collected mother so frenzied. Even on the night Crys mentioned seeing her father, her mother had left Becca's hospital room to clear her head before responding.

"I pursued this, Mom. Markus didn't get to me; *I* got to him."

"But your father introduced you, didn't he? Of course he did. There's no other way for you to get to him. All this time, I thought Daniel still had some good, some kernel of decency, inside of him. But I see now I was wrong."

"He only did what I asked him to do. I needed to talk to Markus. What was I supposed to do? You've been keeping the truth from me this entire time!"

This accusation received a sickened look. "Whatever he told you is not the whole truth."

Crys grabbed her mother by her upper arms. "Then tell me what is. Were you or weren't you a member of Hawkspear?"

Her frantic gaze finally met Crys's. "I was."

A breath caught in Crys's chest at the confirmation. "Why didn't you tell me that yourself?"

"Because the less I think about the society, the more in control of my life I feel. It's been fifteen years since Jackie and I walked away, Crys. Although sometimes it feels like just yesterday."

"Why did you leave?"

Her mother went quiet, her eyes shifting back and forth rapidly as if reliving the memory. "Because Markus is a murderer."

Crys inhaled sharply. "Dr. Vega told me that he thinks Markus killed his father."

Her mother's eyes widened. "You've been to see Dr. Vega, too? I'm seriously going to strangle Jackie when I see her. You remind me of your aunt so much sometimes. She's relentless, too."

"I'll take that as a compliment."

"Okay, Crys. You win." She cleared her throat nervously. "What do you want to know? There's so much to say, too much to tell quickly. My family history is a sordid one, one I prefer not to think about much if I can avoid it."

Crys sorted through the million questions that rose in her mind. She started with what seemed like the most perplexing. "Where did Markus come from?"

"All I know is one day, around sixty years ago, he just appeared out of nowhere, in the middle of my grandmother's bookshop. Here, Crys. In the very same building we're standing in right now. Everyone apparently thought my grandfather was crazy at the time, driven mad by the ghosts said to haunt this building. He was a vigilante who targeted men he thought were evil, and when Markus appeared, claiming to be a god of death, he felt justified in his actions."

Crys stayed silent, listening, her hand now pressed to her mouth as if to stop herself from gasping at everything her mother had said to fill in the blanks of Markus's story.

"My grandmother had become terrified of the husband she'd once loved more than anyone else in the world. And she was frightened of the man he called a god. For the first few days after his arrival, according to Grandma, Markus acted dazed and out of it. My grandfather looked after him. But he and Markus didn't notice that something else had arrived in the bookstore shortly after he did. A book. The Codex."

Crys pulled her hand from her mouth. "The Codex was sent here?"

She nodded. "Like magic. One moment it wasn't here, the next it was. Instead of handing it over to her husband and Markus, Grandma hid it. It remained hidden for years as the men began their society. Grandma became a member, too, not that she was given a choice, but says she never felt the same as all the others initiated—she always felt that something was wrong."

"Why didn't she leave?" Crys asked.

Her mother shook her head. "It's not that easy. But she knew Markus was not the guardian he claimed to be. That the more he used his magic at the meetings, the darker he became to her. Finally, after many years, she went to someone she trusted. Dr. Vega's father. She hoped he could help her understand the book and where it had come from. Markus had never mentioned anything about it before, and she wondered how they might be connected.

All she knew for sure was that the book needed to be kept a secret."

So that was how Dr. Vega's father learned about it. Crys's own great-grandmother had been the one who'd gone to him with the mysterious book. And that information had eventually led to his death because not all secrets could remain secrets forever.

A shiver sped down Crys's spine. "Dr. Vega wrote a paper on the Codex. He's the one who made it public after all those years of it being hidden."

"A very stupid move by a very smart man. If he hadn't done that, Markus might never have found out about it." She let out a shaky sigh. "But Uriah wanted so desperately to please his father—to make him proud. His intentions were not malicious—I know that now. At the time . . . it was all so confusing, Crystal."

Not much had changed in that regard. "Mom, Markus says the book is his. That the magic in it can help him save the world from evil."

If that was true, how could Markus be the bad guy her mother believed him to be?

Her mother stared at her. "Markus mentioned the book to you?"

Crys nodded, her heart pounding. "He knows Jackie found it."

Julia Hatcher's expression turned bleak. "So it seems we'll have to deal with him sooner than I thought we would."

Her voice held both fear and resolve.

Crys still needed more answers, and she couldn't let herself be distracted. "Mom, if Markus is evil like you say he is, why would Dad stay with him? Why wouldn't he be with us instead?"

Julia sat back down at the table. "When one is initiated into the society, Markus gives them a mark on their left forearm. They're given a second if they're accepted into Markus's trusted circle.

Markus carves the marks into their skin with a golden blade, and then he heals them with his magic. The first mark keeps his followers healthy, safe from any physical illness. It also ensures their loyalty to him and the society. The second mark improves their senses. They can literally see in the dark or hear whispers from across a room. The gift had its shortcomings, though, as we soon learned. Bright light becomes unbearable to the eyes and loud noises are deafening." She ran her fingers gently over her skin. "And the arm stays incredibly tender for a very long time."

Crys stared, speechless, at her mother's forearm, the flesh unblemished.

"The effect was always weaker for me than for Jackie and Daniel," she explained. "My senses, my loyalty, my health. I still got sick from time to time. I knew it hadn't worked as well for me, but something kept me silent. It became my horrible secret. When we finally left the society, your father fought against the urge to return for nearly thirteen years before he couldn't fight anymore. He was drawn back to Markus like a magnet because of the magic etched into his flesh. There are times when I also feel that pull . . . a little. But it has much less power over me than it does Daniel."

"What about Jackie? Does she feel the pull of loyalty?"

"No. She hates Markus."

"She thinks you can use the Codex to destroy him."

"She knows the more time he's in a world that's not his own, the weaker he becomes. He needs the Codex to renew his strength, his magic. Right now, he's vulnerable."

"How does she know all that?"

"Because Markus once told her himself."

"Seriously?" Crys's brow shot up. "He trusted her that much?"

Her mother drained her coffee and went to pour another cup.

"Mom?" Crys prompted. "How did Jackie get Markus to tell her something so personal?"

She took a deep breath as she returned to the table, clutching her coffee mug tightly between her hands. "Because . . . once, a long time ago, Jackie and Markus were madly in love."

Again, the breath left Crys's lungs. *"In love."*

Julia nodded. "They kept their relationship a secret, but he soon came to trust her more than anyone else. He told her secrets he'd never share with another, not even my grandfather. But then she learned of his crimes . . . and how he sought to control her, how he sought to control the Kendall line . . ."

"How?"

Her mother didn't speak right away. She took another sip of her coffee, as if it would give her the strength to continue. "When he learned that Grandma had kept the Codex away from him for all those years, Markus was furious. When she wouldn't reveal where she'd hidden it, he . . . he killed her. He killed a harmless old woman."

Crys stared at her, horrified. "Oh my God."

Her jaw tensed. "When my parents learned the truth, Markus had them killed, too, leaving us orphans when we were not much older than you and Becca. When my grandfather died soon after, of natural causes, he left his fortune and his mansion to Markus. Markus is the one who allowed us to keep the bookshop in our family out of the *goodness* of his cold, black heart. How could Jackie have continued to love a man like that?"

It was too much for Crys to even attempt to wrap her mind around. The very thought that this was the whole, actual truth made her sick to her stomach.

But she'd asked for this. She'd wanted her mother to open up, to trust her with the whole story. She couldn't turn back now. She needed to know everything.

"How did Jackie fight the mark?" she asked. "The way you describe it, it sounds like it's impossible. Was it the same for her as it was with you? Did it not affect her as much as the others?"

"No, it definitely affected her. She worshipped Markus, just as he, for a time, worshipped her. But one thing changed everything and made her marks null and void."

"What changed?"

Her mother drained the rest of her coffee, her knuckles white. "Jackie became pregnant with Markus's child."

"*What?*" The word came out as a barely audible gasp of shock.

She wouldn't meet Crys's gaze directly, instead staring down at her mug. "Along with her condition, her mind just cleared, as if it were a side effect of morning sickness—that is, when one is pregnant with the child of an immortal like Markus. Having that very special new life growing within her was all it took to make her marks null and void. It was at that time that she was able to see Markus as what he truly was. She convinced me we needed to get out while we still could. She had a horrible fight with Markus and he told her to leave, that he never wanted to see her again. Apparently, immortal gods can have their hearts broken."

"But Jackie doesn't have any children," Crys reasoned. *What happened to their baby?* she thought with a shiver. "Did she miscarry?"

"No, she didn't miscarry. And she didn't get an abortion. She had the child. But she knew that if Markus ever found out . . . that he'd take that very special child away to get his revenge on her, on us. The man is capable of anything, and Jackie feared for the child's safety, being half . . . Markus. Whatever Markus really is, past his lies and manipulations."

"So she gave the baby up for adoption."

Her mother hesitated. "Yes."

"This was fifteen years ago," Crys said when her mother fell silent again. "Some teenager out there doesn't realize that her father is an immortal god."

Her mother didn't say another word. Her jaw was clenched so tight that it looked painful, her gaze faraway and haunted.

Fifteen years old. With parents like Jackie and Markus, the child would be beautiful. Blond. With dark blue eyes. Someone who might be touched by magic.

Someone who might be affected by magical objects more than anyone else who came in contact with them.

Crys realized with a sinking feeling that she knew someone who fit that description exactly.

"No, it's impossible," she whispered. "You would have said something. You would have told her. Told *me*."

Her mother remained as still and silent as a statue.

"It—it's Becca." The name stuck in Crys's throat. "Isn't it?"

Julia began to tremble. "Jackie moved away to stay with friends in Alberta for the length of her pregnancy. When she gave birth, she . . . she named her Rebecca, after our grandmother. We knew we had to come up with a plan since her existence couldn't stay a secret. Adoption was the only solution, but Jackie refused—flat out refused—to give her away to strangers and never see her again. We also knew we needed to keep a close eye on this baby—in case the mix of human and . . . and Markus . . . created something bad."

"Becca isn't bad," Crys managed, every muscle in her body now tense.

"I know. But we didn't know that then. I—I told Daniel that I couldn't have any more children, but I wanted to adopt. At the time, he only wanted me to be happy, so he agreed. I handled all the details. He never knew the truth of her origins. I'd planned to tell Becca she was adopted when she turned eighteen." Her mother finally met her gaze with glossy eyes. A tear escaped and slipped down her cheek. "I'm sorry, Crys. I'm sorry you had to find out this way."

As Crys absorbed this stunning information, the world dimmed to the point that she could barely see anything. Blood pounded behind her eyes, in her ears.

"You're not lying, are you?" The words came out as a hoarse whisper. "About any of this."

"I wish I were, but I'm not. Now listen, Crystal. Listen very carefully. You can never tell anyone about this. Not even your father. *Especially* not your father." Her mother reached across the table to squeeze Crys's hands so tightly it hurt. She didn't pull away. "If I'd had any choice, I would have taken this secret to my grave."

Crys swallowed hard, fighting the tears that had been threatening to fall all morning. "So Becca's not my sister. She's . . . she's my cousin."

"No. Becca is your sister, and nothing will ever change that. Do you hear me? *Nothing*."

This shocking, crucial, and previously missing piece of information helped connect the rest of the dots for Crys. And in the wake of all this mind-blowing news, she couldn't help but let out a humorless laugh.

Her mother looked at her with alarm. "What could possibly be funny right now?"

"Only that . . . now I know I never should have opened that package from Jackie."

Julia sighed, looking exhausted. "No, you really shouldn't have."

As her mind began to clear a little, Crys felt like she needed a drink. A strong one. Coffee wouldn't do, but maybe another whiskey sour. . . .

Which made her think of something else, and someone else. "Mom, you don't happen to remember, back when you were a member, if the Graysons were a part of the society, do you? You know, the really rich guy who's always in the news? Edward Grayson and his family?"

She took no time at all to think about it. "Yes. Actually, they were among Hawkspear's most elite members. Why do you ask?"

Seeing Farrell and the mugger together in the limo earlier had been a huge mystery to her, one that had made her doubt her own eyes.

But now everything was beginning to make sense.

Chapter 22

FARRELL

It had been two days since he'd last seen Crys. Farrell had decided that, since she hadn't jumped on the chance to contact him again—despite the brilliant idea of sending her the camera—he had to take action.

He pushed open the door to the Speckled Muse Bookshop. There were several customers inside, a couple at the front register paying for their purchases—there Crys was, behind the register—and some browsing the shelves. The store smelled musty, like any old building might. But it also smelled of the paper, leather, and binding glue of the books. The wood of the shelves.

And . . . strawberries.

He'd developed a strong craving for strawberries over the last few days.

Farrell moved deeper into the surprisingly expansive shop. From the outside, it looked no bigger than a convenience store, but inside it went on and on. He paused in the mystery section and eyed the books so he'd appear to be an actual customer.

A black-and-white kitten peered out at him, seated on top of several Sue Grafton hardcovers.

"Hello there," he said. "Are you the speckled muse herself? Get it? 'Mews'?"

He reached forward to pet it, but the cat hissed at him and raked its claws over his hand, drawing blood.

"Stupid little—" He moved to grab the beast by its furry neck, but it scurried away before he could even touch it.

"Farrell?" Crys said from his right. "Is that you?"

He fixed a charming grin on his face and turned toward her, slipping his injured left hand into his pocket. "In the flesh."

"You're here. Wow. This is a surprise."

Today she wore faded jeans, very tight on her thighs and hips, which he liked, and a ridiculous T-shirt that had an excited-looking sugar cube saying YOU'RE SO HOT to a grinning cup of coffee.

She wore her white-blond hair in a braid and, apart from a coating of pink lip gloss, no makeup. Those pale blue eyes of hers watched him from behind her deeply unfashionable black-rimmed glasses.

"I think my phone must be broken," he said, casually leaning against the shelf and pulling the device from his jacket pocket. "I can't think of any other reason why I haven't heard from you yet."

"I should have called," she said, crossing her arms. "I'm sorry I didn't. I've been so busy. But I got your gift. Farrell, thank you—but it's way too generous. You didn't have to buy me anything. It wasn't your fault my camera got broken. I really can't accept—"

He held up a hand. "I'm going to stop you right there. I insist that you keep it. I don't take photos, not counting mental snapshots, so I have no use for it. Just do me a favor and keep it in your bag so you'll never miss an opportunity to take an important picture. Got it? No argument or I'm going to start pouting."

She let out a small, nervous laugh. "Wouldn't want to make you pout."

"You really wouldn't. It's very unattractive." *This is much better*, he thought. Again, he had her in the palm of his hand. "When do you close up?"

She glanced at her wristwatch. "At six."

His phone told him it was five forty-five. "I'm taking you out for dinner."

"Excuse me?"

"You know what dinner is, right? It's what people usually eat several hours after lunch, when they get hungry again."

A smile nudged at her lips, but she seemed to fight it. "I know what dinner is."

"You have to eat. And I just happen to be here, browsing through all these books and getting hungry. . . ."

"No graphic novels here, I'm afraid. I keep telling my mother to order some in."

So she remembered that little personal detail about him. *Nice.* "I can read books without pictures in them if I have to."

"Good to know."

She was playing hard to get today, but he did enjoy a challenge. He knew he could get every little secret detail of her life out into the open tonight.

"There's a sushi place just around the block if you'd like that," he said. "Or we could go for Italian if you'd prefer."

She bit her bottom lip. "Sushi's my favorite food."

He raised his eyebrows as if remotely surprised by this well-known fact about Crystal Hatcher. "Really? It's my favorite, too. See? I knew we had tons in common. This just proves it. Come on, close up the shop, and let's go."

Finally, she uncrossed her arms and his gaze again went to that silly T-shirt. The breasts beneath it, however, weren't silly at all. She had a much lusher body than the stick-thin Felicity did.

"All right," she finally said.

He felt it then. Victory awaited him, only a few pieces of sushi away.

"Grey Goose on the rocks," Farrell said after they'd been seated. Crys had only ordered a glass of water to go with their appetizer, and he'd decided he wouldn't put pressure on her to order a real drink.

Maybe later.

"We don't stock that brand," the waiter said.

Farrell blinked. "Excuse me?"

"We stock a variety of other vodkas, including Belvedere, but we don't have Grey Goose. Do you really care?"

"If I didn't, I wouldn't ask. I'm not willing to take a substitution."

The waiter shrugged. "Sorry, but I can't help you."

The shrug annoyed him deeply. It wasn't a matter of drinking another brand of vodka when his preference wasn't available. It had happened before, of course.

But Farrell wanted what he wanted.

Presently, it seemed vitally important to him to prove a point, here and now, to this apathetic waiter.

"Actually, you can help me." Farrell reached into his wallet and pulled out a hundred-dollar bill. "Go to the nearest liquor store, buy a bottle of Grey Goose for me, and keep the change."

The waiter frowned down at the bill. "I have six tables to look after. I can't just leave at the drop of a hat."

"I'm not asking you," Farrell growled, hot anger rising in his chest. "I'm *telling* you."

Wait. What was he doing? He glanced at Crys to see a look of growing alarm on her face.

His emotions had been unpredictable since he'd been given the mark. They ran either hot or cold. He'd have to keep a close eye on that.

He forced a laugh. "I'm joking, of course. Belvedere is perfectly fine. Thanks so much."

The waiter slipped away without another word.

"That was such a funny joke," Crys said drily. "You're a regular comedian."

"Sorry, I got a little carried away with the act," he lied. "Too bad he didn't want to play along, it would have been a lot more fun."

The waiter returned soon with their drinks and the vegetable tempura appetizer they'd ordered.

"Sorry about that," Farrell said, pressing the C-note into his hand. "No hard feelings?"

"None at all." The waiter nodded, finally losing the peeved expression as he turned back to the kitchen.

Farrell raised his glass. "We should toast to something."

"Like what?" Crys asked.

"The start of an amazing new friendship."

She clinked her glass against his. "Do you befriend all the random girls you meet on the street?"

"Only the ones who help me tackle muggers." He took a sip from his glass and tried not to let the fact that he hadn't gotten his way continue to bother him.

"You get in a lot of fights?" she asked.

"No, I'm very peaceful. Zen-like, actually."

"Really? Have to say, I did a little online search for you last night, and I happened upon a very interesting video of you pounding the crap out of a drug dealer."

Oh, right. That.

How should I handle this? he thought. "Well, I'm Zen-like unless you mess with my family. That guy gave my kid brother cocaine. That's not okay. I may have lost control, but I swear my heart was in the right place. I'm sure you'd want to protect your sister at any cost, right?"

He heard the clink of her ice cubes in her glass when she took a sip. He could also hear her heartbeat—fast and fluttering. She put on an air of calm, but underneath that T-shirt she was nervous about being out with him. Or maybe she was excited.

Either way, her biology proved that he had a definite effect on her.

"Of course I would," she finally replied. "My sister means more to me than anyone."

"Right. I don't want my brother to walk the same path I've walked," he said, wanting to impart a bit of personal wisdom to draw her even closer to him. "I've made mistakes, I'll admit it, and my older brother tried to look out for me. I always gave him a hard time. But Adam, he's more innocent than Connor and me. I can't explain it. Despite the family he's in, he's so naive to the evils that lurk behind every corner. I know I have to be there to save him, even if he doesn't want to be saved."

"I totally understand."

He watched her carefully as she bit her lip and reached for a tempura-battered asparagus, sliding it through some ponzu sauce, before bringing it to her mouth.

Who knew fried asparagus could be so sexy?

Farrell drank the rest of his vodka and signaled for another.

It arrived with the rest of their meal: a salmon roll, seared scallop nigiri, and sea urchin sashimi. Crys busied herself with unwrapping her chopsticks and mixing a concoction of soy sauce and wasabi into a thin greenish paste. He did the same before he ate a piece of the salmon roll with mock enthusiasm.

He hated sushi.

"We were talking about magic the other night," he said.

"We were."

"Such an interesting subject, isn't it? I'd love to know more about your personal experiences with it."

She traced her finger along the edge of her square-shaped plate. "Have you ever heard of Obsidia?"

He blinked. "Obsidia?"

"Apparently, it's a magic language."

"Can't say I have."

She continued on eating and chatting as if they were having a normal dinner conversation, but Farrell leaned in with perked-up ears, regarding her with increased interest.

She'd finally said something important.

Something Markus would want to know. Perhaps this was why he'd been concerned about this girl who was, otherwise, as ordinary as they came.

Satisfaction swelled within him. It wouldn't be long before he'd earn his third mark.

"This language is found only one place on record," she continued.

"Oh yeah? Where's that?"

"In a very special book," she said without more than a moment's hesitation. "If you know how to read the language, it sounds like you'd be able to channel the magic from the book to use however you like."

"That is fascinating." He was entranced now with every word she spoke.

"Fascinating?" she repeated. "I suppose. But it sounds scary, too. All that power up for grabs, and this book is just out there somewhere, waiting to be used. Who knows what kind of monster could get their hands on it?"

He'd never heard of Obsidia before, but it sounded like something Markus would be incredibly interested in.

Farrell reached across the table and took her hand in his. He met her gaze and held on to it. "Don't be scared," he told her. "This book does sound dangerous, but don't give it another thought, okay? I swear, just like with my brother, I would protect you from anything that tries to hurt you."

She smiled. "Really?"

"Really."

Damn, he was good. This kind of talk would have most girls on his lap by now. She didn't pull away from him, so he kept going, not wanting to miss this opportunity to draw her even closer and gain every last shred of her trust.

He slid his thumb over her hand. Her short nails were painted bright purple and she wore a silver ring with a rose on it. "That's a beautiful ring," he said.

She glanced down at it. "My sister and I exchanged rose jewelry a few years ago. One of our favorite books has a girl named Rose in it. Princess Rose. She saved her own kingdom, by herself, without any help from knights in shining armor."

"Sounds like a good book." *Or a piece of feminist trash.* He continued to caress her hand, turning it over so he could trace the lines on her palm. He smiled inwardly when she drew in a shaky breath.

You are so easy to manipulate, Crystal Hatcher.

"I have to admit something," he said. "And this might change things between us."

She hesitated, then answered softly. "What?"

"When I said I wanted to be platonic friends with you . . ."

"Yes?"

"That was actually a pretty shameless lie. There's something about you, Crys. You're so different from the others girls I meet. You . . . you *do* something to me. Of course, I want you to want to be my friend, but I don't think I want you to be my *platonic* friend."

Cue the blonde melting into a romantic puddle in three, two, one. . . .

"Farrell . . . you're different from any guy I've ever known, too." She slid her hand against his, her fingernails lightly tracing his skin. A shiver went through him. The unpleasant scent of their dinner faded away, leaving only the sweetness of strawberries.

The din of the restaurant grew fainter as their body language officially entered into the realm of public displays of affection. He allowed her to trace her fingers up his arm and watched as she bit her lush bottom lip. And now his own heartbeat was speeding up.

He wanted her.

One night with her would likely get her out of his system, after she'd given him—and thus Markus, too—every last piece of information about this magic book. Then he was sure he'd be fine never seeing her again.

Those fingers were doing things to his arm that made it hard to concentrate on the task at hand. And those lips . . . he wanted to explore them for hours.

"I saw you yesterday," she said, her voice smoky and throaty.

"Yeah? Where?"

"Bay and Bloor. You were in your limo, stopped at a light, and you lowered your window." She continued to caress him, driving him slowly mad with desire. "So strange, though. I could have sworn you were in there with the guy who mugged me."

He stopped breathing.

Then he swore inwardly. In a city this large, and with his ultratinted windows, he never would have expected her to randomly spot him out with Lucas. Mustering all the composure he could, he gave a lighthearted little laugh. "That's crazy. You must have been seeing things."

"That's possible," she allowed. "Or maybe I *did* see you two together. Is he in the Hawkspear Society, too? Is that how you know each other?"

He didn't pull his hand back from hers. He didn't give her any clue that she'd just blindsided him. "What? I don't know what you're talking about. The . . . *what* society?"

"It's funny, everything I've learned over the last week. So much of it makes my head spin. But some facts . . . they're as clear as day. I can't ignore them even if I wanted to."

"Wish I could say what you're talking about was as clear as day to me."

"Apparently, everyone in the society has a mark to show they're committed to the leader's cause." She traced a slow circle on his forearm. "Right here. I've been told that, after you receive it, the spot is tender for a long time."

She clamped her hand down and squeezed, hard.

Pain tore through his arm. He clenched his teeth and tried not to react to it.

"Oops. Did that hurt?" she asked.

"Not at all," he managed.

"Right." Crys smiled. It was, hands down, the most unpleasant smile he'd ever received. "I'm not stupid, Farrell. Everything you've said, it's all been lies to get closer to me, so I'll give up something you need. Otherwise, you wouldn't give the smallest damn about getting to know someone like me. Markus told you to do this, right? Find out Crys Hatcher's secrets and report back?"

"Oh, sweetheart." He finally withdrew his arm from her grasp and fixed a steady smirk on his face. There was no sense in trying to deny this. She knew the truth. "Don't lie. You were all over me—all over the *idea* of me. But, yeah, you're right. I'm way out of your league. Sorry to disappoint you."

She winced, a very small one, but he caught it.

"Thanks for clearing that up," she said tightly.

"My pleasure."

"Can you do me a couple of favors, Farrell?" she asked.

"Depends what they are."

"Tell Markus that if he's going to send spies after me, he should send smarter ones."

Charming. "I'll think about it. And the second favor?"

Crys stood up, took a final sip from her glass of ice water, and then poured the rest onto his lap. "Go to hell."

She left him sitting there, his pants soaked and his cover blown. In another life, he would have found this absolutely hilarious.

Tonight, he didn't. His mind darkened at the edges, his thoughts becoming sharp as knives, as he watched her walk past the window, heading back to her little bookshop.

Chapter 23

MADDOX

This book—the book that belonged to an immortal sorceress—was the same book that had sent Becca's spirit here from her world.

"But how could it be *here*?" he asked her under his breath. "If it's already, um, *there*? It can't be in two places at the same time."

Becca drew closer to it, looking past Camilla's shoulder as the witch flipped through the pages of strange gold and black writing and detailed illustrations of animals, trees, flowers, and landscapes.

"I'm sure of it," Becca said. "Unless this is an identical copy." Doubt began to cloud her expression.

"Camilla, is there more than one book like this?" he asked.

"I highly doubt it, but I suppose . . . there is a slight chance a forgery could have been made, to throw off any potential thieves." She shook her head. "But this is the original. I swear, I feel the hum of its magic, like I'm pressing my hands against a beehive."

But it did sound as if there could possibly be a duplicate somewhere. There had to be a reasonable explanation for what Becca had experienced.

"Look, here's a rendering of the stone wheel." Camilla ran a long, sharp fingernail over an extremely accurate illustration of the wheel in her garden.

"The language . . ." Becca studied the book warily as if it might jump up and bite her. "Can you read it?"

"No." Maddox peered down at the strange words. "What language is this, Camilla? I don't recognize it."

"It's the language of the immortals, of course."

Well, of course.

Barnabas had stayed surprisingly quiet, watching Maddox and the witch, his arms crossed. "Quite a day," he said. "We're alive, we're free, and we finally have the means to destroy Valoria once and for all. I suggest we celebrate."

"I don't know," Maddox said. "We've been traveling on foot for days. I, for one, am incredibly tired and—"

"Now, don't you go and spoil the fun." Camilla slapped his shoulder lightly. "I side with Barnabas on this. To the tavern we go!"

The tavern was called the Battering Ram and was filled to the rafters with villagers, drinking and socializing. The excuse for this particular gathering was meant to be a continuation of the festival celebrating Valoria's reign, but in these revelers' hearts it was anything but. Valoria had recently made a decree that would ban the selling of inebriants and outlaw public drunkenness within the year.

"Here you go." Barnabas slid a gigantic tankard of ale along the table toward Maddox, where he sat at the long wooden bench they'd managed to wedge themselves into, shoulder-to-shoulder with the other patrons. Two women and a man were at the other end of the table, on top of it, dancing to the loud band that played a familiar song about immortals and magic.

Maddox knew the words to this song very well. His mother used to sing it often.

We'll live forever, side by side
We'll stay together, 'neath starry skies
Tonight and always, destiny guides us
Tonight and always, magic binds us

Maddox took a sip of ale—his first. Livius had rarely ever drunk anything stronger than cider, and he'd never allowed Maddox to touch a drop.

"You like?" Camilla asked, grinning lasciviously, showing off her broken teeth.

"It's good," he had to admit.

"Drink up, sweetie," she said as she tipped back her own mug of frothy ale, finishing it in one go. Then she let out a giant and rather impressive belch.

A cry came from across the room. "I recognize that sound!" called out a woman who swiftly approached their group, golden-haired and lovely from head to toe.

"My darling sister!" Camilla rose to her feet and held out her arms. "You've returned to me at long last!"

Sister? Maddox exchanged a surprised glance with Becca.

"You are a sight for sore eyes!" the beautiful woman exclaimed as the two embraced.

Barnabas's posture had improved from his relaxed slouch to a more dignified and formal display. "Sienna, what an absolute pleasure to see you again."

Becca leaned toward Maddox. "Is it just me, or is he practically drooling over her?"

"Can you blame him?" Maddox said under his breath as he drank more of his ale. "She's absolutely stunning."

She bit her bottom lip. "I guess. If you like that type. But she's kind of old. She's got to be at least thirty, right?"

He frowned. He'd never heard any hint of such poison in Becca's tone before now.

"Maddox, this is my younger sister, Sienna," Camilla said. "A sister who has neglected to write to me for far too long as she's traveled to lands far across the sea. I have missed you so much!"

Sienna put her arm around Camilla's shoulders. "I'm back now and plan to stay indefinitely."

"More reason for us to celebrate." Camilla signaled to the barkeep to bring another round.

By his third tankard, Maddox had changed his mind about not wanting to join in on impromptu celebrations in taverns. He now found himself up on the table, dancing with the beautiful Sienna, who clasped his hands and spun him around in circles until he became dizzy. Life was marvelous. And wondrous. And all kinds of sparkly.

"Is this your first time drinking ale?" Sienna asked.

"Oh no. I've had it many, many, many times. This is nothing," he slurred. "It's simply wonderful that you've come back to be with your sister. Are you a witch, too?"

Sienna laughed as she covered his mouth with her hand to keep him from saying anything else. "Not so loud, all right? This place is full of joy tonight, but we never know where Valoria's guards might be lurking. They don't react well to those of us who may be touched with magic."

"*I'm* touched with magic." He pressed his hand to his chest. "*Very* touched."

"Are you, now?"

"They call me the witch boy." As he repeated it, the nickname sounded far more impressive than usual.

She pulled back a little to look at him more closely. "So you're the one I've been hearing about, are you? The boy who can summon spirits."

"I brought one here with me tonight," he said, gesturing toward Becca with his mug. Ale splashed over the side of it and hit Barnabas in the face.

"Hey!" Barnabas sputtered, wiping his eye.

Maddox laughed. "Apologies!" Then he shifted his gaze to Becca, who sat on a wooden bench across the tavern, glaring up at him. Her arms were crossed and her expression . . .

Oh dear.

He jumped down from the table. "I'll be back soon, Sienna."

"Take your time, sweetling," she replied with a grin.

She called him *sweetling*!

He made his way through the crowd toward Becca. "You look deeply unhappy," he told her when he reached her side.

"Do I?"

"What's wrong?"

"Nothing. I'm just sitting here, invisible and incorporeal. Waiting. My sister and mother are probably only desperately worried about me, while you're all here celebrating the fact that you managed to open a locked box. So, no. Not unhappy. Just impatient. With *you*."

She said *you* so sharply it was as if it were a dagger she'd decided to poke him with.

But instead of making him feel bad, it raised his ire. "I know you're in a gigantic rush to leave this kingdom you despise so much, but it'll have to wait until tomorrow."

"Oh really?"

"Yes . . . really. Besides, have you considered for one moment that the thought of saying farewell to you might be painful for me? That having you here as a spirit I can never touch is preferable to me than not having you here at all, even though the thought of kissing you—really *kissing* you, the real, solid you—is all I can think about?"

Her eyes widened. "Maddox . . ."

It was a great relief to have gotten the truth out, but the aftermath made him feel raw and exposed and deeply foolish. "Please forgive my drunken behavior."

He staggered away from her without another word.

The tavern swirled around him—the laughter, the chatter, the music, and the dancing. Everyone seemed happy and joyous.

Yet Maddox now descended into pure misery.

He liked Becca so much, had gotten so attached to her in such a short time, it felt as if his heart might ignite inside his chest.

And if everything went perfectly, he would soon lose her forever.

When they got back to the cottage, Maddox excused himself so he could rush outside and be sick. When he was done wiping his mouth, he noticed he had an audience.

"Better up than down," Barnabas said, nodding sympathetically.

"I didn't ask for your opinion."

"What? I'm here to help you through. It'll take you a while until you're able to handle your drink. But it'll happen."

Maddox pressed up against the stone exterior of Camilla's cottage, then slid down to the ground and rested his head in his hands.

"Oh my," Barnabas said. "You're in terrible shape, aren't you?"

"The worst."

"It's not just the ale. It's the girl, too. Am I correct?"

Maddox rubbed his eyes. "Have you ever been in love, Barnabas?"

Barnabas paused, as if in solemn thought. "Is that what this is with the spirit girl?"

"I don't know what it is. I'm just asking you a question."

That pained shadow he'd seen yesterday crossed Barnabas's expression again.

"Yes, I've been in love. I know how it feels. That all-consuming sensation like nothing you've ever experienced before. The terrifying knowledge that you would live and die for this girl, if only she'd give you the chance."

"Who was she, this girl you loved?"

Barnabas turned his faraway gaze to Maddox and finally smiled again. "We should get you back inside, my young friend. There's a warm cot with your name on it in the back room. You can sleep this off."

It seemed Barnabas didn't want to talk about such private things, which was probably for the best. Maddox knew he'd likely be lying anyway.

"Sleep sounds good," Maddox agreed.

"It certainly does."

It was well past dawn when Maddox finally woke. Opening his eyes, he felt as if someone had placed a thousand-pound weight upon his head while he slept.

"Ughh," he moaned as he pushed up from the cot.

"I bet you have a hell of a hangover this morning," Becca said. She stood by the wall, her arms crossed over her chest.

"I wasn't hanging over anything, was I? Were you"—he hesitated—"watching me sleep?"

"Um." Her cheeks reddened. "More like waiting for you to wake up."

"Is everyone else awake?"

She nodded. "They've been up for hours."

Maddox rubbed his forehead, trying to will the crushing pain away. He peered at Becca through his fingers. "My deepest apologizes for my behavior last night."

"No apology necessary." She searched his face in silence before turning away. "I'll leave you to get dressed."

When she left, he forced himself to get up and get dressed, and reflected on all the idiotic things he'd said to Becca last night. At least, all the idiotic things he could remember. With one last groan, he left his little room to join the others.

Camilla tossed him a roasted chicken leg as he passed through the main room of the cottage. "Get something in that stomach of yours."

Barnabas sat at the table, inspecting the book.

"Are we planning to test the book's magic this morning?" Maddox asked.

"Yes, we certainly are," Barnabas replied.

Sienna entered the room, smiled at them all, then turned to warm her hands by the fire. "Good morning, sister. Good morning, Barnabas, Maddox. A lovely day, isn't it?"

Barnabas closed the book. "Not nearly as lovely as you are, Sienna."

"My, you're a charmer, aren't you?" said Sienna.

"I certainly try."

There was a knock at the door.

"Who could that be?" Camilla asked, frowning and scratching her wart-covered chin. "I'm not expecting anyone."

"Perhaps you aren't," Sienna said. "But I am. Seems they've arrived earlier than I expected. They must have taken very swift horses."

"Who's that?"

"Some friends of mine who are interested in what your friends stole from the goddess."

"What?" Camilla exclaimed. "What are you talking about?"

Sienna closed the distance between them, showing a flash of silver in her grip, and Camilla gasped as Sienna sank her sharp dagger into her soft belly.

"Did you really think you could steal from Her Radiance and get to live another day?" Sienna hissed as she let her sister fall to the floor in a heap.

Maddox watched in silent shock. He met Becca's stunned gaze with wide eyes.

"Maddox," Barnabas yelled. "Run!"

The wooden door split and crashed inward as Valoria's guards poured into the cottage.

Maddox tried to summon his magic, but he was too flustered, and too ill and weakened by all the ale he'd consumed last night.

"That one." Sienna pointed at Maddox, her expression now void of any kindness. "Valoria will need him when she arrives."

The heavy weight of a sword hilt struck the side of Maddox's head, and darkness once again filled his world.

Chapter 24

CRYSTAL

Crys visited Becca Saturday morning. It was just the two of them, and Crys sat in the chair and studied her sister's face.

She's not my sister, she reminded herself. *She's the daughter of an immortal murderer.*

Crys tried to see her differently, tried to feel less of a bond with her. Maybe that would make everything easier.

But it didn't work. No matter how hard she tried, she couldn't see Becca as anything except her kid sister.

And she knew in her heart she never would.

She'd been up most of the night, racked with all kinds of thoughts after her dinner with Farrell the previous evening. She hadn't actually meant to admit she knew his secret so soon.

He'd confirmed her worst suspicions. The guy she'd originally met, the guy she'd actually *liked,* hadn't been real. The one from last night, *that* was the real Farrell Grayson. A smug, overconfident, overprivileged creep who was a part of a horrible organization responsible for evil acts.

Did he know the whole truth about Markus? Or was he just another clueless minion?

Crys didn't care either way. She never wanted to see him again.

When she got back to the shop, she considered confiding in her mother about what had happened last night with Farrell, but before she could say a word, her mother immediately grabbed her purse and jacket.

"Can you close up the shop tonight?" she asked.

"Where are you going? Out to visit Becca?"

"No." Julia hesitated at the doorway.

"Mom," Crys said pointedly. "No more secrets between us, remember?"

She sighed and turned to face her daughter. "No more secrets," she agreed.

"So? Spill."

"I need go to the airport and pick up your aunt."

Crys gasped. "Jackie's here?"

"Almost here. She managed to get a flight out of London this morning. Her plane lands in an hour. She wants to see Dr. Vega immediately, but I haven't been able to get him on the phone to set up a meeting. We'll stop by his office on our way back, and hopefully he'll still be there." She reached for the doorknob. "I'll call when I have Jackie in the car, and we'll let you know when to expect us."

"What if someone follows you?" Julia didn't know that Markus had put Farrell on her trail, and it was entirely possible she was being watched as well.

"Trust me, in the last fifteen years I've learned how to get around without being detected."

"You'll have to teach me that."

"Maybe someday." She squeezed Crys's hand. "I'll see you soon."

Crys locked the door after she left, turned the sign to CLOSED, and searched the bookshop until she found Charlie. She took him up to the apartment, where she gave him half a can of tuna, then made a sandwich with the other half.

He gobbled the fish up in record time, then squeaked out a happy *mew*.

"You're welcome." She leaned over to scratch his head. "So, what do we do now?"

He brushed against her leg, his tail twitching.

"You're right. If I stay here with all this time to think, I'm going to go completely crazy. I need to do something. But what?"

Charlie padded out of the kitchen and jumped up on the carpet-covered climber she'd recently bought for him.

"You're no help at all," Crys said.

A half hour went by before she got so impatient that she decided to head to the university campus. She decided she'd wait in Dr. Vega's office for her mother and Jackie to arrive.

She grabbed her keys and her bag, then eyed the Canon she'd left on her bedside table.

"What can I say?" she mumbled. "It's a great camera."

She tucked it in her bag.

On the way to the campus, she tried it out for the first time, confirming that digital had one very important and helpful advantage over film: She could instantly review the photos she took on the view screen.

However, this convenience would also take some of the fun out of photography for her, robbing her of the surprise that came with seeing what showed up on film when she finally developed it days or weeks later.

When Crys arrived at the campus and began navigating her way along the sidewalks toward her destination, she kept an eye open for anyone who might be spying on her, but came up with nothing. But that didn't mean Markus wasn't around. He could be here today, attending one of his classes.

Unless that, too, had been a lie.

She entered the Anthropology Building and headed up to Dr. Vega's office, only to find an unlocked door and an empty room.

"Can I help you?" another frazzled-looking professor came up from behind and asked, frowning so deeply it looked painful.

"I'm looking for Dr. Vega. Is he here today?"

"No, he's not here. I'm afraid he was taken to the emergency room earlier this afternoon."

She stared at him. "What? What happened?"

"He was mugged and beaten very badly."

Her grip tightened on the strap of her bag. "Where is he?"

"Mount Sinai Hospital. It's not far from here."

She'd already started for the exit. "I know exactly where it is."

Dr. Vega was in the same hospital as Becca.

It took Crys a while to find Dr. Vega's room, and then she had to lie and say he was her father in order to see him.

Luckily, the nurse believed her.

She slowly pushed open the door to find a beaten, bloody man lying in a hospital bed, his eyelids swollen and open only a fraction, but enough to know he was awake.

"Miss Hatcher," he managed to say, his voice hoarse and raw. "I'm so sorry about all this."

"Sorry?" She was at his side in a second, wincing at the sight of the tubes attached to his arms and nose. "For what?"

"I'm such a fool, such a weak, pathetic fool. They've been

watching me, all this time. I've prided myself on my paranoia, feeling it's kept me safe all this time. But they were waiting. Until I had what they needed. I've betrayed you. And I've betrayed your aunt. I only wish I could have been stronger."

"The Hawkspear Society. They did this, didn't they?"

He nodded, then grimaced as if the small movement had caused him great pain. "I tried not to tell them anything beyond what I already revealed in my paper, but they applied some duress, as you can see."

Her stomach lurched. "What did you tell them?"

"The Codex . . . you told me you'd seen it. . . ."

Crys went cold inside. She'd told Markus that she didn't know where it was. "What else?"

"That your sister touched it, and that it sent her into a mysterious coma."

"Damn it." Markus now had all the information he needed to get the book and severely hurt her family in the process.

"I should have let them kill me."

"No," she said fiercely. "Don't say that. You did what you did because they gave you no other choice. Jackie will understand."

"She'll never speak to me again." His eyes filled with tears. "All our work, the amount she's struggled these last several years, all for nothing."

"It's not for nothing. When did this happen?"

"I was on my lunch break. Open-faced roast beef sandwich, gravy, salad. Tea with lemon." He exhaled shakily. "I hadn't taken even my first bite when they arrived."

Part of her wanted to be angry with him, but looking at him now, so baffled and helpless, she wasn't. Markus's minions had tortured the information out of him.

"For your sister to have this reaction to the Codex," he managed, "it means that she must be very important and very special."

"You're right. She definitely is."

After a solemn goodbye, Crys left his room, promising to come back and check on him later.

She went to Becca's floor, her steps quickening as she approached the room and pushed open the door.

Becca's bed was empty.

She turned and grabbed the first nurse who passed by. "Where's my sister? Where's Becca Hatcher?"

The nurse frowned, then grabbed the clipboard on the door, scanning it. "It doesn't say she was moved. . . ."

"She's not here, so she must have been moved somewhere. Where was she moved?"

Confusion crossed the nurse's expression. "I . . . don't know. There must have been a mistake somewhere. I'll look into it immediately."

Crys's phone began to ring. She pulled it out of her bag and looked down at the screen.

DAD

"Crys." He cut her off when she answered. "I know you're at the hospital."

Her legs weakened, and she went to sit down on a nearby chair. "What's going on?"

"Markus was ready to be exceedingly patient with you. . . ."

"Dad—"

"But he knows you lied to him. You've seen the Codex, haven't you?"

There was no point in denying it now. "Okay, yeah. I have. But I didn't lie to him. I really don't know where it is."

"I've been asked to tell you to go get it and return to the bookshop. Someone will pick you up there in an hour."

"Dad, aren't you listening to me? *I don't know where it is.*"

"Yes, I am listening. And now you will listen to me." There was no emotion in her father's cold voice, which had turned her blood to ice. "You brought this on yourself. I don't know what your mother has told you, but she's a liar. She's manipulating you."

"Where is Becca?" she bit out, then raised her voice. "Where is she?"

"She's with us."

Crys went utterly still. "With you? You mean, with you and Markus? What the hell, Dad? Why are you being like this? Is . . . is she okay?"

"She's fine."

"I thought you loved me. I thought you wanted the best for me and for Becca." Her voice broke.

"I do. That's all I've ever wanted." He paused, but only for one tense moment before he spoke again. "An hour. Be ready, have the Codex in hand, and all this will turn out perfectly fine."

Before she could remind him, yet again, that she truly had no idea where it was, he hung up.

Crys stared at her phone, then yelled an obscenity at it so loudly that the nurses and patients in the hallway looked at her with alarm.

Hands shaking, she scrolled through her contacts and called her mother as she headed out of the hospital.

It went directly to voice mail.

"Markus knows that we have the Codex, and he knows what it did to Becca. They took her from the hospital, and now Dad says I need to hand the Codex over. If I don't, I don't know what's going to happen. . . ." Her chest was so tight it was nearly impossible to breathe. "Call me as soon as you get this. I don't know what to do."

She hung up and immediately tried Jackie's phone, which also went to voice mail. She left Jackie a similar message.

Who else could help her? She thumbed through the other names in her phone until she came to one that made her pause.

F. GRAY

She stared at it, her heart thundering in her chest.

DELETE

Crys ran the rest of the way home and started searching.

"Damn it, Mom, why didn't you tell me where you put it?" She had a half hour left to find it—that was it.

She checked under beds and in closets as she sped through the apartment as fast as she could. She even checked inside the oven, since her mother rarely ever used it for cooking. It would make a great hiding spot.

But, like everything else, it turned up empty. Where was it? She didn't even know if it was still in the building. It could be anywhere—a safe-deposit box, buried in the ground, hidden in the hollow of a tree trunk.

No. Her mother was practical and would want to keep it close, just in case.

And where better to hide a book than in a bookshop?

Crys ran down the spiral staircase to the Speckled Muse, nearly twisting her ankle in her rush.

"Come on, *think*. Where would she put it?" Crys turned around in a circle, trying to get inspired. Trying to think like her mother.

She scanned the shelves as she walked up and down the aisles, searching for that plain brown leather spine, but the shop had thousands of titles and the shelves seemed to be more endless than usual. There was no way she could search the entire place in a handful of minutes.

Crys ended up in the children's nook, yanking books off the shelves, searching for hidden compartments she might not have noticed before.

Nothing.

She had only five minutes until her mystery ride showed up.

She wasn't going to find it. Neither her mother nor Jackie had replied to her messages with a miraculous solution to save the day. She was on her own with no clue what to do.

Hot tears of frustration slid down her cheeks before the dam broke and loud, wracking sobs escaped from her. She couldn't hold it in anymore; it was all too much. The pressure of the truth, and all the lies and deception, all the fear and uncertainty she'd encountered on the way to discovering it: It all finally crashed down on her with the weight of a collapsing building.

This was all her fault.

She dropped to the ground, surrounded by all the fallen books—books she'd read when she was younger, when she'd loved the written word and the escape it offered. She ran her hand over a fantasy novel that had been one of Becca's favorites.

"I'm sorry," she whispered, then pulled her legs to her chest and lay there, her cheeks wet, her heart aching. "I wanted to help you, but I failed."

Charlie entered the nook, now at eye level with her. He came closer, and, as if sensing her distress, he nuzzled his face against the top of her head.

"What do I do, Charlie? Please tell me what to do."

He pranced over to an empty bottom bookshelf, where he curled up in a ball and went to sleep.

"Helpful, thanks," she whispered.

Crys kept her eyes on the kitten until her gaze drifted a couple of inches away. From her supine position, she could see a gap between the shelf and the floor.

And that something had been tucked into that small space.

Her chest tightened. "No way."

She crawled over to the gap, pushing the fallen books out of the way, and reached under the shelf to pull out the hidden object.

It was the Bronze Codex.

A black limousine arrived right on schedule. Crys slung her fuchsia bag over her shoulder, clutched the Codex to her chest, and left the store.

The chauffeur wore an unreadable expression as he came around to the back to open up the door for her. She faltered, but only momentarily. Summoning every last shred of courage she had left, she climbed inside.

The chauffeur shut the door behind her.

"I bet you thought we'd never see each other again," Farrell Grayson said. "And yet, here we are."

Chapter 25

FARRELL

If looks could kill . . .

Farrell tried not to grin at the fiery glare he received from Crys Hatcher as she got into the back of the limo. He failed.

Hatred emanated off her in palpable waves as they drove away from the bookshop.

"Don't you feel like chatting?" he asked.

"Why you?" she said through clenched teeth.

"That is a very philosophical question. Why *any* of us? Why do we exist? What is our reason for being here? Is it all just a waste of time?"

"Why did they send *you* and not someone else?"

"Because Markus knows what good friends we've become."

"Cut the crap."

He spread his hands, as if in surrender. "Markus asked me to be your escort tonight. I told him you might not appreciate seeing me again so soon after our date yesterday."

"So he knows I figured out all your secrets."

"Not all my secrets. Just one." He smirked. He knew she wanted him to feel bad, to feel guilty about all this. But he didn't. Which made everything so much simpler.

Crys twisted her silver rose ring. "Why are you doing this?"

"You have something Markus wants. I'm just helping him get it." He eyed the book she held tight to her chest. "Show it to me."

"Fetch the girl," Markus had said when he'd called Farrell earlier. "Bring her to the theater. Ensure that she has the book with her—check for the bronze hawk on the cover. If she doesn't have it, inform me immediately."

Reluctantly, she turned the book around.

There was the bronze hawk, just as he'd described.

"Nice to know you can follow directions when given the right motivations," he said, then cocked his head. "Oh, come on, Crys. Why do you have to be so serious? You work at a bookshop, and now you're delivering a book. Seems like it fits the job description nicely enough."

"He has my sister. Did you know that? He stole her right out of the hospital. She's in a coma, Farrell. A *coma*. And he kidnapped her."

Of course he knew that. He was in Markus's inner circle. "Your point?"

"Do you even have a soul?" she demanded. "Or are you made of pure evil, just like your lord and master?"

He watched her, coolly amused by how hard she was trying to get under his skin. "Go ahead. Compare me to Markus. I'll take it as a compliment."

She stared at him in silence for a full minute, a stare so smoldering it practically burned.

"Like what you see?" he asked, trying to rattle her. "Maybe you're ready to rethink last night's 'go to hell' suggestion and take a closer look." He patted the seat next to him. "Got to say, I'm totally ready to forgive and forget."

He'd expected her to respond with a flustered denial, but she just continued to study him.

"Is this really you?" she asked.

"Not sure what you mean."

Crys shook her head, then took off her glasses and put them in her purse. She placed the book down next to her, then moved across to sit next to him.

He eyed her, now intrigued.

"My mother said the mark you get . . . it can change things. The magic messes with your mind, makes you loyal even though you might feel anything but. Did it do that to you?"

Her mother had said that, had she?

Farrell frowned as he glanced down at his arm where Markus had given him both his first and second marks. He remembered how much it'd hurt as the golden dagger sliced through his skin, the alarming amount of blood that had dripped to the floor. Then the pain of the healing before everything felt better.

He brushed his fingers over his skin. "I'm not sure what I really feel anymore. Sometimes it's difficult to think straight. Do you think that might be because of the mark?"

"Maybe." She searched his gaze, her breath quickening. Then she grabbed hold of his hand. "Maybe it doesn't have to be this way. Maybe you can fight against his power over you. You could help me—me and Becca."

She drew even closer, so close that her addictive strawberry scent enticed him more intensely than ever.

"Do you have any idea how good you smell, Crystal Hatcher?" He reached forward and threaded his fingers into her hair. She watched him carefully, warily, but didn't try to pull away. "And do you know how absolutely beautiful you are?"

"Farrell . . ."

"I don't know what to do. Markus's pull . . . the pull he has over all of us . . . it's so strong. So hard to fight." He moved closer, focused on her lips.

"It must be."

"I have heard of one way to break the power this mark has over me, but I'd need your help. Would you help me, Crys?"

"Of course I would," she said, breathless. "How can I help?"

He'd drawn so close he could almost brush his lips against hers. "To break the mark's control, I need to . . . have sex with a really gullible blonde."

She reared back from him, her expression going from hopeful to outraged in a split second. Then she smacked him, hard, across his face.

"Ow!" He laughed and rubbed his cheek as she scooted back to her side of the limo.

"I hate you."

"Didn't look like it a moment ago. Word to the wise, sweetheart, even if this mark did make me Markus's loyal and unquestioning servant"—he held up his left forearm—"I'd be okay with it. I've never felt better in my life. And as far as how I feel about you? I don't feel anything at all. Markus asked me to bring you to him, and that's what I'm doing."

"So loyal. Like a trained poodle."

There was a time not long ago when an insult like that might have incensed him. Tonight, all he felt was calm. He lit a cigarette, not even registering that she gave him a venomous look as he blew the smoke in her direction.

His phone buzzed and he glanced down at the screen to see a text from Adam.

. *where are you? want to see a movie tonight?*

It seemed that his brother had finally forgiven him for what happened at Firebird.

Sorry, I'm on a date with Felicity, he answered. *Won't be home for a couple hours.*

Sam was driving them to the same cathedral where he'd met Lucas on the day of his fateful meeting with Markus. It seemed like a thousand years ago—back when he'd been full of doubt about what was to come, back when he'd still been so tormented by his older brother's suicide.

So much had changed in a matter of days. Now he barely thought about Connor at all. The dead were gone—no reason to give them any further thought.

Sam pulled the limo up to the curb and opened the back door, averting his eyes as Farrell and Crys got out. The chauffeur knew something was up but was smart not to ask any questions.

"You can head off now, Sam. I'll call you when I'm done," Farrell told him.

"Yes, sir." Sam glanced at Crys for a split second before he got back in the car and drove away.

"All right, let's go," Farrell said. "And just a warning: If you draw any attention to us, you'll regret it. Markus said a blindfold isn't necessary this time, but I'm sure he'd be fine with a gag."

"Screaming my head off right now won't help my sister, will it?"

"I'm glad we understand each other."

He took her by her elbow and directed her to the rear of the cathedral, to the tunnel entrance. He pulled up the piece of plywood, and she stared down at the darkness beneath.

"There's stairs," he said. "Let's go. Markus is waiting."

She drew her eyeglasses out of her bag and put them on,

pushing them up her nose. A quick glimpse inside her bag also revealed the Canon Rebel he'd given her as a gift.

"So I see you're all ready to take the perfect shot," he said.

"It probably won't happen tonight."

"Probably not. Now, those stairs I mentioned a moment ago? Let's start moving."

Crys bit her bottom lip but didn't protest. She slipped past the plywood plank he held up, found her footing, and then began her descent.

He knew how she felt, unsure of her next step, worried she might take a devastating fall. For him it was completely different. It only took a minute for his newly improved senses to kick in, and he could see as well as day in the darkness.

Farrell watched as she fumbled her way down the stairs, a mix of trepidation and determination on her face.

"Chin up, buttercup," he said. "It's not the end of the world."

"Bite me."

"Maybe later."

They reached the bottom of the stairs and moved toward the meager glow of the flickering light about fifty paces ahead. Farrell had come to learn that all these tunnels had been created and maintained by Markus, and that they all connected with one another in an underground maze. One could get from the restaurant to the theater and from the cathedral to Markus's home, and vice versa, if one knew the proper turns, and there were several entrances hidden all over the city.

"Is she giving you a hard time, Farrell?" Lucas was waiting around the next corner, leaning against the wall. He had a bandage across his bruised and swollen nose.

"Don't worry, I can handle her."

Crys stopped walking and stared at Lucas. "You have got to be kidding me."

"It's Crys, right?" Lucas grinned. "Really sorry for what happened the other day. I was just playing a part to help out a friend. Then again"—he pointed to his face—"you did break my nose, so maybe you should be the one apologizing."

She gave him the finger.

"Nice." He laughed. "So that's the infamous book, is it?"

"It is," Farrell confirmed.

"Follow me." Lucas led them to the spiral staircase leading to the iron door covered in symbols. He opened the door and gestured for Crys and Farrell to go through. "After you."

Farrell had never been in Markus's theater when it wasn't filled up for a society meeting. Today it felt cavernous—larger and more ominous than he'd ever seen it.

Crys drew in a sharp breath. "Becca."

Farrell followed her gaze to the stage. The curtains were drawn to reveal a pretty blond girl in a hospital gown and bare feet lying on a table, like an image out of a fairy tale. Too bad there were no Prince Charmings nearby to administer magical kisses.

Crys took a step toward the stage but then faltered as Markus moved out of the shadows and stood next to Becca. He wore a tailored suit, black on black. Accompanying him was the man who'd first let Farrell and Lucas into Markus's study.

"As you can see, Ms. Hatcher," Markus said, "your sister is perfectly fine."

"You call this *fine*?" Crys snarled. "Dad, how could you have let this happen?"

Dad? Farrell and Lucas exchanged a surprised glance.

"You chose this outcome, Crys," the other man said. "But I'm very glad you're here to make this right. Give Markus the Codex."

Crys raised her chin. "Why doesn't he come over here and take it from me?"

Farrell stifled a laugh before another one escaped. What the girl lacked in common sense, she made up for in guts.

A smile now played at Markus's lips. A dangerous smile.

And with that smile, Farrell knew, without a doubt, that Crystal Hatcher was doomed.

Chapter 26

MADDOX

When Maddox woke, he found himself in Camilla's garden, looking up at the stone wheel.

Becca knelt at his side. "Close your eyes," she said the moment he opened them.

He did as she said.

"There are six guards here. They think you're still unconscious, so I'd suggest looking that way as long as possible. Camilla is inside the cottage, dead." Her voice broke, but she kept going. "Sienna is loyal to Valoria. That she'd betray her sister like that . . . it makes me sick. The guards have Barnabas restrained. He's sitting twelve feet to your left. I wish I could tell you I have a brilliant plan, but I don't. And, for what it's worth, I tried to possess a guard, but apparently I can't even do that. I'm completely useless."

He went to shake his head, to tell her she's not useless, when a guard noticed his slight movements and wrenched him up to his feet.

"The witch boy's awake." He leaned closer to peer at Maddox's face. "Warning you, boy. You try any magic and we'll skewer your bearded friend."

Barnabas sat on the ground, his hands behind his back. His attention was fixed on Sienna, glaring at her as if he could will her dead with his eyes.

"I can kill you all with a single thought," Maddox said, his voice raspy.

"Go ahead. Give it a try." The guard waited, then smirked. "Didn't think so. Behave yourself or I'll knock out your teeth."

"Maddox," Becca began. "The ground . . ."

He looked down to see that frost now crept across the grass, coating the flowers in delicate sheets of ice. But Maddox had known frost to occur only on the highest mountaintops, not here at ground level.

"Water magic," Barnabas said. "The goddess has arrived, flaunting her power."

The ground turned completely white, as if Mytica had fallen into a swift winter that had frozen to death all the fresh colors of nature. Valoria approached from this stark backdrop, her dress fully crimson, her ebony hair flowing over her shoulders.

"Your Radiance," Sienna greeted her. "Welcome."

Valoria's cold, unpleasant gaze fell over all of them, one by one, before it finally landed on Sienna.

"Well done," the goddess said. "You've pleased me today. All this has come together so swiftly, thanks to your hard work and loyalty."

Sienna nodded. "As I told you before, my sister has been conspiring with rebels. It was by chance alone that I discovered that the book of the immortals had fallen into her hands. I sent the message by raven as soon as I discovered it last night. I'm thrilled you were able to get here so quickly."

"And your sister?"

"I killed her." Sienna nodded toward the cottage. "She won't cause you any further problems."

"Excellent."

Maddox regarded this pair of beautiful women with hatred. Sienna had murdered the kind and benevolent Camilla, and Valoria had murdered Maddox's father.

He could barely keep from trembling. He craved vengeance on behalf of a man he'd never known, a man whom this evil creature had stolen from him.

Valoria moved toward Barnabas, looking down her nose at him.

"Greetings," he said. "We meet again."

"You killed my cobra."

"Oh, wait. Was that *your* cobra?" Barnabas frowned. "I had no idea. Apologies, many sincere apologies."

She nodded at a guard, who then smashed his fist into Barnabas's jaw.

"Did you really think I wouldn't figure out your little disguise? Now that I see your skin encrusted with less grime, and smell that you've managed to wash away some of the stink that emanated from you before, the memory returns. It's been some time, Barnabas."

"Your memory may have returned, but I'm afraid mine hasn't. I meet a lot of attractive women in my line of work. Did we have a tryst once? I regret that it wasn't more memorable for me."

Another nod. Another punch. Blood now trickled from the corner of his mouth.

"It's been years," Valoria continued as if she hadn't been interrupted. "You've grown older. The beard is new, but the face behind it is the same." A smile now played on her lips. "I know how much you must loathe me."

All pretenses of levity gone, Barnabas's eyes narrowed. "You could never in a million years know the depth of my hatred for you."

"But you helped to create a legend to last through the centuries, Barnabas—you and my sister. The immortal sorceress who fell in love with a mortal hunter. How did you think it would end for you both? That you'd persuade her to live the life of a mortal in a little cottage where you would raise your unnatural spawn?" She laughed. "A love like yours burned bright like the sun but was always destined to end in darkness. You seemed to be the only one surprised by that."

"I swear I'll have my vengeance for what you did to Eva."

"I was not the one to take her life."

"You helped."

"You weren't there. You could never know the whole truth."

"I know what I see before me. I see a thieving immortal who, instead of guarding this world like she was created to do, steals lives and magic."

"I never agreed to be a guardian of anything."

"I will destroy you."

"Given where you currently sit and where I currently stand, I sincerely doubt that. No. You've managed to hide from me for all these years. I promise, you won't escape from me again."

"Do you understand a single word of this?" Becca asked. She hadn't left Maddox's side since he woke.

He'd been listening to them talk in hushed silence, fearful that Valoria would have a guard put a sword through Barnabas at any moment. But then that fear fell away and was replaced by confusion.

Barnabas and the sorceress.

Eva had been the girl Barnabas confessed to loving last night. The one he'd lost.

It was Eva's sixteen-year-old daughter for whom Valoria searched.

Eva and Barnabas's daughter.

A mystery girl who Barnabas had not referenced at all. She wasn't the hidden heiress to the throne. He'd broken into the dungeon to find Maddox. Because he needed Maddox's magic . . .

His head hurt from hurriedly thinking through all this, but he knew he was close to something incredibly important. The answer he needed more than any other.

What if it wasn't a girl at all whom Valoria searched for?

What if it was . . . a sixteen-year-old boy with unusual magic?

His gaze shot to Barnabas.

The thief had told him that Valoria had torn the heart right from Maddox's father's chest. But now that he thought about it, Barnabas had never, not once, said his father was *dead*.

"This can't be true," Maddox whispered hoarsely. "Barnabas, it *can't*. Can it?"

Barnabas drew in a sharp breath, his eyes widening with surprise, as Maddox's unspoken question hung in the air.

The goddess, who'd watched both of them closely, focused then on Maddox, looking infuriatingly smug.

"The witch boy," she purred. "How vastly I underestimated you. Barnabas must have thought he was so clever to fool me so well and for so long."

"What's she talking about?" Becca asked, frowning.

Maddox didn't look away from the goddess. He held her gaze defiantly.

"Yes, there it is," she said with a cool smile. "I can see the resemblance much better when you're not shivering like a frightened child. Your father wasn't much older than you when he fell in love with my sister."

"Eighteen, actually," Barnabas said, his voice tight. "There was a bit of an age difference between us, I admit, but we didn't mind."

"Even now, he plays the fool in an attempt to distract me." Valoria clasped Maddox's chin. "All this time I've been searching for a girl. If only I'd known your true parents' little secret."

"I'm afraid I'm not sure what you're talking about," Maddox replied, fighting to keep his tone steady. "My mother is Damaris Corso. My father was all but a stranger to her."

She patted his cheek. "A nice attempt, but you can't fool me. Not anymore."

"Okay, Maddox," Becca whispered. "I think I understand what's going on here. I can't believe I'm about to say this, but promise you'll listen to me. I know this realization might come as a bit of a, um, shock? To say the least? But look at it this way. . . . You've always considered your magic to be a curse, right? You didn't know where it came from or why you had it. Now you do. Your mother was a sorceress and, by the sound of it, one of the good ones."

"Bring me the book," Valoria instructed Sienna. "I'm ready to finally reclaim my dagger and punish the thief who stole it from me."

"After you stole it from Eva, you mean," Barnabas growled.

"If you think I can help you, you're wrong," Maddox said to Valoria. "I've examined the book, and it means nothing to me. I can't use it to open up a gateway. My magic doesn't do that, and that raggedy old thing certainly won't make any difference."

"No, I don't suppose it would. Not the way you're used to channeling your magic now, at least." She eyed him from top to tail.

"The magic I'm familiar with is elemental—the magic of life. You possess the flip side to this—death magic. Life and death do go hand in hand, after all. How curious it is that Eva, an immortal, would give life to a creature who is exactly the opposite. Usually when those of my kind create life with mortals, they end up with witches for offspring, like my loyal Sienna and her dead sister: women with small holds on elemental magic. You are a rare creature indeed."

"Perhaps I am, but I still can't help you." Maddox tried to summon some of Barnabas's irreverence but knew he came up short.

"Even if you could," she replied, "you'd likely fail. From what I've seen of you, you're too young, too timid. You doubt every move you make and seek guidance and permission before every action you take. What a waste."

Darkness churned deep in his belly, and he balled his hands into fists at his sides.

"She's wrong." Becca shook her head. "You have to know that, don't you?"

"Here it is, Your Radiance." Sienna had brought the book out from the cottage and handed it to Valoria.

The goddess took it, drawing in a long, satisfied breath. "Very good."

"What's so special about this dagger you're after, anyway?" Maddox asked. He'd tried to catch Barnabas's eye, but it seemed the man was trying to avoid his gaze.

"When wielded by an immortal, one can carve loyalty, obedience, and trust into another's very skin. Three qualities that are rarely found in your kind."

"You wish to create an army of slaves," Barnabas hissed. "Don't you?"

"Perhaps you will be my first recruit," she told him. "Yes, I think that would be a fitting punishment for you. Three marks would ensure that you will bow to me, that you will worship me. That you will love me, perhaps as much as you loved my sister, even as the magic eats away at your very soul to sustain itself. Very few can resist the magic of the dagger marks."

"I will resist."

"You say that now. I'll ask you again when you're kneeling before my throne."

She leafed through the book until she came to the page that showed the illustration of the stone wheel.

"It's a spell book," Becca said. "This . . . this gateway magic, it's only a part of it."

"How do you know?" Maddox whispered.

"It's pretty thick for one measly spell, don't you think?"

"This will be the most difficult spell I've ever attempted," Valoria said aloud. "Eva could wield this kind of magic easily, but for the rest of us, we need to be wary. Worlds and time can shift. One mistake and I could open a gateway years before the thief entered this world, or years after he finally faded from existence. I wish to pull him back as close as possible to the moment he was originally exiled."

Valoria's guards stood as silently as statues, watching and waiting for orders. Two more stood on either side of Barnabas, who was still on his knees on the frost-covered ground.

"You are Eva's son," Valoria said to Maddox. "A mutation of her magic runs through your veins and infuses your spirit. That magic is what I need to accomplish this monumental task."

He shook his head. "But I don't know how."

Valoria reached out with one hand and clutched his throat.

"You don't have to *know* anything, my sweet nephew," she said. "I will do it for you."

Coldness washed over him, and then a painful tearing sensation shuddered through his very flesh. He gasped and tried to pull away from her grip, but he couldn't move.

"Shh, be still," Valoria hissed. "This won't take long."

He began to shiver, as if the goddess were draining all of his mortal warmth. When she finally let go of him, Maddox dropped to his knees. A layer of shadows coated Valoria's hand, as if she'd dipped it in black honey.

"I may not be able to absorb your magic, but I can wield it."

All Maddox could do was stare at her, his power of speech currently useless to him. There was now something missing from inside him, leaving nothing but an empty, bottomless hole.

Valoria went to the stone wheel, her right hand still dripping with Maddox's shadowy magic, her left hand holding the book. She pressed her palm against the wheel, glanced down at the page, and began to read aloud. The language felt like a golden melody, an enchanted whisper, which released sparks of energy and power into the air with every enigmatic syllable spoken.

Maddox's stolen magic began to flow from Valoria and spread across the wheel, swirling and entwining the nooks and crannies of the stone surface. The shadows kept heaving and expanding until the entire wheel was cloaked by them, and was transformed to what looked like a swirling black hole.

Valoria laughed. "It won't be long now. Maddox, my sweet, perhaps I shall reward you for this. I may need you again in the future, after all."

Suddenly, all the guards gasped in unison and then crumpled to the ground.

Valoria's insidious grin fell at the sight. "Was that you, child?"

"No," Maddox replied, stunned, as he searched the area for the answer.

Becca's surprised gaze swept over the fallen guards. "Then how on earth—?" she whispered.

Sienna stood nearby, her arms out to her sides. "Apologies, Your Radiance, but this crusade ends now."

Valoria cocked her head. "Sienna. You did this? I'm impressed. You must be more powerful than I thought."

"Don't flatter me. I didn't do it alone."

"That's right," said a familiar voice. Maddox turned around to see Camilla, walking toward them from the cottage. "I helped."

Valoria raised a brow. "I thought this vile woman was dead."

Barnabas laughed, then struggled to crawl over and cut his ropes on a fallen guard's sword. "Imagine that. Mere witches, fooling a goddess as powerful as you."

Valoria stiffened, and the book fell from her hands, tumbling to the ground in a flutter of delicate pages. Bands of translucent, airy swirls wrapped themselves around her shoulders, waist, and knees, trapping her arms at her sides. "Yes, with your puny powers combined, your air magic is quite impressive."

Barnabas approached her. "Just to enlighten you, Your Radiance, this has been our plan for a long time. Sienna gave up two years of her life to work her way into your good graces and earn your trust. But, like you said, without that magic dagger of yours, you can't be sure of anyone's loyalty, can you?"

The goddess's lips thinned. "And what do you mean to do with me now?"

"That's the beauty of it, Valoria. Without your determination to open this gateway with Maddox's magic, we couldn't have done any of this. You yourself have given us the means to rid ourselves and Mytica of you, once and for all. From this point forward, you are exiled. You'll never find a way back here. You are now free to spend eternity searching for your thief friend and that dagger you're so desperate for."

She shook her head. "Barnabas, you can't do this. You can't simply shove me through a gateway and have me disappear!"

He laughed again. "Oh, I believe I can."

He clutched her shoulders and fixed a wild-eyed, victorious stare on her. Then, pushing back on his haunches to harness more strength, he shoved her backward.

She didn't budge an inch.

A slow smile snaked across her face. "Didn't you hear me? I said you *can't* do it."

And with her words, the earth beneath Barnabas's feet swiftly turned to mud, and he immediately sank down into it to his waist. He fought to free himself, but he was in too deep.

He continued to sink farther, now just a little at a time. The more he struggled, the faster the enchanted mud drew him downward.

Valoria examined the air magic binding her. "These wispy chains are impressive, but let's not be silly."

With a violent flick of her wrists, she brushed off the spell, the translucent binds sputtering out into specks of dust, and strode toward the witches. "I hate to repeat a trick twice in the same day, but you both deserve a nice, slow death."

Again, the earth gave way to muck beneath them, and they swiftly sank into mud pits identical to Barnabas's.

It appeared as though Barnabas's brilliant plan—which was a complete secret to Maddox until now, of course—had failed. Rather spectacularly.

"Whatever you're thinking of doing," Becca said, her voice strained, "think faster."

She believed he had a plan at the ready to save them all. She couldn't be more wrong.

But I have to do something, he thought frantically. *Something. But what?*

The goddess might be many things—vain, greedy, impulsive—but she wasn't stupid.

Was it possible that he could reason with her?

As Valoria approached the shadowy gateway, Maddox stepped in front of her. "Wait. We could make a bargain," he said, attempting to keep his tone as calm as possible, given the current life-and-death situation. "If you spare the lives of Barnabas and the witches, I will gladly work for you."

"Oh, you poor boy. Yes, you *will* work for me," she agreed. "That was never in question. But *they've* already chosen death by crossing me."

She shoved him out of her way. He lost his footing, and when he dropped to the icy ground, the silver ring holding the dark forest spirit, which he'd nearly forgotten about, tumbled out of his pocket. Steadily and as if in slow motion, the ring rolled toward the gateway until it made contact with the swirling shadows.

With a blood-chilling shriek, the trapped spirit streamed out of the ring as a sickening plume of darkness and took the form of a shadow creature much larger and denser than the one Maddox had originally summoned. The magic surrounding the gateway had affected it, changed it. Strengthened it.

The spirit turned toward Becca, who staggered backward.

"Becca, run!" Maddox yelled.

"Becca? Who is Becca?" Valoria asked. Barnabas, Sienna, and

Camilla were now up to their shoulders in the mud.

"Oh, that's just another name he likes to call me, now and then," Barnabas called out. "Adorable, yes? Sorry, my young friend, but I can't run at the moment. I'm busy sinking to my death."

Just as Maddox was about to give in to despair, the sound of Valoria's amused laughter drew his attention.

"So sad," she said. "If only you had the kind of magic that could help the living, nephew."

All his life, Maddox had been told what to do, how to act. He'd been trained to be afraid. He'd reacted diplomatically to hardship, dealing with difficulties as they presented themselves, but he'd never taken a stand. Never stood up for himself. Whenever he'd tried, Livius had beaten him down and stolen his confidence, laughed when Maddox felt his lowest.

Livius had never felt threatened by Maddox's magic, because Maddox had never shown him what this magic could really do.

"You're right," he said now to Valoria. "My magic can't help the living. But it can *kill* the living."

With every bit of confidence he had left, he summoned what death magic he had left and focused it wholly on the goddess to give her an example of what it truly meant to be a necromancer.

Valoria gasped, her hands flying up to her throat. "What—what . . . is . . . this?" Her face blanched, her green eyes blazing like fiery emeralds. "Release . . . me!"

He shook his head, slow and stern. A calmness, a strange sense of serenity, had taken over as the magic flowed across his skin. "I don't want to do this. I'm not a killer. But you've given me no choice. My magic is death magic. I don't want to kill, but I can, and I will when I'm given no other choice."

Her eyes widened. He knew she believed him.

Valoria had a hand in his true birth mother's death. And Maddox knew with a deep certainty that he would have a hand in Valoria's.

Just as he was ready to unleash the remaining darkness inside him and crush her throat completely, she turned into water before his eyes. Her liquid form splashed to the ground, breaking free of his mental grip before it gained speed and gathered itself up into a funnel and disappeared into the sky.

"Maddox!" Becca screamed.

He whipped around. Becca had been able to dodge the monstrous spirit while he'd been occupied with Valoria, but it had finally cornered her.

He searched the ground for the ring but couldn't see it anywhere.

"Curse it, I need something silver," he growled. "Now."

The book lay on the ground next to the pulsing gate of shadows. He ran to it, stared down at the bronze hawk on the cover, and held it up in front of him like a shield.

"Spirit! I summon you to me," he snarled. "Get away from her right now."

The mutated spirit froze. With a screeching, deafening roar, it flew toward Maddox in a single stream of darkness, then crashed into the book's front cover, disappearing into the metallic hawk.

"So it does work with more than just silver," Maddox muttered to himself. "That's good to know."

Now what?

Better to be safe than sorry, he thought, then hurled the heavy book into the central eye of the gateway. As it hurtled through, the shadows swirled faster, growing smaller and smaller until what remained of the stolen magic broke free from the wheel and returned to Maddox like an obedient pet ghost.

Maddox ran toward Barnabas and pulled him from the mud pit just before he went under completely. Together with Barnabas, who was coated up to his neck in mud, they helped free Sienna and Camilla. The sisters embraced, sobbing in each other's arms.

"Maddox," Barnabas began, panting from the effort. "We must speak."

"Agreed. But hold that thought." Maddox turned. "Becca, come here."

She was in front of him in a heartbeat, her face aglow with both horror and relief. "That was incredible," she said. "I'm so proud of you!"

"Thank you," he said, his voice hoarse. "Thank you so much for believing in me."

Her smile was so bright that it made him ache. "Anytime."

"I have a gift for you."

She raised her eyebrows. "Really? What?"

He held out his hand. A swirl of shadows, like a tiny storm cloud, hovered over his palm.

Becca's gaze snapped to his. "But the gateway closed. I saw it."

He shook his head. "That gateway wasn't for you. I believe this is enough magic to send you back to your home, but I can't hold on to it for long."

Her blue eyes, now filled with pain, met his. "I wish I could have more time with you."

"Me too."

But I have to let you go.

A shimmering tear slipped down her cheek. "I'm going to miss you so much. I'll never forget you, Maddox. Never."

His throat was so tight it hurt to speak. "Hurry, Becca. I can't hold on to it for much longer."

She nodded and pressed her hand against his.

His gaze snapped up to hers in shock. He could feel her hand in his, warm and real. Flesh and blood.

"What is this?" she asked, breathless.

A smile curled up the corner of his mouth. "Magic."

He brought his other hand to the nape of her neck, beneath her silky braid, and pressed his lips against hers, breathing her in. Tasting her mouth, which was even sweeter than he'd imagined it would be.

And suddenly, as quickly as her earthly form had materialized, it was gone. His arms were empty, and he opened his stinging eyes to confirm it.

"She's gone," he whispered hoarsely.

Barnabas gently clasped his shoulder. "I'm sorry."

"She . . . she needed to go." He tried to nod, to remind himself this was the only truth there could be. "This isn't her real home."

"Doesn't make it any easier."

No, it definitely didn't, he thought, his heart a lead weight in his chest.

"Just so you know," Barnabas said after a lengthy silence between them, "I loved your mother. I loved her with all my heart and soul. I would have done anything to save her. When I lost her, I focused on trying to keep you safe. Part of that involved me having to go into hiding, so I found a place for you where I thought you'd be taken care of and grow up to be happy. I'm so sorry."

"Sorry for what? For wanting me to be safe and happy?" Maddox shook his head. "Don't apologize for that."

"It didn't work out the way I wanted it to. I'll understand if you never want to see me again."

"That would probably be the wisest decision. You're a horrible influence."

"Yes." Barnabas nodded solemnly. "Yes, I am."

Maddox knew he needed something substantial to take his mind off the fact that he'd just lost the girl he loved. A girl he'd never see again.

No, he thought fiercely. *One day, I swear I will find you again, Becca Hatcher. I believe in happy endings, just like you do.*

"You know, Barnabas," he said when he felt ready to talk again. "We still haven't found King Thaddeus's daughter. I suddenly feel the need to go on a quest to recover her and put her on the throne, after we finally defeat Valoria once and for all."

"We?"

"Yes, we." Maddox managed a small smile, even though his heart had just been badly bruised and battered. Becca had helped him believe in himself, in his magic, so he might as well start doing something noble with it. "What do you say?"

"I don't usually need a partner to cause trouble and mayhem," Barnabas replied. Then he grinned. "But I'm happy to make an exception this time."

Chapter 27

CRYSTAL

A photographer can tell a lot about a person by how they smiled.

Farrell Grayson had a few smiles in his arsenal. A self-indulgent smirk; a cold, cruel twist of his lips; and a charming, crooked grin that had managed to work its way into her heart before he'd happily stomped on it.

Markus, however, only had one smile, one that at first glance had seemed to be genuine.

He smiled down at her from his position next to her father and unconscious sister. "The Codex, Ms. Hatcher. If you please."

Farrell took her arm and not so gently directed her up the stairs to the stage. She wrenched away from him the moment he loosened his grip.

"No need to struggle. Just trying to move this along," he said. Lucas remained down on the main floor, his arms crossed, watching her with a chillingly predatory look on his face.

"Ms. Hatcher," Markus prompted when she'd turned to look at Becca, inspecting her sister for new injuries. But Becca appeared just as she had at the hospital: pale, thin, and fragile.

"Fine," she said through gritted teeth. "Here." She held out the book, refusing to take another step.

He stepped closer to her, watching her curiously as if she might try to pull a prank, then gently removed the book from her grip.

Markus brushed his fingers over the bronze hawk. "This once belonged to another immortal, who exiled me for siding against her in an uprising among our kind. Ever since I first heard of this book's existence, I've known that someone had sent it here to help me. If only they'd known how long it would take for me to finally have it in my hands."

He seemed to be speaking more to himself than to Crys and his doting members.

"What does it do?" Crys asked. She couldn't help it; she had to know.

"You met with Dr. Vega," he replied in a thin, almost weary voice. "What does he think it can do?"

The mention of Dr. Vega made her tense. She'd chosen not to bring up his beating, but the thought of seeing him in that hospital bed made bile rise in her throat.

"He doesn't know anything for sure, of course. All his theories about the Codex are only guesses."

"Has he come close to translating it? This language his father called Obsidia?"

Wouldn't he have already asked this question of Dr. Vega himself during the torture session? "No. He's stumped," she lied. "But he did mention something about the magic working as a gateway between worlds, which is how he thinks the book got here in the first place. Is that why you want it? So you can go back to your home?"

"Perhaps one day, but not anytime soon. There is still much for me to do here. And now that I have the Codex to help me, I feel a moral obligation to finish the work I started here. There is much evil in this world, Ms. Hatcher, and I'm determined to do what I can to crush it."

He honestly thinks he's a hero, she thought.

She wasn't sure if that was sad or terrifying.

Crys bit her lip and railed against a great internal struggle to remain in control of her emotions. "I brought you the book like you asked me to. Let Becca go back to the hospital."

"Markus promised to heal Becca and draw her out of this coma if you did as we requested," her father spoke up. "She won't need to return to the hospital tonight."

Crys's gaze shot to the immortal. "Is that true? Can you do that?"

Markus nodded, but his attention wasn't on Crys, it was on her unconscious sister. "Dr. Vega says that her current condition has been caused by making contact with this book, but I'm not sure why that would be. It's a mystery I'd like to solve." Markus peered closer at Becca's face, his brow drawing in at his forehead. "She's lovely, Daniel."

"Yes, she is," Daniel agreed.

"I've never had the pleasure of meeting your youngest before. You adopted a child who fits in perfectly with your family."

Crys held her breath. Markus knew Becca was adopted.

Of course he did. Her father would have told him everything.

Crys felt Farrell's presence close to her. She glanced at him out of the corner of her eye, silently cursing him. She didn't need the distraction.

She focused instead on Markus, remembering what her mother

had said about his getting weaker, how his magic had faded over the years. He was vulnerable now.

"You're sure you can heal her?" she asked quietly. "Are you really strong enough to heal more than a paper cut?"

"Crys," her father snapped.

She ignored his strict tone as easily as she ignored her least favorite teachers.

Markus studied her as if she were a dunce who'd finally said something interesting.

"Are you questioning the strength of my magic?"

She decided it would be smartest to play to his ego. "This world has no real magic that I know of. Obviously yours does. What must it be like for someone like you to end up in a place like this? Maybe your magic is fading, which means you won't be able to play the hero here as much as you want to. That book would be the answer to this problem, wouldn't it?"

His singular smile fell as he sent a sharp stare toward Crys. "I am *made* from magic, Ms. Hatcher."

"Well . . . if someone made from magic starts losing their magic . . . ," she began. "Does that mean you're dying and you hope that book will save you?"

Markus's eyes widened a fraction and something very unpleasant slid behind his gaze, making Crys regret speaking her thoughts aloud.

She was baiting a tiger with sharp claws and teeth.

Suddenly, Becca gasped. With a violent jerk, her back arched up off the wooden table, as if she were having a seizure. Crys gripped her hand as her sister's eyelids fluttered and opened.

"Becca! You're awake!" Crys dove in for a tight embrace.

"Did you heal her?" Daniel asked Markus, his voice low.

"No, this wasn't my doing. Hold this." He handed Daniel the Codex and moved closer to the table, his gaze now fixed on Becca.

"What's going on?" Becca murmured, her voice hoarse. "Where am I?"

That was an excellent question. Where had that tunnel led them? Crys only knew it had to be a theater somewhere in the city, but she didn't recognize it.

"Shh. Don't worry about it," Crys said. "The important thing is you're finally awake. Can you get up?"

"I think so."

Crys helped Becca sit up and then supported her as she stood on shaky legs.

Becca finally glanced around and noticed the gathered group of others watching her. "Um, okay. This is weird." She frowned. "Dad? What are you doing here?"

Daniel nodded at her. "Hello, Becca. I'm glad you're feeling better."

Her gaze fell on the Codex, and her face froze up in shock. "That book . . ."

Crys squeezed her hand. "It's okay. We're leaving. We can talk about everything later, at home."

Crys put her arm around Becca's waist and directed her toward the stairs. Farrell stood in her path.

"Move," Crys growled.

"Not going to happen."

"I'm afraid I can't let you leave, Ms. Hatcher," Markus said.

This was what she'd been fearing the most. She felt foolish now for thinking she might be able to get away so easily. "Are you going to just stand by and watch him kill us, Dad?"

"Kill you?" Markus exclaimed. "Why would I do such a thing?

Especially after you brought me the Codex. Yes, you lied to me, but that is forgivable now."

Right. For a moment, Crys had forgotten that Markus thought he was the superhero star of his own comic book, saving the world, one teenager at a time.

"What do you suggest, Markus?" Daniel asked.

"Your elder daughter has requested to join us in our mission, so I'd like to fulfill her wish by inviting her into my society. Both her and her sister." Markus gestured toward Farrell and Lucas. "We'll all return to my home. They will need a comfortable place to recover."

"What do I need to recover from?" Crys asked warily. Was this why she hadn't been blindfolded? Because Markus had already decided how this night would end?

"You've been exposed to too much, too soon. It takes years for the rare few of my most promising followers to learn as much as you know now. I will have to give you all three marks tonight, which, I'm afraid, will be an unavoidably difficult undertaking for you. And, if you resist in any way, the recovery time will be much more extensive."

"What the hell is he talking about?" Becca asked.

"It's okay," Crys said, even though she knew it wasn't. Having one mark would be bad enough, but three could turn them both into Markus's unquestioning minions.

"Do you take issue with my decision?" Markus asked Daniel.

"No," he replied. "It has to be done."

Crys's heart twisted to hear his unquestioning agreement.

She still hadn't heard from Julia or Jackie. She and Becca were all on their own.

Damn it, what *was* Jackie's first lesson of self-defense? Why couldn't she remember? This might be the last chance they had to attempt an escape.

"Come on, don't make a fuss." Farrell took Crys's arm, but she shrugged him off. He gave her an unpleasant smirk. "Sounds like we'll be seeing eye to eye soon enough. Maybe we'll make this crazy romance of ours work out after all."

She gritted her teeth.

Groin and eyeballs. That was still all she could remember, and it would have to suffice.

Crys's father put the Codex under his arm and fished his buzzing cell phone from his pocket, glancing at the screen. He answered it, frowning.

"Who is it?" Markus asked.

Daniel glanced at him. "Jackie Kendall. She says she wants to speak to you."

Crys looked right to Markus, eager to see his reaction. But there wasn't one. His expression had gone completely blank, as if someone had pressed his Pause button.

Why was Jackie calling Markus?

Finally, Markus held out his hand and took the phone. He flicked his wrist at Farrell. "Leave me. All of you. *Now.*"

"Let's go," Farrell said. His grip on her was crushing, and she almost dropped her bag as he pulled her off the stage. Lucas took Becca's arm and guided her toward the exit to the tunnels.

They descended the spiral staircase, then started down a tunnel forking in a different direction than where they'd come in.

"I'm waiting for you to try to appeal to my softer side again," Farrell said after a few moments. "Feel free to give it a shot."

"I know now that it's a waste of my time," she replied.

"It's too bad you can't see the benefit of everything Markus has to offer. It would make everything easier."

"That's my goal, Farrell. To make everything easier." She tried her best to ignore him and focus on her sister. "How are you feeling, Becca?"

"I've been better," her sister admitted.

This section of the maze-like tunnels had only a few fluorescent lights set into the ceiling to guide their way before they were plunged into inky darkness. Perhaps this was a less traveled section of Markus's subterranean maze? She kept looking to her left, to her right, trying to see anything, any clue to help her untangle herself from this mess and escape with Becca.

Escape.

Yes, that was definitely the magic word.

"Hey, Becca, remember last summer, when Jackie gave us a few lessons?" Crys whispered.

"Yeah."

"Do you remember lesson number one?"

"Of course. Don't you?"

"I have a few lessons I can teach you, Becca," Lucas said. "Just let me know when and where."

There was no mistaking his leering tone. "She's only fifteen, you creep."

His only response in the darkness was a withering laugh.

Crys nudged Becca again, reminding her of the self-defense question.

"Well? My brain isn't a computer like yours," Crys said.

"She called it the git-ho."

Git-ho? Crys strained her memory for the next dozen steps she took.

Then it dawned on her.

She actually laughed under her breath, but it came out more as a dry cough. "How could I have forgotten that?"

Becca met her gaze and nodded.

"Be ready," Crys told her firmly.

"Stop talking," Farrell snapped.

Lucas and Farrell walked swiftly and with certainty while the girls stumbled along with them through the darkness.

"Once you get the marks, you'll be able to see as well as we can," Farrell said. "And you won't need to wear those ugly glasses anymore."

"They're not ugly."

"Yes, they are. Like, super-ugly."

"You didn't like my old camera, either, so you clearly have terrible taste."

"I like your new one much better."

"Right." She fished into her bag, knowing that he could see her in the darkness with his improved vision. "Well, I do have to admit one thing about it. . . ."

"What's that?"

"It's nice to finally have a flash." She held the camera up to his face and pressed the shutter, sending a piercingly bright light flashing directly into his eyes.

Farrell clamped his hands over his eyes and roared in pain. Lucas lunged for Crys's arm, but before he could reach her, she flashed his sensitive eyes as well.

While both of them grappled to recover from the unexpected bursts of blinding light, Crys grabbed Becca's hand. "Now."

Jackie's lesson number one wasn't a specific karate chop or a roundhouse kick—some physical response to a violent threat. It had been much simpler than that. *When in doubt, GT-HO.*

Get The Hell Out.

Any way possible.

They sped down the tunnel until it finally brightened again, taking any turn they could. Left, right, left . . .

"I don't know how to get out of here!" Crys managed. "Look for a door, anything."

"There's nothing here. Nothing!"

They ran around the next corner and skidded to a halt. A boy around Becca's age stood in front of them holding a flashlight.

He beckoned to them. "You two, follow me."

Crys hesitated. "Who are you?"

"No time to explain. Just hurry up, okay?" He turned and, without waiting another moment, started running down the tunnel.

"Works for me," Becca said, tugging at Crys's arm. "Come on."

They raced to keep up with the boy as he weaved through the tunnels like they were second nature to him.

Finally, they came to an elevator. He pressed the button.

"This leads up to a restaurant," he said.

"Why are you doing this?" Crys demanded. "Why are you helping us?"

But before he could answer, Farrell and Lucas skidded around the corner and came to a stop.

"There you are," Farrell said, smirking. "Nice trick with the camera, by the way. I wouldn't have expected . . ." He trailed off, a look of concern where his smirk used to be. "Adam? What the hell are you doing here?"

Crys looked back at the kid. *Adam?* Of course. Now she recognized him from that magazine photo spread. He was Adam Grayson, Farrell's younger brother.

Adam glanced nervously at the elevator doors before facing his brother, squaring off with him sternly. "This is wrong, Farrell. I know you can't see it, that you're all messed up, but it is."

"You need to get out of here." Farrell's voice was low, his tone wracked with danger. "This isn't your business."

"It is my business."

"Kid's a troublemaker," Lucas said, his arms crossed defensively in front of his chest. "Not good, Farrell. Control your brother."

"Trying to."

"Try harder. And as for you." Lucas glared at Crys. "You need to learn your place."

"Oh yeah?" She laughed in his face at his pompous statement. "Come closer and say that."

"Crys . . . ," Becca hissed.

But Lucas did come closer. Crys grabbed his shirt and brought her knee up as hard as she could, but he twisted out of the way before she could do any damage.

"Nice try." And in an instant, he grabbed her face and slammed her back against the wall. "You think you're so tough, but you're nothing but a weak, insignificant girl. Are you going to force me to teach you a lesson right now?"

Before she could respond, he backhanded her, hard, making her ears ring.

"Enough. Let's get them to Markus's," Farrell growled. "Adam, I'll deal with you later."

"I'm not nearly finished yet," Lucas replied. "Got to say a proper thanks to your girlfriend for breaking my nose."

He shoved Crys again, this time smacking her face against the concrete surface. Her glasses broke. Pain reverberated through her whole body, and hot blood trickled down her forehead as she collapsed to the ground.

Lucas kicked her in the stomach and she cried out.

"Stop it!" Becca tried to grab his arm to pull him back, but he pushed her away with the slightest effort.

"I told you, *enough*," Farrell snapped.

Crys looked up through a veil of pain. Her broken glasses lay in shards next to her, the left lens completely shattered.

"Lucas, what the hell do you think you're doing?" It was Daniel Hatcher, walking toward them. He still had the Bronze Codex tucked under his arm.

"Your daughter doesn't know how to behave," Lucas explained. "I'm teaching her a lesson."

Daniel looked down at where she lay on the floor. "She's always been a bit difficult. Stubborn and argumentative to a fault."

"She sure is."

"Hold this, please." He handed the Codex to an annoyed-looking Farrell. "Lucas, I have to tell you something very important. Are you listening?"

"Sure."

"If anyone hurts my daughter? I'll kill them."

He took Lucas's head between his hands and twisted. The sound of his snapping neck echoed brutally off the walls.

Lucas fell to the ground beside Crys, his eyes still open, cold and staring.

Farrell took a step backward. "What the hell are you doing?"

"Excellent question," her father said. He twisted the gold ring on his left index finger to reveal a short needle, then clapped his hand against Farrell's neck.

Farrell stared out at them in shock before dropping to his knees, then crumpled over to his side, unconscious.

The elevator doors finally opened up.

"Get on the elevator. Adam, lead them out of here." Daniel came to Crys's side and helped her to her feet. "How badly are you hurt?"

"I'll survive," she groaned. "What's going on, Dad?"

"Markus has his inner circle monitor all the society members closely, unbeknownst to them. Adam, when I saw that your dagger mark wasn't affecting you properly, that you still had doubts about Markus and Hawkspear, I knew that what was happening to you was the same thing that happened to Julia. Girls, your mother wasn't totally affected by the marks, either. Those who have a natural resistance to Markus's magic are appalled by what happens here. It's slowly made me question the validity of my loyalty to this man. To his mission. What I feel, what I think, what I believe . . . it's all wrong. I've been corrupted by his magic. I know that now with more certainty than ever before."

Hope welled in Crys's chest. "So does that mean you can break away from him now that you're thinking clearly again?"

"No. My thoughts are still as unclear and unreliable. I'm afraid the marks continue to affect me deeply, just as they're meant to. I chose the society, Crissy, because what Markus has done to me has made me complicit in his actions. But what I've seen over the last week . . . after you became involved in all this . . . somehow it's managed to wake me up from a very long slumber. I couldn't let him hurt you or Becca." He gently squeezed Becca's hand. "And I won't let you follow me down this path of darkness. Get out of here while you still can. And take this." He grabbed the Codex off the floor and handed it to Crys. "If it's true that Markus will die without it, then let him die."

Crys clutched his hand as he helped her into the elevator. "Come with us."

He shook his head. "I can't. I've made my choice." He stroked her cheek, then reached over to do the same to Becca. "I love you—both of you. Please, never forget that."

The elevator doors closed.

Chapter 28

FARRELL

When Farrell came to, Daniel Hatcher was still standing next to Lucas's dead body. He thought for sure the man was waiting to kill him, too.

"Let's go see Markus," Daniel said instead. "I'll tell him Lucas was to blame for everything. The escape, the stolen book. Everything."

"Why would I lie about that to protect you?"

"Because I don't think you want your brother's name dragged into this."

What the hell was Adam doing here? Farrell thought.

Farrell pushed up from the ground. "Fine. You do the talking."

"I will."

Daniel and Farrell stood before Markus, who sat at his desk in the library. Daniel had the immortal's full attention as he related his side of the story.

"We'll get your Codex back," Daniel finished. "I swear we will."

Markus's expression was unreadable, but getting the book he'd wanted more than anything and then losing it again in record time . . .

Farrell knew he had to be absolutely livid.

"I never would have predicted Mr. Barrington's betrayal tonight," Markus said evenly. "But I certainly agree that his death was earned and deserved."

Farrell relied on the cool steadiness of Markus's marks to keep from fixating on what had really happened. He focused on his breathing, slow and steady, on his mind, clear and calm.

If Markus asked him, point-blank, what had happened, he had decided to tell the truth.

He would beg for his brother's forgiveness and hope Markus would be lenient.

"Two things still trouble me, Daniel." Markus rested his elbows on the desk and joined his fingertips together in a temple.

"Which are?"

"What could have possibly motivated Lucas to help two girls he didn't even know? And even if Mr. Barrington were, in some kind of stroke-like fit of irrational empathy, to assist your two daughters in escaping out of sheer kindness and goodwill, why in the world would he let them get away with the very book he knows I need?"

"I don't know what came over Lucas," Daniel replied. "And I didn't bother to ask him before I broke his neck."

Markus nodded. "Perhaps I didn't phrase my questions correctly. You know this already, but Mr. Grayson does not, that there's an aspect of the marks that can be very helpful. Whenever I ask someone who bears two or more of my marks a direct question, they will be compelled to answer truthfully."

Farrell's chest tightened.

"So let's try again, shall we? Did you have any part in helping Crystal and Rebecca escape?"

Daniel's jaw tensed as if he were fighting the compulsion to answer. "Yes," he finally grunted.

"I see. And am I to understand that you've begun to fight against the marks I've given you?"

"Yes." The word was a hiss.

"If I were to give you the option, given the extenuating circumstances that have come to light, would you wish to leave my society and return to your family?"

"Yes."

Markus continued to show not a hint of emotion, whether he found these answers shocking or not.

"One last question, Daniel." Markus leaned back in his chair, regarding the man before him with narrowed eyes. "Is Rebecca Hatcher my daughter?"

Daniel's eyes widened. "What? Is she—?" He shook his head, as if trying to give an adamant denial, but the words didn't come out. "I . . . I don't know."

"No," Markus replied. "I didn't suppose you would."

Markus stepped out from behind his desk and stood before one of his most loyal circle members. "You betrayed me tonight. You, whom I trusted more than anyone else."

Daniel said nothing, his jaw hardening to a defiant line.

"What do you think, Mr. Grayson?" Markus asked. "What judgment shall we pass on this man who has put everything I stand for at risk? Who has worked against me to deny me something I need to continue watching over this world to keep it safe from evil? What should our verdict be?"

Farrell glanced back and forth between the two. Suddenly, he felt like he was in a society meeting.

"Guilty," he said.

"And what punishment does a guilty verdict incur?"

Farrell's mouth felt dry. "Death."

Markus opened the wooden box on his desk and drew out his golden dagger.

Daniel eyed it, his expression resolute but tight with inner turmoil. "They're my family, Markus," he choked out. "I had no other choice but to try to protect them."

"I know." Markus regarded the blade before placing it into Farrell's hand. The golden hilt was cool against his hot skin.

"Markus?" Farrell asked, uncertain.

"Show me you're worthy of taking his place," Markus said simply. "I need someone by my side in whom I can believe."

Farrell looked to Daniel, who stared back at him with an expression of placid strength.

He waited for Daniel to confess everything to save his skin, to say Adam had really been the one to rescue the girls, not him or Lucas. He waited for Daniel to implicate him.

"Go ahead," Daniel said instead. "Do it. But always remember: I once stood where you are right now."

It sounded like an omen. Like a curse.

Was this who Farrell had become? Did Markus's marks control his actions? All he knew for sure was that this choice he now had to make, with the cool weight of the golden blade in his grip, would define him forever.

It's too much, he thought. *I can't kill him. This isn't who I am.*

He swore he dropped the weapon, but he didn't hear it clatter to the floor.

It was still in his hand.

He thought of his tattoo of the movie quote: *Bright is life. Dark is death.* It meant to choose good over evil, even in one's darkest moment. But it seemed he had no choice anymore. And part of him, the larger part that wasn't screaming far off in the distance, didn't seem to care.

Farrell locked gazes with Daniel as he thrust the blade into his chest. Daniel gasped but didn't cry out. The life slowly faded from his eyes until the last flicker went out.

He pulled out the knife, and Daniel's body slumped to the floor.

Red blood dripped from the tip of the dagger.

Suddenly, the air was charged with magic. It pulsed with the same energy that always invigorated Farrell after the Hawkspear trials. And other than that, Farrell felt . . . nothing. No remorse. No regret.

Still, one singular thought from that small and distant version of himself did manage to eke its way to the surface.

What's happened to me?

Markus nodded. "Very good, Mr. Grayson. Give me the dagger."

With only the slightest of hesitations, he did as instructed, and Markus wiped the blade off on a cloth.

"Now give me your arm."

Farrell obeyed, pulling back his shirtsleeve.

"You have proved yourself well to me tonight," Markus said as he carved the third mark into Farrell's flesh.

This time, Farrell barely felt any pain.

"Tell me, Mr. Grayson, have you come to care for Crystal Hatcher?" Markus asked.

The truth escaped him before he could stop it. "Yes."

"Did you help her escape tonight?"

"No."

"Good." The mark finished, fresh blood now dripping to the floor to mingle with that of Daniel Hatcher's, Markus gripped Farrell's arm and healed him.

What gifts would the third mark bring? He could barely wait to find out.

"She's become a serious problem," Markus said. "For you, for me. For all of us."

He nodded. "I know."

Markus watched him carefully for any flinch, any sign of distress. "If I asked you to, if I decided it would be the best decision for the future of Hawkspear and for my mission . . . would you kill her?"

Farrell held his leader's gaze steadily as the distant scream of the boy he used to be faded away to a mere whisper.

"Yes, Markus. I would."

Chapter 29

CRYSTAL

The elevator doors opened, and, just as Adam had promised, Crys and Becca found themselves standing in a fine restaurant. After running around down in the tunnels and the empty theater, Crys found the sound of voices and laughter and the rich scents of authentic Italian food disorienting.

"Take this." Adam handed Becca a plastic shopping bag that he'd grabbed from behind a potted plant. "I stashed it here earlier. Your father said you'd need some shoes and something to wear. They're my mother's. Probably not your style, but they'll do."

"Thank you," said Becca wearily but gratefully.

They didn't linger in the restaurant. Once they were out in the street, they stopped at the nearest corner, where Crys shielded Becca so she could quickly change and discard her hospital gown. The blue silk dress Adam had brought was loose on her and far too formal, but the shoes were flats and seemed to fit her well enough.

"Thanks again for your help," Crys said to Adam. Her head and rib cage ached from the pounding she'd taken from Lucas, but she tried not to think about it.

"I know you probably hate my brother," Adam said as they walked, as casually as possible so as not to attract any attention. Crys didn't know where they were going, but Adam walked with purpose down an unfamiliar route of side streets and alleys, and she'd officially decided to trust him. "But that's not really who he is. Markus gave him another mark that changed him into something he's not, something dark and hateful."

Was that true? Was this Farrell who Crystal knew someone who only existed because of what Markus had done to him, just like her father?

She had no time to consider this. Besides, it's not as if it mattered. Farrell had chosen his side. They both had.

"We're here." Adam nodded at the white Honda Accord idling at the side of the road. There were rental stickers on the bumper.

Aunt Jackie leaned out the window. "Thanks, Adam. I'll take it from here. Girls, get in the car right now."

Crys gave Adam another grateful nod before she and Becca climbed into the backseat.

"Jackie," Crys began, "I've never been happier to see anyone in my entire life."

"Right back at you." As soon as she laid eyes on the book in Crys's arms, Jackie let out a huge sigh of relief. "You still have it."

"Yes." *Thanks to Dad, we do,* she thought. "Where's Mom?"

Jackie got the car in gear and started to drive. Becca watched through her window as they passed Adam Grayson, who was now walking back the way they'd come, his hands deep in his pockets, his attention on the sidewalk. "Making arrangements for us. She sent me to pick you up while she figures out our next move. We can't go back to the Speckled Muse right away, not with the Codex on us. That'll be the first place he'll look."

Crys immediately perked herself up, but regretted it when her body cried out in pain. "We can't leave Charlie there all alone!"

"We can't? Well then, it's a good thing I have him up here with me." She patted the small pet carrier on the passenger seat, which Crys hadn't noticed before now. "Don't worry. Your mom made sure to tell me which essentials to bring."

Despite how lighthearted she was being, Crys could see the worry in her aunt's eyes reflected in the rearview mirror.

"You called Dad looking for Markus," Crys said. "Why?"

"I got your messages, but I also got one from Daniel. Which is how we were able to arrange all this with Adam. You know, I was more than ready to write your father off completely, and then he has to go and do something selfless and brave like this. I called on a signal from Daniel to distract Markus so you two would have a chance to escape. Luckily, for all of us, it worked. I wasn't totally sure it would."

"What did you say to him?"

There was a momentary silence, one that felt heavy and pained. "It doesn't matter. What matters is we're together. Now, sit back, try to relax, and let me do the driving."

Just as she'd attempted to see Becca differently now that she knew the truth, Crys tried to look at Jackie through the lens of her newfound knowledge about her aunt's past.

Becca's birth mother. Markus's ex-lover.

"Are you okay?" Becca asked Crys.

"You're asking *me*?" Crys said, rubbing her aching head. "I'm going to be, I think. What about you?"

"Just trying to keep breathing." She hesitated. "Crys . . . when I touched that book, it sent my spirit to another world."

Crys blinked. "Excuse me?"

"I know how crazy it sounds—believe me. Maybe my body was here, but the rest of me was somewhere very, very different." She let out a shaky sigh. "And . . . I met a boy there."

"While you were in a coma, and your spirit was in another world, you met a boy. Wow, your social life is way more vibrant than mine. The only boy I met was only talking to me because someone carved an evil spell into him."

Becca didn't speak for a moment, but her bottom lip began to quiver. Crys reached for her hand. "Sorry, I shouldn't joke. Tell me more about this boy."

"He was special. In such a short time, he became so special to me."

"You fell for him hard, huh?"

She nodded, her eyes moist. "I can't believe I'm never going to see him again. There has to be a way for me to find him again. There *has* to."

"Of course there's a way," Crys replied.

Becca's eyebrows shot up. "How can you say something like that?"

"Because, my blond bookworm, this week I've come to believe in magic. And if *I* can believe in magic, then, damn it, anything's possible."

Becca laughed softly, wistfully. "Okay, then I guess I'll believe right along with you."

"I've come to believe in something else this week, too. It's been in front of me all this time and . . ." She shook her head. "And I've been so stupid and blind not to see it so clearly before."

"What?"

"You, Becca." Crys drew in a deep breath and took a firm hold of her sister's hand. "I believe in you."

ACKNOWLEDGMENTS

Since Falling Kingdoms has come out, I've been lucky enough to experience more enthusiasm from readers than ever before in my writing career. I'm so excited that you're excited! That is what gets me out of bed early(ish) in the mornings and at the keyboard. That's what sees me through into the late, late nights when I'm editing or proofreading or trying to make a deadline. You—yes YOU—are seriously everything to me, and I can't thank you enough!

Thank you to my mother, my father, my sister Cindy, and my BIL Mike. I couldn't ask for a better support team and pep squad; plus you feed me regularly since you know I can't cook. A million thank-yous.

Thank you to Bonnie Staring, Eve Silver, and Juliana Stone for being there for me as my friends and my kindred spirits in writing. You are three shining stars that I'm so very lucky to have in my life.

Thank you to my gift and fabulous editor Elizabeth Tingue; thank you so much for helping me take this book from a meandering first draft to a finished book I'm proud of. I thank the Muses every day that we are on the same page (pun fully intended!). Thank you to Jim McCarthy, my darling agent of a decade-plus now who is truly the best. You both rock!

My eternal thanks to Ben Schrank for allowing me to take a detour into another part of Mytica and for helping to point me in the right direction when I misplace my writer GPS. And to Laura Arnold for originally wanting me to write more books apart from the main series. I miss you! Thanks also to Casey McIntyre, Anna Jarzab, Jessica Shoffel, Erin Berger, Mia Garcia, and Colleen Lindsay, to name only a few fabulous Penguins who make All Things Possible. Also, to Tony Sahara, Irene Vandervoort, Anthony Elder, and Shane Rebenschied, who make beautiful cover art together. Penguin Young Readers and Razorbill are the bomb dot com. Truth.

BECCA HAS RETURNED SAFELY FROM MYTICA,

but dangerous magic still lurks, and the darkness is far from over.

Turn the page for a sneak peek of

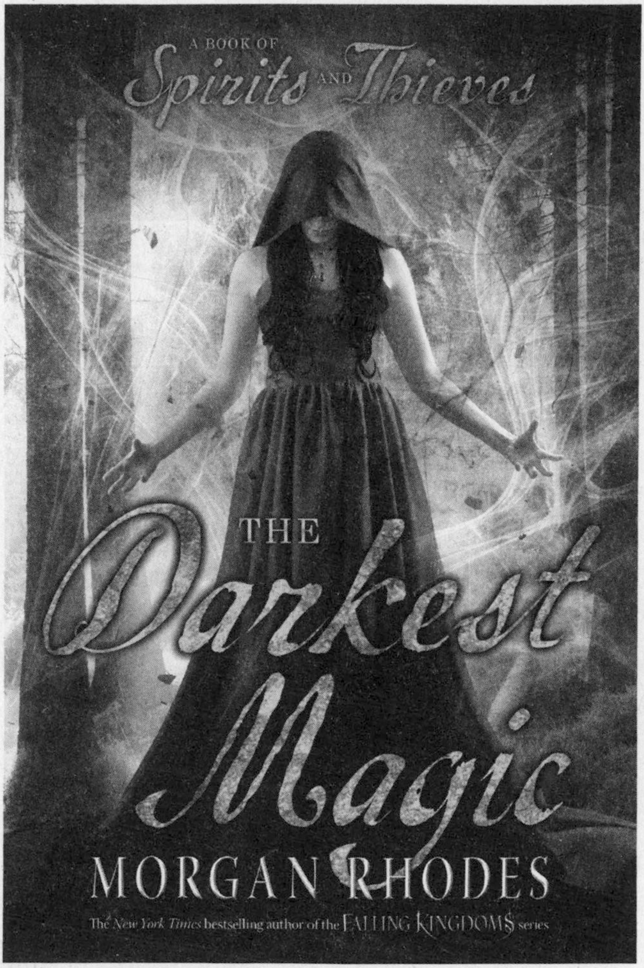

A BOOK OF
Spirits AND Thieves
THE
Darkest
Magic
MORGAN RHODES
The New York Times bestselling author of the FALLING KINGDOMS series

The thrilling second installment in the

BOOK OF SPIRITS AND THIEVES

series by *New York Times* bestselling author Morgan Rhodes!

AVAILABLE IN HARDCOVER SUMMER 2016.

Chapter 1

MADDOX

NORTHERN MYTICA

Each step he took was torture.

It was as if a curse from a vengeful goddess had turned his flesh to fire. Still, he knew he had to be brave—to bear it as long as possible.

Maddox's companion eyed him with curiosity as they strode along the dirt road that cut through the village of Silvereve.

"It's the boots, isn't it?" Barnabas said.

Maddox's jaw stiffened. "I don't know what you're talking about."

"You're limping. And I'm sure I just heard you whimper." Barnabas frowned. "You should have let me take care of stealing the boots. I would have found ones that properly fit you. But no. You wanted to do it *yourself*."

Perhaps Maddox hadn't hidden his error as well as he'd hoped. "I didn't whimper."

Barnabas grinned, white teeth glinting in the moonlight. "Admit you're a terrible thief. Go on. Don't be embarrassed."

Maddox gritted his teeth. Perhaps he couldn't blame *every* difficulty he faced on the goddess. "Very well, if that's what you want to hear. I'm a terrible thief, and I desperately need new boots."

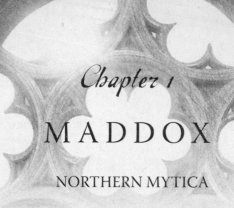

"We'll get you some tonight. Promise. A fine leather pair fit for a royal prince." Just then, a burst of boisterous voices sounded from the center of the village, which was lit up with torches and lanterns. Barnabas turned to look. "I thought you said Silvereve was a quiet place."

It usually was, which was why Maddox now took a long, hard look at the stone-sided shops and landmarks that made up the otherwise familiar town square to be certain they hadn't taken a wrong turn and ended up in another world altogether. He could barely focus thanks to all the shouts and laughter, singing and hollering.

It was so loud, and he was concentrating so hard, that he didn't notice the man with a large round belly, bright red cheeks, and ear-to-ear smile who had approached. "Welcome, friends!" He boomed, slapping Barnabas on his back and handing him a tall green bottle. "Wine flows freely tonight. Drink up!"

Barnabas tossed a skeptical glance at the bottle in his grasp, then fixed a crooked grin on his face. "Thanks, *friend*. What inspires such generosity on this otherwise mundane evening?"

The man's bloodshot eyes bugged out. "Haven't you heard? Only today, Her Radiance announced that she has extended her anniversary celebrations from a mere season to a full year! Not only that, but in gratitude to her loyal subjects, wine touched by her magic will flow like water throughout the celebration."

"Really now." Barnabas's smile faltered, and the friendly light in his eyes became cold and hard. "A full year? Well, that's our radiant goddess for you. So generous and kind to us all."

"She is, my good sir." The man slapped Barnabas on his back again. "She certainly is. Praise her name: Valoria, goddess of earth and water! And wine!"

The drunk man turned away, and Barnabas tossed the bottle away from him as if it had been overflowing with maggots.

"*Touched by her magic*," Maddox repeated with disgust. "The wine has been *tainted* by her magic, is more like it."

A year of celebrations in honor of that creature of darkness. The thought made Maddox sick to his stomach.

"Precisely what I was thinking," Barnabas said. "As much as I enjoy a good bottle of wine, I'll make sure not to touch one again until next year. Come. Let's fetch your mother and be gone from this place."

After they found Damaris and ensured her safety, their plan was to capture and interrogate Valoria's scribe, who'd spent the past several months by the goddess's side.

His job, according to Barnabas's witch friend, Camilla, was to rewrite the history of Mytica and fill it with lies that would fool generations to come. Among the dozens of historical records the scribe had already altered was the account of King Thaddeus's truly heroic reign, as well as the very existence of the rightful heiress, a young girl named Princess Cassia, whose throne Valoria had stolen when she'd murdered the king.

Camilla was certain that this scribe would know Valoria's weaknesses.

Everyone had a mortal weakness. Even an immortal goddess.

They continued on their route to the cottage where Maddox had been raised, the revelers in the village echoing all the way. Maddox tried to concentrate on anything other than Valoria—or his abused feet. So he decided to focus on his companion.

Barnabas was as tall as Maddox. The thief had let his dark hair grow out long and wild, and now he had it tied back from his face with a scrap of black leather. A short, thick beard covered half of his tanned face. This was a man who could skillfully play the part of the fool when circumstances called for it, but apart from the sparkle in his dark brown eyes, the man looked every bit as dangerous as Maddox knew he was.

And he had even more reasons to hate Valoria than Maddox did.

That hate grew stronger with every step he took. It gave him strength and purpose as they neared his home.

They finally arrived at the cottage to find it empty and dark, with no fire burning in the hearth.

"Don't panic," Barnabas said, which only made Maddox worry more—if Barnabas knew to calm him preemptively, that meant he was concerned for the safety of Damaris Corso as well.

"I'm trying my best not to."

"Good," Barnabas said. "Likely, she's in the midst of the celebrations."

Maddox shook his head. "Not likely," he said. "She despises the goddess. Always has."

"Ah, but these festivities give her the chance to pretend she feels the opposite. You know as well as I that right now it's much safer to blend in with the rest of the ignorant fools in this kingdom than to call attention to your reasonable beliefs. We'll find her, I promise we will."

Barnabas's assurance gave him some relief, but now they needed a plan. They'd continue searching for information in the main market area and ask those they passed for help in their search.

To Maddox, every inch of this section of Silvereve was haunted with ghosts. Right now he was haunted by memories of a mother who worked hard from dawn to dusk to support her only son, to keep the dangerous secret that he could see spirits, could coax the dead from their graves without even trying. If Damaris had one fault, it was that she had been vastly overprotective, keeping Maddox at home most of the time and scaring away potential friends who were curious about the strange, pale boy with the dark, haunted eyes. There were times he'd resented it, wanting to be as normal as any of the others. But that wasn't what he was thinking about now. Instead, he thought about how she would hold him when he had nightmares, promising that he was safe. How she'd read his favorite books to him, make crisp biscuits topped with melted sugar—his favorite—when he was scared.

She'd taught him to read and had inspired his love of books—the kinds of books that Valoria had recently banned. The goddess claimed her decision to allow only approved publications containing what she deemed to be useful, practical information—rather than fantastical tales that did nothing but rot the minds of the young and make them believe in nonsense—would improve the intelligence and overall lives of her citizens.

Thirteen years he'd lived here, rarely straying farther than a couple of miles away to visit the neighboring village of Blackthorn with his mother. But then came Livius, who had discovered Maddox's abilities and decided to use them for his own gain, stealing him from his home and his mother with the lie that they were only going to Blackthorn for the day. Maddox hadn't known he wouldn't see her again for nearly a year.

"You will do exactly as I say," Livius had hissed at Maddox after they'd left Silvereve. *"Otherwise, when you next return here, you will find your mother dead. And you'll have only yourself to blame."*

It was easy to frighten a thirteen-year-old with barely any experience in the world. He'd believed in Livius's threats, and so he'd done exactly as he'd said: traveled with him across Northern

Mytica convincing nobles that their villas were besieged by evil spirits and that only the witch-boy and his guardian could help them—for a price, of course.

Every now and then, Maddox did have to deal with a real spirit. But those encounters were rare, and he soon learned that nobles were remarkably easy to fool.

All his life, Maddox had hated this dark magic that drew these frightening, shadowy spirits to him.

But recently, all that had changed.

Because not all spirits were the same, he'd discovered. He'd come to know one that was beautiful, helpful, and kind: a spirit girl named Becca, who claimed to be from another world.

Sadly, Becca had returned to that world long before he was ready to say farewell. Now it seemed their handful of days together had been only a dream.

But she wasn't a dream, he told himself firmly now. *She was real—as real as I am. And one day I will see her again.*

Maddox held on to this hope, refusing to think about how truly impossible it was.

At last they reached the crowded village square. Hundreds of men and women strode past them, laughing and drinking from bottles and flasks. Maddox and Barnabas scanned the area for any sign of Damaris but saw nothing. When Maddox tried to stop revelers and ask if they knew her, all he received were drunken shakes of heads and incoherent mumbling.

His worry over his mother's safety grew with every moment that passed.

Maddox caught the shoulder of a man with a red face and stringy black hair. "Pardon," he said, "but can you tell me if you know of a woman named Damaris Corso?"

“Damaris Corso, you say?” The man then let out a loud crack of a laugh. “I know her.”

“Excellent!” Maddox tried to smile, keeping his hand on the man’s shoulder to keep him and his foul-smelling breath from getting too close. “Do you happen to know where we might find her? We have an urgent matter to discuss, and she’s not at her cottage.”

“No, I don’t suppose she would be. She’s keeping everyone’s bellies full at the Serpent’s Tongue. Lovely thing, she is. Got to grab a handful of her skirt earlier this evening before she managed to slip away from me.”

“Did you?” Barnabas said low and evenly while Maddox clenched his fists at his sides, outraged by the man’s claim.

The drunken man winked. “Give me time and I’ll get all I want from that woman.”

“I’m sure.” Barnabas nodded, then slugged the man in his face. He dropped like a bag full of hammers to the ground, grunting and grabbing his nose, which was now gushing blood.

If Barnabas hadn’t hit him first, Maddox was sure he would have.

“What”—the drunk sputtered—“what was that for, you arse?”

Barnabas glowered down at him. “You insult my sister, I break your nose. It’s a fair price to pay, I think.”

Maddox blinked. *Sister?*

“Your sister”—the man clumsily got back to his feet, his eyes blazing with fury—“isn’t much more than a common whore.”

This time, Barnabas punched the man with enough force to knock him unconscious. Then he swept his gaze over him from head to foot.

“Nice boots.” Barnabas nodded at them. “I think they’re your size, Maddox.”

Maddox just stared at him. “Your *sister*?”

Barnabas's expression turned tense. He dropped to his knees and hastily untied the boots. "Yes. Haven't I mentioned that?"

"I think I'd remember if you did."

"Yes, well, I have now. It's true. Damaris is my sister, therefore one of the very few people in this world I trust—despite her unfortunate decision to hand you over to Livius."

"She didn't exactly hand me over."

"Regardless, that's a matter I'll make sure to discuss with her."

Maddox's mind was still reeling. "Your *sister*," he said again.

"You already said that," Barnabas said.

This was truly unbelievable. Why wouldn't he have mentioned something so important before now? "How many siblings do you have?" Maddox asked.

"Only two—that I'm aware of. Damaris and Cyrus."

Maddox remembered Cyrus. He was a rebel who had found work as one of Valoria's guards, a position that gave him access to information and sometimes allowed him to help fellow rebels who had been arrested.

"And before you chastise me for keeping secrets," Barnabas said as he threw the pair of heavy black boots at Maddox, "know that this is simply what I must do. Out of necessity, to survive. I keep secrets. I trust very few in this world, and that's not going to change any time soon."

Maddox eased off of his blustering, but only by a fraction. "Don't you trust me?"

"I do. Of course. I just—" Barnabas groaned. "I keep secrets from everyone. You're not the only one. So," he said, clearly trying to change the subject, "what's the Serpent's Tongue, anyway?"

"A tavern. It's not far from here."

Barnabas nodded. "Lead the way."

The newly stolen boots fit Maddox perfectly, as if they'd been made especially for him. But Maddox wasn't ready to gush with gratitude just yet. He was deeply annoyed that Barnabas had waited until tonight to reveal that Damaris was his sister—and that he'd only done so in reaction to the taunts of a drunken man.

It was especially tough considering that Maddox was still coming to terms with the new knowledge that the only mother he'd ever known wasn't connected to him by blood. His birth mother had been an immortal who'd fallen in love with a mortal man.

His family tree was getting more crooked and confusing with each day that passed.

It didn't take long for them to reach their destination. Maddox had never ventured inside the Serpent's Tongue before, but he'd passed by it many times and would recognize its exterior anywhere. Carved above the heavy wooden front doors was the head of a snake, its mouth open in a hiss, the points of its sharp fangs only an arm's reach above the heads of patrons entering the dark and crowded establishment.

Tonight, at an hour when many would have otherwise already taken to their beds, the tavern was packed from wall to wall, long wooden tables loaded to capacity with both locals and visitors participating in the celebrations.

"Do you see her?" Barnabas asked.

Maddox scanned the multitude of sweaty faces, all seemingly drunk and happy. "No."

"Let's take a seat."

"Where?" Maddox asked, gesturing at the completely full taproom. "They're all taken."

Suddenly and with little effort, Barnabas shoved two men off the wooden bench to their left. "What were you saying?" he asked as he sat down.

"Nothing useful, apparently." Maddox continued to search the crowd. Nearby, a woman smoking a cigarillo sent a cloud of rancid smoke into Maddox's eyes, making them start to water.

He rubbed them and kept looking, his gaze moving past face after face. Despite living here all his life, no one looked familiar. And no one looked at him as if they might recognize him.

A fat man spun a laughing woman around in a circle to the music of a fiddler standing on top of a table. Some others were clapping in time to a song that Maddox didn't recognize. Three men pounded on their table, shaking it, to garner the attention of a barmaid.

"More wine!" they called.

The barmaid appeared, elbowing her way through the crowd. She smiled and nodded and promised that she would be back as soon as possible. One man slapped her on her bottom, and she spun around and scolded him, but she was laughing as she turned from the table and locked gazes with Maddox.

"Mother," he whispered, his heart swelling. He raised his hand in greeting and found that his cheeks already hurt from how widely he was smiling.

Even though she looked different tonight in her tight white bodice that showed far more of her bosom than Maddox was used to, and a long black skirt that hugged her hips, he would recognize her anywhere. Her smile, her laugh, the kindness in her eyes—even when dealing with thirsty heathens, it would seem.

Damaris Corso quickly weaved her way through the crowd toward him and threw her arms around him, hugging him close to her.

"My sweet boy! I've missed you so much!"

"I've missed you too," he said, his throat tight with both happiness and relief at finding her. He cast a look over her shoulder at Barnabas, still seated, who nodded his approval. "When you weren't at home, I thought . . . well, I didn't know what to think. And now, you're here and . . . you're a . . . a . . ."

"A barmaid. Yes, it's true." She sighed, but her smile didn't falter as she kissed both of his cheeks. "With all these celebrations, it's the easiest way to earn my coin." Her eyes were kind, but it wasn't until now that Maddox saw how tired they were, and he felt guilty for feeling any shame over his mother's new occupation. "Oh, I'm so glad you've come home!"

Yes, it was possible that his heart might burst. "Me too," he said, smiling so as not to shed a tear.

Then, Damaris's joyful expression shadowed. "Where is Livius?" she asked in a low voice.

"Not here, thankfully," replied Barnabas.

She turned her surprised gaze to Barnabas as he rose from his seat and drew back the hood of his cloak so she could fully see his face.

Damaris's mouth fell open. She appeared to grapple for the right words. "You . . ." was all she managed.

Barnabas nodded. "Yes, it's me. How've you been, sister?"

In one lightning-fast motion, she slapped him, hard, across his left cheek.

Barnabas winced, stroking his face gingerly. "I suppose I deserved that."

"Sixteen years! Sixteen years without a single word from you! I thought you were dead!" Then she grabbed him into a tight hug. "I've missed you so much, you horrible thing!"

Barnabas grasped her shoulders and gave her a grin. "The feeling is mutual, Dam. Now we need to get out of here."

"What? I can't leave. Do you see how many people are in here? On a night like tonight I can earn enough to live on for at least a month! Go back to my cottage, stay as long as you like, and when this place closes up I'll come home, and we can catch up on all that has happened."

A man with a shaved head in a red tunic climbed on top of a nearby table and raised his tankard high in the air. "To our radiant goddess Valoria!" he slurred. "May she reign for a thousand years! And a deadly curse upon the dark goddess of the South! We would rather spit than speak her name!"

A deafening cheer followed this toast, and patrons pounded on the tables to show their approval. Maddox watched all of this uneasily. What would they do if they knew the horrible truth about their beloved goddess?

"More wine for everyone!" the drunken man called out.

"I can't talk long," Damaris said, gesturing at the eager patrons rushing to the front with their goblets and mugs. "But I promise to return as soon as I can."

Maddox grabbed her wrist as she turned away. "I know, Mother. I know everything."

Her face blanched, and her gaze found his again. "As soon as I saw Barnabas . . ." she sighed. "If he found you, I knew it had to mean . . ." She swallowed hard. "You know *everything*?"

He nodded solemnly.

"So you know that Barnabas is . . . is . . ."

"My father," he finished, still struggling to believe it was true. "And that you're not really my mother, even though you . . . you *are*. I've been thinking about this for days on end. You will always be my mother. You kept me safe my whole life, with no one to help you, even though you've always known who I am. *What* I am.

I love you for that—I'll always love you for that."

Damaris drew in a shaky breath, her eyes brimming with tears as she pulled him close and stroked the hair on the back of his head. "I wanted to tell you, Maddox, but it was never the right time. I wanted to assure you that your . . . abilities . . . came from a good place. Not from evil. Never evil." Maddox didn't want to let her go, but when he finally released her, she sniffed and rubbed her hand under her nose. "When Livius arrived, I thought that if he knew at least part of the truth, then perhaps he could help me protect you. I trusted him, foolishly. I was so stupid. I'm sorry. I'm so sorry for all the misery that man caused both of us."

Maddox grasped her hands and squeezed them. "It's all in the past. Really. That part of our lives is over. But I must urge you to come with us now."

There was no time to tell her everything. That Livius was dead, killed from a poisonous bite from Valoria's pet cobra. That Maddox and Barnabas had attempted to exile Valoria to another world but had only met with failure and the promise of a goddess's wrath. That now the plan was to capture and interrogate Valoria's scribe.

Damaris's brows drew together. "What is this? Barnabas, what's going on?"

Grim lines had settled into Barnabas's expression. "Maddox isn't the only one who knows the truth now, Dam."

She stifled her gasp with the back of her hand. "Valoria."

He nodded. "We need to get you somewhere safe. It's no secret that Maddox has been with you all these years. Now that she knows who he is, it's not beyond her to use your safety against him. She wants his magic for herself. For him to be at her disposal at all times."

"She can't have it," Maddox gritted out.

Damaris was quiet for a long moment, until finally she nodded firmly. "Very well," she said. "Let's go."

Without another word, the three of them made their way through the crowd toward the exit. Thanks to his good boots and knowledge that his mother was safe, Maddox now walked without any pain in either his feet or his heart.

"Not staying for another round?" The man in red who'd toasted to the goddess on top of the table now stood between them and the door.

"Afraid not, friend," Barnabas said. "I guess that means more for the rest of you."

"For the rest of *them*," he said, gesturing at the drunken crowd with a jerk of his chin. "I stay away from inebriants myself. They cloud the mind. Don't you agree, Barnabas?"

Barnabas drew the dagger from the sheath at his belt. "Who are you?"

"My name is Goran."

"How do you know my name, Goran?"

Goran glanced at Maddox, whose heart had started racing in his chest. "And you're Maddox, are you? I wasn't expecting more than a mere boy, but look at you. Practically a man."

"Let us pass," Maddox growled as Damaris gripped his arm.

Goran glanced at the weapon in Barnabas's hand. "Not a good idea to wave that about, Barnabas. Some innocent person in here could get hurt."

"I'm not planning to hurt any of them," Barnabas said. "Only the person who prevents us from leaving."

"Perhaps you wouldn't like to hurt anyone. I, on the other hand, would kill everyone in here without blinking an eye."

Barnabas narrowed his eyes. "What are you? An assassin?"

"I was. But I've recently been specially chosen to follow a worthier path."

Barnabas cocked his head. "Let me guess. By Valoria?"

Goran smiled. "Her Radiance told me what happened. Did you really think this could end any other way? The boy comes with me tonight. If you try to stop me, I will kill you and everyone else in here."

"That would be a mighty feat for even the most skilled assassin."

"You thought this would be that easy?" Maddox snarled at the bald man. "That you'd just take me out of here and walk away and all is well?"

Goran raised a brow. "I've heard about your magic, boy. I know that as soon as we leave here, you will try to kill me. Therefore, I'll be sure you're not conscious for the journey."

Maddox glanced around anxiously. No one else in the tavern seemed aware that there was a life-or-death negotiation going on in their midst. His stomach churned, but the amused expression on Barnabas's face helped to keep him calm.

"Valoria has sent a single assassin after us," Barnabas said, casually shifting his dagger back and forth between his hands. "Well, damn. It seems as if we're defeated."

"You speak mockingly," said Goran. You shouldn't."

"Oh yes, you're right. I'm incredibly intimidated." Barnabas inched close to Goran and stared him straight in his eyes. "Get out of our way, or I'll send you back to your radiant goddess in pieces."

"There's no need for violent threats," Damaris hissed, her hold on Maddox's arm growing stronger. "There is a peaceful solution to be found here."

Maddox almost smiled at that. His mother was always searching for peaceful solutions. How often had he found a large spider on his bed, only to watch his mother carefully scoop the creature up in a cooking pot to set it free while he'd been searching for something to kill it with.

"Every creature deserves a chance at life," she'd tell him. *"Even the ugly, eight-legged ones."*

But an assassin working for Valoria could surely do things much uglier than any spider could.

Maddox examined Goran closely. He had tattoos on his neck and muscular forearms, some sort of writing in black and gold. Maddox couldn't read the language, although it seemed oddly familiar to him. He pulled his gaze away when he felt the assassin notice him looking.

"My tattoos," Goran said, holding out his arms. "The ink is so fresh it's barely dried. They are gifts from the goddess herself. She told me that if she had her dagger, she could have made the marks deeper, more permanent than she was able to with her earth magic alone. Though these will work just fine."

Among all the items she greedily sought, the one the goddess prized the most highly was a golden dagger. This dagger, she believed, had the power to turn mortals into slaves if it was used to carve special symbols into their flesh.

For a while now, Maddox had suspected that these symbols were words written in the language of the immortals—the same language and symbols that filled the magical book that had sent Becca Hatcher's spirit to Mytica.

"How fancy," Barnabas said drily. "But your little drawings change nothing. And you're still standing in our way. I suggest you move."

He raised his dagger to Goran's throat, but the assassin didn't even flinch.

"When you return to your goddess with your tail between your legs," Barnabas said, "kindly tell her she can kiss my arse."

Goran moved with supernatural speed, grabbing the dagger out of Barnabas's grip. Barnabas looked down at his empty hand with shock. He didn't have time to so much as look up before Goran picked Barnabas up and threw him across the room, as if it took no more effort than tossing a small rock into a river. Barnabas hit the wall hard and landed on a table, sending plates and goblets flying in all directions. Damaris shrieked and let go of Maddox's arm. Everyone in the tavern fell silent and turned with surprise toward the violence.

Maddox didn't wait another moment. He clenched his hands into fists and summoned his death magic. Enough to harm, but not to kill. It was like a shadow rising within him, filling his limbs with dark strength, and he focused this mere taste of his magic on his foe.

"Yes," Goran grunted. "I feel it. Like a hand thrusting through my chest to grip my heart. It's just as the goddess warned."

From the corner of Maddox's eye, he saw Barnabas push himself to his feet and draw closer.

Goran staggered forward one step. His next step was much smoother. And then he took another.

No one had ever been able to push back against Maddox's magic like this before.

This was no normal man.

"Maddox, be careful," Barnabas warned.

"Not so strong, really," Goran said through clenched teeth. "Is that all you have in you, boy?"

The earth magic in Goran's marks, Maddox thought. Could that be what was dulling the effect of the magic?

"No, not all," Maddox bit the words out.

Maddox drew more magic to the surface. It was a cold sensation running through his veins, his limbs, but perspiration began to drip down his forehead at the effort. He hadn't needed this much before, and he wondered how much of it he had. Would it be enough?

He clenched his teeth and fisted his hands, his muscles tensing down his arms enough that he began to shake from the effort of trying to stop this man from drawing closer to him.

"Enough of this," Damaris said. "Maddox, stop!" She moved to stand in front of him. She held her hand up, palm out and facing Goran. "I won't allow anyone to be hurt here tonight. Leave here now. Tell the goddess that if she wants Maddox, then she can come here and face us herself."

"Step back from him," Barnabas hissed at her.

She kept her attention fully fixed on the assassin. "No, Barnabas, let me handle this. You've done enough."

Goran stopped, an arm's reach away from Maddox and Damaris. A smile curled up the corners of his mouth. "You mean what you say, don't you? You wish to find a peaceful solution to this."

Damaris raised her chin. "I do."

"I don't have many weaknesses, especially not now," he said, looking down at his fresh marks, "but one of them is for brave women who stand up for what they believe. Who protect what they love. I admire that more than I can say."

Amazed, Maddox watched this exchange. Would his mother be able to stop this assassin, using only words as her weapons?

Damaris nodded firmly. "Good."

Goran's smile widened. "Luckily, I learned to ignore my weaknesses long ago."

The silver blade caught the flickering lantern light as Goran slashed Barnabas's dagger forward, cutting Damaris's throat in a single, deep line.

"Mama, no!" Maddox caught her as she dropped to the floor,

her hands flying up in vain to try to block the flow of blood. She sought Maddox's gaze, her eyes full of pain and regret. Barnabas was there too, next to his sister and clutching her hand.

Goran glared down at him. "Come with me now, boy, and no one else has to die here."

Maddox tore his gaze away from his dying mother to send a wave of cold death toward this murderer. Goran's eyes widened in pain as he dropped the bloody dagger and clutched at his throat. He staggered backward, his face convulsing and turning red.

"What—?" he gasped. Your power . . . it's so much . . . stronger. . . . "

He fell to his knees as Maddox twisted the magic like a black knife, and blood began to pour from the assassin's nose.

The tavern had transformed from a den of wine-soaked revelry to a pit of chaos. The patrons had realized their lives were in peril, and they flooded toward the exit, blocking Maddox from the killer. By the time they cleared out, Goran was nowhere to be seen.

The assassin had escaped.

"Damn it," Barnabas said, his voice pained and shaky. "Damn it all. And damn Valoria for this!"

Hot tears streaked down Maddox's cheeks. Damaris weakly clutched his arm.

"I'm sorry," Maddox choked out. "Mama, I'm so sorry. Forgive me."

He gazed down at Damaris for as long as he could. Apart from the pain in his mother's tear-filled eyes, there was only love. Peace.

And then her gaze went blank, her expression still and lifeless.

Maddox pulled his mother's limp body against him and sobbed against her shoulder. The sheer force of his anguish reached outward, and his magic shattered every window in the tavern.